IT WAS NO PLAGUE OR CHEMICAL, IT WAS SOMETHING MUCH MORE EVIL . . .

He didn't expect to find anyone, but still he knocked. When no one answered, Officer Williamson let himself in. It was a small town, folks rarely locked their doors. Still, something didn't seem quite right.

Wary, he entered the living room.

Williamson flinched when he saw John Glover on the couch—the man's skeletal form was dressed in old, familiar work clothes, but they were black with dried pus and decay. The figure was outstretched in obvious agony, although the moment of its torture had long passed. Its hands clutched at the cushions in a futile struggle to resist death. The corpse might have been three or four days old. The black bile had almost entirely eroded through the flaky gray covering its skin. The eyes had shriveled and fallen within the sockets.

The hardened lawman was shaking. He still had a whole house to search, and John Glover had had two children.

Oh God.

DEMONIC COLOR

PAULINE DUNN

ZEBRA BOOKS
KENSINGTON PUBLISHING CORP.

ZEBRA BOOKS

are published by

Kensington Publishing Corp.
475 Park Avenue South
New York, NY 10016

First printing: October, 1990

Printed in the United States of America

To the other half of my writing team, my sister, Susan K. Hartzell, without whom this would not be the book it is.

Additional thanks to Judy Post for reading through our manuscript and making suggestions.

And also to our editor, Ann LaFarge, for believing in our work and for all the nice things she's said about us.

Friday, June 9

*. . . it fed not only on his body,
but upon his very soul . . .*

Chapter One

He could smell it from half a mile away.

Jimmy Arnold kicked at dusty clumps of dirt lying on the edge of the road with the toes of his sneakers, shoulders hunched forward, hands thrust deep in his pockets, fingers wrapped around the wood-grained plastic handle of his new jackknife. The blade was longer and sharper than that of his other knives. He was anxious to try it out.

Ahead, a thick canopy of gnarled hickory branches stretched across the rutted land and blocked out most of the searing afternoon light. He sauntered along, slowly making his way through the sun-dappled shadows toward the town dump. It was cooler in the shade, and a slight breeze raised the hair on the back of his neck.

Abruptly a shrill, taunting whistle burst from the nearby side road, and he whirled about just in time to see Hank Stoddard glide past on his glossy black BMX bicycle. Hank flipped up his middle finger and laughed arrogantly, then turned onto State Street, riding toward the center of Town (it didn't have any other name; everyone simply called it Town).

Jimmy stuck out his tongue at the rapidly diminishing shape of his classmate. Who gave a fart about dumb old Hank Stoddard anyway?

It was Friday, June 9, the last day of school. All the local kids were headed home for summer vacation, but

Jimmy was taking the long way around because he had business to attend. His thumb pressed over the grooves in the knife. By next fall, when classes began again and he started middle school, he was going to have a brand new BMX like Hank Stoddard's.

See if I don't, he thought bitterly.

His dad wouldn't pay for a new one—"not when you've already got a perfectly good bike rusting away in the garage."

Perfectly good bike! A peeling green twenty-incher with a banana seat and dented handlebars. His older brother had used it for twelve years to run errands down at the store before finally going into the army and leaving Town forever. Jimmy could hardly be seen riding that piece of trash.

He was approaching the dump, and the stench was worse than usual. Somebody must've dropped off an abnormally odoriferous load. He liked the word odoriferous. Hank Stoddard would be odoriferous when he caught up to him.

Broken pieces of glass and bits of garbage that hadn't quite made it into the pit lay scattered throughout the surrounding area. He stooped over and examined a cracked vase. He had the whole summer ahead of him. He would fix up some of this junk and sell it to folks to earn the money for his new bicycle.

He'd show his dad. He'd show them all.

A bent metal sign in front of the dump threatened a $500 fine for unauthorized usage. He'd been warned to stay away, that this wasn't a place for kids. But Jimmy and his friends had been here lots of times; it was absolutely safe. You could find a lot of neat stuff and spear a few rats. They were fun to kill. They'd squeal and kick their skinny little legs.

Oh, there had been a big fuss a few years ago. He remembered his dad talking about it. A company out of Indianapolis had used this site for disposing of radioactive materials. Several women had miscarried, and a couple of people in Town had come down with leukemia. The papers compared it to a place called Love Canal. There was a long court battle. The chemical company was forced to come in and clean it at their own expense, and his dad had said it cost them plenty of cash. But finally, it was all taken care of and people started using the dump again.

Jimmy swatted at an insect that buzzed around his ears. He couldn't see it, but he could sure as heck hear it. The buzzing grew louder. He couldn't seem to chase it away. He was about to move to another spot, one with less bugs, when he saw something shift in the center of the heap. A light stirring of debris in a paper bag.

A rat.

He crouched and pulled out his knife, the excitement building in his chest. Silently, he folded open the blade and held it poised in his hand, ready to throw as soon as the creature stuck out its ugly head. The muscle tensed in his right arm.

Jimmy had excellent aim. He had speared more rats with fewer misses than any of the other boys at Shadeland Elementary. What Mrs. Wilcox said about being good at the things you really loved must be true, he thought.

From the furious movement of the bag, he figured it had to be one queen mother of a rat. He hated their cold, black eyes and wormlike tails. They deserved to die. They carried disease. They . . .

He held his breath tightly as it neared the edge—but it wasn't a rat that emerged.

The buzzing became a roar in his ears. Jimmy stared in shock and let the knife drop. It was on him before he could move. He was utterly surrounded by the dense, swirling kaleidoscope of demonic color that poured from the bag like some hideous, low-lying fog.

For a moment, there was only an icy chill that pierced his spine in cold waves of inexplicable fear. Then he felt it—excruciating pain as he'd never imagined—seeping

11

into his pores, invading his body, permeating and diffusing throughout his bloodstream. Agony raged like fire through his veins. His mind carouseled out of control.

His organs were collapsing. He was being consumed . . . digested from within. His body protested violently in a futile attempt to combat the nameless intrusion. The sound of his scream was cut off as masses of digestive fluids erupted out of his mouth. He doubled over and fell to the ground.

He couldn't breathe. He tore at his face, clawing at his nose and lips to let in more air. The corrosive liquids filled his lungs and burned his eyes, continuing to eat away at the tender inner core of his being.

His senses exploded in sheer torment. His mind no longer functioned except to register new sources of pain. He thrashed and groped in the dirt, his fingers digging into the hard, unyielding earth.

A heavy blackness crept into the corners of his fevered mind, growing larger and darker. As he was slowly absorbed, it fed not only on his body but upon his very soul, threatening to swallow him entirely. And through his mind's eye, he saw the horrors that were to come. . . .

Slowly his skin began to shrivel, to turn gray and brittle, tightening as the monstrous mist sucked the life from him. His taut, dry flesh cracked and split. The thick, viscous bile that his vital organs had become oozed forth.

Monday, June 12

. . . it was something much darker
and deeper, more primitive . . .

Chapter Two

i.

Specks of dust hung motionless in the beams of sunlight streaming through the window. Abigail Morton paused and glanced uneasily around her oversized kitchen, acutely aware of the stillness. The boardinghouse was seldom this quiet.

In the back of her mind she knew something was wrong, though she couldn't say what. She looked over the dirty breakfast dishes in the sink and the sterilized bottles lined up on the cupboard, helpless to give her anxiety a name. Neither could she shake it.

There was an unpleasant odor she'd only just begun to notice. She couldn't quite define it. A faint stench of decay, acrid and clinging, not like anything she'd ever smelled before. She puttered about searching for the cause, checking the drain, examining the waste can under the cupboard, all without success.

It occurred to her then that it might be the weather. Old houses were like that in the summer. The heat was stifling, more like August than June. She could scarcely breathe. Maybe if she let in a little more air.

Abigail pushed open the window above the aging gas stove and shoved in a square, ten-inch metal fan, then plugged it in. The thin, curved blades began to spin, picking up speed with each revolution. One of these days

15

she would pay to have air conditioning installed in the ancient house. That would put an end to any nasty odors.

She was wearing her navy blue funeral dress. It was hot and sticky, and the cloth clung to her back in a growing patch. Sweat rolled like oil down her plump face and wide, loose arms.

It was only in the last few years, since Homer died, that she'd really put on the pounds. The curves of her body were gently rounded testimonies of her flare for cooking, as her seven boarders could well attest. Watching her move around the large Victorian kitchen was like watching the sand shift on the beach or a platter of gelatin being carried across the room.

Her coarse brown hair was beginning to fray from the tightly wrapped bun at the back of her head. She tucked the loose strands into place and fanned herself with the latest edition of the weekly Town paper, which was nothing more than a series of For Sale ads and a sounding board for its editor, that elderly poop, Ezra Hunt.

On the worn Formica table in front of her sat a straw hat and a sturdy black purse. Her equally sturdy black shoes squeaked as she pulled out a chair and sat with her legs spread slightly apart to allow for a greater flow of air. The thick, humid current being pulled in through the window brought little relief, and the smell was getting no better.

She reached over and grabbed a paper napkin from the center of the table and used it to blot the moisture from her face. Then she patted under her arms. Her stout padding of flesh made the heat even more difficult to tolerate.

The clock in the dining room chimed twelve o'clock noon. The funeral was set for one. Virginia Hollingsworth wouldn't be picking her up for another twenty minutes. It was probably a combination of the rising temperatures and the day's somber activities making her so tense.

It was a shame, she thought, about the Arnold boy. His folks were honest, decent people. At least they had two other children, one of them still living at home.

That new doctor — he'd set up practice in Town less than three years ago — couldn't say for sure what it was that had killed the boy. Many hours had passed before they found him, and the rats, the bugs, and the sun had all taken their toll. His body was found on the ground in a clump of trees near the dump, a rotted, grotesque lump of pulp and bone. He was a dried blackened mass that had to be literally shoveled into a bag.

Abigail shuddered. Virginia had relayed the story, and then Abigail had called the sheriff herself to get the rest of the details. So sad. They didn't think foul play was involved. It must've been some kind of terrible accident.

Dr. Corliss had wanted to do a full autopsy, but Mrs. Arnold didn't want them touching her boy — and there wasn't much left. The family just wanted him buried as quickly as possible so they could put their grief behind them and get on with their lives. Abigail suspected it was best. Dr. Corliss was a young man, and he'd never had a family. He didn't know how it was to lose one of your own. Abigail knew; she understood perfectly. She'd buried an infant son many years ago, and then her husband, Homer, six springs back. All she had left was her daughter, Laura, who'd probably be leaving soon to go off to college or a job in the city.

Abigail did her best to ignore the growing odor in the kitchen. Virginia would be here shortly. When they got back, maybe the two of them could figure out what was causing it.

She stared down at her ankles, swollen and overlapping the sides of her shoes. It was the damned heat, the root of her troubles. Like an oven in this house. But she loved the house. It was more than her home; it was her business and the center of her world as well.

What her own life lacked in interest, she was able to make up for in the comings and goings of her boarders.

17

From this kitchen she kept her finger on the pulse of all the activities in Town. Little escaped her attention. Like a spider sitting on a web, she watched and waited, ever alert. She let the only rooms for miles around. If you needed to rent a place south of Indianapolis, between Martinsville and Franklin, you had to stay here.

Five rooms were occupied now. Two were rented by single women, spinsters, both exceedingly dull. Louise Simmons, the librarian, and Kate Jaffe, a schoolteacher. There were never any callers to either of their rooms and seldom a noise to be heard after nine o'clock at night. There couldn't be two quieter, less obtrusive tenants in all the state.

George Reidy had the room across from Abigail's. He was a shameless drunk, frequently needing to trade his services as a handyman in exchange for his rent. Oh, he had been respectable once, before the bottle bled him dry. He had been a forcman down at the canning factory, very popular. Everyone had liked him, including her husband, Homer. Though when Homer was away after dark, Reidy used to come around and sit on the porch with her in the swing. She had never told Homer about those nights, about that simmering wave of electricity that passed between the two and said something might happen—though it never did.

Her eyes drifted down the hall toward his door with regret. No, it never did, but for a long time she had thought it might.

You got caught up in the river of time as it dragged you along through the sluggish seasons that viciously ate at your body. The next thing you knew thirty years had passed, and none of your dreams had ever been realized. It was too late now. There was little to do but continue on in the trickling stream that was her life. The only comfort came with the knowledge that most of the world had also suffered the same course.

Upstairs, the room at the back of the hall was occupied by a man she didn't like and, furthermore, didn't

18

trust, a newcomer. Stephen Myers. He'd arrived in Town only five days before the Arnold boy's death. He claimed to have spent four years of his childhood here when his father was laid off from the steel mills. Though it was possible, Abigail didn't remember him. She'd grown very good at sizing up a person's character in the first few minutes after meeting, and she didn't doubt that she'd gauged this one right.

He was tall and thin, and pasty, like he never got any sun, like he spent all his time cooped up in the dark doing nasty, secretive things. Abigail didn't trust people who spent too many hours alone. Solitude bred insanity. She knew. After all these years of living and observing, Abigail considered herself an authority on people.

Myers had a shock of unruly black hair and intense, boiling brown eyes. The moment you looked in those eyes you knew he'd seen plenty of trouble—bad trouble. There was a deep violence in them, the kind that no matter how many years passed, it wouldn't go away. When she met him on the stairs, it made her blood run cold.

She honestly couldn't say why she'd agreed to rent him the room. Perhaps because young Henry down at the store had vouched for him. The two had become friends at college. Or perhaps because nothing had happened around Town in a long while and she had a craving for a little excitement to come along and ruffle the quiet settling of Town. Ruffle, not bulldoze.

The longer he stayed, the more frightened she became. She had heard him pacing late at night. It kept her awake, wondering what he was up to. She never saw anyone enter his room. He stayed in it nearly all day. He seldom talked to the local folk, just Henry, and Henry insisted the fellow was simply the quiet kind and overly serious.

Overly serious about what? Abigail wondered. Was he running from the law? Was he into drugs?

She'd been tempted to suggest to the sheriff that he call the FBI and have this Stephen Myers checked out, but then the Arnold killing had come along and she hadn't gotten the chance. He was up there now, making no noise, doing whatever it was he did day after day. She hadn't been inside his room since she gave him the key. He didn't want her to come in even to clean.

It made her nervous. What kind of revolting acts did he commit up there? Her pulse quickened. Dirty and illegal. She made up her mind then and there to have him investigated. She hoped it wasn't too late.

The last of her boarders was a young married couple, the Hendersons. They had both grown up on farms outside of Town. John was a good, responsible boy who had planned on making something of his life, but he had allowed himself to be led astray by Sallie Ann Folger. Sallie Ann had always been a bit wild, bleached her hair, wore tight-fitting jeans and T-shirts with no bra. John should've known better than to get mixed up with a girl like that.

It was all over Town that his mother had caught them together in the barn. What a sight that must've been! The pair of them groping and rolling around in the hay, going at each other with nauseating lust.

Abigail drew a deep, steadying breath from the sultry summer air.

Sallie Ann had turned out to be pregnant a month afterward, and John had given up his hopes for college to take a job at the feed and grain. Abigail didn't normally rent to couples with children, especially those with babies, but in their case she had made an exception—an exception she now regretted.

That baby cried night and day. But then, no one had expected Sallie Ann would turn out to be much of a mother. Abigail had told them they would have to leave, and they were saving their money, looking for a place. They couldn't be out soon enough to suit her.

The baby was usually in an uproar by now, and suddenly she realized that she hadn't heard a peep out of it all morning. Why not? Her flesh tightened as her feelings of anxiety returned. Why wasn't the baby crying? She was so used to the constant wailing that she'd come to expect it.

She glanced at the bottles resting on the cupboard. Sallie Ann hadn't been to the kitchen to fix anything for the baby since last night. She hadn't been down for herself, either.

Abigail wondered if they were sick. Maybe she ought to check on them before Virginia arrived to take her to the funeral. Sallie Ann wasn't very smart. She might not be capable of taking care of the child if anything serious was wrong. She might let it lie up there and die just because she didn't feel like coming downstairs. In fact, Abigail wouldn't put it past the girl to do something purposely harmful to her own child if it suited her nefarious motives. Sallie Ann had pinned up posters of movie stars on Abigail's antique wallpaper and was always dreaming about Hollywood.

Hollywood!

The fifty-one-year-old woman heaved herself out of the chair and headed for the stairs, straining to hear any sounds from above. All she detected was an odd sort of thumping on the floorboards.

The first step groaned as Abigail set her foot on it. That repulsive stench was even worse here, and she realized it must be coming from upstairs. It smelled as if someone had let garbage pile up in their room, probably Sallie Ann—the girl was as lazy as they came—but Abigail couldn't imagine anything that would create this much stink.

She started up, then hesitated, fear beginning to dominate her senses. Sallie Ann wouldn't really do anything to the baby, would she? Maybe that was the . . .

Sweat broke out anew across her lined forehead.

Old woman, you're letting your imagination get the better of you. Sallie Ann's a local girl. Ain't never been anyone around here that would harm a baby.

She braced herself against the handrail and continued

21

to ascend the stairs. She'd read in the paper where a woman in California had drowned her infant in the toilet.

The thumping became louder as she drew closer. Three-quarters of the way up she stopped and called out. "Sallie Ann, are you all right?"

Abigail knew she had spoken loudly enough for her voice to carry through the heavy wooden door, but there was no answer, only that peculiar noise.

She paused outside the closed room. The smell was so bad she had to cover her face with her hand. Dear God, what was in there? Suppose Sallie Ann really had killed the baby and she walked in and caught her? What would the girl do then?

Her mouth went dry. Should she turn away, simply go downstairs and pretend nothing was going on? Maybe she ought to call the sheriff. But about what? Because of a noise? A little garbage?

This was her house. She wasn't going to be intimidated—not by an eighteen-year-old girl!

Thump . . . thump . . . thump . . .

She grasped the brass knob with a shaking hand. She had no right to intrude. The girl might be engaged in a private act, but on the other hand . . .

In one solid, determined move she thrust it open. "Sallie Ann, I just thought—"

Abigail froze.

It was utterly unbelievable. At first she couldn't even comprehend what she saw; then her breath caught sharply and she staggered backward, recoiling with horror from the terrible scene before her.

On the floor near the rug, the gnarled form of the baby lay sprawled in a darkening puddle of glutinous fluid. Small glassy eyes stared sightlessly up at her. Its tiny body was hideously discolored, dry and crumbling, the skin recessed and pulled tightly over the bones. It was split in numerous places, huge jagged tears dissecting the misshapen miniature arms and legs, trailing all the

22

way into the fine feathering of downlike hair. The large, open lesions revealed a mass of yellowish slime that continued to vomit out of the wounds like lava as the baby's ashen flesh caved in further.

Abigail stood numbly in fear-choked disbelief. Her pulse beat wildly in her throat. It couldn't be real. Her mind blocked out all other thoughts. Nothing this horrible was possible. Then she saw the mother—Sallie Ann.

The window was open—no screen in it—and the young girl's emaciated, gray body, clothed only in a T-shirt and bright red panties, writhed spasmodically on the sill, half in, half out. Her head thumped uselessly against the porch roof. Her fingernails had left deep, notched scratches in the paint on the ledge. Sallie Ann clutched and convulsed, tangled in the white lace priscillas. Her brittle shape had begun to disintegrate and collapse inward. Abigail watched aghast as deep gashes erupted and carved their way across the girl's anguished frame, spewing a gruesome abundance of mucus.

Abigail was helpless to drag her gaze from the spectacle of the poor girl's dying struggle. Finally a scream burst from the fear-constricted passage of the old woman's throat. The sound bounced off the quaint Victorian wallpaper, while the plastic smiles of movie stars leered secretively at her. Her knees grew weak. She clenched her hands in despair.

Sallie Ann thrashed soundlessly, except for the sickening thump of her shriveled body against the ledge. There was one last movement, then the girl lay still.

Abigail staggered out into the hall and collapsed in a heap.

ii.

The ten-inch fan cranked around and around in the window, but made little headway against the heat in the kitchen. Sweat dripped from their faces and soaked through their clothing, but none of the other three seemed to notice. All were in a state of shock as they sat waiting for the doctor. Every window in the house was open, but you could still smell the pervasive odor creeping down the stairs. Stephen figured it would take weeks to get rid of it completely.

He leaned back in his chair and wiped his neck with a handkerchief. He was clad in faded jeans with the beginnings of holes wearing through at the knees and a plain white cotton shirt, rolled up at the elbows. His heavy, black hair looked as if it had been raked with his fingers rather than combed.

Stephen had already reckoned with and accepted the fact that it would be many nights until he got the picture of that room upstairs out of his head. He'd seen corpses before, but none like this. None so completely ravaged. There was damn little left up there that was recognizably human.

He watched the girl, Laura Morton, as Sheriff Robert Foss questioned her mother, Abigail. The girl was seated across from him: pale and tight lipped; long, slender fingers folded together atop the Formica table; big, somber green eyes. He liked her eyes.

She was pretty in a clean, wholesome way, the type who would never have spoken to him in high school or college, who would've avoided him on the street in his hoodlum days. She was one of those so-called nice girls—out of his league. He regarded her kind as a rare species of bird—something to be ogled and admired, but not experienced. In that pose, with her sober expression of fear, she would have made an excellent portrait. She was attractive. Honey blond hair, high forehead, graceful chin, remarkably clear complexion . . . a good model.

During his week's stay here, they hadn't said more than hello to each other—nor did he ever expect to—but when they met there was always the slightest hint of a smile at the corners of her mouth. He couldn't help wondering why, if perhaps they had met someplace before.

She turned and caught him staring at her. An expression of surprise crossed her face. She looked away flustered, hesitated, glanced back again, then returned her focus to her mother.

The sheriff questioned Abigail as Stephen awaited his own turn to be drilled. He hadn't known Sallie Ann, had never seen her other than in death, and doubted there were any clues he could give as to the cause of her bizarre demise.

His landlady grabbed a napkin from the plastic green container in the center of the table and loudly blew her nose.

"You're sure you didn't hear anything earlier?" the sheriff pressed Abigail.

The older woman shook her head. "I didn't hear anything until I started up the stairs." Abigail dabbed at her eyes with another napkin. There was a soggy, wadded-up pile in front of her.

The daughter listened without comment. She hadn't been up to the room where it happened. But Stephen would never forget. It was the stuff nightmares are made of. The sight of that tortured woman, twisted in the drapes. Her body sunken in, an ashen mound of flesh, covered with slime. And the smell . . .

"What do you know about this?" the sheriff asked, directing his attention to Stephen.

"Not much," he said cautiously. He was a stranger here and didn't want any trouble. "I heard Mrs. Morton scream. When I came out of my room, she was standing in the other woman's doorway. Then she fainted. That's when I saw the bodies. I helped Mrs. Morton downstairs and dialed the operator."

"You didn't hear anything either, then?" Foss insisted. "Before Abigail's scream, I mean?"

"No."

Foss turned back to the landlady. "How about your other tenants?"

She shook her head. "No one else is home during the

25

day."

The sheriff pulled at his chin and studied the stairs to the left.

"From what mother said," Laura spoke, "isn't this something like Jimmy Arnold's death?"

"But how could it be?" Abigail objected. "Wasn't his death an accident?"

"Maybe," Foss responded tersely. "Had they been down to the dump recently?"

Abigail shook her head. "What would they go to the dump for?"

"To drop off trash."

Laura had risen from the table and handed her mother a tall glass of ice tea.

Abigail took a long sip before answering. "Not Sallie Ann," she said firmly. "I don't mean to speak ill of the dead, but that girl wouldn't have gone out of her way to swat a fly. She never even did the diapers. She sent them over to her mother's house for cleaning. Three times a week, John hauled 'em over."

Foss nodded. "Maybe when the doctor gets here, he can put the pieces together. I'll be damned if I can figure it out. I've never seen anything like it before. Two corpses—three counting the boy. There's got to be a logical cause."

Stephen studied the husky, sunburnt sheriff as the lawman drew out a cigarette and lit it. There were tiny laugh lines around his eyes and deeper ones etched about his mouth. His face was mildly pitted, though that was fading with time. He had to be in his late forties or early fifties, and had probably spent his entire life in this Podunk town.

Stephen was sorry now that he'd come back. The change of scenery hadn't helped like he'd hoped. He had remembered this place through the idealized view of a child: corn, open fields, woods, freedom. The reality did not match up. He was no more free here than anywhere else. Yesterday was gone forever. He should've known.

26

Slowly, he drew his hand over his face and rubbed his eyes. He hadn't been able to sleep the last couple of nights.

The girl leaned toward him, concerned. "Want some coffee or ice tea?" she offered.

He straightened and smiled grimly. "Coffee, thanks."

"What about you, Sheriff?" she asked.

The big man shook his head. "Not now, honey."

Stephen watched with interest as the girl got up to fix him the coffee. It reminded him of his late wife Kat and how it felt to have someone who cared enough to do those little things for you. But this girl was different—innocent—untouched by the darker sides of life. He hoped she would remain that way. He planned to avoid her. Getting involved was too painful. He wanted to be alone; he needed time to heal.

Stephen Craig Myers was thirty-three years old, an ex-carpenter, an ex-boxer, and most recently an artist. But he no longer loved painting as he once had. Now it was merely the way he paid his bills and earned his keep. One way or another he had always made his living with his hands.

The Chicago neighborhood where he had grown up was as different from this place as China from Africa. He had been a skinny white kid in a nearly all black area, using his fists and his wits to survive. There had been only a few short years, when his family had farmed in Indiana, that he had glimpsed a more peaceful lifestyle; then his parents had moved back to the city and divorced. He never saw his father after that, and his mother died young—from too much work and worry.

He dropped out of high school at sixteen, like most of his peers, and hired on where his uncle worked as a carpenter. From there he went into the service for three years and became a trained boxer. He'd gone to college on the G.I. Bill and studied art, which had led him to Kat. But she was dead now. Murdered. There was a homicide committed nearly every day in Chicago. They

27

were costly and time consuming to pursue. No one cared about a cheap two-bit artist's model, and so the killer had never been apprehended.

It was all in the past now. He tried to forget. His dreams had ended when he learned that dreaming could be fatal.

He stared down at the cup between his hands. The coffee was hot and bitter, and he didn't really want it, had accepted it only to be polite. A silence nearly as heavy as that which hovered over the two grisly bodies upstairs had fallen over the kitchen.

The sheriff stepped forward and ground out his cigarette in a saucer. "I'd better call over to the feed and grain and talk to John," he said. "I don't know what I'm going to tell him. Sallie Ann and the baby. It couldn't be worse. I sure as hell wish Mike would get here. Maybe then I could tell that boy something about this that would make sense."

The phone rang.

Foss reached out one of his hamlike hands to answer it. "Sheriff, here," he boomed. His eyes narrowed. "Hold on."

He covered the mouthpiece and handed it to Stephen. "It's for you. Don't say anything about what happened. I don't want John to be the last one in Town to get the news."

Stephen nodded and pushed back his chair. At the same time, they heard a vehicle pulling up to the curb out front.

The sheriff slapped on his hat and turned down the hall to see who it was. Mrs. Morton and her daughter left the kitchen as soon as Stephen put the phone to his ear. Normally, he would've spent the day stripped to the waist, alone in his room, trying to push away memories and struggling to paint beautiful, serene images—pictures he could sell easily.

He stared out the window, past the whirling blades of the fan, at the neat, trim, fenced-in backyard, like the

28

one they had hoped for. Kat whispering softly, desperately, in the purple twilight of their bedroom: "It's ugly. I hate this city. One of these days we'll leave and never come back. I mean it. Everything will be good then. You'll see." And he had believed it; they both had. But with her death, their plans had become a nightmare destined never to end.

"Steve, are you there?"

He recognized the voice on the other end immediately. It was Henry Gorkenoff, and he sounded upset. "Sorry, Henry. I was lost in thought. How are you?"

"Not so good. Got bad news, I'm afraid. I can't figure out how it happened. We've never had this kind of trouble at the store before." Henry paused, then spoke again. There was no mistaking the genuine misery in his tone. "It's about those paintings you left in the storage room."

Stephen heard him swallow.

"I went up a few minutes ago to get a stepladder and discovered that someone had broken in. They utterly trashed the place. Tossed the canvases around. Ripped some of them up. Burned holes in others. Jesus, I don't know what . . ."

Stephen sucked in his breath so sharply it made his lungs ache. The paintings were all ones of Kat.

"You all right?" Henry asked.

"Yeah."

"I know how much they meant to you, but I figured it was better to let you know before you saw them. God, it's a mess. Cigarette butts, beer cans, piss all over the floor. Even left an old jacket. No ID, though. Whoever it was must've been there a couple of days. I can't figure out how they got in. Christ, it's three stories up. The only access is through the store, and nobody has a key to the room itself 'cept me and my dad. I feel really shitty about this. I don't know who would've done it or why. We don't get many vagrants 'round here."

"I'll come over and take a look."

"Sure. I'll be here. And Steve . . ." Henry hesitated.

"I'm sorry."

"It's okay."

Stephen replaced the phone on the hook, stunned. First Kat, then his paintings of her . . . all he had left.

"Trouble?" It was Laura Morton, standing beside him, so close he could feel the heat rolling off her body.

He stared down at her, unable to speak for a moment. He was certain the pain must've shown on his face, and he hated that, didn't like for anyone to know what he was feeling. He tried unsuccessfully to push it away, but it simply hurt too damn much.

The girl frowned, searching his face for an answer. Her eyes widened, big and green, luminous pools of sparkling emerald. For an instant he could almost pretend that he'd never had another life, that there had never been anything else . . . but no. This place wasn't going to be any good for him. No better than the last.

He cleared his throat to take the edge off it. "There's been some vandalism at Gorkenoff's Market."

"Vandalism? In broad daylight?"

"They aren't sure when it happened. It wasn't much. Some of my paintings that I had stored there," he said, digging the keys from his pocket. "I told Henry I'd be right over."

He turned and headed toward the back door as the sheriff was coming downstairs. "Where you going?" Foss asked sharply.

Stephen stopped and smiled. It was a hard, cold smile. He had control of himself now. "Over to Henry's. Don't worry, Sheriff. I'll be back."

"I'll need your statement for the inquiry."

"Well, you know where I'll be."

Without waiting for a reply, he stepped outside and let the old wooden screen door bang shut behind him. A hot breath of air ruffled through his hair.

Things never get any better, he thought, and let out an audible sigh.

The smell was nauseatingly ripe and full.

Dr. Michael L. Corliss entered the room alone; it had taken him several minutes to build up his courage. Nothing in medical school had prepared him for this. He drew out a mask and fastened it over his face, then pulled on a pair of latex gloves.

The sheriff had taken one glance at the gruesome spectacle of splitting, oozing bodies and decided against any further investigation on his part. He had immediately declared it out of his realm of expertise and gone back downstairs.

This was obviously out of Michael's line, too. He was a general practitioner, used to delivering babies and prescribing antibiotics. Only three years out of medical school, he wasn't prepared to take on anything so bizarre and frighteningly lethal by himself. He planned to call the university as soon as he got back to his office.

What if he made another mistake, another wrong diagnosis, and more died because of it? He blamed himself for not realizing with the Arnold boy what kind of tragedy they were dealing with. The mode of death was definitely the same. He shouldn't have let them talk him out of doing the autopsy. There might have been something to alert him to the danger sooner.

He looked over the shriveled remains surrounded by an abundance of sticky mucus, surprised not to see any blood. It didn't seem possible for the human body to so viciously self-destruct. Whatever it was, it was spreading. Three dead already. Almost a normal year's toll. Enough to turn life upside down in the peaceful little community of Town, or worse.

Both Mrs. Morton and the sheriff had been shocked by the dire fate of Sallie Ann and her child, but only Dr. Corliss could truly comprehend the terrible potential of what he was seeing.

He stepped over the baby, poor child—its future so horribly shortened—around the bed to the woman's contorted body.

His eyes filled with unexpected tears, and he brushed them aside with the back of his glove. He knew how many of the townspeople felt about this girl, but he had liked her. She had been so young and full of life, so wonderfully spontaneous and filled with silly dreams. Now it might be his fault that she and her baby were dead.

His sadness turned to anger, and then despair. What had killed them? Poison, disease?

The heat was accelerating the process of decay. Sallie Ann's once beautiful body was now grossly deformed, shrunken and riddled with gaping gray tears. He scanned quickly over the parchmentlike surface of her crumbling skin. The corpse had continued to fold inward upon itself, flaking and bursting with a multitude of lesions. A syrupy yellow residue wept slowly from the open wounds, congealing into a dark, tarlike puddle.

Half in, half out, her head lay thrust back against the shingles on the roof over the porch, her lovely cheeks and nose hollowed in and pulled tightly over her skull. Her lips were curled back in their futile attempt to stretch across her face.

Even now, he could still remember how beautiful she had been. His heart ached with regret. Such a waste. She was always so attractive, a pleasure to behold, even at the height of her pregnancy.

His gaze roved over the scratches in the paint and the drapes that were entangled around her skeletal arms and waist. Her back was violently arched, her brittle hands outstretched in frozen terror. Her blackened eyes were sunk deep within their sockets. She had put up a desperate struggle against death. Whatever claimed their lives had to have been brutally painful—and extremely horrifying.

Why had she gone to the window? Had she been trying to escape the plight of her flesh, intending to leap

32

from the ledge and end her suffering? Or had she been trying to shut something out before it attacked her?

He studied the scrapes of paint and her ragged nails, then glanced about the tiny apartment. He opened the bathroom door. The bathroom was empty. There was no evidence of anything out of the ordinary, but for some reason he felt threatened. An involuntary shudder of sudden fear rippled down his spine. Unspoken danger loomed on the faces of the two victims.

Anxious to be on his way, he opened his medical bag and took out several vials necessary for gathering on-site samples. He hoped they might yield clues later as to the cause of these monstrous deaths.

He reached down to pull Sallie in, handling her gently, as though she were yet alive. One hand wrapped around the back of her neck; the other grasped under her knees. He lifted, then felt an intense burning in his right hand and dropped the body back against the sill.

Searing pain shot up through his fingers to his shoulder.

He stared in dumb horror at his gloved hand. It looked as if the gummy mucus had literally eaten through the latex. He ripped off the glove and dashed to the bathroom sink, but already scaling gray patches were forming on his fingertips.

His thoughts raced while the icy water washed over his skin. His breath caught, then whistled from his throat in a silent scream. His testicles drew up. His belly felt as though it had turned to molten lead. Whatever it was they had died of, he was now infected.

Chapter Three

Stephen had decided to walk instead of driving the eight blocks to Gorkenoff's Market. He wanted a chance to let his head clear and his emotions settle. The gruesome enormity of this morning still weighed heavily on his mind. He didn't want Henry to think that he blamed him in any way for what had happened to the paintings. The Gorkenoffs had lost as much as he.

The storage room was at the top of a long, narrow staircase, and the only way to the stairs was through the Gorkenoff's workroom in the center of the store. It was difficult to imagine how anyone could've gotten into that room unnoticed, or why he would've made the effort. There was little of value in the garret, and it seemed an unlikely place to hide out, the risk of getting caught being so high.

Stephen stopped in front of the post office to wait for the light to change. It was one of just three signals in the entire county.

Town in either direction was only a couple of miles wide, a brief stretch of the legs. Every inch of it could be walked in an afternoon. The streets were lined with huge knotted shade trees and stately ornate houses that dated back a hundred years or more. There were no modern examples of architecture, except for a two-acre trailer park on the west side. The community claimed to have the oldest bank and the oldest church in the region.

34

Inside the antique storefront facades, the shops sold merchandise you would expect to find in ordinary stores, electric blankets and Nike sports equipment, while on the outside the buildings resembled those of a nineteenth-century village. The town elders hadn't planned it that way, but from a combination of historical events and economics that was how it had ended up. Visually, it was a slice out of time.

He crossed onto Mulberry Street and headed toward Main, keeping a brisk pace. His arms swung loosely at his sides. The sun glinted into his eyes as he stepped in front of an old woman on the corner. Her head turned, and she regarded him with obvious suspicion as he passed by.

No good, not even here, in a town so obscure it didn't have a true name. Everywhere the faces were faces of strangers, yet it made no difference. He carried the real enemy inside. There is no escaping who or what you are, he thought. It was as though the cobblestones themselves had memories—and they knew. The hate, the violence, the aching rage were written in his eyes.

The crooked brick streets and Victorian edifices were the same ones he remembered from his youth. It was a sharp contrast to the gray modernity of Chicago. He recognized the road signs, recalled this or that landmark, but it was all changed. Older perhaps, more worn. Less grand. Or was it he who had changed and matured? He couldn't be sure. Maybe a little of both.

He could not recapture that feeling of sheer enchantment he'd had as a child, and he could see the mistake now in looking back. He realized that he must not look back, at Kat, or at anything that was even an hour out of sight. For it was a race, a race to the end—to death and whatever lay beyond.

He might never actually have returned if it hadn't been for a chance meeting with Henry on the campus of Northwestern six years ago. Henry had been studying accounting. He was this crazy, second-generation Greek

35

with a head full of wild ideas for different businesses he could start up when he finished college. Nearly every week Henry had come to him with a new approach to success. One of them was to open an art gallery, featuring Stephen's work.

But then toward the end of Henry's senior year, his father had suffered a mild heart attack. Henry had gone straight home after graduation, and Stephen and he had gradually lost contact—until after Kat had died. Then, with nowhere else to go, he had remembered Henry and called him. He was ready for a peaceful, low-key lifestyle. Nothing bad could ever happen in a place like this. Nothing too terrible anyway.

It was going to be hard to confront those paintings again. He had planned to store them out of sight until he'd had time to recover. He wasn't ready to see her face again. The pain was too great, too fresh. Someday, he knew, he'd want them, want to hold onto the only shred of Kat he had left. But not yet. To look at them now would be like staring through the open lid of her coffin.

Kat had been the most beautiful and willing of all his models, clothes on or off. She could have gone to New York and been one of those faces that smiles up seductively from a magazine cover. But Kat had no ambitions of the monetary sort, and fame meant nothing to her. She screwed around—literally and figuratively—in the artists' quarters of his old neighborhood.

Like her name implied, she was long and lean and sexy. He had come to Kat's bed relatively naïve, or rather Kat had come to his bed. She had known all the secrets, and soon he had become convinced that she was all he truly desired from life.

More than anything Kat wanted to be innocent. She felt life and poverty had robbed her of it, but she intended to get her innocence back. She wanted to get away from the fury of the city, to achieve her own little piece of the All-American Dream, that house with the white picket fence . . .

Stephen stopped on the corner of Main, swallowing the bitterness that rose in his throat. His gaze moved slowly to the upper windows above Gorkenoff's Market and finally to the gable peak which hid the garret.

Henry stood sweeping the sidewalk in front of the large, plate-glass display window, amid tipped-up cartons of fresh fruits and vegetables the Gorkenoffs had on special. He mopped the sweat from his face with his shirtsleeve and glanced down the street. His eyes fastened on Stephen's.

Henry's long, narrow face looked tight and flushed in the heat. His heavy, bristly brows were knit in one continuous dark line across his forehead and nose. The curly black hair and protruding brown eyes made him look younger than his twenty-eight years.

In the years since college Henry had done none of the stupendous things he'd planned with such enthusiasm at Northwestern. Instead, he was working for his father, helping to run the family business.

"Hi," Henry said tiredly as Stephen approached. He leaned the broom in the corner against the window. "Come on in. I'll get you something to drink. My folks are waiting inside. They're pretty upset, too."

Henry stepped back and pulled open the narrow glass door. A brass bell tinkled above them. The aromas of fresh-baked bread, deli meats, and cooling pies enveloped them. A huge fan with greasy, black blades whirled noisily on a high stool in the rear doorway.

The store was filled with polished mahogany, crown molding, and marble-colored tile. An old-fashioned brass cash register with a little red No Sale tag graced the main display case. A couple of kids with foot-long submarine sandwiches sat at one of the tables.

Mrs. Gorkenoff stood in a large flowered housedress behind a row of glass shelves full of bakery goods. There were plates of cookies, cakes, pastries, and marzipan candies fashioned into the shapes of all kinds of colorful fruits. She smiled broadly when she saw the two enter.

She looked like Henry, only much, much plumper, and reminded Stephen a little of his landlady as she brushed a strand of damp gray hair from her cheek.

"I'm so happy to see you again," she said to Stephen, but then her smile faded. "It was a terrible thing that happened. I cried when I heard. I can't go up there. I won't be able to sleep tonight."

Her husband emerged from the back workroom, side-stepping the fan. He was clad in a white shirt, with a navy silk tie held fast by a simple gold stick pin, and dark suit pants, and wore a powdery apron fastened around his waist.

"How're you doing, Steve," he said quickly, moving around the counter and wiping his hands. He spoke rapidly with a thick accent that was sometimes hard to follow. "I can't believe my eyes. What it looks like up there! I've never seen such a mess. Who would do such a thing? It's a nice town. Nothing like this ever happened before. We don't have that kind of hoodlums around here. Nobody ever steals anything, they don't break the windows, or pop off your hubcaps. No, I can't believe this. In my heart . . ." The old man thumped his chest with an expression of sorrow, as if to say whoever had done this had broken his heart.

Stephen extended his hand and firmly clasped the old man's. "I'm sorry, sir. If there's anything I can do . . ."

Cecil Gorkenoff raised both arms and shook his head. "It's not your fault. A black day. We must try to forget. You want a sandwich, something to eat?"

"No, thank you."

"A cookie, maybe?" Mrs. Gorkenoff offered. She held one out over the top of the counter. "Chocolate chip. Everybody's favorite. You try it." Her lively brown eyes were both sad and happy at the same time.

Stephen took the cookie. It was big and round, nearly the size of his open palm.

Mrs. Gorkenoff nodded appreciatively as he bit into it, and her husband waved them toward a marble and wrought-iron table in the corner. "How about bringing us a couple of beers, Ruthie?"

Mrs. Gorkenoff brushed her large flat hands on a towel and waddled toward the cooler.

"They didn't take anything," the old man continued, "just broke everything up. I don't understand that kind of crime. Who wins? We come here to get away, to avoid this type of thing, and what happens? But we don't have trouble like they have in the big cities." He used his hands to suggest what he thought of big cities, which wasn't much. "Nobody here would do anything like this—." Then he stopped and took a deep breath, because somebody obviously had. "We sold six of your new paintings. The people love them. You paint some more."

"Yes. As many as you want."

"That's good. The ones upstairs. Henry tells me they were of your wife."

Stephen nodded. His throat was too tight for words.

"She was very beautiful. My son told me what happened to her. Chicago's a bad place. You find another girl soon." The elder Gorkenoff dug into his pocket. "I want to pay you. I feel very bad. Money can't make up for something so terrible, but . . ."

"No," Stephen interrupted. "You don't owe me anything. You were doing me a favor. I didn't have anywhere else to store them. Please."

Mr. Gorkenoff nodded, then grinned, revealing black rotted and yellow tobacco-stained teeth. "You got a nice friend here," he said to his son. "I buy you lunch. My wife would be very insulted if you did not eat with us. Excuse me, please." He rose to attend a customer who had burst through the door.

Henry sighed. "I thought my dad was going to have another heart attack when he saw that room. This place means so much to him."

"I like him," Stephen said. "I hope he won't be offended, but I'm not hungry. I'd like to see the paintings now."

39

"Sure. He'll understand."

Henry scooted the chairs into place under the table and led the way toward the back stairs. Stephen had been up to the garret only once, when he'd first brought over the paintings.

They passed through the rear workroom. It was packed with huge cooking utensils, confection ovens, large vats, a slicer—everything the Gorkenoffs needed for the deli side of their business. The couple also sold canned goods, yard goods, and unusual items such as porcelain dolls imported from France—Mrs. Gorkenoff's passion. The business was a mishmash of the family interests.

Henry opened a door at the far end of the workroom, and they stood staring up at the dark, enclosed staircase. Henry reached up and flipped on a light switch above the rail. A single naked bulb emitted a dim, yellowish glow at the base of the stairwell. The steps were lined with layers of dust. Several sets of shoe tracks, leading up and down, were stamped one overlapping the next. Long black shadows loomed threateningly over the stairs like jagged teeth.

Stephen hesitated a second, then grasped the handrail and followed Henry. The air grew denser and more stifling with each step.

Although there were landings at each of the three floors, this passage was the sole access to the fourth floor, which was a finished-off attic. The steps were steep and old, but they were the only ones that went all the way up. The main stairs inside the house went no farther than the third floor.

It was hot, and getting hotter as they ascended. Sweat poured from every gland. Stephen's shirt clung to his back and chest. Moisture dripped from his forehead.

The stench of urine was nearly overpowering in the confines of the narrow corridor, but there was an even more sickening odor rising above it. Putrid, like spoiled meat.

Stephen wiped the perspiration from his eyes with his

sleeve. That smell . . . decay hung fetid and foul in the air. He thought of Sallie Ann, her body shattered with ugly surging gashes. The smell was much the same. Christ. He tried not to breathe too deeply.

His canvas shoes made hollow slapping sounds on the rough planks. It echoed back dully, emptily. His heart pounded heavily, not just from the climb. He felt decidedly uneasy as they neared the top. Looking back, he could barely see the faint glow at the bottom.

Then, it began to grow lighter again, the hazy grayness giving way. His eyes rapidly adjusted. He could feel a breeze.

Following in Henry's path, he moved slowly off the stairs into a tight landing. A stream of light sliced into the darkness from a partially open window at one side.

There was a room on each side of the stairs. The door to the left was open several inches. Henry pushed gently. The rusty hinges creaked as it widened. The space reeked of death. Stephen half expected to find another corpse. But as his eyes scanned the debris he did not immediately see one. The mess was unbelievable.

Henry's face tightened. "They didn't have to do this. They could've slept here without tearing the place up."

The contents had been completely devastated. Lawn chairs were bent and slashed. A box of stored clothing had been literally cut to ribbons. Stray pieces of fiber coated the room with a layer of fuzz. And there were matted places of darkness—urine and feces.

Stephen walked slowly around the wreckage, toward the inner wall. "My God, how on earth could they have done this without anyone hearing?"

Henry shrugged. "It could've been anytime. The shop's a pretty noisy place, and it's three floors down. We'd never have heard." He stopped and drew a breath, then grimaced. "It's bad, isn't it?"

Stephen nodded. He could see his paintings from here, on the other side. They were tossed together in a jumbled heap of splintered frames and ripped canvases, a massacre of faces, arms, and legs. He tried not to look — not yet.

He picked up a blanket littered with cigarette butts and brushed them off on the floor. The intruder had even taken an axe and chopped wedges out of the wooden ladders.

It made no sense, Stephen thought. A crime of this sort. But even more disturbing was the sweet-rottish odor of decomposition. Because it was so familiar. So like the room where Sallie Ann had died. Her baby . . . What if whoever had trashed this room had also been suffering from the same thing?

Then a corpse would be here, and it wasn't. All the other victims had died quickly. None of them had even been able to call for help.

So what was causing the smell?

The stench was strongest in the corner. He picked up the tattered denim jacket Henry had referred to. A film of powdery gray soot covered the floor beneath it. The odor from the jacket was utterly repulsive.

As he tossed it back down, he spotted a yellow receipt from the hardware store.

"I saw that, too," Henry said. "I don't know if it'll do any good, but I thought I'd give it to Foss."

"I'll help you clean up," Stephen volunteered.

"It's kind of overwhelming. Where do we start?" Henry asked.

"I don't know." Stephen paused, thinking of the window. "How do you suppose they got in?" Curious, he stepped out into the hall and looked to see if anyone could've climbed up the side of the house.

Henry was right behind him. "It's a straight drop," he said. "They'd have needed a crane to get up here."

There were no dings or scrapes on the siding. No fresh mars in the paint. But somehow they had gotten in.

Stephen could think of no answers. He pulled away from the window. He wasn't going to be able to figure it out alone. It was beyond his powers of reasoning. Like the sheriff had said, maybe the doctor could. Right now, he was anxious to get away from the sight and the fetor of it all.

He walked back into the garret and gingerly took hold of the first painting. . . .

Chapter Four

His hand was unsteady. Instead of gripping the bottle of vodka on the desk before him, he knocked it on its side. The colorless liquid splashed over the notes he had made, smearing the ink.

"Damn it!" Dr. Michael Corliss cried out in frustration.

He didn't usually drink, but today he couldn't help himself. He set the bottle back up and went into the bathroom for a fistful of paper towels, then looked with dread at his injured hand, the one that had contacted Sallie Ann. He couldn't believe it had happened.

The flaky gray sores on his fingertips had started to spread even before he left the Mortons. There in that room, with the two corpses watching, he had immediately given himself an injection of cortisone and bandaged the hand.

His fingers had begun to wither for awhile, but now, five hours later, they were nearly normal again. The unnatural color remained, however, the ulcerous patches festering and oozing a cloudy, yellow mucus occasionally. He frequently checked to see if they had grown or increased, expecting at any moment that it might begin taking over his body as it had Sallie Ann's and the baby's. He had come up with no reason yet for why his glove had not protected him.

It was impossible, and yet the seepage from her corpse had seared like hydrochloric acid through the latex, while her clothes and the curtains were both unaffected. But how?

He pounded his fist against the desk. He fought to stay calm and approach the situation logically as his medical training had taught him. He knew there were substances that would break down plastic without affecting cloth, such as petroleum. But how could any element formed by the human body have had such a violent response to latex?

He had spent these last hours desperately poring over textbooks, compiling notes, and running the results through his home computer. Nothing made sense. There had to be an added ingredient. No chemical known to man could have produced this reaction.

He'd debated everything possible—poison, plagues, toxins, bacterias. The results were unreal. In fact, he was sure he must've made a mistake. The mucus itself appeared to be not the normal defensive mechanism of the body's immune system, but the by-product of digestion.

The autopsies had proven even more baffling. When he'd examined Sallie Ann closer, he'd found that not a single internal organ remained. The victim's interiors were literally consumed from within, and all that remained was a combination of bones and gastric juices encased in her twisted, sooty skin. There was no blood. He'd run numerous tests on the corrosive secretion. It was high in many common enzymes, but there were other ingredients in it, too, ones that he was unable to identify as of yet.

What freakish catalyst could Sallie Ann and the Arnold boy have come in contact with to cause this?

He kept hoping it was all a bad dream, that he would awake in a few hours to discover it was nothing more than his overworked imagination. He was just preparing

45

to go over the lists another time, for any details he might have missed, when he spilled the bottle.

He had been drinking all afternoon to numb the pain and drive out the gruesome reality of what had happened. He knew he shouldn't combine alcohol with the cortisone already in his system, but he had to get a grip on himself.

With shaking hands, he lifted the soggy papers and dumped them into a metal waste can, then mopped up the mess on the desktop. He would have to start over, and he wasn't sure how much time he had. The injury on his hand had made him a walking time bomb.

Be a doctor, son. Make lots of money. People will think you're smart; they'll give you respect. You won't have to peddle your ass all across the country like your poor old dad.

He'd done everything they'd told him to, worked hard, stayed away from women and booze. He'd paid his residency dues changing bedpans and performing tonsillectomies at the county hospital.

He had the grades and the recommendations to have gotten into a fine practice in Indianapolis, but he hadn't gone into medicine for the money, as his father had suggested.

He wanted to work on his own. This was his personal struggle against evil, against the corruption of the mind and tissue. From the moment of its conception, the body was a doomed machine, destined for disease, old age, and eventual death. The great deprivers of the human spirit. The insidious cripplers that turned spunky, robust twelve year olds into frail, bitter old men.

He was young, only thirty-one. Not ready to die. Life was just opening up for him. Eight years of medical school, then two years of residency. He couldn't let the door close yet. There was so much he had planned to do, so much he'd missed out on. He hadn't any wife or kids. No one to mourn him, no one to carry his genes into immortality.

He grasped the black vinyl address book from the corner of the desk. He had to have help to fight this thing. 317-555-7792. Dr. Philip Thompson, head of biology and forensic sciences at the university in Indianapolis. The good professor would know what to do, how to save his soul from hell.

As he reached for the phone he heard a knock at the office door.

It was after 6:00 p.m.; his office closed regularly at 5:00, but today, on account of the deaths, he had closed even earlier.

He put down the book and glanced at his hand. No change. He would get rid of whoever it was quickly.

The knocking came again.

Loud and forceful.

It might be an emergency.

He grabbed a stale cup of coffee and swished it around in his mouth to mask the alcohol on his breath, then glanced at himself in the bathroom mirror on his way past.

The pounding outside his office door continued.

"I'm coming," he shouted. "Just a minute."

His sandy hair was tousled. He smoothed it with the palm of his good hand and tucked in his shirttails. His skin felt clammy. His heart was racing. He didn't know if it was because of the infection or the mixture of drugs and alcohol, but what did it matter? Sweet Mother of God, what did anything matter?

He slid back the dead bolt and opened the door. Sheriff Foss stood on the other side, smoking a cigarette.

"Evening, Mike. I was wondering if you'd come up with anything on those bodies yet."

"No, uh . . . I . . ."

"Mind if I come in?"

Michael hesitated. He was suddenly overcome by the pressing desire to conceal his damaged hand. If people knew he was infected, he wouldn't be allowed to continue his work. He'd be put in the hospital, stuck in isolation,

47

away from his patients and everything that mattered.

He quickly hid the hand behind his back as he pulled the door wider. He could feel the vicious burning begin anew and tried not to wince.

"This thing has me scared," the sheriff said. "And I'm not the only one. The phone's been ringing off the hook down at the station, people wanting to know what happened. I got a call over to the Gorkenoffs. Their attic was torn up. I don't know if it's got anything to do with the rest of this, but Steve Myers said it smelled just like the room where that girl died. They half expected to find somebody dead up there, but they didn't. I don't mind telling you this situation's got me stumped. Folks are wanting some answers, and I don't know what to tell them." He tapped the ash from his cigarette into an empty vase on the receptionist's desk.

Michael wanted to shout: "Get out! Get out, and leave me alone." Somehow, he managed to stay cool. But time . . . time was running out.

"You're asking me for information I don't have. I'm trying to isolate the cause. As a matter of fact, before you showed up I was about to call one of my colleagues from the university for advice. So if you don't mind . . ."

"You've got to understand how people feel."

"I'm concerned, Sheriff. That's why I'm anxious to get on with my work." He was ushering the broad-shouldered lawman toward the door.

"Let me know what your friend says, will you?"

Michael nodded. Get out. Get out.

Foss started through the door, then turned back. "Say, you all right? You don't look good."

"I'm fine." Michael smiled to prove it, but the smile cut across his pale face like a rubber slit.

Foss hesitated, then started down the walk. "See you t'morrow, Mike."

Corliss couldn't let him go, not without some kind of warning. "Oh, Bob—"

48

The sheriff stopped.

"Tell Mrs. Morton not to clean that room. I'll drop by tomorrow and do it myself. No one should handle any of the fluids that came from either of those bodies. They're highly corrosive."

"Okay. I'll tell her." Foss stood for a moment looking puzzled, as if he was waiting for more, but the doctor shut the door.

Corliss stared at his hand. No change. In spite of the renewed burning, no change. There still might be time.

He rushed to his office, picked up the book, pushed in the number. Ringing, again and again. Goddamnit. He has to be home. A click: someone answering the phone. Please, not an answering machine. No. It was a live voice. Young. Friendly. Female.

"Dr. Thompson's residence. May I help you?"

"This is Michael Corliss." He tried not to hurry, to keep the flow of words natural. "I was a student of his, and I have a problem I need his help with."

"I'm sorry, but the doctor's not in right now. Is this an emergency?"

"Yes, it is."

"Dr. Clancy will be seeing Dr. Thompson's patients for the rest of the week. Would you like the number?"

"No. I have to talk to Dr. Thompson. Would you tell him it's desperate? Three people are dead, and there may be another soon." His voice stumbled over the last few words. "Please, tell him."

"I'll try to reach him."

"Thank you." He gave the girl his number and hung up.

The sheriff's visit had sobered him considerably. He knew he had to get back to work. His wasn't the only life at stake here. He had to quit feeling sorry for himself and go in there and resume searching for an answer. He had to confront Sallie Ann again, and the voraciously malign thing that had killed her.

In his mind, he knew there had to be a rational cause,

a logical explanation for the shocking way they had died. But from further down in his spinal cord, a black fear emanated in mounting waves, telling him it was something much darker and deeper, more primitive.

Chapter Five

i.

Laura rocked in the swing on her mother's front porch, her long bare legs gently pumping it back and forth in the dark. The rusted chains squeaked softly above her with each slow movement.

She glanced warily into the deep black shadows hovering at either end of the long narrow stoop. It was infinitely cooler out here, but the gloomy twilight made her feel uneasy, more vulnerable, especially after what had happened to Sallie Ann.

The night was filled with a continual chirping and croaking that rose and fell all around her. Normally she would have enjoyed such a warm, tranquil evening, but not now. Even the traffic on the highway had lessened and muted itself for the night. She told herself it was typical for 9:00 p.m. on a Monday in town, though that didn't help. The sweet scent of June roses drifted across the yard from the white, fan-shaped trellis, but she found no comfort in it. The stench of death still lingered in her nostrils.

She had forfeited modesty for comfort by wearing a pair of brief, ragged, cut-off denim shorts. Her short, midriff T-top hung loosely over her breasts, exposing her tanned, lean waist. It had been a difficult and tedious afternoon with no memorable moments. Not a great

51

start of a summer vacation.

Her mother had oscillated throughout the long daytime hours between heavy periods of somber reflection and hysterical outbursts about how it was all that trashy country girl's fault. Curious neighbors and relatives had made numerous visits to exchange shocked reactions to the frightful news. When her mother had finally seen the last of them away and dozed off to fitful slumber on the living room sofa, Laura had breathed a sigh of relief.

Somehow she made it through the day, but tomorrow would be just as bad. Going up there to that apartment, helping to pack the dead woman's belongings and the baby's crib.

Oh, God. It didn't seem possible that such an awful thing had really happened.

Sallie Ann's husband had come running over from the feed and grain as soon as they told him. He went up to their room, though the sheriff had forbidden it. Heartwrenching sobs tore from his throat in wild gutteral pleas. He'd come down an hour later with a bleary-eyed expression of disbelief, and that was the last she'd seen of him.

A queasy, disturbing sensation settled into the pit of her stomach as she thought how the same thing might have happened to any one of them. Sheriff Foss made it clear they didn't know the cause of death. It might have been something Sallie Ann touched—something she ate. Laura shivered and stared out into the velvet sky laced with stars.

Down the street, a dog barked. It provoked another into the same kind of thoughtless response. In the distance, a car horn honked. There were crickets, and occasionally a voice, one of the neighborhood kids passing through their yard. Nothing more than usual noises, nothing to betray the ominous events of the morning.

She stretched her arm along the back of the wooden slats and rested her head against it. A light went on in a window across the street and then back out again; within seconds the house was plunged into darkness. A pair of car lights turned off Vine and headed up Elm. Maybe she should go up to bed, she thought, feeling herself grow wearier. Long day . . . long night . . . her mind drifted into a world of murky images and uncertain fear.

"Laura?"

She awoke when she heard her name and quickly sat up, startled to see Stephen Myers leaning against the railing in front of her. He was holding his shirt in one hand. His hair was damp and his shoulders covered with a sheen of sweat, as though he'd been working out or jogging.

"It's late," he said. "You ought to go inside."

"I know." She stifled a yawn. She had lost track of time. "But it's still so hot in the house. Did you just get back from the Gorkenoff's?"

He nodded. He looked drained in the pale sodium glare from the street lamps. "The garret was trashed. I stayed to help Henry clean up." He paused, and she glanced up into his eyes. Whatever he was feeling, he kept it carefully concealed.

"This might sound strange," he continued, "but I've been meaning to ask you—do we know each other from someplace else?"

"Sort of," she answered, a little embarrassed. "I met you at one of your art shows in Chicago."

"Oh?" His eyebrows raised.

"Yeah. It was in a small, ritzy brick building with a pink and yellow striped awning."

He thought a moment, and she laughed nervously. "I'm sure you don't remember."

"I remember the building."

"But you don't remember me."

"No," he admitted. It was a soft, drawn-out sound. "I was fairly busy in those days, and most of it's a blur."

He shifted his weight against the post.

"You look tired. Do you want to sit down?" She indicated the empty seat next to her on the swing.

"Thanks." He sagged down beside her.

They swung in absolute silence for several minutes. She was intrigued by his mysterious past and had been hoping to get to know him ever since he showed up at the boardinghouse. He was good-looking, she thought, and she wouldn't mind going out with him.

Laura broke the quiet first. "You know, I can't figure it out. Whatever possessed you to pack your bag and come to town? Why did you leave everything? I would've thought you had it all."

"Looks can be deceiving. I had my reasons." His gaze shifted toward the ground. He seemed to be studying the varying degrees of shadows that flickered across the cement.

"I'm sorry. I didn't mean to pry."

"No, it's okay. My wife died, and . . . well, I just couldn't make it work any more. The two of us had been trying to buy an old farmhouse in a place like this, planning to fix it up. I came here looking for a change of scenery. At least that's what I told myself."

"And?"

"And it's not turning out to be quite what I had envisioned."

"I know what you mean. It's a trap here. Everyone doing nothing, going nowhere. I can't wait to go away to school in the fall."

"Where are you going?"

"University of Iowa. I haven't decided on a major yet."

"What are you considering?"

"You name it, I've considered it. Business Administration, Computers, Chemistry. I haven't been able to find anything that I really want to end up doing the rest of my life."

"But whatever it is, you don't plan to do it here?"

She tipped back her head and laughed. "Never in a

million years. My mother's always telling me I should become a teacher, but I could never do that. I don't have the patience. You went to college, didn't you? That's where you met Henry, right?"

He nodded. "I only took classes now and then. I never graduated."

The silence resumed for a few moments, then she asked: "What about now? Had enough of life in the boondocks?"

He shrugged. "I haven't really given it a chance. It's only been a week."

"That would be enough for me ... especially after this morning."

He nodded.

She waited for him to say something more, but he didn't. They sat staring at the sky. It was well past midnight. The moon was nearly out of sight. She was hoping he'd kiss her. Finally she found the courage to break the silence.

"I like you, Steve. Very much."

"I like you, too."

He leaned forward, putting one arm around her shoulder to draw her closer and the other against her waist. His mouth pressed lightly on hers.

Laura closed her eyes. His lips were firm with the hardness of teeth behind them. The kiss fluctuated, light then strong.

He pulled back and smiled. "It's late. You'd better go in. Your mother doesn't trust me as it is."

"Yeah. I'm sorry about that."

"It's okay."

She looked around as he held the door open for her and thought she saw someone watching them—a man in a light colored flannel shirt—but the figure drew back and blended with all the other night shadows, and she wasn't sure she'd seen anything at all.

ii.

In his room at the far end of the hall, Stephen undressed in darkness and climbed into bed. He worried about the evening. He had vowed not to get involved again, and then he had. Laura was a nice girl, but it wouldn't be fair to either of them. He wasn't yet recovered from Kat.

He lay down and wished for sleep, but it was difficult. He caught sight of his easel and the canvas he'd been working on. It was splashed with shades of charcoal and midnight blue: a thunderstorm over the lake. But as he studied it in the blackness of the room he thought it looked more like a hurricane.

That night he dreamt of Kat. He relived the last hours they'd spent together—when she kissed him good-bye and left for the modeling assignment from which she never returned.

Wednesday, June 14

The nether world beckoned . . .

Chapter Six

i.

Piggy Woodhouse and his new friend, Hank Stoddard, let their bicycles fall on the rutted trail that ran alongside of Town Creek. Piggy had been very pleased when Hank called him up and asked if he wanted to go along. Piggy didn't have a lot of friends. In fact, he didn't have any—not at the moment—not until this afternoon.

He was an oversized youth—just under six feet and going into the sixth grade next fall—with buck teeth and thick glasses. He had a lot of soft, white flesh and a sluglike belly that lapped over the edge of his pants, like Pop's, only smaller.

It was because of his size, he told himself, that most of the other kids didn't like him.

Jimmy Arnold's funeral had been two days ago, and Piggy was about the only one in his class who hadn't attended. It was a frightening thing to have somebody you saw every day in school, somebody you stood behind in the lunch line and threw wads of toilet paper at in the john, suddenly wind up dead.

Piggy wasn't even sure what dead meant, except that he knew it wouldn't be pleasant. He had watched bugs and spiders die. He'd tear off one of their legs or squash part of their juicy bodies, and they'd limp along, still kicking and pulling, dragging the damaged parts after them. He could tell it was difficult for them; they were straining and struggling and they didn't usually go too far, but he couldn't tell just what it was like. They showed no emotions.

He'd seen a couple of dead cats and dogs by the edge of the highway, but that didn't tell him much, either. They were pretty picked over by the maggots and weather by the time he had gotten to them. The thing that impressed him most was the cold, dull stare they all had. He'd watched once while flies crawled over a dog's eye. It didn't even blink. That was dead for you.

Hank was busily untying his gear from the back of his bike. They had brought their rods and tackle boxes with them. Fishing was one of Piggy's favorite pastimes. It didn't take much energy. He could lie on the grass all afternoon, soaking up the sun, and actually get something back for his effort.

The creek wasn't very deep or wide. It was a tributary from the Big Blue River, but by the time it got to Town there wasn't much left. The stream continued through these woods, finally trickling into a small pond on the east edge of Town. But it was good enough for catching steelies and pickerel, which was all that mattered.

Piggy was wondering just how he had happened to get so lucky as to be invited along on this little sojourn when Hank called out, "Let's set up down here."

Hank had put his box atop a large boulder and was baiting his line. It was a nice sunny spot across the bank from a grove of water oak. Anywhere else it would've been a hot, sticky afternoon, but the air rolling out of the woods was moist and cool. Piggy hitched his pants and waddled down to the water's edge with his rod and red plastic tackle box.

"You ever smoke grass?" Hank asked.

Piggy shook his head, and his chin quivered like jelly.

The water churned past them in a clear, bubbly stream, so clear he could see the smooth pebbles on the bottom of the bed, but no fish.

It was a funny thing, because he hadn't seen any ants or bugs crawling through the grass, either. He didn't hear any birds calling out or squirrels scampering between the trees.

It was odd.

Piggy had been down here many times, but it was never this quiet, never this still, never this empty.

Goose bumps rippled down his padded spine. He wanted to go home, but couldn't. He couldn't let Hank know he was scared. And scared of what? he asked himself. He had no answer, except for maybe the terrible stillness. The utter lack of movement screamed with its very presence that something was horribly wrong.

He awkwardly lowered his bulk onto the ground beside Hank, who was busily rolling a joint. The plastic bag of pot and packet of rolling papers had been concealed in his tackle box.

"This is s-o-m-e potent weed," Hank said. "I got it from my sister's stash. She and her boyfriend are always getting high. You're lucky I share with my friends."

"Yeah," Piggy echoed, but he wasn't feeling too lucky any more. He didn't want to get into trouble, and this looked like it could be. He'd never so much as smoked a cigarette or lied to his mother. He didn't even swear.

Hank lit up the joint and passed it to Piggy. "Here. Take deep breaths. You got to draw it way down in your lungs to get the full effect."

Piggy pinched the crinkled paper between his fat fingers and did as he was told. He took several long breaths, ignoring the burning at the back of his throat.

They slowly finished the first, and Hank rolled a second. Both boys leaned back against the boulder with their poles in the water. Within fifteen minutes, Piggy was thinking how fine he felt, how he hadn't ever felt so fine in his whole life. The sun seemed to grow warmer, and the whole day had mellowed out. He no longer felt afraid. He was like a tub of warm butter melting on the creek bank, absorbing the sun's energy and becoming aware that for all these years he had always underestimated himself. He was not such a bad fellow at all.

He smiled at Hank.

"You feel good, Piggy?"

"Real good."

"I'm glad. I like my friends to have a good time when I'm around."

"Yeah." Piggy let the pole slip from his hands. His eyelids were growing heavy.

"I hear you eat anything, Piggy."

The fat boy shrugged.

"I hear you'd eat your own shit if your mother would let you. Isn't that so?"

Piggy didn't answer.

"I said, isn't that so."

"I guess." Piggy was beginning to feel a little sick to his stomach.

Hank reached into a Tupperware container full of night crawlers and drew out a fistful. "I want you to eat these for me. I ain't catching no fish, so I want you to eat 'em."

Piggy looked at the worms wriggling in Hank's muscular fist, and swallowed nervously. They looked kind of like raw hamburger.

"Eat 'em, Piggy."

"I don't want to."

Hank handed him another joint with his free hand. "Smoke this, and then eat 'em."

Piggy took the marijuana and sucked the smoke down. Tears stung the corners of his eyes. Hank wasn't his friend. He'd invited him out here so he could make fun of him like all the others. But at least Hank *had* invited him. Maybe if he ate the worms, if he did what Hank told him to, Hank would learn to like him. They could be buddies and Hank would *make* all the other boys like him.

Piggy let the stub of the joint fall from his fingers. He heard a loud buzzing like a swarm of mosquitoes. It was the first noise he'd heard besides their own since entering the woods. And there was a smell, too, not dead fish or algae like the creek usually reeked of, but something worse. He held out his plump white hands, and Hank filled them with wet, slithering worms.

He'd close his eyes, Piggy thought, and it wouldn't be so bad. If he just didn't think about them moving and squirming.

Piggy looked up one final time to see if Hank was really going to make him go through with it. The dark-haired boy was grinning, actually laughing. Piggy brought the night crawlers closer to his face. The buzzing grew louder.

He saw a weird, iridescent shadow behind Hank that seemed to hover and then move forward. He wondered what it could be. Hank's expression was filled with morbid anticipation as he waited for Piggy to swallow the worms. But Piggy's eyes widened in dumb horror—then the swirling gray vapor surrounded them both. . . .

ii.

Angela Stoddard was going places. But first she had to find her snot-nosed little brother. It was almost dark, and he still hadn't come home.

She tramped over the field toward the woods and the bright glaring rays of the setting sun. Darn that insufferable brat. She'd been upstairs dressing, shaving her legs and smoothing them over with a musk-scented body lotion, when her mother had hollered up for her to go out and find Hank. She was planning to see "him" tonight, and if Hank made her late she'd slug him.

The brittle weeds and dried grass broke under her glossy black pumps. There was a path worn where all the kids in the neighborhood rode their bikes down to the creek. Angela hated her brother and his gross friends, and she hated the woods at night. The long shadows and creaky old branches gave her the willies.

How come Hank couldn't look out for himself? How come she had to have a little brother, anyway?

Maybe he'd fallen in the water and drowned. It wasn't very deep, but just maybe. Or, maybe some sex pervert had nabbed him. Just as long as she didn't ever have to put up with his smart-assed remarks again.

Yesterday he'd come bursting into the bathroom as she was stepping out of the shower. He had stood ogling her with his mouth agape, until, naked and wet, she had forcefully shoved him out the door. He'd claimed he hadn't known she was in there, and their mother had let him get away with it, but Angela knew he had done it on purpose. The little creep.

Though Angela was only a high school junior, she already knew a lot about life—like how to get what you wanted. She'd been blessed with a curvaceous body that would've been the envy of any thirties or forties pinup queen. She had boobs, large, full ones like Jane Russell that bounced when she walked, a trim waist, and saucy hips.

Her assets were firm and compact and filled out the lines of her blue summer shift to perfection. There was only the tiniest bulge at her tummy, but soon it would be growing. That had her worried. She had to settle her business quickly. If her father found out, it would mess up everything.

Something moved in the bushes ahead. She let out a gasp and jumped. A skinny brown rabbit dove from the undergrowth and sprinted through the purple-shaded trees.

Angela put her hand over her heart to slow its wild pounding and watched the rabbit scurry into the distance. For a moment, she wished she was that rabbit, free to simply run from its troubles. But it was destined to spend its days hungry, scrounging and digging for food, and Angela was not.

She and her lover would discuss "the problem" tonight.

If he wanted her to get an abortion she would, in fact she'd rather, but first he would have to file for divorce. She wasn't leaving all her eggs in one basket, though. If Pokey . . . that was the pet name she had given him, and he liked it because poking was the name of their game . . . if Pokey failed to come through with the divorce, she'd settle for money if it was enough. And if worse came to worse, she could always blame the pregnancy on her boyfriend, Ned, though they had never had sex.

Pokey had insisted she keep seeing Ned, though he knew a boy like that would never interest her. It was part of their cover, so the world would never suspect what was going on between the two of them. In public she was Ned Charmichael's girl, but in truth she could never belong to him.

Ned was a simpleton like the other boys she'd met in high school. He might object a little to paying for somebody else's good time, but he was in love with her. A fatal mistake in Angela's book. She'd never allow herself to fall in love with anyone.

Ned could sell his motorcycle to pay for the abortion, and Angela would promise to be true to him from here on out. She'd even be sure to screw him so he didn't feel gypped. If Pokey wasn't willing to marry her, she didn't want to have babies and spoil her figure, and she wouldn't consider marrying Ned.

She hoped to marry Pokey, and she'd have his babies if that was what he wanted, whatever turned him on. Someday, he was going to be governor of this state and Angela intended to be there at his side—as his wife. Maybe he'd even go on to become president. Pokey had what it took to get ahead in this world and so did Angela Stoddard.

But Pokey was more than money to her; he was the best. He knew how to make a girl feel right. He could make her soar as none of those kids she had laid with before ever had. He could turn her inside out with that fabulous cock of his, but if Pokey fucked her over he'd be sorry. She held all the power cards. She could ruin his life with what she knew. Pokey was her ticket to the top. She wouldn't allow him to let her down.

The sun was dropping below the level of the trees, leaving a wake of magnificent bloody-orange streaks in the sky. She came to the place on the trail where her brother had abandoned his bike. There was another bike, too, a more dented up one beside it.

Her hands tightened into fists. Where were those damn fools?

She walked in a small circle around the bikes, looking for tracks. It would be dark in half an hour, and she didn't want to be here alone when dusk fell. The woods were full of long, jagged shadows and snake holes and such. It made her uneasy. She wanted to go home. Pokey would be waiting at their spot.

She heard a loud buzzing and froze. She couldn't tell which direction it was coming from.

She cringed and moved back toward the creek, thinking she must have inadvertently stumbled upon a wasp nest or a beehive.

Dear God, but she wanted to get out of this spooky place. It was a bad place. Nothing good could happen here.

The strange buzzing noises seemed to follow her, and she noticed an obnoxious smell. She glanced around nervously.

No sign of the boys.

Well, she was going home. Enough was enough. Hank could find his own way back. She had important things to take care of.

Then she heard a hideous sucking sound and stopped in midstep, her shoes sinking part way into the muddy creek bank. Her heart thumped painfully in her chest. The sound came from the grove of trees on her left.

"Hank?" she whispered.

Slowly, she turned about. Something *had* happened to her brother. What was her mother going to say?

Angela squinted into the hazy gloom of the approaching twilight. Two shapes writhed and shivered on the ground like a pair of wounded animals, skin crumbling and flaking off in huge ugly patches, exposing a thick yellow drainage underneath that wept out in lumpy streams. It was her brother and his friend.

Bile immediately rushed up through her throat, and her hand flew to her mouth. She swallowed the bitter fluid back down, coughing and gagging.

Hank was crawling toward her on misshapen knees and elbows. Tears mixed with the globs of tarlike liquid pumping down his cracked face. His whole body was wasting away, totally collapsing in upon itself as he tried frantically to draw a breath of life-saving air. There was a monstrous bright color shimmering around him. The buzzing in her ears had become a deep rumble.

Angela drew back, terrified. "What's happened Hank? What did you do?"

Air whistled horribly from his recessed lips. He couldn't speak. He was dying. Hank was dying! He reached out his mangled hand toward her, slimy fluid dripping from it.

"Jesus! Stay away from me!"

Angela tripped, losing one of her shoes in the soft ground. She didn't stoop to pick it up. "I'm warning you, Hank . . ."

She stopped, realizing how ludicrous her words were. "I'll get mother. I'll get help."

But before she could move, something reached out behind her and grabbed her skirt. She screamed and turned around. She saw that she had backed into a sticker bush. Her dress was tangled in the canes.

"Shit." She tried frantically to pull the fabric free.

"Just a minute, I'm caught." She glanced back at Hank as she struggled to free herself; she didn't want her brother to come any closer.

Her hands fell from the dress. The huge luminous mass was moving away from Hank—he lay motionless in the dirt—and heading toward her.

Her mouth hung open in fear. She wrenched herself loose and fled down the trail. She had lost both her shoes now, torn her dress, and had blood running down her long, sleek legs from the stabs of the pricker bush, but her mind turned heedlessly from those things and concentrated desperately on escape.

The woods were completely black, and she couldn't see. She plunged headlong through thorns and bushes, and she didn't care. She was scratching and bruising herself, but she had to get out of these woods. It was chasing her.

She reached the edge of the woods, where she finally had starlight to guide her, but the shadowy fog caught up to her. The buzzing was all around her. The fine mist wholly enveloped her body. So close, she could feel it pulsating and pounding around her.

She howled in pain as the glittering substance crawled over her flesh, permeating her pores. Torment shot through her veins. She staggered and fell, striking her head on a stone, but hardly noticed it. She rolled in the grass and tried to push the undulating mass off, but it was like putting your hands through water.

She could feel her insides revolting, yet succumbing to the violent intrusion. Soon she'd be filled with it. Her lungs, heart, and kidneys were caving in under the fierce onslaught. Her skin was shriveling, contracting and pulling taut over her frame. Her organs and blood were being consumed, digested, and replaced with a solution so caustic that it threatened to burn through the thin, brittle covering that her flesh had now become. The pressure was overwhelming. At last, the wounds began to erupt, leaving the vicious venom to surge madly into the open field.

Her eyes bulged in terror. She couldn't breathe. Her collapsing body jerked and bucked and strove to survive against the toxic invasion. Her mind swam. The stars danced overhead. She felt as though her soul was being drained out of her. The nether world beckoned, its evil chill beginning to erode her essence. It was cold, so cold and dark.

Above the desperate pain, above the sheer agony, there was one earthly thought left: Pokey is going to win . . . Pokey is going to win. . . .

Thursday, June 15

. . . it crawled up from the bowels of hell . . .

Chapter Seven

i.

Stephen jerked, then bolted upright on the mattress, his mouth caught open in a half-scream. Rivulets of sweat tracked down his chest. The ghoulish vision of gnarled bodies and gray, rotting faces vanished as he sat staring into the black depths of his room. Somehow the deaths of Sallie Ann and Kat had become intertwined in his sleep.

He caught his breath and swung his legs over the edge of the bed, knowing it was only a dream.

Only a dream.

Yeah. But part of it wasn't. Part of it was real.

He shuddered, certain if he closed his eyes again it would all return.

The thin cotton curtains at the window gaped slightly. A narrow stream of silver moonlight flooded in over the hardwood floor and the small, neat pile of clothing folded on a chair beside the dresser.

In the distance, downstairs, he heard the phone ringing.

Stephen stood and reached for his shirt on top of the pile. He buried his face in the familiar fabric, then mopped the sweat from his stubbled cheeks. His heart pounded heavily. She had been gone a year. Wasn't that long enough? When would the nightmares end?

He pulled open a drawer in the spindly-legged night-stand next to the bed and heard the plastic bottle of pills roll backward inside. He clasped them firmly in his hand.

Maybe they wouldn't stop. Maybe they'd just go on and on like some godawful movie you couldn't walk out of. How much time does it take to grieve? On what day can you say it is over at last and you have permission to forget and go on, that it is all right that I am alive and she is dead?

He pushed down the cap and began to turn, then heard a knock at the door.

"Steve?" It was Laura's whisper. "Steve, are you awake?"

"Just a minute," he croaked. His voice was groggy with sleep.

He took yesterday's jeans from the pile and slid them on, then stepped to the door. As he eased it open, the light from the hall spilled into his room. He blinked and ran his fingers through his hair.

Laura stood in a white nylon robe, her face pale and vulnerable, still not fully awake. They stared at each other blankly.

"Henry's on the phone for you," she said. "He says it's important."

"What time is it?"

"Almost one. Henry sounds upset. Someone's died. I know they have."

"Don't panic."

He grabbed his shirt and closed the door. Laura followed as he padded barefoot past the other rooms, down the stairs, and into the kitchen. The receiver lay on the counter. The old woman's door was partially cracked, and he knew she would be listening to every word.

Laura pulled out a chair and sat tugging nervously on the ends of her belt.

He put the phone to his ear. "Hi, Henry. What's the matter?"

Henry was breathing hard. "Three local kids are missing. Their parents are going out of their minds. The sheriff is organizing search teams. He asked me to call whoever I thought might be willing to go out and help."

"Sure. Where do we meet?"

"Bob Foss is going to swing by here in a few minutes. We'll pick you up next. Wear heavy clothes. They think the kids are lost in the woods. It's pretty wicked down there. I'll bring an extra flashlight."

"Okay. I'll be ready." He heard the click on the other end before he hung up.

Laura looked up anxiously.

"A couple of kids are missing," he said, trying to play it down. "I'm going to help look for them."

"Did he say who they were?"

"Sorry, I forgot to ask."

She nodded with understanding. "You know Sallie Ann was the same age I am. We would've been in the same graduating class, but she dropped out when she got pregnant." There were tears in her eyes as she spoke. "It's like a dark sign has fallen over all of us," she said, "an evil omen that won't let go until it's had its fill of vengeance."

"You're tired."

"Yes. I am. But will it seem any better in the morning?"

He couldn't answer, for he knew, at least where he was concerned, it seldom did. Days wore hard, and nights wore harder. He wished he could reassure her otherwise, but he feared it would only get worse before dawn.

ii.

None of the three spoke as they climbed out of the squad car into the night and headed down the rutted trail toward the blackened woods. In hopes of covering a maximum amount of territory, they separated and spread

75

out, about twenty yards apart, still within calling distance—Stephen on the right, Foss in the middle, and Henry to the far left. Each carried a flashlight and a short-handled axe.

Foss followed a narrow bicycle path that was commonly used to traverse the dense path of woodland, while the other two began hacking their way through the tangled briers and lowhanging branches on either side. There were four other groups combing the neighboring fields and barns on the outskirts of Town.

Earlier a hysterical Mrs. Woodhouse had told the sheriff that the boys were supposedly out on their bikes. She was in such a state of panic—Piggy had never stayed out all night before—that she couldn't be sure of anything the boys had said, but she thought they had gone fishing.

In view of the information, the creek seemed the most likely spot to start, and so the three commenced working their way in that direction as fast as they could. The water was lower than usual this time of the year, barely three feet in most places, making the possibility of drowning fairly remote.

The sheriff believed there was still a chance of finding the boys alive and had allowed Mr. Woodhouse and Cal Stoddard, both of whom refused to sit idly by, to join the teams searching the northern section of the stream, up along Haggarty's Meadow.

Stephen swung the piercing beam of his flashlight in a steady arc through the layers of deepening shadows. Brambles and weeds tore at his clothes. In self-defense, he wielded the axe vigorously back and forth to carve out a path. He moved rapidly, hunting for signs of the three kids, but there was no indication that any human had ever come this way before.

The woods were pitch black. Moonlight never touched these hidden knolls or hollows. The trees grew too thickly and their trunks too tall and spindly for healthy wood. It would've been bad enough spanning this section by day, but at night it was a nearly impossible task.

Though it hadn't rained in a couple of weeks, the stones and fallen logs were covered with a spongy coating of dank green moss that looked black in the heavy darkness. The ground gave slightly beneath the pressure of his canvas shoes with a soft, crunching sound. The damp, earthy smell of infinite years of decay grew stronger with each step and permeated his lungs with its rich, loamy scent.

Without conscious thought, a visualization of the brutal deaths of Sallie Ann and her child crept into his mind. There was no reason to believe the same fate had befallen these three. It was just a feeling he had, a gut reaction he couldn't suppress, that if these kids were alive they would've turned up by now. But that wasn't necessarily true, he tried to tell himself. Kids don't think. They pull all sorts of crazy stunts without ever stopping to realize the trouble or concern they might be causing, and he hoped it was the case tonight. Still . . . he didn't think so.

They had gone about a hundred yards. Stephen glanced to the left, where he saw the other two beams cross the underbrush in random swings. He couldn't see the men, only their lights, but that was enough to reassure him that he was not alone. He had no intention of becoming lost out here himself. It wasn't a friendly woods.

There were some like Brown County that put you at ease, that gave you an immediate back-to-nature feel and invited curious strangers to wander their trails. But this one was oppressive and grim, laden with long thorny vines that stabbed like knives at your passing.

Stephen pushed forward, staying in line with the others as they progressed toward the water. The stealthy darkness absorbed their shadows. Each was utterly alone with his own somber thoughts.

The hunt reminded Stephen of the night everyone on Jay Street had gone looking for Joey Peachtree. Instead of skeletal trees and clinging undergrowth, there had been crumbling brick buildings and garbage cans lining the dim alleys. He remembered the sound of his footsteps echoing along the dark stone corridors and being bitterly afraid, not so much of the night or the criminal elements who lived in his neighborhood, but for the fate of his friend.

At that time, Joey was the only person he'd ever been really close to. His parents had always had too many problems of their own. There had been no room for him in their lives, and so he and Joey had formed a brotherly alliance to see themselves through the bad times.

Stephen was surprised how many people turned out that night, all the fathers and older boys from the neighborhood, the cops, and even a few socialites from the towering lakeside apartments. It seemed for awhile the whole north end of the city had revolved around that one single cause. All the old divisions were temporarily vanquished. One child had brought them together in a way nothing else could.

The search had lasted five days, with posters of Joey's picture being continually circulated and more volunteers called on. Then, they'd found Joey's body floating in the river. It had been there at least three days, and something was said about him being sodomized. That night had marked a turning point in Stephen's life.

As they neared the creek the air grew more fetid, with a strong algae smell and something more powerful. Stephen knew what it was immediately—the stench of corrupted flesh—and his hopes sank. He knew what they would find, and he dreaded it immensely. It took considerable effort to force himself onward to confront that sight again. Maybe it would turn out like the attic, though, and nothing would be there.

He wondered if Henry and Foss recognized the fetor, too. Surely, they did. The odor grew worse until he was forced to cover his mouth and nose with the sleeve of his shirt. He glanced at the others. They kept moving forward. But he was afraid, afraid for the fate of Joey Peachtree and the three local kids.

The solitary ray from his flashlight sliced into the funereal gloom, revealing the dry brown leaves of last fall and an occasional rotting log. But no trace of the kids. Then . . . a glimpse of color. He held the beam steady on the prickly stalks of the thicket directly in front of him.

"Over here!" he shouted. His voice was thick. He could feel his throat tightening. He stepped forward.

It was a piece of sky blue cotton.

Henry and Foss rushed to his side. All three flashlights focused on the same point.

"Wasn't the girl supposed to be wearing a blue dress?" Henry asked.

"Yeah, that's what Cal said," the sheriff muttered.

Stephen shone his light around the area, on down the trail. "There's more," he said. "The same color, I think."

The others followed. It was just a few threads this time, but of identical cloth.

"It looks like she was running," Foss observed.

"That doesn't necessarily mean they're dead," Henry insisted, voicing their common fears.

"No," Foss agreed. "But it's not looking good."

"None of the others ran," Stephen said.

Henry wiped his face. The stench was nearly overwhelming. It brought tears to their eyes.

The sheriff tucked the bits of fabric into his pocket. "Come on. Let's keep looking. She must've been headed this way."

Stephen braced himself. It was Joey Peachtree all over again. They weren't going to find these kids alive.

They veered away from the direction of the creek, following the traces of Angela Stoddard's flight. The smell got better for awhile, then worse again.

The sheriff stopped abruptly, then drew back toward them, forcing Henry and Stephen to do the same. "Oh shit," Foss exclaimed. "Oh God." He turned about, his face pale and cadaverous in the yellowish glare from their flashlights.

"What is it?" Henry croaked. He made no attempt to cover his fright.

Foss's mouth moved, but made no sound. He stumbled and fell to one knee. His tanned face wrenched into a mask of shocked anguish.

Stephen's hand dropped on the lawman's shoulder as he stepped toward the edge of the woods. Henry stood frozen. Stephen aimed his flashlight into the field.

There lay the body. Her gnarled corpse had shriveled within the dress, crumbling and leaking a putrid fluid that soaked her entire torso. It looked almost as though she were melting in the heat of the night. Bits of gleaming bone were revealed where her ashen skin had completely peeled away from her frame.

A strange fear crept over Stephen, a primitive sense that whatever it was that had killed this girl, it could not have been more evil had it crawled up from the bowels of hell itself.

He heard Henry emit a strangled sound, then swallowed the lump in his throat and turned away. "Are you all right?"

Henry nodded.

Foss rose slowly. "Let's get back to the car. I want to tell them we've found her."

"What about the two boys?"

"We'll get someone else over here to help. I've had enough. We aren't going to find them alive."

"No," Stephen admitted.

"What the hell is it, will you tell me that?" Foss demanded.

"I wish I could."

iii.

It was a hot, sticky night.

Flora Malcolm kicked off the sheet, and at the same moment realized she was fully awake. She lay prone for several minutes, gathering her senses. For the past eighteen years, ever since marrying Hubert Malcolm, she'd been troubled with insomnia. Her back ached, and her knees, too, a bit of arthritis, though she was only forty-five.

It was totally dark in the room except for the night-light plugged in under the curtains. She wondered what time it was. It had to be early yet, only four or five o'clock. She'd drink a glass of milk, then try to go back to sleep.

Her husband lay snoring next to her. She wondered if she could get out of bed without waking him.

Gently, slowly, as though scared of disturbing a sleeping lion, she began to scoot toward the edge of the mattress.

Hube turned his head and mumbled.

She caught her breath and stiffened. She waited. All quiet. Cautiously, she moved again.

Hube's hand lashed out like a snake's tongue and caught her right thigh under her nightgown. The fingers kneaded her flesh. "Where you going?"

Fingers crept up toward the deep cleft between her legs.

"To get some milk."

"Not yet. I got something that will put you to sleep. Make you sleep like a baby."

Hube always awoke with a hard-on and liked to relieve it before he got out of bed, even before using the bathroom or rinsing the night's bitterness from his mouth. She never refused him, afraid he'd look elsewhere if she did.

He was a man with a powerful need. The past six months he'd been even more demanding than usual, acting like a teenager, staring at himself in the mirror, wanting her to do things he'd never asked for before. But she never refused, no matter how perverted the request.

81

Whatever Hube wanted. That was the way to keep your man.

If his constituents only knew. If all those people who thought Hubert Malcolm was so wonderful only knew.

Flora understood how others must see him, his curly blond hair, those sparkling blue eyes, that boyish smile, the dimples in his cheeks. He had husky, broad shoulders and a flat narrow waist. People said he looked thirty-five, and it was true. You'd never guess he was two years older than she. She envied him that. Oh, there were signs of his aging: a few creases, a slight receding around his temples; but he had that look of eternal youth that somehow convinced everyone this man would never grow old.

His breath was horrible. He snorted and sucked on her neck like a vampire. He shoved up her nightgown and squeezed on her breasts till she let out a gasp of pain. She only wanted to get this over with, so she could go downstairs for her milk.

He'd come home last night in a particularly foul mood. Slamming doors and drinking himself into a near stupor. She'd been terrified to ask what was wrong. Anything at the office, dear? Traffic? A budget cut? He'd growled and criticized her cooking. Told her what a dumb, stupid piece of shit she was; how fat she was getting; how gray; how tough it was to bring himself to sleep with her.

And yet he was constantly at her.

But that was just the way Hube was. She worked hard to ignore those remarks and go on with her life, doing whatever he asked whenever he asked. Most of the day he was gone, and she was free. It didn't seem like too much of a price to pay for the comfortable lifestyle she led.

She turned her head away as he spread her legs and knelt between them. With disgust, she felt her body becoming moist, making itself ready for his entry—

The telephone rang.

Hube swore, then groaned and climbed off. He staggered awkwardly to the phone, his erection poking stiffly up through the drawstring waist of his pajama bottoms. Hube had a lot to offer, and he wasn't a gentle man. Often it hurt. But after eighteen years, she was used to it. Her biggest fear was that Hube would tire of her, that she wouldn't be enough to satisfy him.

Flora slid out the other side of the bed. She was safe for now; she could do what she wanted. She wandered toward the bathroom.

"This is Mayor Malcolm," Hube said in a deep, bellowing voice.

He had a different tone and inflection for every occasion. He should've been an actor instead of the four-time mayor of Town. But Hube claimed he was on the way to the White House. He was gathering the recognition he needed to begin his career in earnest.

Flora washed her hands and stared at herself in the mirror. He was right: she was getting old. She leaned closer. Her chestnut brown hair now had more than a sprinkling of gray in it. Knotty blue veins stood out like wires in her neck. Her skin was wrinkling and sagging. Those awful bags under her eyes . . .

The tone of Hube's voice suddenly drew her back.

She felt afraid, though she didn't know why. The phone rang so often lately, and at odd hours, but whenever she answered there was never anyone there.

What if Hube was having an affair? No, it wasn't possible. She was a good wife. She took good care of her husband. Hube wouldn't do that to her.

He was pacing back and forth near the window, red in the face. A frown furrowed deep creases into his forehead. His expression grew solemn. Something was wrong.

He lifted his gaze to meet hers, and she could tell there was something he needed to discuss that he didn't want her to hear. He covered the mouthpiece. "Go start me some coffee," he barked.

It wasn't a request; it was an order.

She nodded obediently and slipped on her robe. She closed the bedroom door, then paused outside.

"Yeah, she's gone now," she heard him say.

There were always political secrets, deals he didn't want her to know about; but this was different. He'd been so changed lately, so secretive. He was gone almost every evening. Yet his sex drive hadn't diminished. If he was having an affair, he wouldn't be hammering away at her every night and morning, too. No, it had to be something else. But what if it wasn't?

She headed down the stairs. Her mind was awhirl with the intenseness of her feelings. It *had* to be something else.

The extension downstairs sat on the coffee table, tempting her like forbidden fruit. If he caught her listening he'd be furious. She always did exactly what he said. She'd never given him any cause for complaint.

But she had to know. The fear would consume her. She wouldn't make it through the day if she didn't find out what the phone call was about. There was an aching sense deep inside of her. It had to be something else.

Carefully, Flora lifted the handset, keeping her thumb over the button. Then even more carefully, she slid her thumb away.

"I've got to call the families. Then get some more men over here." It was Bob Foss.

"Wait. Give me a minute to think," she heard her husband respond.

"About what? You're off the hook now. Angela's dead. Your stinking little secret will be safe in the grave."

"You can't let them autopsy her."

"What?" Foss exclaimed.

"She's pregnant," Hube explained. "I was going to get it taken care of. . . ."

"Jesus Christ," Foss muttered under his breath. "You fucking bastard. You goddamn slimy prick . . ."

"That's enough." Hube's voice was firm. "They can au-

84

topsy all the others, but not Angela."

Flora felt herself reel. Angela Stoddard. Oh God. A seventeen-year-old girl. One of their daughter's best friends. Her stomach lurched. She struggled to hold back her sobs.

"I don't think you appreciate the situation here," Foss said. "We've got six dead of this thing now. I won't interfere with whatever is necessary to get it stopped."

"You'll do what I tell you."

"Forget it, Hube. What was going on before was none of my business, but this—"

"Listen to me, you son of a bitch. It was my money that got you into office, and I can use it to take you out—just as easily. At your age it could be tough to start over again. How'd you like to go back to that job you had over at Duncan Stables?"

"At least the shit was clean, and it didn't turn my stomach."

They were both silent a minute, then Foss spoke again. "Corliss should be here soon. I'll see what I can do."

"You'll damn well keep them from doing the autopsy!" Hube slammed down the phone.

Flora replaced the receiver. There had to be some other cause for Hube's reaction. It couldn't be what it sounded like. Not after all these years.

Her hands trembled. Eighteen years. Every night and morning. Never had she refused him, not even when she was sick or having babies.

If . . . if it were true, then that meant he was screwing that girl and coming home a few hours later and putting it into her. A young girl, without any gray hair or . . .

Flora pushed the images from her mind. It couldn't be true.

She stumbled away from the table into the kitchen to make his coffee. Her knees were shaking so badly she could barely walk. Her intestines were tied in knots. She could hear him upstairs, rushing around.

It wasn't true. No man would . . . and then come

home and . . .

Hube lumbered down the steps. He picked up his keys from the cupboard. "Got to go. Got an emergency. I'll see you tonight."

He walked out and banged the door closed. She heard the engine rev on his little sports car. He hadn't noticed how pale she was, the way she stood bent over, holding her gut as though she'd been shot.

iv.

Stephen leaned against the right flank of Foss's patrol car and took a long swallow from a canteen he'd gotten out of the trunk, then passed it to Henry. A coppery glow was just beginning to pierce the eastern sky. It had been a long night. Both were bone weary from their efforts in the woods, but the hunt was not over yet. There were two more bodies to find. They were waiting on Foss to finish his calls from a cellular phone in the front seat.

Others were starting to arrive. Stephen counted six vehicles emerging through the hazy gray dawn: two station wagons, two smaller compacts, a pickup, and a four-wheel drive. None of the owners' faces meant anything to him, but Henry performed brief introductions amid the clamor of opening and shutting doors.

Stephen caught the name Cal Stoddard—the girl's father. He was a big man, easily six foot seven, bull shouldered and barrel chested, with a florid complexion.

Bob Foss had finished making the last of his calls and slid out to join the group congregating on the berm. He stepped up to Stoddard. "I'm sorry, Cal," the sheriff said. "We haven't found the boys yet."

The large man nodded sternly. His eyes were red as though he'd been crying, but he wasn't now. "I appreciate everyone coming down here to help."

Dr. Michael Corliss had joined them. One of his hands was bound in gauze. His face was almost as white as his

86

bandage, his hair was uncombed, and he was sporting three days' growth of beard.

Foss turned to Corliss. "You look like hell. I wasn't sure you were coming. Your receptionist said you've been laid up."

The doctor studied the lawman through bloodshot eyes. "Burned my hand on the stove," he mumbled. "Infected. Hurts like the devil."

The mayor interrupted. "Excuse me. I need to talk to you, Bob. Did you get a chance to ask Dr. Corliss about that little matter we spoke of earlier?"

"No, not yet. It's going to have to wait."

The mayor smiled nervously. He was the only man there who was wearing a jacket and tie and looked like he'd had a decent night's sleep. "Mike, if I could have a minute before you—"

Dr. Corliss held up a shaking hand. "I'm sorry. Maybe later. We need to get going. The more time lost before I examine the victims, the harder it will be for me to figure out what's causing this."

"Of course. It's just that . . ."

Cal's voice cut through the group. "What can we do to help?"

Foss responded. "I need about ten of you to divide up and continue searching along the creek. We found Angela about forty yards to the south. Cal, if you'd rather—"

Stoddard shook his head. "No, I'll go with them. If my boy's out there, I want to find him."

Foss nodded. He turned to Stephen. "You and Henry grab the stretcher, those insulated gloves, that blanket, and follow me and Mike."

They headed toward the woods, and the mayor returned to his Porsche, swearing to himself under his breath.

The sheriff jammed a cigarette into the corner of his mouth and blew out a stream of blue-gray smoke as they tromped through the weeds. "The girl was killed the same as Sallie Ann," he said, "but she was obviously running from something. Tore her dress, lost her shoes, didn't stop to retrieve them. That's the part I don't understand. What have you turned up on this stuff?"

Beads of sweat dotted the doctor's face. "Not much. I've called a colleague of mine, and his office says he'll be down in a few days." His voice was thin and strained. "I also notified the state board of health and made inquiries to see if any other counties have turned up similar cases. And there's none so far, but if my guess is right, there will be."

"Damn it, Mike. We've got to get this stopped."

"I know," the doctor said tiredly. "I'm doing the best I can. Everything in my power."

They came out on the other side of the woods, where Angela Stoddard's corpse lay twisted in the parched field of grass. By daylight the sight was even worse. Except for the blue dress, they wouldn't have known who she was. Her body had ruptured and contracted to such a degree that not even her sex was obvious. Her hair had all fallen out and lay in fine, brittle clumps scattered near her blighted scalp.

The doctor supplied the four with filter masks. "Remember not to get any of this stuff on your skin. It'll eat right through it," he warned. "It won't penetrate the specially insulated material of these gloves, but watch out for your arms."

Stephen passed each of them a pair of the heavy metallic gloves.

"Look at this," Foss pointed.

Corliss leaned closer.

Stephen craned his neck to see what they'd uncovered; there were several sets of boot marks right next to the girl's legs.

The ground all around her was muddy and should've produced an abundance of tracks had anyone been following her, but there were none, other than the girl's own bare footsteps. They searched the area to no avail.

"Looks like she struggled with someone," Foss said.

"The tracks must be old ones," Corliss insisted. "There's no way to tell how long they've been here."

"Maybe," the sheriff grumbled.

Corliss frowned. "The cause of death is disease, not murder."

"What if the killer injected them with something?"

"I doubt it." He knelt next to Angela's emaciated frame. "I think these people are coming in contact with massive doses of some toxin or germ."

"Couldn't a killer be injecting them with poison?" Foss pressed.

"Not likely."

The two men halted their argument at the approach of the group sent out to locate the boys. Foss stepped forward. "Cal, I don't think you ought to . . ."

The giant stopped the sheriff abruptly. "We found my boy, and the Woodhouse kid, too." His words were halting, strained with grief. He walked around Foss.

"Cal—"

The broad-chested man stared down at his daughter's crumpled remains.

"Please, don't touch anything," Corliss implored.

Stoddard nodded. "I need to tell her mother." Then he turned away, back into the trees.

"I hate this," Foss muttered, drawing another cigarette out of his pocket.

It was nearly 11:00 a.m. by the time they had finished loading all the corpses into the van. Every joint in Stephen's body ached. He had been up most of the night and was anxious to return to the boardinghouse and fall into bed. No painting today. He imagined the others were exhausted as well. Henry and Foss had been up even longer, and they knew the families involved. That had to make it worse.

All of the cars were gone except for the mayor's, the

patrol car, and Corliss's van. Malcolm had waited. He stood in the heat, leaning against his Porsche and wiping the sweat from his face with a limp handkerchief. Whatever it was he had wanted to discuss before, it had to be damned important, Stephen thought.

He watched Foss take off his straw Stetson and tap it against his thigh. The mayor and Foss exchanged quick glances, then the sheriff spoke. "Mike, I hate like hell to ask this, but I don't want you to do an autopsy on that girl. You ought to be able to get what you need from the others. God knows we've got enough corpses."

"Are you going to tell me why?" The last few hours had taken their toll on the doctor, and he looked as though he might pass out.

The lawman hesitated, and Stephen recognized the look in the sagging man's eyes. It surprised him. He had not thought Foss was the kind, but whatever it was he wanted to say he was planning to lie about it. The sheriff was not very good at covering his emotions, and Stephen had had plenty of experience with lying. It must be to protect the living, he guessed, for the girl was beyond hurt.

"There's a local boy she's been seeing, and it seems Angela was in trouble. If all that comes out . . . Well, how do you expect the families will feel? I don't think Cal knows, and no good can come out of his finding out now. It might make him feel worse than he does already."

Corliss took a deep breath and let it out slowly. His expression was tense, and Stephen sensed that he had other things on his mind. "I may or may not need to autopsy her, but I'll keep the knowledge of her pregnancy between us."

"I appreciate that."

Henry cast a look at Stephen, and it was enough to tell Stephen that Henry wasn't buying the sheriff's story, either. Stephen wondered how it involved the mayor, because it obviously did.

Abigail ripped open a packet of Nutrasweet and poured it into her ice tea, then stirred. She wiped a tear from the corner of her eye. It was awful, just awful. So many people dead.

She carefully placed a sheet of aluminum foil over a chicken cassarole she was planning to take out to Hannah Stoddard. Poor woman, she had lost both her son and daughter.

Abigail had talked to Cal on the phone. He hadn't given her any details, but had simply said they were dead, both of them. It was hard to imagine. She hadn't liked Hank, but Angela had been such a cultured girl. Whenever she came to visit, she had always said, "Please, Mrs. Morton" and "Thank you" and "What a lovely house you have." She'd had a future ahead of her and was not the least bit lazy. Angela had been a cheerleader, an honor roll student, and queen of her junior prom.

That Cal was a cold man. Abigail would have to talk to Hannah to find out exactly what had happened, where the bodies were found, what they looked like, and what the kids had been doing before they were killed.

Stephen Myers had come in an hour ago, dirty and reeking of that same foul odor of death. She'd tried to pump him for information about the search, but he'd been less than polite, skirting her questions and going directly up to shower. She worried about him and Laura. She had seen them together much too frequently lately. They were becoming too close. She hoped nothing serious was going on between them, that her daughter wasn't becoming overly interested in the Chicago native.

Abigail picked up her glass and started out of the kitchen, then heard the doorbell buzz. "I'm coming!" she hollered, setting the drink down again.

The large walnut door was propped open to let in

more air, and she saw Flora Malcolm through the screen. "Why Flora, how good of you to drop by. Everything is so hectic. I've barely had time to catch my breath."

She flipped the handle and swung out the screen. Her gaze fastened on the woman's tightly pinched expression. Her hand flew to her throat. "Oh my lands, what is it? It isn't another . . ."

Flora shook her head. She sucked in a sob and braced herself against the doorjamb.

Abigail grasped her arm. "Here, dear. Why don't you come into the parlor?" Abigail almost never used the words "living room." Parlor was so much more refined.

Laura was on the sofa, reading a book. She looked up as the two entered, and her smile faded. She dropped her book and stood, alarmed. "What's wrong?"

Abigail led Flora to a chair. The woman seemed to have no strength of her own. "Are you ill, dear? Should I call the doctor?"

"No, I-I'll be all right. I just need to sit a minute."

"Can I get you anything?" Laura asked.

Flora swallowed and shook her head.

"It's probably these killings," Abigail clucked. "It's got everybody upset."

Flora reached out and pressed Abigail's hand. "You've got to tell me . . ."

"Tell you what, dear?"

"I heard a-about . . . t-t-that girl's death."

"Angela Stoddard," Abigail affirmed. "Isn't it horrible? I couldn't believe it myself. Such a sweet girl. Her poor mother. I can't imagine what she must be going through."

Flora stifled a sob and turned to Laura. "Y-you were a . . . a friend of hers weren't you?"

Laura nodded.

"She was a good friend of Kelly's, too, you know, but we never really got the chance to talk. I-I liked her. She seemed s-s-sincere." Flora was having trouble saying the words. "Maybe you can tell me something about her."

Laura hesitated.

"Did she have a regular boyfriend?" Flora persisted. "Someone she saw steadily?"

"Well . . . yes." Laura glanced at her mother, puzzled. "She and Ned Charmichael had been going together since the eighth grade."

"She wasn't the kind who would've cheated on her boyfriend, was she? I have to know," the older woman whispered.

"She . . ." Laura looked to her mother for support, but there was none. "She did tell me there was someone else. She didn't want to hurt Ned. He's kind of quiet and shy, and thought the world of Angela, but she was very in love with this other man. She really couldn't help herself."

"Who was this . . . man?"

"I don't know. She never said."

Flora leaned forward, all the color gone from her face. "Was she having sex with him?"

Laura flushed, obviously uncomfortable with the topic.

"It's very important. You must tell me," Flora pleaded.

The woman's desperation was obvious. Laura weakened. "Angela came to me a few days ago. She was very upset. She made me promise not to tell, but she was pregnant."

Abigail gasped. "She seemed like such a nice girl!"

"I have to know. This man she slept with, was he the only one, or were there many others?" The tears rolled freely down her aging cheeks.

"Angela was very particular. She wasn't a loose girl." Laura paused. "Mrs. Malcolm, you're not thinking Tommy had anything to do with it, are you? Tommy is two years younger than Angela. The two hardly ever went to the same places. I really don't think—"

Flora pushed herself up from the chair, trembling, her gaze fixed on the carpet. "Y-y-yes, it was Tommy."

Abigail nearly choked. The boy was only sixteen.

"I overheard Hube asking the sheriff not to do an autopsy on the girl because it would all come out."

Laura looked directly at the woman. "I'm sure it couldn't have been Tommy. I had the distinct impression it was an older man she was seeing. A man with money. Those things meant a lot to Angela. Did Tommy say anything?"

The woman turned away as though she were ready to leave. "It was Tommy."

"I just can't believe it."

"Nonetheless it's true," Flora said sharply. "I have to go. I have so many things to do."

"Oh Flora," said Abigail as she walked her to the door, "if there's anything I can do . . ."

"Don't tell anyone I was here. Don't tell them what we talked about."

Abigail pressed her lips together. "Not a word."

But they both knew by morning it would be all over Town.

Flora nodded and stepped over the threshold into the glaring sunlight.

Abigail forgot all about her other plans for the day and rushed straight to the phone.

Friday, June 16

It sparkled with demonic intensity . . .

Chapter Eight

i.

Stephen worked with great energy all morning, completing two canvases, and though neither came out entirely the way he intended, he was satisfied with the effort. He took a break and left the boardinghouse, for a change, to have lunch in a local diner.

The restaurant was a refurbished hotel from Town's days of greater glory, he guessed, with cracked plaster ceilings, gloomy eight-inch walnut trim, checkered tile, a dusty chandelier, and high wooden booths. But it was filled with noonday noise, cigar smoke, and clinking glasses, which made him feel a part of the world again.

When his hamburger arrived, the bun was soaked through with grease. The waitress was wearing jeans. She plunked down a bottle of ketchup and asked: "Will there be anything else?"

"No, thanks."

She wrote up the bill and dropped it on the table. "Have a nice day."

He sat frowning at the burger, wondering whether it was actually intended for consumption, when Sheriff Foss waved to him from across the room. The lawman ambled over. "I wanted to thank you for your help the other night. I never did have a chance to ask what you prefer to be called. Is it Steve, or is it Stephen?"

"Either is fine."

The aging lawman folded into the opposite side of the booth. "I've just left Corliss's office. Busier 'an hell over there. He looks like shit. On top of his usual patient load, he's trying to get to the bottom of those deaths." He took off his hat and wiped his forehead. "Hey, Mary, bring me a Coke!"

The waitress put one hand on her hip and shook her finger at him, then winked.

Foss's smile faded quickly as he continued. "We're issuing warnings for folks to stay around home, to avoid the creek, the woods, any unusual shrubbery, and advising they call the doctor's office at the first sign of illness. We're also warning them that the victims of this stuff excrete a corrosive fluid."

The lawman paused, and Steve could tell that he was choosing his next words carefully.

"Corliss had some strange findings from the tests he's run. He doesn't know what to make of them, so he's called in help. We may be in for a whole lot more tragedy if we can't get this thing stopped soon. You know that substance the bodies are expelling?"

Steve nodded.

"Evidently it contains digestive juices among other things. Enzymes, he said. Kind of like what you'd find in the human stomach, only disproportional amounts. I don't know if I can explain it—it was all pretty technical—but he said this stuff was higher in pepsin and trypsin and the other catalysts that control the digestion of meat. He found one other substance that really has him stumped, too, a derivative of a complex carbon chain he's never encountered before. He's running more tests, trying to break it down into carbon rings so he can identify it, all without success so far."

"What does it mean in terms of finding a cause?"

Foss shook his head. "I don't know. The really scary part is, when he autopsied the bodies, there wasn't an organ or a single drop of blood left in them. Just bones and that obnoxious slop we've been smelling. It seems they're literally filled with this carbon chain as well as the enzymes, but he can't begin to imagine how they got that way. No way could the body have manufactured this carbon crap on its own."

"Then how can he think this is a disease or toxic reaction?"

"My question, too. Which leads us to my theory. You probably think I'm crazy, chasing after red herrings and all, but remember those boot prints we found by Angela?"

"Yeah, but I thought you decided they were unrelated."

"Well, I called the county forensic expert out there anyway, on a hunch you might say."

"And?"

"Angela definitely struggled with someone. Her bare footprints overlapped the boot prints and vice versa. No question. Beyond a doubt, Angela fought with someone at that spot, someone who managed to leave no tracks coming or going.

"I know that Corliss is convinced that this is a disease," Foss went on, "and that may be, but I'm positive there's more involved here." The sheriff leaned back and peeled the paper from the straw Mary had delivered with his Coke. "I hope that specialist has some answers when he gets here. I've been sheriff for a long time now and I've seen a few gruesome killings throughout the years, but I've never had such a bad gut feeling about anything."

"I know what you mean." Stephen wrapped both hands around the sandwich. A small puddle of grease had congealed on the plate.

Foss grimaced. "You're not going to eat that, are you?"

At 8:30 p.m. Stephen quit for the day and set his brushes in turpentine to soak. He arched his back at the shoulders, then released the muscles with a slow, deliberate stretching motion. The light through the window was growing dim, and though he could have flipped the switch on the overhead lamp, he had never found artificial light adequate to paint by. In this way, he was temperamental about his work.

He surveyed the canvases spread across the bed to dry. It had proved his most successful day in months. He hadn't had such a day since leaving Chicago.

It was hot as hell in the room. Laura had brought him supper around five o'clock, and it sat on a tray by the door, largely untouched.

He was in the mood to get out of the house for awhile. He showered and put on a clean pair of jeans, the shirt he carried slung over his shoulder. He would ask Laura to go someplace nice for dessert.

He trotted downstairs and noted the silence immediately. He called out several times. "Laura? Mrs. Morton?"

No answer.

On the kitchen table he found a note: "Dear Steve, have gone to the memorial service with mother. Love, L."

He had not thought, but of course there would be services for the latest dead. He had heard the sheriff's warnings on the radio in the afternoon and wondered if the local folk would obey. Nearly everyone would want to see the deceased off to the grave.

"Hmmm," he muttered, toying with the note. Finally, he slapped it down on the table. He was still anxious to go out, though it was clear he would have to go by himself.

He slipped on his shirt and headed down the street on

foot toward a tavern Henry had told him about on the edge of Town. It was supposedly the hot spot of the county. Perhaps he would find some company there.

Danny's Saloon was actually an insulated barn. Above the entrance, there was a hand-painted sign of a gigantic bottle of bubbly champagne being poured into a cardboard glass. He opened the huge, crisscrossed door and to the right was a bar, complete with a plate glass mirror behind it and rows of long-stemmed wine glasses hanging overhead. Beside that was a bandstand where a country and western group was setting up. The rest was taken up with tables. There were rusty farm implements adorning the walls and artfully placed bales of hay to compliment the decor.

Stephen glanced around, surprised by the fanciful and spacious atmosphere. The place was almost empty, though. Only two tables were occupied. He took a seat in the center, close to the band.

A woman—he could not have called her a girl because she was too old for that—in a short, ruffled, red-and-black saloon dress came up to him. Her smile was painted on with thick red lipstick. Her layers of eye makeup and fiery orange hair were done up to make her look younger than she truly was.

He guessed her age at somewhere between thirty-five and forty. She still had a very good figure. The mounds of white breast that were pushed up above either side of her red lace corset were sprinkled with freckles and told him that her flamboyant hair color was natural. Her shapely legs were shadowed in black fishnet hose.

She leaned on his table, and a strong musky scent filled his nostrils. "Okay, Sam, what'll you have?" she asked hoarsely.

"A pitcher of whatever you've got on tap."

She smiled. "Not too particular, huh? I don't remember seeing you before."

"You haven't. I'm new in Town."

"All alone?"

101

"For tonight."

"Where you from?" Her leg brushed his thigh as she shifted her weight.

"Chicago."

She laughed. "Isn't that fine? I'll be right back with your beer, Chicago."

He settled into the chair and watched the musicians tuning up. There was a singer in a fringed cowgirl jacket with long, stringy blond hair. He wondered if she was any good.

A few moments later the waitress returned, balancing a beer-slopped tray with two mugs and a foaming pitcher which she set down on the table. The band started playing, low and soft. There were two other women in the same brightly colored saloon dresses leaned against the bar, looking bored.

The waitress picked up the pitcher to pour his beer. "Business is slow tonight," she said, cocking her head. "All them damn killings have scared everybody off. I suppose if I was smart I would be, too. But I don't know. It just don't seem worth it. Somebody gets cancer, another has a heart attack, someone else gets knifed. The story always ends the same. Nobody wins, not really. You know what I mean?"

"Unfortunately."

"Tough, ain't it? Today's my birthday, and not one good thing's happened yet. I could use some company. You mind if I join you?"

She walked like she'd already had plenty to drink, and he figured she probably celebrated her birthday every other night, but he nodded anyway. "Have a seat." He pushed out a chair without getting up.

"Thanks. You're a real gentleman. I been on my feet for hours." She dropped heavily into the chair, scooting it over close to him, and filled the other mug. "So where are you staying?"

"The Morton's boardinghouse."

"Good God, that old bag! I see that fat old bitch sitting on her porch, them sharp weasel eyes watching everybody else's business. I'll bet you ain't having any fun over there." She cackled and sipped the foam off the top of her mug. "I don't think a girl should have to work on her birthday, do you? I think she ought to be able to relax a little."

"Is today really your birthday?"

"Of course, it is. Do you think I'm a liar? Oh—I know what you're thinking, but yeah, it really is. I'd tell you how old I am, but you look too young."

"What's your name?" He'd finished his beer and was beginning to feel less tense.

"Didn't I tell you? It's Marie Sheldon O'Neal. Now what do ya think of that?"

"Pretty."

She snorted. "You're a gentleman all right. I've got so I can tell, except . . ." She leaned forward, studying his eyes. "I think that maybe sometimes you aren't."

Up close, her face looked hard and more lined than it did from a distance. It showed a lot of wear. In Chicago he had met quite a few like her.

She wrapped her arm around his shoulders and began running her fingers through his hair, then leaned over and kissed him. Her greasy lipstick smeared between their lips. "If you're ever lonely, I live at 131 Mulberry Street, and my door is never locked."

She stood up. The pitcher was empty. "I got to get back to work, but I'll be around again. You want another?"

He nodded, pulled out a ten, and said, "Keep the change."

She grinned and tucked the bill into the front of her corset, then waltzed away, the ruffled hips of her dress swinging broadly.

Stephen wiped his mouth with his sleeve. The place had begun to fill some while they talked. Through the din he saw that more than a dozen tables were full, and there might have been more up in the lofts, which were fixed like balconies. There was a staircase at the rear of the long room and another door with a neon sign that read: Exit.

He noticed a man at the bar, half turned around, glaring at him. It wasn't anyone he'd met, nor did he think he wanted to. The guy was big and burly, at least 220 pounds. Mean looking. He wondered if this was the saloon's bouncer.

The front door banged open, and Henry stepped through, looking bedraggled from the heat. "Hey Steve," he called, making straight for the table. "God, do I need a drink."

Henry flopped into the chair Marie had vacated. He seemed depressed and a bit worn from their grim search the night before. There was an aroma of stale flowers about him, and Stephen wondered if he had been to the memorial service.

Marie had seen Henry come in. "Hang on to your pants, Henry!" she bellowed across the room, drawing a few laughs from the other tables. "I'm on my way." She dropped off another pitcher, without staying to talk this time.

"I'm buying," Henry said. "I'm grateful to have the company. I figured I was going to have to drown my sorrows alone. I feel like I've been walking around in a haze all afternoon."

"I need a change of scenery myself. How's the store?"

"Lousy. Papa's cussing. He isn't making any money. And Mama's upset. She helped arrange the flowers for Sallie Ann's funeral today. I just got back from the grave site."

"Sallie Ann? I thought they were burying the Stoddards."

Henry grunted and shook his head. "I was told Dr. Corliss hasn't completed his examinations yet."

A heavy, black lull settled over their table amidst the music and general noise in the room. Stephen's expression darkened. All day he had worked to push the images

104

of Thursday's hunt from his mind, but now it all came rushing back like an unbound river with an increased sense of dread: the gray, ulcerous bodies of the young woman and her baby, the two misshapen boys on the creek bank, and the utterly obliterated form of Angela Stoddard.

Stephen stared blankly at the amber liquid in the heavy glass mug.

When he spoke, Henry's voice was solemn and filled with pain. "I came here to forget. You know what I mean?"

Stephen nodded.

"Sallie Ann's parents were there, her dad hugging her mom, and her mom trying not to cry, sniffling into her handkerchief. She finally collapsed, and they had to carry her away. I saw John's folks, too. They were pretty much in the same shape. But John wasn't there. I heard he left Town. Nobody seems to know where he's gone, and it's tearing his mother up.

"I couldn't do that to my folks. No matter how bad it got, I'd hang in there. But I'm not condemning John, either. I guess nobody *knows* what they'll do until the time comes." Henry tipped up the mug and finished the dregs of his beer.

They plowed through two more pitchers. The noise in the place was becoming an annoying drone in Stephen's ears. He knew he'd had about enough.

Stephen rose and plodded carefully toward the little door marked Restrooms under the stairs. He was trying not to weave. He saw Marie oscillating among the tables, men tucking tips into her garter. He had been watching, and frequently she made a clean sweep of it, folding all the money into her corset and starting over.

For as nice as the rest of the tavern was, the john was a pit. There was only one bathroom for both men and women. It smelled strongly of urine and a powerful lemon cleanser. A tampon machine and one for condoms hung side by side above the single stool as though united

105

in some kind of warped marriage.

Stephen felt himself sway as he turned to the sink to wash his hands. He staggered back out into the filtered light, barely able to negotiate the doorway. It was definitely time to think about leaving.

When he got back to the table, Henry had ordered another pitcher. Henry refilled both mugs. "The whole world is going to hell in a handcart, you know that?"

While they worked their way through the pitcher, Henry's mood swung back and forth between silly giggles and glowering, hate-filled declarations. Stephen figured it was Henry's method of venting the pent-up emotions he felt about the killings, and drank patiently with his friend. A couple of times, Stephen almost stood up and left, knowing that he was getting thoroughly soused, but with each swallow, his limbs grew heavier and the effort seemed increasingly useless.

"To William Shakespeare. God rest his soul," Henry toasted, then tilted the pitcher up and discovered it empty. "Another round!" he bellowed, looking for Marie. The more he drank, the louder and more aggressive Henry became.

She swung through the smoke-darkened room, a tray with three more pitchers wedged against her waist. She dropped two of them off along the way. Her face was flushed. Sweat crawled over her shoulders and down between her cleavage. As she drew near, Henry reached out and pulled her onto his lap, almost spilling the beer. She cried out with pretended shock, then giggled and slid her arm around his neck.

"Where've you been, Sam?" she laughed, caressing his hair. "I've been looking all over the place for you."

Henry hugged her tighter and smiled. "Right here, darlin', waiting for you."

"Today's my birthday. I don't think a girl should have to work on her birthday, do you?"

"It's criminal, that's what it is!" Henry declared emphatically. His hand settled onto her thigh and rubbed up and down with careless ease. "Where's Bill tonight?"

Marie pouted. Her words were so badly slurred Stephen could barely make out what she was saying.

"We're through. I ain't never gonna let that man in my door again. He said I was a stupid slut. He called me a fucking whore. I don't think that was right, do you? I treated him good, better than anybody's ever treated him before, an' then he's got the nerve to call me a whore. I don't think that's fair."

"Neither do I. You're a hell of a good girl. To Marie," Henry said and tipped up his glass again.

She swayed on his lap and nearly fell off before Henry caught her. "Today's my birthday," she repeated, leaning against him. "I don't think a girl should have to work on her birthday, do you?"

"No, not at all." Henry lowered his head and began kissing her neck. Her hand crept up his thigh and fondled the bulge between his legs.

Stephen poured himself another beer. The big burly man he'd noticed at the counter earlier slammed down his drink and stormed out of the bar.

Marie nuzzled her face next to Henry's ear. "Did you bring me a present? Today's my birthday."

"Sure, I got a present." Henry grabbed himself and made an obscene gesture.

Marie tipped back her head and laughed. She roared with laughter until her whole body shook. Suddenly she stopped. She stared straight ahead with a blank expression, then her eyes rolled back in their sockets.

Stephen saw it coming. He lunged forward, but his reactions were slowed from the booze.

Marie landed with a thud, face down on the floor, out cold.

Henry and Stephen rose from their chairs. The bartender and one of the other waitresses rushed over. "I knew this was going to happen," the bartender mumbled as they hauled her away. That was the last the two saw of her.

iii.

Stephen had completely lost track of the hour and number of pitchers by the time they left. It had taken considerable persuasion to get Henry out of the tavern and started on his way back to the store. They said a drunken good-bye at the door and promised to repeat their performance again another night.

Stephen proceeded alone, walking languidly through the hushed streets, stopping now and then to catch his balance. He probably shouldn't have drunk so much, but it had seemed like a good idea at the time. In spite of the ringing in his ears and the dull pressure at the base of his skull, this was the most relaxed he'd felt in months.

A muggy blackness blanketed the town. The air was oppressive and weighted, like the atmosphere inside a dark, steamy sauna. There were no lights on in any of the houses he passed. No stars in the sky, either. Only dense, ponderous clouds that moved slowly over the moon, a full white moon, that gleamed brightly when it was not caught behind the celestial fog.

It was an effort to put one foot in front of the other and keep himself headed in the direction of the boardinghouse. He was tempted, instead, to lie down on the grass and nap like Rip Van Winkle, to awaken, he hoped, in a better place and time. His mind drifted in a bleary alcohol haze as he wandered the sleep-drenched Town.

His brain was nearly nonfunctioning when a familiar voice called to him out of the darkness.

"Where have you been?"

His eyes widened and focused. It was Laura. She was wearing something navy colored and short; he couldn't quite make out what. Her arms were folded across her chest. He looked up and saw that he'd made it all the way back to the boardinghouse.

"You shouldn't be out here," he said. "It's dangerous." He was not so far gone that he had forgotten his unsettling conversation with Foss.

"I'm not sure I'd be any safer in the house. Sallie Ann's room is right next to mine."

He sensed that she was unhappy, but in his befuddled state he couldn't figure out why. "Is something wrong?" he asked.

"No, not really. I'd been hoping we might go out, but it's kind of late now. Didn't you get my note?"

"Yeah, but it didn't say anything about going out. . . ." Stephen felt himself reel. "Maybe we'd better sit down."

"Sure. Can you make it up the steps to the porch?"

"No problem."

She smiled as they started up the walk. "Why is it I think you've been patronizing Danny's Saloon?"

"They must call you astute," he said, tripping slightly over one of the steps.

"Among other things," she retorted. "You know that tavern has an awful reputation. I wouldn't go there."

"You can't. You're underage."

"Well, I wouldn't go even if I weren't."

"Henry recommended the place," he said, stumbling onto the porch, "and it seemed okay to me. We had a pretty accommodating waitress, too. I think she liked us." He tried to wink and nearly fell over. "It was her birthday."

"Marie O'Neal," she sighed. "I hate to tell you this, Steve, but Marie likes everyone, particularly husbands. She's had three of her own. She has a notorious past. Shall I go on?"

"I'm all ears."

"Men are money to her," Laura explained, steering him toward the swing. "They're a way to keep her in booze another month. One night there was a van parked outside the tavern with the rear doors open. There must've been ten men lined up to have at her. New ones came

109

and went all night. So, you'd better not let her accommodate you too much," she added with a teasing grin. "She's liable to give you some kind of nasty venereal disease."

"Hmmm . . . I see what you mean."

Their laughter was brief, an easy release of all the pain that had entered their lives recently. But it died abruptly when their eyes met.

He leaned into her as they dropped onto the swing. She was warm and soft and sweet smelling. He was having a hard time concentrating, but still it wasn't too bad. He was enjoying the muggy mellowness of the evening, the mood, the company—

"Do you like her?" Laura's words broke into his thoughts.

"Who?"

"Marie!"

"I didn't dislike her."

"Men always like naughty women."

Naughty women . . . he thought of Kat. Kat was the epitome of a naughty woman, and *how* he had loved her. But God, now he wanted nothing more than to forget. The alcohol swam in his brain. Maybe it was time. There had been no one in over a year, no one since Kat. . . .

He blanked her from his mind—she was dead—and stared down into Laura's upturned face. Her eyes were bright and shining and vulnerable. She shivered under the intensity of his gaze, but didn't draw away.

He took her in his arms, and they kissed—lightly at first, testing. Her mouth was pliant and willing.

She clutched him tightly, her fingertips kneading the muscles of his back. She pressed her mouth firmly against his, thrust her tongue deep, and instantly their kisses became hot and demanding.

His mind whirled, floating in gallons of beer. The swing began to rock, gently to and fro. It was like being lost at sea. The blood pulsed through his temples.

He knew it was happening too fast, out of pure lust

and desperation. She was not the kind to love casually, and he didn't want to hurt her, but something snapped in him, and in her, also. Their passion was suddenly blazed by animal urgency. They clung to each other with a hungry, almost frenzied desire.

She drew away slowly, her mouth leaving his with reluctance. Her face was flushed. "Not here," she whispered, taking his hand and pulling him toward the house. "Come up to my room."

Slowly, as though under water, he followed her up the stairs, past the other closed doors. They paused on the threshold to kiss again, then stumbled inside, shutting out the rest of the world.

It seemed more dream than reality. Filtered streetlight seeped through the ghostly curtains billowing gently at the window; the room was cast in shades of amber and blue. A crackle of dry lightning pierced the sky like a long skeletal finger. The scents of exotic perfume lent the atmosphere an air of fantasy.

Stopping at the foot of her lace-covered bed, they grasped at buttons and zippers, hastily throwing off their clothes. Touching her transported Stephen, brought him out of his long-dead past. Each caress of her flesh sent a deep, radiating heat searing through him.

There was just enough illumination for him to see the highlighted features of her face, the exquisite curves of her body. His beer-soaked brain was beginning to clear. She was utterly beautiful.

The downy coverlet sank beneath them. They responded to each other in a nearly frantic manner, squeezing, stroking. He rolled her over and kissed her breasts. She nibbled his shoulder. The feverish gyration of her body was all-consuming. The rustle of sheets. Her lips and hands. He gripped her buttocks and brought her to him. Her breasts pushed against his chest, her hips grinding against his. Their whispers and moans were low and fervid. They flexed and grasped, tensing in perfect rhythm, as though they were not only coupled but

111

melded. For an unmeasured time, the only sounds they made were throaty groans and short gasps of pleasure.

Laura arched her slender, willowy frame and wound her legs around him, tossing her head back on the pillow. Stephen repeated her name as he emptied himself into her, and it was as if his guilt and fear from the past jetted out of him along with his seed.

Exhausted, they lay side by side on the rumpled bed. She took his hand, and he squeezed it. He could have stayed with her, like this, forever.

He slept for awhile and had no idea what time it was when she finally woke him.

She touched her finger to his lips. "It's late," she said.

He nodded.

"Mother's going to be waking up soon. It sounds old-fashioned, but she'd be mortified to find you here in my bedroom. She still thinks of me as her little girl."

"Okay." He smiled and reached out to kiss her. "I can take a hint."

She laughed softly. "We'll see each other in the morning."

Stephen rose and grabbed his jeans from the floor. She slipped on a robe to walk him to the door. They lingered in a last embrace.

"You're not sorry?" he asked.

"No. I'm glad."

Then he eased the knob and pulled it open.

That was as far as he got. When Stephen turned about, his eyes riveted on a sight of unbelievable suffering. He heard Laura's gasp of fear next to him. In the adjacent doorway, a woman's quivering form struggled desperately against an unnatural blanket of hideous color surrounding her. It was Louise Simmons, the librarian.

Already the frail little woman had turned an ashen, sickly gray. The wavering, iridescent mist continued to linger over her, swirling and pulsating as her limbs thrashed in frantic protest. It sparkled with demonic intensity as it crawled over her flesh, penetrating and invading her writhing body.

Stephen stood transfixed as her skin began to draw inward. Scaling patches formed and spread across her entire figure. Jagged lesions erupted, a glutinous cloudy fluid surging forth. She caved in further, her arms and legs contorting and crumbling. Her features distorted as powdery flakes peeled off her face. Her mouth was caught open in a silent scream of eternal terror.

He recoiled in horror as the savage wounds continued to burst, oozing the deadly residue onto the carpet. A vile stench filled the hall. He remembered Foss's words "highly corrosive" and knew there was nothing he could do to help the woman.

He heard a door slam and someone rush to the bottom of the stairs. It was Abigail. "Laura!" she cried.

"Don't come up!" Stephen yelled. "Call the sheriff. Quick!"

He listened to the sound of her footsteps scurrying away, then turned back toward the disintegrating woman.

The evil luminous shadow had begun to move. It crept toward them with sinister menace. The air around him was filled with a maddening buzz. For a moment, he swore he could detect a pulse—an actual heartbeat within the cloud—hear it breathing, feel the essence radiating off of it. The effect was almost mesmerizing.

Laura tugged at his sleeve, and Stephen recovered his senses. He pushed her back into the room, slamming the door behind them.

"Come on!" he shouted, hurrying to the window.

He flipped up the lock and heaved open the glass. Long, curling tendrils of the fiendish vapor were whisking in under the door and with them a sickening odor of death.

They were almost out of time. Stephen helped Laura onto the roof of the porch, then climbed out after her. They scrambled toward the edge of the roof. He grabbed onto the gutter and flipped himself over, then hung full length and dropped to the ground. He was surprised at his own agility, but the grisly scene in the hall had sobered him considerably.

He quickly recovered his balance and held up his arms to Laura. "Hurry!"

She closed her eyes and reached out to him with both hands in front of her as her body fell into nothingness. Her chin struck his forehead, and they tumbled backward onto the grass. He leapt to his feet and pulled her up. She threw herself into his arms, trembling.

Above the porch roof he saw the undulating mass drift out and disappear into the midnight sky.

Saturday, June 17

. . . whispering of supernatural evil . . .

Chapter Nine

i.

Although it was early, not quite 7:00 a.m., the parlor was filled with morning light. Stephen sat in dismal silence listening to the birds chirping outside the window and the labored ticking of an antique clock atop the mantle. His head ached from all the beer last night, and he regretted it now. A bottle of aspirin and a cup of coffee rested on the marble table in front of him.

He could hear Mrs. Morton in the kitchen on the phone to an unfortunate neighbor, half sobbing, half ranting, as she shared the gruesome story of how yet another of her tenants had died.

Stephen rubbed his hand across his eyes. He had seen the whole thing—and still didn't know what it was. A whirling mist. A kaleidoscope of the most malevolent color he'd ever seen. Undulating and hovering over that woman. Sucking the life from her. Somehow corrupting her flesh and eating her from the inside out.

His immediate reaction had been pure terror, as though this were evil itself incarnate in its most vicious form, a prehistoric fiend from the realms of utter darkness. But in the bright light of day, he knew there had to be another, more logical explanation. He'd been trying to convince himself of as much ever since.

When Foss and his men arrived, they'd found the librarian weltering in a puddle of foul-smelling drainage, rapidly deteriorating, and becoming a heap of gray pulp right before their sickened eyes. The sheriff and Dr. Corliss had spent most of the night at the boardinghouse, studying the scene of the woman's demise. The malign shadow that had overtaken her had been expedient, deadly, and efficient in its devastating task. Little remained that was lifelike.

He and Laura had been the only witnesses to her actual death. Through the long hours, they'd had to retell the story several times. Town's diabolical enemy now had a form but no name.

Stephen glanced out the window and felt his gut tighten. Laura's 83 Volkswagen still had not returned. She'd been gone over an hour, delivering the news to the librarian's relatives. He hoped she was all right, but surely . . . It was difficult after last night not to be extremely wary. Laura had been awfully upset at first, as they all were, but she'd gradually regained control. In fact, he was surprised at how well she had recovered.

She had surprised him in a number of ways. He thought of the frenzied passion of their desperate lovemaking. Her desire had easily matched his own. That intense longing had obviously been building in both of them prior to their acquaintance and culminated in last night's encounter, fulfilling their different needs. He did not delude himself into thinking it was more than it was. Perhaps in time. Kat was finally slipping away from him, but in her wake she left a void—an aching that would take years to fill.

He reached out and took a swallow of the coffee in front of him, then grimaced at the cool, bitter taste. The screen door at the front of the house opened and shut. A few seconds later, Sheriff Foss stepped through the archway of the parlor.

"Morning," the lawman grumbled drowsily and sagged into one of the winged chairs. "Get any sleep?"

Stephen shook his head.

"Me, either. Christ, what a night. I've got more bad news, too. I need you to come down to the municipal building with me."

Stephen ran his hand through his tousled black hair. "Why?"

"The mayor's called an emergency meeting. They want to hear your version of what this thing was for themselves. I'll warn you, though, it may go kinda rough. There's a lot of skepticism about your account. You being a stranger to Town."

"Laura saw it, too." He had managed not to tell them about being in her bedroom and only relayed that they had both been awakened by the loud buzzing.

"Yeah, I know," Foss answered. "It's just the way things are in a small town. It doesn't help that you showed up only a few days before all this started."

A muscle twitched in Stephen's cheek. "They don't think I have anything to do with it, do they?"

Foss shook his head. "No. 'Course not. Not after what Mike said about the autopsies." He shoved his bulk up out of the chair. "Well, we might as well get going. They'll be waiting. Life is going to be hell around here for awhile."

They settled into Foss's brown-and-tan cruiser and headed slowly toward the center of Town. It was only a few blocks away, but neither man was anxious to get there.

Stephen gazed out the window. The trim Victorian houses with their fishtail siding and ornate gingerbread woodwork seemed cold and withdrawn, as though they harbored a century's worth of hidden pain and secrets. He wondered how long it would take to bury the latest outbreak of terror, and when it would end.

Of all the inhabitants in this place, he was the freest. He owned no property, had no family here, no business, nothing that tied him to this inconsequential bit of Indi-

119

ana flatland. But, he was a witness to the horror and had been asked to remain available. There was Laura, also.

Foss reached across the dash for his package of Pall Malls and pulled out the cigarette lighter. "I've been thinking about the way you described this thing," he said between puffs, "and trying to put it together with what I've gotten from Mike."

"Did you come up with anything?" Stephen asked.

The sheriff frowned. "Nothing that makes good sense. And that bunch of pansy asses down at the city building aren't much help, either. Malcolm's too damn scared about covering his own butt, making sure he makes the right political moves so that none of this mars his brilliant career. He can't see what the people of this community are going through. He hasn't even thought long enough to realize his own family could die from this shit. I've had my fill of politics. When all of this is over, I'm getting out."

Foss blew a long stream of smoke against the windshield. The man was clearly discouraged. His shoulders slumped, and he seemed to sink further into the vinyl seat. "I can't blame the council members for being skeptical. The whole mess sounds unreal. If only I had more definitive facts to work with, then I could draw it all into some type of theory, a lead I could follow."

"Dr. Corliss think it's a disease."

"But you say it's a cloud, and I was damn sure there was an individual behind this. Where do we go from there? It's all got to figure together one way or another."

Stephen nodded thoughtfully. "Maybe the cloud contains germs that are causing the disease."

"And Angela was running from it," Foss finished. "But how does that explain the fact she struggled with someone, because I'm darn sure she did."

"Maybe this person, whoever he is, is releasing a canister of the germs."

"But he never catches this crap himself?" Foss shook

his head.

"Wait a minute. That's easy enough. He's either immune himself, or he wears a mask. And it might not be germs. It could be poison."

"Yeah. You know, we might have something at that." Foss pulled alongside the curb and parked the vehicle, still smoking and making no move to get out. "Angela could have discovered him when he was releasing the stuff, and then they struggled. But how did he get into the boardinghouse twice? Somebody would've spotted him."

"He just releases it nearby."

"Possibly. Corliss said the bodies were full of digestive fluids, not a single organ or drop of blood left. Do you think poison or germs could have caused that?"

Stephen cleared his throat. "Are there any government labs around here?"

"Indianapolis. Why?"

"Are there any that might deal in germ or chemical warfare?"

The sheriff stiffened and stared straight ahead, his voice tight as he responded. "I see where you're going. That shit is illegal. The president made a deal with the Russians and the U.N. to ban all our testing."

"But that doesn't mean they did."

"No, but—"

"There are other alternatives, too," Stephen said, sensing the man's reluctance. "It could be just one individual."

"What do you mean? That a loony tune decided to test this stuff on our own people? That's pretty farfetched."

"It may or may not have been done on purpose. What about an accident, a dropped flask, a stolen formula?"

"That doesn't account for whoever struggled with Angela."

"Well . . . Town is a small, out-of-the-way place. They might have decided to forfeit one insignificant community for the benefit of the whole."

121

"No. I can't buy that. As corny as it sounds, I've believed in this country all my life and I still do. Not that I can think of anything else." Foss paused, as though giving it careful deliberation. Finally he said, "Where does this cloud go? Why don't we see it hovering in the sky? Why isn't everyone dead?"

"It could just dissipate, but we have no way of knowing. It could be that one of these days we'll wake up, and everyone will be dead."

The sheriff ground his cigarette into an ashtray under the dash. "Not if I can help it. Whether it was done on purpose or not, if this thing came from a government lab, I've got a chance of finding out who's responsible and how to go about stopping it. At least, it's something tangible I can go on. Before . . . it was like tracking a ghost."

"We still might be wrong. It's all guesses, like you said, pretty farfetched ones at that."

Foss exhaled noisily. "But it makes sense. What I was thinking earlier—that didn't."

Stephen waited for him to elaborate, but the lawman glanced at his watch instead. "We'd better get inside," he said.

They opened the doors and stepped out onto an old brick sidewalk. The municipal building, as Foss called it, was sandwiched between two more ancient structures. All three were austere brick edifices that had been painted gray and laden with heavy black cornices and window caps. When they got closer, he saw there were iron bars on the inside of the upper windows of the municipal building. No doubt it served as a part-time jail. He couldn't imagine there were many arrests in Town. Maybe for pig stealing or lewdness late on a Saturday night. But he doubted if any murderers had spent the night behind these bars.

"The council's a rather close-minded group," Foss said. "They hear what they want to hear, and it may take them awhile to believe something like this is even possible. But

I'll run it all by them and you jump in if you've got anything to add."

Stephen wasn't sure how—perhaps because they'd been together on the search for the Stoddard and Woodhouse kids—but at some point along the way he had earned the broad-shouldered lawman's trust.

A large, muscular man in a deputy's uniform came toward them as they approached the steps. He wasn't as tall as he was hard and solidly built. His biceps were knotted like lumps of steel beneath his beige, short-sleeved shirt. Stephen recognized him as the glaring stranger in the saloon who had stormed out when Henry pulled Marie onto his lap.

"Stephen Myers, this is Bill Leland," Foss said. "Bill's been my right-hand man in this county for twelve years."

Stephen extended his hand, but the stocky deputy did not respond. His huge fists remained unflinchingly at his sides. Foss seemed puzzled by the man's reaction.

"Malcolm, Peters, Hunt and the rest of 'em are already up there," the deputy said curtly, staring at Stephen with obvious dislike.

For a moment Foss looked as if he might say something, then he let it go.

"Cal Stoddard called, too," the deputy added.

"Okay," Foss said slowly, still perplexed. "While we're in this meeting, I need you to go over to the office and get me the name and number of every government lab in this part of the state, and find out who's in charge. Scan the bulletins and see if any spills or leaks have been reported recently. I want to know of any experiments involving toxic agents, such as germs or poisons."

Bill nodded rigidly and headed toward his car. As soon as he had crossed the street, Foss turned to Stephen. "I wonder what's got into him? Bill's not usually that way. He's always been pretty much of a loner, but he plays cards and goes out regularly with me and some of the boys over at the saloon. Not the overly friendly type, but a good man. I don't understand it."

123

They ascended the steps into the dark corridor of the building. The wooden stairs were worn down in the middle from years of intensive use.

"I might know the problem," Stephen volunteered as they continued to climb. "Is he a close friend of that red-haired waitress at Danny's?"

"Marie Sheldon O'Neal." Foss shrugged, pondering the question. "She's a sore point with him. They've gone out. Bill's wife left him about a year ago, and he's had a rough time of it. He gets lonely sometimes. I remember him making a comment about wanting to get married again, but I don't think he's that serious about Marie. She's got all sorts of problems. She's not the kind of girl—"

Stephen smiled. "Yeah, I know."

By the time they reached the third story, both their shirts were clinging to their chests. Stephen pushed the damp hair from his forehead. Foss led him to a large council chamber that encompassed the entire floor.

The ceiling was low and the compacted air on the top level held the odor of old age, cracked plaster, and dry rot from the woodwork. The windows were open at opposite ends and a slight breeze blew across the length of the long suite, bringing a little relief from both the confined atmosphere and the heat.

There was a large, scarred table in the center and several dilapidated leather chairs and sofas along the walls. A water cooler hummed softly in the front corner under the windows, and a coffee machine stood next to the door. A group of eight men, all but two of them over sixty, wearing varying shades of dark trousers, and white shirts rolled to the elbows, were gathered at the streetside windows. Several held wrinkled, cone-shaped paper cups from the cooler. Their voices dropped and heads turned as Foss and Stephen entered the room.

Stephen saw Dr. Corliss among the group. The doctor looked no better than he had the other day at the woods. His face was drawn and deep circles rimmed his eyes.

While the others assembled around the table, taking their designated places, Mayor Malcolm moved straight toward Stephen and Foss. He checked his watch, an expression of annoyance on his round, boyish face.

Stephen couldn't help noticing his perfectly straight white teeth, his expensive suit, and the rich scent of aftershave that lingered around him.

"It's eight-thirty already," Malcolm grumbled without greeting either one of them. "I hope we can get this over with quickly. I've got a lot to do today."

"We all do," Foss replied shortly. "Steve and I have come up with several ideas."

"Good. Then let's not waste any more time," he said, gesturing them toward the center of the chamber.

Foss grimaced and stepped over to the table with the rest. There was obviously tension between him and Malcolm.

Three councilmen were present, as well as the mayor, the doctor, Ezra Hunt—publisher of the local paper—the sheriff, and Stephen.

"All right, gentlemen," Malcolm said, as he took his seat at the head of the table and looked each man in the eye with an air of seriousness. "We'll speed this meeting along as fast as possible. I know you're all very busy, and it's been a long morning already. These are difficult and trying times for everyone. I want to extend my condolences again to those of you who have lost family members and friends in this recent tragedy. Be assured I am doing what I can to bring the situation under control, but we must pull together." He emphasized his words with a tightening of his fist and a tone of heartfelt concern.

Malcolm, sitting rigidly in the hard-backed chair, aimed his gaze at a wizened old man to the far right. "I appreciate your cooperation, Ezra, in keeping this out of the papers. The level of fear in the community is high enough without purposely repeating and exploiting grisly details."

The leathery old man nodded grimly. "But the folks 'round here won't stomach it for long. They want answers. They want ta know what's being done ta protect their families an' land."

"I agree," the mayor stated, his earnest blue eyes moving over each face at the table. "And we'll let them know as soon as we can. The governor called. He's offered additional manpower if we need it and the complete cooperation of the board of health. We should determine just what assistance is required before we respond. Bob, can you give us your report?"

Foss pushed himself back from the table and dropped a package of cigarettes beside an ashtray on the scarred surface. He took out a memo pad and cleared his throat.

"Starting with the Arnold's boy, there have now been seven mortalities attributed to this malady. All the victims appear to have died the same—a complete breakdown of the body's tissues and organs. Stephen Myers and Laura Morton both witnessed Louise Simmons's death last night and said there appeared to be a cloudlike substance surrounding her. It remained over her until after she had died, then shifted toward them. They fled through a second-story window, and the substance drifted out into the sky."

The three councilmen wore expressions of doubt.

Ray Fawley traced his finger over a line of grain in the table. "How does this 'cloud' fit into your theory, Doctor?" he asked without raising his eyes.

Corliss coughed. "I haven't had time to fully consider the matter. I've only just finished the autopsy on Miss Simmons."

"I see," Councilman Fawley said. "But off-hand, is there any scientific explanation you could give us for it?"

Foss interrupted. "Steve and I were going over that on the way here, and we've come up with a guess."

Fawley now lifted his angry brown eyes and glared scathingly at Foss. "I was asking the good doctor, if you don't mind."

"I'd like to hear what Bob has to say," Corliss said.

Fawley objected. "I don't want to hear guesses! We need facts. My wife's sister lost both of her kids, and I wanna know why!"

The sheriff slammed his fist against the table. "Damn it, Ray. That's what I'm trying to tell you. I think we may have come up with the answer."

"How could a cloud have killed seven people?" another of the council members demanded.

Murmurs of dissent arose from around the table, and it was plain to Stephen that these men were running scared. They were farmers and merchants and factory workers, not scientists, and they wanted to know what was terrorizing their homes.

Malcolm called for attention. "Please. It's hot, and we're all under a great deal of stress. Tempers are short, but this isn't helping. If we remain patient, we'll get finished a lot faster. Sheriff, will you please tell us what you and Mr. Myers discussed?"

Foss nodded. "You all know me well enough to realize I don't take my job lightly. It's clear there isn't any ordinary explanation for this. What Steve and I came up with isn't very pleasant, but it's something to go on. We were thinking about all those chemical plants and government labs there are up in Indianapolis, and how a few of them aren't too careful. Mike, is there any chance the events of the past ten days could be related to an industrial spill or germ warfare of some type?"

Corliss hesitated. Finally, he said, "Yes. I suppose there is."

The rest of the group was visibly shaken. It was suddenly clear to them that they might once again be the victims of the big-city giants, who with their megamillion-dollar deals and greedy land grabs were stealing away the countryman's ability to earn a living.

Everyone remembered the days after they discovered the Town dump was contaminated, the fear that had struck at the soul of every man and woman as they wondered who had been affected — who was due to come down with a deadly form of cancer. As time went by and the dump was cleaned up, they had begun to rest easier, and now this. . . .

"It couldn't have been a chemical spill," Fawley insisted feebly. "If it was, we'd have heard about it."

"Not nec'ssarily," Ezra reminded him. "I've been in the newspaper business a long time, seen all kinds of scandals, an' believe me — not nec'ssarily."

"But . . ." Fawley faltered, unable to cope with these new revelations.

Malcolm was the first to recover. "I understand what germ warfare is, but what are you suggesting? A communist attack?"

"Well," Foss hedged, "it could be an accident. Somehow this cloud — potentially the carrier of a lethal germ — might have escaped from one of the area labs. Or then again, it might be intentional testing. There's evidence that the Stoddard girl struggled with someone, which increases the likelihood that this poisonous gas is being purposely released."

Ezra Hunt struck a wooden kitchen match against the underside of the table and lit his pipe. "Seems to me," he drawled, "I recall a story like that on the wire. Seems 'bout thirty years ago the gov'ment approved a test of germ warfare on a small California town. 'Course wasn't nothing 'bout it released till at least twenty years after the fact. I don't recall that anybody died, either. Seems the test was a failure. Jus' made ev'rbody good an' sick."

"We don't want to jump to conclusions," Malcolm said.

"We can't ignore the possibility, though," Corliss argued. "I examined the bodies. There's nothing I know of that would cause these results. I would say there's a very good chance Bob is right." He shivered and hugged his bandaged hand closer to his chest. "I should've thought of it myself. In massive doses, this germ must cause the whole body to go haywire. Within minutes the body be-

128

gins forming gastric bile so corrosive that it literally dissolves the victim from the inside out."

Corliss paused and glanced uneasily at his friends. "If we are correct, then this is no disease in the regular sense, but a sophisticated, manmade germ. Not the kind easy to find a cure for. God only knows if one is possible. We need to find out where it came from. Otherwise, our hopes of finding a cure are almost nil."

"You're convinced, then, that we've stumbled onto the cause for these deaths?" the mayor asked.

The doctor nodded gravely.

The eight men sat in stunned silence, overwhelmed by the magnitude of what these theories could mean. It was too much to absorb at once. The deeper they probed into this mysterious plague the more horrifying it became. The results could be frighteningly far reaching. If it spread, there might not be anyone, anywhere, who was safe.

How could any human being create something so lethal to be used against his fellow man? Even Steve found himself shaken by the conclusions they had drawn. Unlike the sheriff, his faith in the system was not so strong, and he believed there was a real possibility that the government could be involved.

Fawley's face reddened with outrage. "By God, they won't get away with it!"

"Are there any other suggestions as to what this could be?" Malcolm asked.

No one spoke.

Foss squared his shoulders with determination. "We're going to need a plan of action and a way to protect ourselves until this is over."

Malcolm responded. "As I said before, we can definitely get assistance from the state, whatever we need. There's no question that this qualifies as a major threat to the well-being of the community."

"A colleague of mine will be arriving this afternoon to help," the doctor said. "I've sent him skin and fluid samples from the victims. The man has a lot of contacts in the government and with the local labs. He does research work for both. He's an incredibly gifted diagnostician. I think he can give us the answers we're looking for."

"I've already got Bill calling every lab in the state trying to track this down," Foss said.

"I doubt you'll get any of them to own up to it," Malcolm said. "It isn't going to be easy to get someone to take responsibility for this. And, we can't go around pointing our fingers without evidence. This might take years."

"We'll have to do what we can by ourselves," Foss said.

"Panic is going to be a problem," the doctor added. "We might all have been exposed to this without realizing it. While massive contact results in immediate death, minute quantities of it may not even affect the victim for awhile. People might start leaving Town and spread this germ across the country. A quarantine might have to be imposed. It may only be a matter of time."

"Do you think that's likely? That we've already been exposed I mean?" Foss asked.

"I have no way to know," the doctor said. "Although the toxic cloud Steve spotted last night was easily visible, trace amounts of this germ may float airborne without being detectable."

"Christ alive! I don't believe this." Malcolm tightened his grip on the edge of the table, and Stephen saw that he was beginning to lose his cool at last. "Let's not blow this out of proportion. We've got to keep our wits. It can't be as serious as that."

"It can't?" Foss questioned. "Why not?"

The mayor paled and glanced at his watch again. "Ezra, you understand the importance of continuing to keep as much of this out of the paper as possible? The situation's bad enough as it is."

"I'll do what I can," the old man groused. "It ain't easy. I'm playin' it down, but a reporter from the city called me this mornin' wantin' to know what it was all

130

about. I put 'em off, but . . ."

"People don't need a paper to tell them what's what," Fawley grumbled.

"We'll confine the facts," the mayor ordered. "All deaths will be reported to me first. We'll isolate the sites, and I'll issue an official statement concerning each one."

"Should I broadcast a warning telling people to stay indoors and keep their windows shut?" Foss asked.

"It wouldn't do any good," Stephen muttered. "I saw the cloud come in under the door last night. It even crept in through the hinges and around the knob. I doubt if there's a single window in Town that'll seal tightly enough to keep this thing out."

The room fell silent. Then the mayor cleared his throat. "I think we're doing all that we can for the moment. We'll continue to give warnings on the radio, listing the symptoms of this disease and advising people to seek prompt medical attention. We'll instruct them to report any sightings of this lethal gas and to keep an eye out for strangers. The more gruesome details can be kept to ourselves until we have more facts to go on. Our town, our property, our lives depend on everyone doing their job." Malcolm paused a moment. "Are there any other questions?"

When no one spoke, he turned to Corliss. "Anything you care to add, Doctor?"

The doctor shook his head.

"That does it then." The mayor gathered the papers in front of him, and they all rose from the table.

The doctor winced as he pushed out his chair.

"You okay, Mike?" Foss asked.

Corliss nodded, hugging the bandage against his chest again. "Yeah. It's only this burn. I'll be all right. Don't worry."

Foss frowned. "From the look on your face, I'd say it was more than that," the lawman insisted.

"No. Really. I was just thinking about what we discussed."

"You *do* think we've come up with the cause, don't you?"

"Probably. We need more tests to be certain."

"But?" Foss waited impatiently.

"When I did the autopsy on Louise Simmons, I discovered this." He reached into his shirt pocket and produced a small plastic bag with a clump of dark, matted hair. "I found it clutched in her hand."

"That just about clenches my theory that the victims struggled with someone."

"Not all the victims."

"What are you saying, Mike?"

"I'm not sure."

"If someone's purposely letting this stuff go each time, then it's murder."

Corliss shrugged. "Could be, but it doesn't make sense. How does the killer get away without getting caught? Why hasn't he been seen? We're still missing the mark. It's my guess that not all the pieces to the puzzle are here. Either that, or we're overlooking something vital in our research."

ii.

Hubert Malcolm rushed down the long wooden staircase ahead of the rest of his companions, who still lingered in dismal discourse over the appalling revelations of the council meeting.

Malcolm was depressed, too. He could see his dreams and plans withering before his eyes. He could feel it in his guts. More lives would be lost. Town would become plagued with reporters. It would become the focus of national attention. Everyone would remember him as the mayor whose city was utterly ravaged by a toxic, man-made germ. They would not remember his efforts to save Town, nor how courageously he fought the chemical companies and government for compensation. People always remembered the bad, never the good.

So it was time to think of himself.

The bright sunlight struck his eyes as he exited through the side door. He was on his way to his lawyer's office in Indianapolis to discuss how to best save his securities and land investments. They had to act fast, with absolute secrecy. Word that he was bailing out and selling his holdings must not get out—not yet.

He'd do what he could for Town, then pack up Flora and the kids and move someplace new. Maybe to a different state. Where they could live down all the lies that were bound to surface. He was still young enough and had a lot of charisma. In the last election, he'd drawn great attention. Papers statewide had called him another Jack Kennedy. And so, he would be. He'd run for office again. Congressional office next time. No more playing around, wasting his resources on small potatoes.

He shoved the key in the lock of his shiny beige Porsche and settled in behind the wheel. It hit him then, as he looked over the pavement at the rows of quaint shops, antique lampposts and benches, that he was going to miss this place. He'd worked hard to get Town back on a sound economic track and make the most of its historic image. In his six years as mayor, they'd gone from a decaying village to a state landmark. They owed him a lot—but no one would remember.

His eyes moistened. It was a pity. He had done nothing to deserve this pain.

As Malcolm started the engine, a young girl in a tight red skirt passed by and reminded him vaguely of Angela. He felt renewed sadness. In the thirty years since high school, Angela Stoddard had been the first real risk he'd ever taken.

It hadn't been planned. She'd come to his house one afternoon in shorts and a skimpy halter top asking to see his daughter. But neither Kelly nor Flora had been home. Angela had offered to wait and seated herself beside him on the sofa. He remembered every delirious minute of it,

133

her stroking his crotch, unzipping his pants, wrapping her lips around his cock.

Nothing that exciting had happened to him since high school, but Angela made him realize it needn't stop. He was a vital, attractive man, one who could make a young girl happy. . . .

But now there'd be only Flora. Fat-assed, gray-haired, dried-up Flora.

He tightened his hands on the wheel. He knew he couldn't afford to take another chance. He'd barely gotten away with the fling with Angela. She had been so mature, so sure of herself, and even she had allowed what could have been a tragic mistake.

The girl in the tight red skirt was now out of sight. Malcolm pulled away from the curb. He shifted into third and headed for the interstate, trying not to remember what had been and never would be again.

Chapter Ten

i.

It was nearly noon. Stephen declined Foss's offer of a ride back to the boardinghouse in order to stretch his legs after the long conference. He was slowly making the adjustment from the heavily populated, bustling streets of his own home turf to these sparse, provincial crossroads.

The enormous old houses could look both intimidating and charming at odd turns. It was unsettling in some ways, and yet he was beginning to get back a little of that feel he had come here for. He could understand why Henry and the other residents would be willing to fight for a place like this—unlike his own neighborhood, where you fought to get out.

Yet as he strode the heat-baked, dusty sidewalks he didn't see another soul. The park, that had only a couple of days ago been filled with raucous kids the moment school let out, was now deserted. People were taking the warnings seriously, as well they should, but he remembered Dr. Corliss's words. Would it do them any good? Were they all, including himself, already infected?

He stepped across the broken bricks at the entrance to the alley behind the boardinghouse, and a figure moved out of the sun-sharpened shadows between the buildings. It was the muscular deputy, Bill Leland.

"I want to talk to you," Leland said gruffly.

Stephen stopped, squinting directly into the big man's steel gray eyes. The deputy obviously hadn't grown any fonder of him in the last few hours. Leland might be Foss's right-hand man and a jolly good fellow in everyone else's esteem, but he had seen little evidence of it.

"What can I do for you?" Stephen asked, trying to be polite, though it was plain this was not a social call.

"To start with, you could get out of Town."

"I could, but I don't plan—"

Without warning, Leland grabbed the front of Stephen's shirt and shoved him into the alley, slamming him against the rear of one of the buildings. Stephen's skull collided with the rough siding. The world spun briefly in and out of focus.

"I don't give a damn what you had planned," the deputy growled. "I said you can get out of Town."

Stephen shook off the man's grip. A cold sweat broke out across his chest, and adrenaline pumped like fire through his veins. "Listen, friend," he said tightly. "I haven't the vaguest idea what your problem is."

"Then let me fill you in. Marie is my girl. She's going to be my wife."

"Well, that's between you and her, isn't it, pal?" Though his assessment back at the municipal building had proved correct, Stephen had difficulty imagining it was a relationship destined for the altar.

"I'm giving you a warning," Leland threatened, shoving Stephen to emphasize his words. "It's the last you're likely to get. You keep your hands off, and you tell Henry the same."

"Beating the crap out of me isn't going to solve your problem. There was a whole bar full of men stuffing money into her garter."

The big man's face drew closer to Stephen's. His

136

breath alone could've made Milwaukee famous. For whatever reasons, Bob Foss's right-hand man was losing his grip. Leland's eyes were filled with murder. He had a grudge to kill.

"You don't think I can control my woman?" the man challenged.

"If you're looking for trouble—"

Stephen saw it coming, a huge fist aimed straight at his jaw. He ducked and moved in quick, hitting the deputy in the middle with his right. Leland swung, but his reflexes were too slow. Stephen sidestepped the punch and struck him again an inch or two above the belt buckle. The deputy doubled over, a deep retching sound escaping his throat, but he wasn't through yet. He kicked out at Stephen and caught him behind the shins. The thirty-three-year-old artist went sprawling onto the pavement, his hands and face scraping the abrasive surface. Piercing stabs of Technicolor pain shot through his body.

Within seconds Leland was on Stephen's back, pounding his forehead against the cement. The lawman was in a rage and out of control. Stephen arched and swung his elbow around hard, jabbing the deputy in the kidney and knocking the huge baboon off his back. Leland lunged at him as he was pushing himself to his feet. Stephen drove his knee into the lawman's groin. The big man collapsed and fell to his side. He lay puking on the road.

Stephen squatted on his haunches, getting his wind back. He felt sorry for the guy. The man was fighting and lashing out, but he was never going to win with Marie. Stephen understood women like her. He'd met a lot more of them than he had the other kind, the kind like Laura.

He staggered back, wiping a trickle of blood from the corner of his mouth. The inside of his lip was puffed up and his forehead tender, but he'd live. The next time he'd be prepared. A knife was easier to conceal and carried less of a penalty than a gun if he got caught. He dusted off his clothes and headed toward the boardinghouse.

ii.

The outer door of the doctor's office opened, and the gray-haired nurse at the desk glanced up with annoyance as she phoned in prescriptions to the local pharmacy. There were already twenty-five patients crowded into the tiny waiting room.

The sheriff's announcement yesterday on the radio, advising all those who noticed any unusual symptoms—especially ulcerous sores, flaking, or discoloration of the skin—to seek immediate medical attention, had created pandemonium in the small clinic, and Helen Worman had developed a corresponding headache. She replaced the receiver and glared with impatience at the elderly gentlemen who had just tottered in. He was no one she knew.

"What can I do for you?" she asked flatly. "We're rather busy."

The frail man leaned heavily on a knobby cane and gazed in at her through the open receptionist's window. He appeared to be in his late sixties, with a small, hunched frame and a few thin strands of wispy white hair draped back from his forehead across his balding scalp. He wore a long-sleeved shirt and baggy woolen trousers. In this heat, she thought. He must be nuts.

"I wish to see Dr. Michael H. Corliss," the old man said.

"Do you have an appointment?" she asked nasally.

"No . . ."

"We have at least a three-hour wait, but if you take a seat, the doctor will be with you as soon as possible." She reached up to close the window.

With surprising speed the old man rammed one of his scrawny hands into the opening.

"Sir, if you please."

"I'm Dr. Philip Thompson. Doctor Corliss phoned me several days ago on an urgent matter."

"Oh. Yes. Well, you should've said so," she answered, refusing to be either flustered or rushed, and punched one of the buttons on the intercom with stiff efficiency. "Dr. Corliss, Dr. Thompson is here." She swung back around to the window. "Now if you'll please take a seat, I'm sure—"

The inner door to the examining rooms burst open before she could finish. Dr. Corliss stood in the entry, disheveled and harried, his white lab coat slightly askew and his sandy hair falling rakishly across his forehead. Helen didn't approve at all. These last few days the doctor had made an abrupt transformation in both his appearance and actions. He seemed in a constant state of agitation. It marred the dignity of his profession. What would the patients think seeing him so?

"Professor Thompson," Doctor Corliss said. "Please, come in."

Helen watched as he ushered the elderly man into the inner office sanctum and down toward the private quarters, a four-room apartment attached to the rear of the main building.

"I'm glad you could make it so quickly," she heard Dr. Corliss say. "I need time to finish up here, then I'll be right with you."

"Of course."

"Make yourself at home. There's coffee by the stove."

The old man nodded. "I'll be fine." Then he moved off with a jerking gait, maneuvering his cane over the threshold.

Dr. Corliss hurried back to the receptionist's desk. Helen was ready. "Bring me the charts for whoever we've got waiting," he said abruptly, "and close the office. Cancel the rest of the afternoon's appointments, and refer any emergencies or new calls to the patient center at the county hospital. Get the sheriff on the line, too, Helen."

"Yes, Doctor."

She sniffed indignantly. They didn't run things this way when old Dr. Bower was here. None of this rushing about. None of those fancy tests, either, CAT scans and ultrasounds. Old-fashioned X rays and penicillin were good enough for Dr. Bower

After informing those seated out front that they would be seen soon, she posted the appropriate emergency message on the outer door, then grabbed the files Dr. Corliss had requested and took them into his office. There were dozens of calls to be made canceling all the appointments. It was going to be a nerve-racking afternoon.

"Doctor, I've got the sheriff on the phone," she said. "Line one. And Mrs. O'Connell is waiting in room four."

He took the files from her without so much as a thank-you. That was gratitude for you. Corliss punched the button on the speakerphone as he flipped through the folders, jotting brief notes.

"Bob," the doctor said, "Professor Thompson is here, the man I was telling you about this morning. I thought you'd want to come over and hear what he's got to say."

"Right," the sheriff answered. "Hang on just a second, would you?"

Michael frowned as he was put on hold. When Foss's voice returned, the doctor asked, "Is something wrong?"

"We're swamped down here. I can't get a hold of Bill. Apparently he's had a run-in with Steve Myers."

"What about?"

140

Helen whisked in and out. With the modern speakerphones, she could hear every word, though she tried not to listen. It was none of her business, after all. She prided herself on crisp professionalism.

"Don't know," the sheriff said, "but the two of them really slugged it out."

"Anything serious?"

"No, no. They're both all right. Listen, Steve's here with me now. I want to bring him along. He's agreed to help out while we're shorthanded. Tell me, does this . . . what's his name?"

"Professor Thompson," Michael answered.

"Does he know anything about germ warfare?"

Helen started when she heard the words: germ warfare. Good Lord, was that what this crisis was about?

"He's worked in government labs all over the country," Dr. Corliss went on to explain, "including D.C. During the seventies he studied the aftereffects of Agent Orange and other chemicals used during the war. He has top level clearance. I'm certain if any man in the state can find out what's going on around here, he can. He's head of biology and natural sciences at the university in Indianapolis. That's where I met him. Professor Thompson's very well respected."

"Good. I hope he can solve this for us. Be right over."

"No hurry. It'll take me close to an hour to finish up here."

"Okay. See you then."

Michael turned off the speakerphone.

Helen cleared her throat. "Mr. Kaymeyer is waiting for you in room one," she said.

"Thank you."

It took Dr. Corliss exactly forty-five minutes to finish with his patients and clear the office. He had Helen

Worman lock the front door on her way out.

For the first time in days, he had real hope that they would beat this thing. And yes, if he was going to be totally honest, a chance of saving his own life as well.

He removed the bandage and examined his injured hand. The intense burning was mostly gone, so were the open lesions. They had not spread as he had first feared. Though it appeared to be healing, there was an inexplicable coldness that traveled up his arm to his shoulder and chest, not like the numbing stabs of a heart attack, yet equally frightening. He was horribly aware that, while the pain was fading, all was not right. For the disease was not gone, it was inside him now.

He could feel it, insidiously working its way into his vital organs, day by day, blood vessel after blood vessel. At odd times, he experienced sudden headaches and chills, blurring of vision, a pounding tenseness in his veins. Then it would all go away, and he would feel better, almost totally well, and yet . . . It was never completely gone. He was never allowed to forget. And, the spells were increasing in frequency as well as severity.

What did it mean? How long would it last? He had asked himself a thousand questions, but still had not one answer.

Perhaps he had been infected by a small enough dose of the germ so that he was actually developing a sort of immunity which might lay the groundwork for vaccinations or possibly a cure. He was researching along these lines, but he couldn't be sure it wasn't planting the seeds for a worse, even more drawn out and agonizing illness.

The human existence was incredibly frail. Mortality was devastatingly simple. He saw it every day. It didn't take much to snuff out life. One high fever could wipe out an intelligent, animate child's mind. This disease could run rampant over them like a supersonic jet.

But he wouldn't let that happen. His battle with evil had truly begun in earnest. He had lived his entire life for this moment. This was his great purpose—his reason for being. All of society would benefit. It was better this way, that the many should benefit from the sacrifice of one individual. He was doing the right thing, he assured himself, and that comforted him. His life would not be wasted.

With shaking hands, Michael reached for the half-empty bottle of vodka stashed behind the manila folders in his personal file cabinet. His appetite for food had greatly diminished since this crisis began, but his desire for liquor . . . He quickly bolted down several mouthfuls. The alcohol did more than steady his nerves, it soothed the icy tingling of the disease and gave him the strength to fight back.

Time was running out. He replaced the bottle, locked the cabinet and pocketed the key, then headed down the darkened hallway toward his apartment in the rear of the building.

The old man had seated himself on a black leather davenport in Corliss's makeshift living room and was leafing through a medical journal he'd found on the side table.

The journal was insufficient to hold his interest, and his gaze shifted about the apartment. It was small and sparsely decorated. Bare, white walls. Plain gray blinds at the windows. Nothing but the essentials for getting by. It suited the needs of a man who was deeply involved in his work and little else.

He had often wondered what would become of Michael Corliss. Michael was one of the brightest students he'd ever had, industrious, quick thinking, determined—obsessed. A man should have more in his life than work. But with Michael medicine had always been more than a profession: it was a mission.

That worried Dr. Thompson. For it created a certain sort of instability that was dangerous, that went against the natural course of events which ought to shape a man's life. But what concerned him more were the terrifying, preternatural circumstances transpiring in this little community.

From the moment Michael had begun describing the situation over the phone, the professor had a deep feeling of dread. He had immediately urged Michael to send along samples and dropped everything else to struggle with identifying the peculiar hydrocarbon derivative Michael had detected.

As soon as he'd run the preliminary tests, he'd realized just how right his initial reaction had been. He didn't need to look at the autopsy reports to understand how precarious and explosive this thing could be, how easily it could reach beyond its present confines and how wide the repercussions might be.

He was not surprised by its appearance either. He had been expecting something like this for years. In fact, he had written a book on the subject and spoken before large groups of fellow scientists and physicians.

But no one had listened.

The scientific world varied widely in its beliefs of the origin of the earth and universe. Thompson's research had led him to his own conclusions and to the hypothetical discovery of a component he referred to only as a latent primitive force. This force concerned him. For he knew all it needed was the right receptacle to set itself in motion, and he now feared it had found one.

He had a sixth sense about these things. The same way a psychic might know who was standing on the other side of a closed door, he knew that what was happening in Town would change life on earth forever.

He had hoped when it struck it would not be so close to home, or that he might already be dead. He had not wanted to be around to say I told you so. . . .

The door swung open. Michael entered, looking tired and drawn. His eyes burned with a feverish tenseness.

"I called the sheriff," he said, unbuttoning his lab coat and hanging it on a hook in the closet. "I thought he ought to be in on our discussion."

"That's good." They would need all the help they could get, the old man thought.

Michael lifted the steaming pot of dark brown liquid from the stove. "You didn't have any coffee. Is there anything else I can get you?"

Dr. Thompson shook his head. "I'm on a very strict diet."

"Oh, that's right. Was it your daughter? No, your niece who told me that you'd been ill. I hope you're feeling better."

"As well as can be expected. I had more therapy before I left."

"Cancer?"

Dr. Thompson nodded.

"I'm sorry."

"It doesn't matter. I'm an old man. I'm ready to die."

Michael glanced nervously at the door. "They should be here any moment. Frankly, I was surprised not to see them when I walked in. I thought they might've come through the back."

"How are *you*, Michael?"

The sandy-haired doctor nodded grimly. "I'm fine." He plucked at his bandaged hand. "I burned myself on the stove, but it's almost well now. I never was any good at . . ." He stopped, a fiery blush creeping up from his neck.

Thompson knew Michael was under a considerable strain from what was happening in Town, but still he was worried. He had a genuine fondness for his former pupil and sensed he might have some kind of personal trouble. But before he could question him further, the door burst open. Two men strode in, one young, one middle aged.

"Dr. Philip Thompson, this is Bob Foss, and a newcomer to Town, artist Stephen Myers. You may have seen his paintings in Chicago or the art magazines."

"I wish I had. There never seems to be enough time for the things I enjoy. Pleased to meet you, gentlemen."

Dr. Thompson didn't rise from the davenport. The effort would have cost him valuable energy he needed for other endeavors, and it wouldn't have been appreciated. At this point in his life, he had learned to conserve what little strength he had.

The artist looked as if he'd been in a fight. Michael automatically took hold of Myers' chin and examined his battered face with a critical eye. There was a large bruise on his forehead and a purple and blue knot forming around the left side of his mouth.

"Move over into the light," the younger doctor directed.

Stephen complied.

"He got you a good one all right." Michael pulled down Stephen's swollen lip. "It looks okay, though. Be sore. Keep a watch for infection. It should heal in a couple of days. No stitches needed."

"Thanks."

"I'll talk to Bill tomorrow," Foss promised. "Let him cool down first. He's been alone since Ellen left, and I expect it's just gotten to be too much for him. But he'll come around. It isn't entirely his fault. Marie's trouble. A woman like that can drive a man to distraction. I arrested her once on charges of prostitution, but it wasn't much use. You aren't going to change someone like that by throwing her into jail for a couple days. I

146

suppose every town's got to have one like her."

They had each taken a seat in the meagerly furnished living room.

Dr. Thompson waited patiently. He was unsure just how to explain his suspicions. It would take time to phrase it in a way that they could understand.

"Several new facts have been disclosed since I called your office," Michael said. "Another woman has died, and Steve was witness to it. We think it may not be a disease after all, at least not in the conventional sense, but a reaction to a chemical, possibly germ warfare. Nothing about this seems to be commonplace."

The old man listened quietly as they described to him the events of last night and this morning, ending with their conclusion that something of extraordinary proportion was happening to the citizens of Town. He couldn't agree with them more, except it was not germ warfare or a chemical spill as such. He was impressed, though, with what they had come up with on their own. News of a cloud was enlightening, too, and he began to put it together with the theories he was already formulating in his mind.

"We thought—if you were willing—that you might be able to help determine who's responsible for this," Michael finished. "We don't know where else to start."

They stared at him expectantly, believing he held the keys to the solution of their problems, though he did not.

He began hesitantly. "I ran a complete battery of tests on the samples you sent," he said. "Most distressing was the consistent presence of the particular polynuclear hydrocarbon derivative you had mentioned and its identification."

"Were you able to break it down?" Michael questioned anxiously.

Thompson nodded. "More or less. I ran an infrared as well as a nuclear magnetic resonance spectrum on it, and came up with a molecular formula anyway."

"And?" Michael pressed.

"It's an incredible chemical hybrid, one that I would never have thought possible. I wouldn't even begin to know how to go about synthesizing it in the lab, and neither would anyone else, I fear."

"So you're telling us this isn't a man-made germ, is that it?" the sheriff interrupted.

"Yes . . . in a sense. It's very complicated. Formally—according to its structure—this molecular chain would be called tolylcyanobenzanthracene. To abbreviate the nomenclature, you take the first initial from each of the major components. Which would be TCBA.

"This chain is made up of elements that have always existed within the earth's soil, but they are considered to be highly *un*reactive with each other. In nature, all things take the path of least resistance. This applies to chemicals as well. They combine with the molecules around them that are the easiest targets. They only recombine when they encounter a more desirable molecule. Am I making myself clear?"

Michael nodded, but the other two looked confused.

"Sometimes," the professor explained, "you end up going through a massive sequence of reactions in order to synthesize the compound you're after. Other times, it's not even possible. No matter what you try, the molecules just don't want to hook up with each other in the combination you're after. That should be the case here. This synthesis of TCBA should never have taken place.

"But something has caused these molecules to bond together, forming this deadly combination. A powerfully unique catalyst would have been required, a force capable of changing the electrolytic characteristics of the molecules. Not one that could have been generated in a lab."

"You're sure," the sheriff questioned, "that this

148

couldn't be some new experiment, something you haven't heard about yet?"

Thompson nodded. "Quite certain. We are decades away from that point. It would be like trying to create a star. Nature does it, but man doesn't have a shot at duplicating it with technology as it now stands. This is not to say, however, that I don't think mankind has played a role in the formation of TCBA. I found traces of unreacted benzanthracene in the fluid samples you sent me. Benzanthracene has been linked to some of the most powerful carcinogens known to man. It is also frequently associated with industrial waste."

"I don't understand," Michael said, shaking his head. "Where did the benzanthracene come from?"

"Precisely what I was going to ask."

Thompson stared at the three as they looked to each other. Both Michael and the artist were relatively new to Town. It was the sheriff who finally spoke.

"I don't know if this is what you're looking for," he said, "but about fifteen years ago there was some illegal dumping that took place on the east side. A company out of Indy was using the gravel pit to dispose of toxic waste. But we took 'em to court, and they cleared it up. All the ground was gone over and pronounced clean by a team of federal experts."

Thompson's eyes narrowed to fleshy slits. "Are there any facilities nearby involved in chemical use? Any supply firms or solvent manufacturing? Maybe heavy-duty pesticides?"

Foss shook his head. "Nothing more than a can of Raid."

Michael leaned forward. "How is the unreacted benzanthracene getting into the victim's systems? From the cloud?"

"The benzanthracene itself could have come from a number of sources. This gravel pit you spoke of is one possibility," Thompson said.

149

"And the cloud?" Michael asked.

"My guess is that the cloud described is actually a gaseous form of this new hydrocarbon derivative, TCBA, and that's how it infected your people. The question is where did the cloud come from? I suggest we visit this gravel pit to determine whether either TCBA or benzanthracene are present. I've developed a couple of quick on-site tests we could run."

Michael agreed. "But how is the TCBA causing such massive bodily destruction in such a short time?"

"I'm not certain. We know that TCBA is a component of the corruptive fluid as well as some common enzymes, but beyond that we have no answers. That'll require more research."

Thompson was hesitant to expound upon his theory about the invisible force involved. It was all so new, so unexplored; but he was sure he was right. Just as a black hole in space is controlled by a force so primitive and strong that not even a massless photon of light can escape its grasp, he suspected this catalyst—this spark that caused nature to defy itself—was equally primitive and, he feared, equally strong.

"We are dealing with a volatile situation that until this place and time in history never existed before," he said. "Resolving it will regrettably include much grief to you and your community."

"Is there a risk of this spreading? From person to person I mean," Foss asked.

"I honestly don't know."

"What about an evacuation?"

"I can't say what the risks would be. Perhaps after we visit the gravel pit we'll have a better idea."

The old doctor picked up his cane and rose painfully from the davenport. "Gentlemen, shall we get going?" Without waiting he proceeded toward the door, and the others followed.

"We'll need a couple of volunteers to go over the

area, and something to dig with," he said. "I'm not able to get around well myself. There is some danger of exposure, but you should be safe with the protective suits I brought. We'll want to be careful, though. God only knows what we'll find out there."

iii.

The four were silent during the short drive to the dump. Stephen and Dr. Thompson sat in the back of the ten-year-old patrol car. Gravel ground ominously under the tires as the sheriff pulled through the wide rusted opening in the chain link fence and turned onto the dirt lane that led directly up to the pit. Stephen could feel the tension building in the car, though no one spoke a word. He didn't understand all the implications of what Thompson had said, but he shared the old man's sense of foreboding about their task.

He listened to the sound of the engine strain as the sedan rolled up the rutted trail. It was a dry, hot summer. Dust crept in through the windows and air-conditioning vents. Stephen drew his sleeve across the dampness tracing a path through the stubble on his cheeks.

Foss brought the car to a stop and put on the emergency brake. They were parked at a steep upward angle in the dirt road on the side of a hill.

"This is it," the sheriff said, opening his door.

The smell from the pit wafted over to them. It rose from the ground and clung to the hot, lifeless air. The nauseating fetor of decay encircled them in an almost visible effluvium. It was the same malodorous scent they had encountered many times now and in itself proved that there was or had been something here connected to these deaths.

Foss reached into his pocket for a handkerchief.

"Christ, this is going to be bad."

They all lumbered out of the car, including the old man, who leaned carefully on his cane. He rested his aging frame against the side of the cruiser, but showed no signs of retreating. He didn't look well, but Corliss looked worse, Stephen thought as he saw the two doctors standing side by side.

Corliss's face was drained of all color, and his skin had an anemic gray cast. Stephen was surprised to realize just how much the young doctor had changed, how sallow and gaunt and almost withered looking he'd become in the last week.

Foss unlocked the trunk and swung open the lid. Back at Corliss's office they had loaded it with the professor's gear and the things they would need for the dig. The sheriff yanked out four white airtight suits of space-age material, similar to those developed for NASA, complete with helmets and filter masks.

Stephen and Corliss had agreed to go into the pit and gather the necessary samples. After they finished, the space-age apparel would be disposed of properly in case of contamination. Stephen wondered at the cost and about who was going to foot the bill.

He felt ridiculous donning the bulky suit, but was more than glad to have it. He'd seen enough of what this TCBA, or whatever it was, could do. No one knew how much of this stuff it took to kill, and he didn't want to find out personally.

Stephen could no longer smell the putrid stench once he was sealed up inside the protective garment, but it was hot as hell. Thompson handed him and Corliss each a shovel, a long, pipelike tool, and a slotted tray of empty beakers to fill with dirt.

"If I had known we'd be searching for the contamination in a garbage pit, I would have brought slightly different equipment," he explained, "but we can make do with what we have. You'll need to work your way around opposite sides of the pit, digging down at even intervals—say two feet apart."

Stephen glanced over the crater-sized trash heap. It would take a couple of days to cover the entire area, wallowing in all that . . .

"Use this pipe like an auger," the professor continued. "Push it into the dirt and twist, then tap the clod into a beaker. Number each beaker with these." He pulled a pair of black markers from his pocket. "Here," he said, handing them each a bundle of small orange surveyor's flags. "Write the same number you put on the beaker on a flag, then use it to mark the spot so we'll know where you got it from. Do you understand?"

They both nodded.

"Good. Bring the trays back when they're full, and we can test them while you're gathering the next batch."

"Are you ready?" Corliss asked Stephen.

"Yeah." With the helmet on, Stephen could hear the sound of his blood rushing in his ears.

"Be careful," Foss warned, walking with them toward the perimeter of the wide pit that was once a gravel quarry. "There's all kinds of shit in there. Pieces of glass. Shards of metal. Watch where you step. If your suit gets torn, get the hell out of there."

Stephen didn't need to be told twice. At the first sign of trouble he'd scramble out over the edge.

He and Michael slid cautiously over the brim and immediately sank to their knees in garbage. It was a nauseating experience.

The hole was filled nearly to the top with the dregs of civilization. It wasn't well maintained, and most of the refuse was exposed to the open air. It resembled a bombing site, with broken lamps, cast-out refrigerators, appliances, building supplies, clothing, disposable diapers, rusted autos, and unidentifiable lumps of brown rot that squashed under his feet. The thought of encountering another of those clouds amongst this stuff filled him with dread, and he began asking himself why for God's sake he'd gotten involved in this.

Thompson's scientific explanation of the phenomena made it seem more rational, if not less threatening. Stephen told himself it was merely a chemical, deadly but nonetheless a gaseous vapor and not the demonic menace he had perceived it to be in the Morton's hallway. It was only the woman's grim struggle and the sickening corruption of her flesh that had made him think it was more. His words were useless, however, in his effort to slow the rapid beating of his heart or ease the anxiety building in his mind.

He followed Dr. Corliss's example and began to dig, marking each beaker and flag as he'd been told. He moved cautiously through the debris, stopping every two or three feet to retrieve another inch of soil. There were twelve beakers in the tray. It wasn't long before he had filled them all.

Stephen climbed out of the pit, being careful not to break any of the containers, and carried them back toward the patrol car. Thompson and Foss had set up a makeshift field lab on the ground, utilizing the professor's chemical cases for tables. A folding chair from Foss's trunk served as a place for the old man to sit.

When he got there, Corliss was just leaving with a fresh set of beakers. The two older men were busily emptying the glass jars and testing the contents. They looked up only briefly as Stephen approached. There was a row of brown bottles on one case, labeled toluene, acetone, benzoic acid, and methyl orange. These were among the battery of reagents they were using to test for the presence of benzanthracene and TCBA. Without a word, Foss handed Stephen a fresh tray of beakers and he headed back toward the pit.

It was a tedious process. Stephen soon fell into a

routine, giving less thought to his fears, but becoming increasingly repulsed by the never-ending piles of garbage. Among all the rot it was impossible to distinguish any dangerous change in the soil from site to site, and he wondered if their effort would not all be in vain.

The heat was miserable inside his suit, but he realized the outside temperature was gradually lowering as the day lengthened. The long evening shadows made it even more difficult to see objects on the ground. He glanced over his shoulder and saw Foss watching expectantly, shading his eyes against the setting sun. Stephen hurried on, determined to cover as much of the area as possible before dark. He dreaded coming back a second day.

He had tramped almost a quarter of the way around when he tripped and fell. He picked himself up. Thick, gooey remnants of garbage clung to his metallic suit. Stephen wiped himself off with disgust, then climbed forward. He was almost through with another tray. Corliss was working his way over a rusted car.

Stephen had lost count of the number of trips he had made to the makeshift lab. He tapped the pipe and filled the last of the beakers, then headed out.

As he drew near the lab, he saw that Foss and Thompson had stopped their work. Both their expressions were grave.

"What is it?" he asked.

"We found evidence of TCBA in the last batch."

"Corliss's batch?" Stephen asked, for he had seen nothing unusual, though he had no idea what it would look like.

"No, yours. Marker 151."

Stephen tried to recall the exact spot. It was close to the rim.

"We'll need more," Thompson said. "I want to send a sample to my lab in Indianapolis for further analysis.

155

Take these jars and fill them."

Stephen nodded. A cold premonition swept over him and he shivered. The tray hung at his side like a lead weight.

If this stuff gave off a deadly vapor, why hadn't he seen it as he filled the beaker?

He approached the contaminated site feeling more than a little trepidation. He could see the orange flag, 151 clearly written on it. There was nothing . . . nothing out of the ordinary.

He knelt beside the marker and began to loosen the soil. Would the suit truly protect him?

The earth was damp, wetter than it had been in some other places. He saw a thick, clear fluid oozing out as he shoveled the dirt into the bucket. This might be it, he thought. TCBA. It looked harmless enough. Almost like liquid glue.

Stephen handled the tray as though it were made of delicate china. He held it away from his body, watching for any sign of a vapor or mist within the jars. Nothing.

He mounted the piles of garbage and headed as fast as he dared toward the cruiser. He stumbled and caught his balance, climbing over an abandoned dining room table that stood in his path.

The daylight was fading. It was difficult to see. He looked toward the lab. Corliss was there, Foss was shouting something he couldn't hear. They were waving their arms, beckoning him to rush. All the chemicals had been repacked. The old man was sitting inside the car.

Stephen balanced the tray on the edge of the pit and clambered out.

Corliss ran to meet him. "Hurry," he said, taking the sealed jars from Stephen. "I'll put these in the trunk. Get your suit off."

"What's wrong?" Stephen asked.

156

"Another death."

"God, no." He began pulling off the bulky garment and stuffing it into the disposal bag.

He and Corliss rushed toward the car through the deepening twilight. Foss was behind the wheel, talking into the transmitter. When he saw them, he motioned out the window. They could see the misery in his eyes.

Stephen and Corliss swung open the doors and slid inside.

The sheriff flung the transmission into reverse and pulled out in a burst of gravel and dust.

"Who is it?" Stephen gasped, short of breath.

"Henry Gorkenoff."

iv.

Foss brought the cruiser to an abrupt halt beside the curb outside Gorkenoff's Market. He jumped out, followed by Corliss. The old man moved slower, supporting his weight against the cane.

Stephen stood stunned. From the walk, he could hear Mrs. Gorkenoff wailing. Her cry was a mixture of terror and overwhelming grief. Stephen felt a deep sense of loss. An enormous weight of sorrow wedged itself in his chest. He dreaded going inside. He didn't want to see Henry's defiled body.

After a few moments, he was able to force himself to wrench open the door of the market. The brass bells at the top clanged harshly against the glass.

The deli was empty. Mrs. Gorkenoff's cries continued to resound from the living quarters.

Stephen stepped past the whirling fan at the rear of the store and into the darkened house section. Mrs. Gorkenoff leaned over the toilet in the bathroom, sobbing. Another woman crouched beside her, holding her hand. Around the corner, in the hall outside one of the

157

bedrooms, he saw Foss and Corliss. Stephen moved up behind them, then stopped short, confronted by the gruesome destruction of his best friend.

His guts clenched and turned cold. He swallowed the bitter taste in his mouth, filled with instant rage. Henry had fought his grisly fate. The room looked as though a hurricane had blown through. The dresser was overturned, and the mirror smashed. The models of classic cars that Henry collected so meticulously lay fractured into bits of wasted plastic. The carpet and bed were soaked with the putrid sediment that spewed from Henry's ravaged corpse. Darkening yellow pus congealed in a puddle around his body. The air hung heavily with the obnoxious stench.

"Sweet Mother Mary," Foss gasped.

"I don't understand it," Corliss echoed. "This is unbelievable."

In the center, twisted on the floor, lay Henry, or rather the shrunken, quivering, tangled mass that he had become. His body was knotted and withered, and although he was quite dead, his arms and legs continued to draw up ever so slowly as his skin shriveled and tightened against his skeleton. He was rent with ulcerous tears that continued to burst and spill forth the corrosive fluid in slimy, gelatinous lumps. It slid through the torn lattice openings with a soft, sloshy sound.

His stiff fingers were tangled in the thick plush of the rug. His eyes bulged forward as the lids pulled gradually back and away from them. The terrified desperation captured by his facial expression had begun to distort and recede as his features disintegrated.

Thompson came up behind them as they stood in grim shock outside the door. "May I get closer?" he asked quietly.

For a moment Foss and Corliss acted as if they hadn't heard; then they parted to let him pass.

"Remember not to touch anything, Professor," Corliss reminded him gently.

"Don't worry. I won't forget."

They stared in horror at the mottled gore that had been their friend as the old man hobbled about the edges of the room. "It almost looks as though—," Thompson said, then stopped. "I need photographs taken, so I can go over them later."

Stephen didn't think he would need a photograph. Every detail of the sight would be burned forever in his memory. Dear God—Henry.

Foss and Corliss turned away. Stephen heard them questioning Mrs. Gorkenoff. Had she seen anything peculiar, a mist or thickening of the air perhaps? No, nothing. Henry was tending the shop alone. She and her husband had both gone out on separate errands. When she came back—this was what she had found.

It was hard to believe this was caused by a mere chemical vapor, Stephen thought. It looked more like a slaughter.

He gazed around the interior of the room. How had the poisonous gas gotten to Henry? There were no windows in the room. Had it seeped into the store under the crack of the door or through a window in the deli? Had he seen it coming? From the looks of this room, he had. But what good would an overturned dresser have done against such an illusive substance?

Then he remembered Foss's theory that someone was purposely letting this lethal vapor go. Henry's actions were those a person would make to keep out an intruder. But that did not fit with their conjecture that the fumes were being emitted from the ground; and the dump had tested positive for the TCBA. So what *was* it then that Henry had fought against?

Last night, he would have sworn that the toxic cloud had come directly at him. It had not seemed like an accident. Perhaps it was attracted to heat, like a missile. Perhaps something in their bodies drew it. . . . The whole idea was insane, and yet . . . He recalled Thompson's words: "Until this time and place, it never existed . . . it would have taken a unique catalyst . . . a spark, a powerful force of nature." But the professor had never truly elaborated on what that spark was, and now Stephen wondered. Was such a thing possible? Or were they looking down one more dead end?

He stared at the overturned dresser. Henry had not done all this in his struggle with death. No, it was obvious—to Stephen at least—that he had tried to block someone or something's path to prevent its entry. What the hell was going on?

Stephen was not a religious man. He didn't believe in an afterlife, or spirits, or heaven, or anything he didn't have absolute evidence of. He could only relate to that which could be touched or proven through physical means. In his mind, the existence of intangible elements governing the universe was doubtful at best, yet he could not squelch the awareness that lurked at the outer perimeter of his consciousness, whispering of supernatural evil. It bordered on lunacy. Still, he could not deny Henry's mutilated corpse.

He was vaguely aware that the phone had been ringing. His disturbing reflections were interrupted by Bob Foss. "For you," the sheriff said, inclining his head toward the front of the store.

Stephen nodded and pivoted around.

He saw Corliss and the neighbor woman helping Mrs. Gorkenoff from the bathroom. They each had a hold of one arm and were leading her toward the living room. There was vomit on her dress. Her doughy face was red and puffy beneath the red splotches from crying.

Stephen headed down the hall into the deli. The receiver lay off the hook on the counter. He picked it up.

"Hello?"

"Steve, are you all right?" It was Laura, her voice filled with concern. "I was worried about you. Mother said—"

"Henry's dead," he blurted out.

He heard her gasp, then mutter, "Oh, no. Not Henry." There was silence, and he waited for her to recover. Finally, she asked, "Was it the same?"

"Yes."

"I'm sorry. I don't know what to say. Are his parents there?"

"His mother is." Stephen's throat was so tight he could barely speak.

"Poor woman. Is there anything I can do?"

"No. She's got someone here to help her."

"I was with Mrs. Simmons's family most of the day. It was awful. They were devastated by her loss. It seems like everyone is dying. I want to get out of this town. I can't help it. I just want to leave."

"I know." He was feeling much the same.

"After seeing that cloud . . . what it did to Louise, I don't think I can live here any more. I don't even care where I go. I talked to Mother and told her we ought to leave, but she won't. She's so stubborn. She says this is her home. How can anyone call a place like this their home! Please. You've got to help me convince her." She paused, getting a hold of herself. "Has anybody said what's causing it?"

"No. Not for certain, anyway." Stephen considered telling her the theories Professor Thompson had presented, but there was no proof that they were right and he had his doubts.

"Are you sure you're okay? Mother said you'd been in a fight, that your face was covered with blood."

"I'm fine. Just a few bruises."

"I wish you were here," she said.

"Me, too."

161

"Will you be back soon?"

"I don't know. I'll try."

"I'll wait for you."

"Okay."

He stared at the receiver for several seconds after he'd hung up. It felt strange to have a woman in his life again. They were so different, years and worlds apart. Right now, it worked, while there was so much pain and fear pushing them together—while their need was great—but what about later? Could there ever be anything permanent between them?

The county undertaker had arrived and was taking pictures of the body. Stephen watched from a distance. Thompson's handling of the scene was quick and efficient. There was no mistaking the fact that he knew his business well. He gave orders, and the others followed. The attendants wore thick, insulated gloves to load Henry's corpse onto a gurney.

Thompson asked several times whether anyone had directly contacted the slimy yellow pus excreted from the victim's bodies.

"No, sir," the undertaker repeated. "It was purely by chance, though. When I went out to pick up that boy at the dump—he was a godawful mess—"

"Worse than this?" the old man asked.

"Darn near as bad, except he was dried out. Didn't find him till better than twenty-four hours after he died. Folks looked everywhere."

"But you didn't touch him?"

"Well, he was so far gone. I wore my heavy digging gloves, and Russell and I shoveled him into the box. Couldn't have fixed him up if we'd have wanted to. Turned out lucky for us. Then Dr. Corliss called to warn us about the acid on the bodies before we went to pick up that girl and her baby."

"I see," Thompson said. "Thank you for your help."

"No problem."

Stephen wondered what Thompson thought might've happened if someone had touched the bodies.

"I think I've got everything," Thompson said at last, closing a case of carefully labeled samples from the site.

"You can take the body now," Foss announced to the undertaker's men.

Stephen watched as they carried Henry out on the gurney, draped with a white sheet. Already the darkening puss was soaking through.

Sunday, June 18

. . . the hideous thing invaded . . .

Chapter Eleven

i.

The sky was a high, even blue, the trees blowing gently in the breeze—a nearly perfect day, except that Stephen's mind was dark with thoughts of death and revenge. It was useless, he told himself. Revenge. Revenge against what? Henry was dead, but still . . .

He shut off the engine and glanced up at the porch. It was two o'clock. He had spent all morning at Foss's office manning the phones. A hundred calls from distraught citizens, all frantic, wanting to know how to protect themselves. What was there that he could tell them?

Better not to think about it.

He got out and started up the steps to the boardinghouse. Laura was seated with a group of her mother's cronies. Their voices lowered as he approached, and he realized they were discussing Henry's fate.

Laura caught his eye and smiled weakly, apologetically. He nodded, understanding, and ambled on inside. He didn't really want to talk to anyone right now.

The smell of Mrs. Norton's fresh-baked muffins filled the house, but it was not enough to rouse any pangs of hunger in his clenched stomach. Stephen went straight up to his room. He was still reeling from Henry's death last night, so sudden, so pointless, so violent.

167

Anger flooded his mind with renewed fervor as he visualized the lurid killing in paralyzing detail and hideous, shattering color. Work was the only remedy he knew, the only way to forget, to regain control over the part of him that desperately wanted equal reprisal for what had been done to his friend. There wasn't anyone he could blame.

He drew out several new canvases, already stapled to stretcher frames, and started immediately to paint. He furiously penciled in dark charcoal sketches and lined them with long streaks of vivid color, creating images from his tormented brain, not needing a model or photograph to fill in the background.

The air was suffocating. He flung open the window, knowing it gave him no protection against the insidious lethal vapor anyway, and stripped off his shirt as his concentration intensified. Rage poured out through his pores. The legs of his jeans were soon damp with perspiration, but he worked with maniacal speed, channeling all of his energy into art, trading off brushes and brandishing each with fevered skill.

Disregarding his usual attention to light, he painted well through the gray twilight until night fell and he found himself straining to see in the shadowy darkness.

Finally, he flipped on the light switch. The yellowish glare of the naked bulb revealed a repelling, gory caricature of humanity. Stephen stared at the canvas. The savage memories of these last ten days were displayed before him now in graphic, surrealistic carnage. Even the faces were grotesque parodies: blue tongues, bulging eyes, dangling veins, and twisted flesh.

Stephen stepped away from the easel and wiped his face with a towel, hating himself for his own inner well of violence.

He knew that every member of this community must be going through similiar emotional turmoil. Some had lost much more than a good friend, and he guessed

168

that before it was over hardly a person in Town would have gone untouched by the specter of death now stalking the area.

He clenched his palette angrily, then threw it, splattering greasy oil paint on the wall.

Almost as if in retaliation, a knock sounded on the door.

"Who is it?" he asked.

"Sheriff Foss."

He slowly reined in his emotions and opened the door—only as much as he had to—not wanting the lawman to see the effects of his fury.

But the aging lawman looked as if he were experiencing comparable feelings. "I stopped by the office," he said heavily, "but you'd already left. I wanted to thank you for your help with the phones."

"No problem."

Foss sighed. "It's been a long day. I haven't been able to let go of what happened yesterday at the Gorkenoff's. I called Mike's office. He's still in the lab with the professor. You want to go get a cup of coffee or something?"

Stephen nodded. He understood perfectly, and he wasn't going to get any more done here. Maybe if he got out and walked, let his head clear, the rage would go away, but he didn't hold out much hope. He seemed to be slipping in deeper everyday, into a hell he would never be able to extricate himself from.

"Just let me put on a shirt," he said.

"I'll meet you outside on the porch."

Stephen told Laura good-bye, then climbed into the patrol car. He and Foss rode in silence to a diner on the edge of Town. It was a square, one-level building, a mom-and-pop business of the type erected in the early fifties, which clashed vulgarly with the eighteenth-century surroundings of Town.

There should have been a crowd left over from the

169

supper hour, but the restaurant was nearly deserted. Only one other table was occupied.

"I eat here every night, and it's never like this," Foss said. "Nobody's going out if they don't have to. Other cities, everyone might've just taken off, but they're not like that around here. It'll take more than this to move most of these old-timers from their homes. People here have faith in the system, faith in their neighbors. They'll go do down fighting, but they won't run out. It's not our way. You know what I mean?"

"I think so."

They seated themselves at a table in the back. The waitress brought menus, but neither man was hungry. "Just two cups of coffee, honey," the sheriff said, then pulled out a cigarette. "Heck of a day," he sighed.

Stephen agreed. "Where do we go from here? It looks like we were wrong about the germ warfare idea."

"Yeah. It sounded so damn likely this morning. And Mike went along with it. I really thought we were onto something. Everything fit together, but now . . . All that stuff about new-formed chemicals — TCBA. That shit blows my mind."

"He was right, though. We did locate a site of contamination at the dump."

"Yeah, but I didn't see any haze or fog, nothing like what you had described." Foss let out a stream of blue-gray smoke. "I'm not sure he's right. I'm just not convinced. I had the feeling the professor was holding something back. But why? And what? It doesn't make sense, does it?"

Stephen shrugged.

"We'll have to wait till he's run his tests, then see what he says. Mike's got all the confidence in the world in this guy." Foss shut his eyes and sighed, then opened them again. "Never figured to find myself in this position. In twelve years I've never had to do more than pull over a half dozen speeders a summer, give a couple

170

of safety lectures at the school, and lock up a few drunks. This is totally out of my league."

"I don't think any law enforcement agency in the country would be prepared for a situation like this."

"That's so, I suppose, but I can't help feeling that no matter how much I do it isn't enough. People keep right on dying. I sure as hell hope when all this is over I can still live with myself."

They passed several minutes in silence, listening to the hushed conversation from the other table, each lost in his own thoughts. Stephen could tell from the lawman's pained expression he was taking each loss personally.

The waitress came and refilled their cups.

Foss shifted and gazed out the window, puffing pensively on his third cigarette. "I suppose you heard all the rumors about the dead girl's pregnancy," he said, obviously having shifted to another subject. "We were planning to keep it under wraps, but these things have a way of getting out."

Stephen nodded. "The mayor's wife dropped by the boardinghouse. Laura said she wanted to know about Angela Stoddard, who the girl dated, that kind of information. Apparently, she thinks her son was involved."

"That's the crappiest part of the whole mess. People are blaming the boy when it was actually the father."

"Malcolm?" Stephen recalled the mayor's cool, self-satisfied demeanor at the meeting. The man hadn't seemed like the type; he'd seemed far too conscious of his every move. But the guy was good looking and smooth. He spoke with absolute confidence, a real showman. Stephen could see a young girl easily falling for that type of imagery. Malcolm had what it took to get ahead.

"Yeah. The worst of it is Cal Stoddard's got wind of it, and he's out for blood. I can't blame him. If it was

171

my daughter, I might be ready to hit somebody too, but it wasn't Tommy."

"What are you going to do?"

"Try to talk to him. See if I can calm him down. Tell him the truth if necessary. Only when he learns it was Malcolm's doing he's likely to get even madder. It's one thing to think of two kids getting carried away in the back seat of a car. Another entirely to think of your little girl being taken advantage of and used by a middle-aged snake like Malcolm. Cal's likely to kill him."

"I see what you mean."

"I also hate like hell for word to get back to Mrs. Malcolm. She's already suffered enough. I've known that fellow for twenty years, and Hube Malcolm is no bowl full of cherries to work alongside. I can imagine what kind of hell he'd be to live with. He's the most egotistical, self-serving man I've ever met. Every year I've watched Flora's self-esteem sink lower. There can't be much left at this point. I'd never treat a woman like that."

"Have you ever been married?"

"Never really had the opportunity." The barrel-chested man shifted uncomfortably and resumed staring out the window.

Stephen thought of Kat, the good days and the bad. A lot of marriages ended in an all-out declaration of war. He could only wonder at what would've happened between the two of them if they'd had longer together.

"I still have difficulty reconciling the fact Bill Leland took a punch at you," Foss said, changing the subject again.

"Several punches."

"Yeah. Guess the heat and tensions 'round here are taking a toll on people's tempers. All that fear and anger's got to come out somehow. Things could get even rougher, I'm afraid."

The waitress came up and handed Foss a note. "Fella

172

jus' called an' left this message for ya," she said. "He says it's an emergency."

Foss glanced down at the paper. "I've got to go. You want me to give you a lift home?"

"No. It's okay. I can walk."

"All right. I'll see you tomorrow." The sheriff picked up the bill and paid on his way out.

ii.

Stephen finished his coffee, then left. He took the long way back to the boardinghouse. He wasn't quite ready to face his empty room. His talk with the sheriff had done nothing to alleviate his melancholy mood. Rather, he found himself sinking further into depression.

He passed by the saloon—it was Sunday, so the doors were locked—and stopped for a moment to stare at the darkened, unlit exterior. Ominous lakes of blackness separated the small pools of fluorescent light from the street lamps. The last time he'd been to the tavern was with Henry. It was going to take time to recover.

There were few in his eventful past he would have called friends, but Henry was one. Their acquaintance had struck quickly and firmly. Though their lives had little in common, they'd found they could talk, share dreams, and relate to each other without the rivalry that usually evolved from college friendships.

He stared at the shadowed lot across the street, his mind wandering from Henry back to his conversation with Foss. The sheriff wasn't alone in his feelings of helplessness before the monstrous, overwhelming power of this thing. He realized that last night very little had stood between him and the most grisly death he could've imagined.

Which one of us is next? he wondered. He could get

in his car and leave, simply drive away from it all. But as the sheriff had said, it wasn't that easy. Already he had begun to care about these people. Their fight was becoming his.

All his life he'd been a man without roots. Leaving school, going off to the army, returning to Chicago, then fleeing again. A lifetime of running. But to what? From what? It hadn't even really stopped during the brief time he'd been married. Both he and Kat had continually looked for something more. Now, for the first time in his life, he was ready to stop, though he couldn't say why.

Stephen was so engrossed in his memories that he failed to notice the sudden wind rising until a piece of newspaper blew over his shoes, breaking his concentration. He jammed his hands in his pockets and sauntered on. If the tavern were open, he would've gone inside and drunk until his brains were pickled and he could no longer feel.

As he headed down Plum Street, he thought of Laura. He liked her, liked her a lot. She was a nice girl, one of the few truly nice girls he'd ever met. No one would have called Kat a nice girl, not in the traditional sense. She had been fun loving and playful, but troubled. She had never known her father, and her mother had been an abusive alcoholic. Kat had become a model at twelve. He'd seen pictures, and even then she'd had a sultry, erotic beauty like you rarely saw in real life. She generally went for older men. They were father images for her.

He was one of the few lovers she'd taken who was her own age. He thought it must've been because of how serious he was in those days. It had been a challenge for her to see whether or not she could get him between the sheets. It was not that he didn't want to, but he had been desperately afraid of letting down his guard, even for a night. But Kat had kept after him

174

until he couldn't stand it, until she was all he thought of every hour of the day.

Making love to her had been a turning point in his life, and he had never questioned whether or not she still slept with other men, though he suspected she did. It didn't matter. For Kat, sex was a way of reassuring herself of her own self-worth, and he understood that. Painting was the same thing for him. But he hadn't been prepared for her death. He could never have been prepared for that.

The detective in charge of the investigation had been certain that Kat's last client that day had also been her murderer, but no one cared enough to pursue it. She wasn't important enough. No one cared any more, but him. . . .

Stephen was jolted back to the present by a muffled cry from somewhere ahead in the darkness. At first he thought the pained noise was that of an injured animal, but as he drew closer he realized it was human.

An icy chill wormed its way down his spine. He crossed the street and hurried toward the sound.

It came from a narrow brick alley between two of the closed storefronts. He stopped and peered warily into the thick black shadows. The street lamp on the other side illuminated only the barest features of the gloomy passage. He was unable to make out any definite shapes.

Then he saw a figure crawling on the ground. The dim light revealed a glimpse of red hair. His mouth went dry. "Marie?" he whispered.

The woman drew back, sobbing.

"What happened?" he asked. He was too far away, and he still couldn't see her distinctly. "Are you hurt?"

She shook her head, cowering against the wall. "I'm all right."

But he didn't believe her. He moved closer. "Let me help," he said gently. He doubted she remembered him

175

from before.

"Just leave me alone," she sobbed, struggled to her feet. Then she fell, crying out in pain.

Stephen rushed forward. He could see the blood now, all over her arms and legs. Her face was scratched and blackened with grime from the alley. He could tell she'd been beaten. She was wearing a denim skirt and a braless tank top, no less suggestive than the ruffled black-and-red dress she'd worn at the tavern. Her shirt was dirty and torn. One strap dangled loosely from her shoulder. She shook uncontrollably and inched slightly backward as he approached.

"I won't hurt you, Marie," he repeated. "I only want to help. Do you want me to call an ambulance?"

"No." Tears rolled freely through the dirt on her cheeks. "I-I w-want to go home." The words tore at her throat. She tried to pick herself up again and winced.

"I can't walk," she cried.

"It's all right. I'll carry you."

She drew a deep breath and looked away. "I told him to leave me alone. I tried to get up the fire escape, but he pulled me back down." She choked on her sobs.

"I'll help you. Where do you live?"

She pointed through the alley. "I live in that little gray house on the corner."

"Come on," he said. She clung to his neck as he pulled her into his arms.

iii.

Marie sat on the sofa in the shadowy darkness of the living room, cradling a glass of bourbon in her hands. She had bolted down the first two drinks he'd given her. The only illumination came from a hidden fluorescent strip above the kitchen sink. She'd asked him not to turn on the light.

176

Stephen leaned against the counter and poured himself a shot of Jim Beam. Even from a distance, he could see her trembling. A clot of blackened blood had dried on her scalp, and the cascades of disheveled red hair fell tangled onto her bruised shoulders.

He studied the line of her jaw and her high cheekbones. She'd once been a beautiful woman, but life was treating her rough. Too much booze and possibly drugs. Her face was becoming thick and sagging. The puffy, dark circles under her eyes and the tiny broken vessels about her nose were permanent now. In another five years, she'd be an old woman. But with makeup, in hazy lighting, she'd still be pretty for awhile to come.

He felt sorry for her. "Are you sure you don't want to go to the hospital?"

She laughed sourly. "Thanks, but I lick my own wounds. Don't worry. I can take care of myself. I have for a long time."

"Assault is a crime."

She shook her head. "It wouldn't do any good, sweetheart. You can't fight it. You just got to live with it and go on." But in spite of her tough words, tears rolled from the corners of her eyes. Her head lolled back against the sofa, and she turned her face away.

Stephen reached into the cupboard and pulled down a metal mixing bowl and filled it with warm tap water. He'd doctored a good many cuts and bruises. He found a basket of laundry on top the washing machine. "You mind if I tear up this sheet to make a bandage?"

She shook her head and held out her glass. "Can you get me another drink?"

"Sure."

He brought over the bottle of bourbon, the bowl, a bar of soap, and the strips of sheeting.

She splashed bourbon into her glass as he lifted her ankle up on his knee; then she looked across at him with a puzzled expression. "Who the hell are you?" she

177

asked.

"We met at the saloon the night before last," he said, examining her leg.

"Oh. Did we do anything else?"

He smiled. "No."

"I was just wondering."

The ankle didn't look broken, but sufficiently swollen to give her difficulty getting around for a few days. "I'll wrap this as tight as I can to make it easier to walk, but you ought to get an elastic bandage tomorrow and stay off it as much as you can."

She stared at him without recognition. "You weren't the one who drove me home, were you?"

"No."

"Too bad."

He had finished with her ankle, and she grabbed a crumpled package of cigarettes from the table beside her. She managed to find one last smoke inside. Her hands trembled as she flicked open the lighter. Stephen took it and lit the cigarette for her.

More tears spilled down her face. She tried vainly to wipe them away, but the flood was too great. Her breasts heaved as she cried.

"Oh damn it," she gasped. "I got what I deserved — that's what you're thinking."

"Not actually."

"Well, I did. I've made a mess of everything I've done. It's my own fault. I'm a whore, and this is what happens to whores. Nobody asks any more, they just take what they want."

Marie drained her glass and poured another. "I made a mistake of getting involved with Bill." Her voice cracked. "I knew what kind of guy he was. I've known him and his prissy ex-wife since grade school."

She took a large gulp of bourbon. "Bill started dropping by the saloon a couple of months ago, coming every night, bringing me presents, driving me home,

178

stuff like that. He wouldn't come into the house, though, because he said it wasn't right. He knew about the others, and he told me I'd have to settle down, that he'd have to be the only one if we were going to continue. I knew what he was about."

She smiled sadly. "Nobody's thought about me and marriage in the same breath for a long time. It's been eight years since I divorced my third husband.

"It was kind of nice, having somebody treat me like that again. You know what I mean? I didn't really like him much—he's kinda cold, not much fun. But I thought: why not? There aren't going to be many more chances. And I thought maybe I wanted a regular life before I got so old men wouldn't want to look at me any more. What would I do then? Marriage never worked before, but I was younger in those days. Now I figured I was desperate enough to make it work.

"And I've tried. But I never can seem to cut down on the booze and the coke. No matter what I do. And to be truthful, maybe I really don't want to. But Bill, he doesn't understand. He thinks I'm doing it just to hurt him."

She ground out her cigarette in the ashtray. "Tonight, he shoved a pistol in my mouth and told me he was going to blow my brains out. I thought he would. Then he dropped the gun and screwed me instead. I don't know what to do. I can't go back with him. It ain't gonna work."

She stopped and finished her drink. The bourbon was gone, so were her tears. "God, I don't know why I told you all that."

"It's okay."

"No, it ain't. You ain't the one getting beat up in alleys and having a gun shoved in your mouth. Christ, he's going to kill me. I know he is. You didn't see the way he was. He's gone crazy. Something inside him has snapped."

"Why don't you leave Town?"

She laughed. "And where would I go that would be any better?"

Stephen leaned forward in the darkness. "I have a place in Chicago where I lived with my wife. It's just sitting empty. You could go there if you want."

Her hands twisted nervously. "I ain't never lived no place but Town. Christ, I'm scared to go, and I'm scared to stay. I want a cigarette. I need another cigarette."

She pushed herself off the sofa and hobbled toward a cabinet against the wall. She pulled open a drawer and began rifling through it.

"There's got to be another pack here someplace. Oh, damn it." She pulled out the drawer and flung it on the floor, then dropped to her knees, sorting through papers and rubber bands that had fallen out. "Oh, damn it."

She rocked up and down on her knees, screaming and wailing, the same injured sound he'd heard in the alley.

Stephen grasped her shoulder. "Marie?"

She threw her arms around him and sobbed into his neck. Stephen put one arm under her knees and carried her back to the sofa.

"I'll go out and buy you a carton of cigarettes. Okay?"

"No. Don't leave. Please. He'll come back, and he'll kill me this time."

"All right. I'll stay. Why don't you lie down? You'll feel better."

They stretched out together, side by side on the sofa, arms wrapped around each other. Her head nestled under his chin. He wondered if Leland would return. He had a switchblade in his pocket, but it would be of little use against the .357 the deputy sheriff packed.

He closed his eyes and tried to sleep. He had the

feeling it was going to be a long night. Her fingers dug into his sides and drew him closer.

"I'm here," he whispered. "Don't worry. I won't leave."

He thought of Laura waiting for him at the boardinghouse. He hoped she'd gone to bed. He felt bad. As much as he wanted to change for her and take on a different life, it just wouldn't work. It wouldn't work. . . .

Chapter Twelve

Bill Leland rubbed his eyes and focused on the dark, winding stretch of country road in front of him. Woods and soybean fields passed in a blur outside the windows.

Goddamn that bitch! He tipped up the bottle of beer in his right hand and swallowed. Well, fuck her. Just go ahead and Jesus fuck her. The stupid whore.

The car veered into the left-hand lane, and he gradually brought it back over. There wasn't any traffic this time of night, so it made little difference.

He pounded his fists on the steering wheel. For years he'd endured Elaine's cheating and ridicule in silence, while she degraded him in every way possible. Then on the night she finally left, all he'd done was cry like a baby and beg her to stay. Now, Marie wouldn't get off her rotten drugs, and he was sure she was sleeping around. That was the nature of the animal after all. But no more, goddamn it! The fire raging inside of him had built and built, until it was a black fury he could no longer control.

He wasn't sorry about what he had done tonight. In fact, he wished he'd done more. He wished he had blown her fucking brains out, because that was the only way he'd ever be free of her seductive influence. It was worse than alcohol, worse even than the primal need that had brought him to her.

The pistol lay on the seat beside him. His hands twitched.

Then the radio crackled.

He knew Foss was trying to reach him and had been trying all day. They didn't work regular shifts. Each of the tiny burgs in the county had a part-time deputy sheriff, and Foss was the head man over the whole operation. It was Leland's misfortune that Foss happened to live on the edge of Town and was thereby able to keep in closer contact with him than with the other men.

Well, he'd make up some kind of cock-and-bull story. He was out on patrol, out around the farmlands, keeping a watch for any suspicious clouds. He laughed and belched at the same time, then rubbed his crotch. Tonight was only the beginning. He'd show that bitch.

Another swallow of beer.

The cool liquid felt good rolling down the back of his heated throat. Marie was the first woman he'd been with since Elaine. He'd tried not to. He'd tried to stay away from women, most of all Marie because he knew what she was, but she kept drawing him back. The way she swung her hips when she walked. The way her fat, ripe breasts pushed out above the top of her dress. But she offered herself to any and every dickhead willing to buy her enough booze and coke to get her thoroughly stoned. She didn't care nothing about him or how he was suffering.

Bill wiped his eyes with the back of his hand. Stupid cunt. Rotten piece of shit. He'd given her a chance. He'd put it all on the line for her, everything he had. He'd offered to make her his wife and elevate her to a decent status in life, but she wasn't good enough. She wouldn't quit the lousy drugs.

The car swerved onto the edge of the road and bumped along the gravel berm till he drew it back onto the blacktop. He'd go back and drag her out of her house. He'd take her to the farm and chain her up like the goddamn animal she was. He'd keep her under lock and key till she learned different. Wouldn't nobody be able to get at her out there. Wouldn't nobody even know where she was.

He tipped up the bottle.

Yeah. That's what he shoulda done before. All the rest, taking her flowers, talking sweet to her—all that was a waste. You had to talk a language women understood. Cocks and fucking. She understood that. She clawed like a wildcat when he gave her the business.

He remembered the look in her eyes when she'd seen him standing outside the alley. It was the only pleasure he'd had in weeks, seeing that look of sheer panic. He'd grabbed her by the hair and dragged her into the darkness. She'd screamed, and he'd belted her. Then he'd belted her again to teach the slut her place. He was taming the shrew.

She had almost made it up that fire escape, but when the owners heard her coming, they'd snapped off the lights and pretended they weren't home. It was lovely the way one neighbor would help out another.

He'd latched onto her ankle and pulled her down the stairs, smiling when her head hit one of the steps. Nobody, 'cept one busybody across the street, even acknowledged the noise she made. He'd shouted out a simple "police business," and that was the end of that.

By the time he had her on the ground she was pretty well spent, but he punched her a few more times to make sure she didn't give him no more trouble. If he'd done the same to Elaine, she might not have walked out. Women enjoyed a bit of pain; they wanted to be punished when they knew they were bad, just the same as little kids.

Marie had whimpered like a kitten when he'd stuck the .357 in her mouth. Then he'd shoved up her skirt, and she'd begged him to take her instead. She'd yielded to his flesh like warm butter sliced by a knife. She'd wrapped her legs around him and moved her ass as though it was going to be her last fuck, giving in to what came natural, gruntin' and groanin' and slappin' her thighs against his like she couldn't get enough.

She certainly knew how to do it right. She wasn't afraid of nasty smells or getting messy. She was patient and did whatever was necessary to turn a man on. While she'd never have the class of a woman of Elaine's quality, she was a bigger comfort in other respects. If only it weren't for the damned drugs . . .

He stared ahead at the road as he started to take another swallow of beer, then saw a flashing red-and-blue light. He hit the brakes hard. Tires squealed, and his car nearly spun into the grass before finally lurching to a stop.

He turned up the radio to catch the transmissions.

"One fatality. No ID." It was Foss's voice.

They would have heard him stopping.

He glared up through the windshield again. Nobody coming yet.

He rolled down the window on the passenger side and pitched the bottle into the woods, then wiped his mouth. He would tell Foss he was taking the night off. Personal troubles. It was the truth, wasn't it? He belched again and straightened his shirt. Stinkin' whore. Then he drove slowly and cautiously toward the scene.

Foss's patrol car was parked the wrong way on the right-hand side of the road. There was no accident as he had expected to find, only a battered, dark green pickup pulled off on the berm across from the sheriff's car. No driver in either vehicle, and no fatality.

He pulled up behind Foss and cut the engine. It was goddamn queer, and he didn't like it. He saddled the .357 into the holster on his hip and swung his legs out of the car. The crackle from both police band radios continued. Chrissy's bored, monotone voice gave instructions to the poor, son of a bitching deputy sheriff in neighboring Mirror County, something about another victim having been found.

The gravel crunched under Leland's boots as he walked around the other two vehicles. No sign of trouble. Nothing out of the ordinary. He put his hand on the hood of the truck. The motor was still hot. They couldn't have been parked here long.

Then he noticed a faint light in the woods to the right. That had to be them. But what were they doing out there? He squinted through the dark, but couldn't make out anything from this distance.

His first notion was to just take off, but suppose Foss was in trouble? All hell would break loose if anyone found out he'd gone by and hadn't bothered to help.

He'd have to check it out. For twelve years he'd had this job and been damn good at it. People respected him. He'd been written up in the paper four times for courageous action above and beyond the call of duty. He wasn't going to let any bowlegged whore screw things up for him.

He entered the woods cautiously, heading in the direction of the light. As he drew closer he heard Foss's hand unit crackle, and low voices. There was a bad smell, too, rotten and fetid, like an old piece of meat. Foss and another man were standing around something on the ground.

Bill sucked in his breath and prepared to confront the sheriff. A dozen excuses for neglect of duty raced through his mind.

Foss turned when he heard him coming and shone the light in his face. Bill shaded his eyes. "It's me," he said.

Foss lowered the beam. He didn't look angry. If anything, his expression was one of pure fear.

Bill stopped and stared at the ground, then nearly let

186

out a yell. The air caught in his throat, and for one brief, agonizing moment he thought he would vomit. The beer churned madly in his belly.

The grossly twisted body of a teenage boy lay sprawled in the weeds. Even in the dim moonlight filtering through the canopy of trees, the corruption was evident. The boy's wet, gray flesh glistened with a hideous silvery sheen, a deteriorating tangle of ruined arms and legs. Sticky pus left dark brown splotches on the cracked ground. New fissures continued to cleave his body and spill forth more of the putrid substance.

"Got an ambulance on the way," Foss said, his voice betraying signs of distress. "We're not sure who he is. Mr. Peters," he gestured to the man in bib overalls on his left, "was out looking for a stray colt. He thinks this might be a neighbor boy from the Weisser place, a couple miles to the east."

Peters, a husky, red-faced farmer in his late sixties, nodded grimly. "Them boys been using my shed down in the orchard to smoke and drink where their folks won't catch them. I find all kinds of cigarette butts and empty cans. I reckon he's one of them, all right."

The sheriff shook his head. "Let's get back to the road. We can't do any more here, and I'm sick of this sight. I'll call around, try the Weisser residence first, see if I can get some identification on him."

Bill kept silent, waiting for Foss to ask him about his attack on Stephen Myers or why he hadn't called in all day. His stomach was still rolling over from the sight of that kid. There was a dull pounding behind his temples. He thought of Marie, and his anger rose all over again. She was poison.

When they reached the road, Foss told Peters he could go. The farmer got in his truck and drove away, then Foss turned to Bill. Bill opened his mouth to protest his innocence, but before he could utter a word Foss's big hand clapped down on his shoulder.

"How are you doing, Bill?" he asked. There was genuine concern in his voice. "I know you've had a rough time since Elaine left."

Bill nodded.

"We should go out more," Foss continued, "and have a bit of fun, neither of us tied down. I'm sorry I ain't been around much. This job eats away your time."

"Yeah. I know what you mean." Bill smiled cautiously. It was incredible. Foss was apologizing to him!

They stood under the trees by the edge of the road, waiting for the ambulance. It would take awhile because it had to come from the county seat. Foss took out a package of cigarettes and offered him a smoke. Bill accepted.

"You know if you got any problem you can come to me," Foss said. "I haven't always been there, but I'll try to be in the future. We've got to look out for each other. Now more than ever. This thing," he waved his hand at the night air, cigarette glowing, "this poisonous gas or whatever it is that's causing all this death, it forces a man to stop and think about what really matters. What's truly important when you weigh everything out."

"I been thinking on that, too," Bill said. "About what happened yesterday . . . I don't know. I saw that new fellow and Henry with my girl the other night—"

"Marie?" Foss interrupted.

"Yeah."

"You're still seeing her then. I'd hoped for your sake that it'd blown over by now. You know what kind of woman she is, Bill, the problems she's got. You can't expect to change her."

"She ain't the same. I swear it." He could feel his voice rising, but he couldn't help it. His left eye began twitching. "She don't have any interest in them others. But they won't leave her alone. It's them damned drugs she's hooked on, that's the real trouble."

"She's hooked because she wants to be."

"That ain't true. She wants to change. She told me so. She only needs somebody to show her how."

Foss put his hand on Bill's shoulder again. "Simmer down. I believe you. Anything's possible, but you got to give these things time. It won't come easy. You got to give people time."

"She wants to change," Bill repeated stubbornly.

"I hope she does. I've tried to help her myself, but well . . . Maybe it's different this time, like you say. I'd love to see her make a fresh start."

"She will. You can take my word for it."

"I'm glad to hear it. I hope things work out for you two. But in the meantime, no more fistfights, huh?"

Bill nodded sheepishly.

"There's no problem. Myers isn't going to press charges, but I don't want to see you get into trouble. You're a damn fine lawman, Bill. One of the best this county's got. We need you."

"Thanks. I ain't never lost my temper like that before."

"That's why I'm not making out a report on it, but next time . . ."

"I understand."

"Good. We don't need any more trouble. This county's about three breaths away from a panic as it is. People are scared, damn scared, and they're depending on us to see them through this."

"Has anything new been turned up about these deaths? I heard a professor from Indianapolis arrived yesterday."

The sheriff sagged. "Professor Thompson. But he hasn't got anything definite for us yet. Henry Gorkenoff died last night. Mike and Thompson collected samples and are working on it. Maybe tomorrow. Mike has faith in this guy. But we can't keep sitting around waiting for more victims to be found."

189

Bill agreed.

They heard the faint wail of the approaching ambulance and stepped out into the road to meet it.

Chapter Thirteen

It was close to midnight when Dr. Michael Corliss awoke. He lay curled on his side in bed, shaking and sweating profusely. The glowing red numerals of the alarm clock above him glared unwaveringly.

Off and on throughout the evening he'd suffered from stomach cramps, but now the pains were suddenly quite severe. He had difficulty breathing. His whole chest constricted. Bile rose like poison in his throat. Fever raged through his veins.

He managed to roll from the bed and stagger weakly into the bathroom. His trembling limbs seemed barely able to support his weight. He crouched beside the toilet in the dark, waiting for the inevitable gorge to wrench itself from the pit of his stomach. If this was flu, it was the worst he'd ever had.

His body convulsed in incredible pain. The spasms gripped his guts, and he leaned forward across the stool. But instead of the half-digested mixture of last night's supper that he'd expected to see, a hot, black, oily slime gushed from his mouth in a thick stream that bubbled and hissed as it hit the water.

The doctor's eyes widened in alarm, but there was nothing he could do. He was held captive as his body heaved and heaved, regurgitating an ever-increasing flow of the noxious black fluid.

Chapter Fourteen

Long velvet shadows sliced across the gloomy darkness between the rooms. Stephen checked his watch again: 3:00 a.m.

He hadn't been able to sleep for hours. He had an unnerving sensation of deep foreboding, a feeling that somehow with the passing of the last few hours all of their lives had secretly and drastically changed. He could almost sense the evil growing outside in the streets, walking the sidewalks, peering in windows.

It was not unusual for him to have trouble sleeping. In fact, it had become the norm since Kat's death. But his nightmares tonight were of a different nature. Instead of reliving the grisly night of Kat's murder and his summons to a Chicago morgue to identify her body, when he closed his eyes it was Laura he saw — with that strange iridescent cloud hovering over her — struggling uselessly and pathetically to push it away as the hideous thing invaded her body. He was forced to watch inert as she screamed and pleaded to him for help.

After his last failed attempt at sleep and the repeat of the same nightmare, he'd given up. He had worked his way out from around Marie's prone form and off the sofa without disturbing her, then taken a seat in a chair across from her to wait for dawn.

With each passing hour his tension mounted. He wished Corliss and Thompson had been able to come up with more on this deadly vapor mysteriously afflicting the county. It felt as though time was slipping away from them all, himself included. The sheriff had said there would be no more word from either of the doctors until morning, which was at least two hours away yet. But he knew that, out there somewhere, while the rest of the Town slept, the toxic gas still drifted over the countryside, picking new victims with uncanny deliberation.

Stephen stepped to the window. It was a dark night. Only a sliver of moon was visible. There had been no traffic past the house since he'd gotten up.

Marie was still sleeping. Occasionally, she cried out in her slumber. Her dreams were apparently not pleasant ones, either, but he didn't wake her. She needed whatever rest she could get.

He hoped she would be all right in the morning. If not, then he would have to find someone to stay with her, and that might not be easy, considering how most of Town felt about the woman. It seemed either they really liked you here or they hated you, and if they hated you they showed no mercy about it.

In a community this size there were few havens a person could retreat to, and Marie had found them all: booze, drugs, and sex. The three refuges of a troubled life.

He glanced at his watch again: 3:10.

The minutes crawled by.

Stretching, he yawned and arched his back. From out of the blackness he saw a pair of headlights emerge. He moved back from the edge of the window. The car crept slowly into view, over to the right, then pulled up in front of Marie's house. He could see from the yellowish haze of the street lamps it was a tan-and-brown patrol car. The driver's door popped open, and a large, brawny man slid out.

Stephen stepped in front of the glass, hoping if the

193

deputy realized the lady had company he might change his plans.

The figure turned toward the house, spotted Steve, then quickly got back in his car. The engine revved, the vehicle pulling away with a loud squeal of tires.

Stephen moved back from the window again, releasing a silent sigh of relief. He was in no mood for a fight. He stared down at the small, red-haired woman on the sofa. For the time being at least, he had forestalled another confrontation, but in the long run he didn't know how much he would be able to do. To the biggest degree it would be up to Marie to help herself. Without that, she would surely be lost.

Monday, June 19

. . . a horrifyingly lethal form . . .

Chapter Fifteen

i.

Stephen had fallen asleep in a chair. He awoke when he heard Marie cry out, and immediately bolted onto his feet, thinking there must be some imminent danger. The morning glare streaming through the window pierced his eyes.

He saw Marie sitting on the sofa with her knees drawn up, and his sleep-drenched brain fought through the haze of weariness.

"I'm sorry," she said.

"Are you all right?"

"Yeah. I-I just ha-had a bad dream." She pushed the damp hair out of her eyes and hugged the sheet he had draped over her.

He walked over and sat beside her. She reached out and squeezed his hand.

"You're sure you're all right?" he asked again.

She nodded. "Did you get any sleep?"

"Some," he lied, knowing he couldn't have been out more than a few minutes. It was now 5:58.

"I'm sorry I've caused you so much trouble."

"Don't worry about it."

She swung her legs down and grabbed for the crumpled package of cigarettes, having forgotten it was empty. "Oh, damn."

197

"I'll go out and get you a carton."

"No, don't bother. You've done enough already."

Deep purple circles rimmed the undersides of her eyes. She gazed nervously about the room and twisted the sheet in her hands. "Christ, this place is a mess. I feel like I must have a hundred knocks on the back of my head. Our local deputy sure knows how to show a girl a good time." The joke came out flat and she laughed tensely. There was an unmistakable look of fear on her face, though she was trying desperately to conceal it.

She rose and headed into the bedroom. When she returned, she had pulled on a pair of jeans and an old ragged T-shirt that read: Cheerleader. Her thick hair was twisted back in a fifties-style ponytail. A huge bruise swelled on the right side of her jaw, and there were scratches and bits of dried blood on her cheeks and neck.

She went directly to the cupboard and pulled out another bottle of bourbon. "You want some?"

"No, thanks."

"After last night I think I need it." She poured the bourbon into a ceramic mug and drank it straight down, then poured another. "Let me fix you some breakfast before you go. It's the least I can do."

Stephen agreed, not because he was hungry, but because he was afraid to leave her alone.

ii.

He ended up leaving Marie's earlier than he would've expected. Rather than wanting him to stay, as he had anticipated, she seemed anxious to be rid of him.

Throughout breakfast she had talked rapidly, forcing a smile and trying to pretend all was well, though it obviously wasn't. Several times she'd glanced around

198

nervously, and he figured the moment he left she was either going to get high or drunk, or possibly both. But it was her life. She was scared and seeking refuge where she felt the safest, or at least where she wouldn't know what was happening.

Once he'd eaten, she had quickly ushered him to the door, seeing him off like one of her boyfriends, with a brief kiss on the lips and an invitation to "Come around again real soon, sugar." The aftereffect of those words lingered in his mind like a bad taste.

He saw Foss sitting on the porch in the swing, as he walked up the steps to the boardinghouse. "Morning," the lawman said glumly, grinding out his cigarette.

"You waiting for me?" Stephen asked.

"I was hoping you'd get back before I had to leave."

"What's up?"

"Found another body in the woods north of here, a teenage boy, and three more in Mirror County."

"Where's that?"

"Just a little south of here."

"Yeah, I remember."

"The Mirror County coroner called my office early this morning," the lawman said. "She had read about the deaths on the wire and wanted to know what new information we've got. Thompson and Mike are organizing another meeting to fill everybody in on what they've turned up so far."

"That sounds promising."

"The situation couldn't get much worse. It's too bad they couldn't've come up with the answers before these others had to die. I hope like hell never to lay eyes on one of those pus-filled bodies again."

"Have they made much progress?"

The sheriff shrugged. "I don't know, but I sure hope so. These killings are really escalating. Two counties now."

Stephen was silent.

The lawman continued. "Since you were helpful enough to dig around in that garbage pit yesterday, I thought you might like to be included in the meeting today."

"Are you sure I won't be in the way?"

"Actually, Thompson requested that I bring you along. You and Laura are still the only two who've seen this toxic cloud."

"Okay. I'll get ready. How much time do I have?"

Foss jammed another smoke into the corner of his mouth and struck a match against the bottom of the swing. "About ten minutes. Oh by the way," he said between puffs, "I had a talk with Leland last night. You won't have any more trouble from him. He's just having a rough time."

Stephen almost told him about Marie, then decided against it. He had the feeling the lady wouldn't get much sympathy from Foss. She was never going to make it in this town.

iii.

Mayor Malcolm and Ezra Hunt were already waiting when Foss and Stephen arrived.

They met on the third floor of the city building in the same room as the day before, but this time they were smaller in number. The long, narrow chamber held an air of secrecy, for the realization that something truly horrifying was happening to their town had dawned on them. Malcolm and Foss had apparently made their peace. There was less of a sense of argumentation and more of an air of desperation. They were losing control of Town, relinquishing it to an evil they couldn't even name.

The group was soon joined by Professor Thompson, who hobbled through the door with his cane, looking as though he had spent all night in his clothes and gotten little, if any, sleep. The old man was followed by Dr. Corliss and another companion—a tall, slender woman in her late forties, with gentle eyes and traces of gray in her neatly pinned black hair.

Corliss motioned tiredly to the small gathering. "This is Dr. Mildred Cook," he said. "A specialist in the field of biochemistry. She's come from her clinic in Mirror County to assist us in this crisis. One of the young women found yesterday was her daughter."

Foss thrust out his hand. "I'm sorry about your loss," he said. "But we're certainly glad to have your help."

Malcolm echoed the sheriff's sentiments, but Stephen said nothing. He was utterly shocked by the drastic overnight change in Corliss's appearance. He had lost so much weight now that the flesh literally clung to his skeletal frame. The doctor was almost unrecognizable. His skin was nearly translucent, and there was a cadaverous look to him. But the bandage was gone from his left hand, and not a mark remained to indicate that he'd ever been injured.

Foss bore a look of extreme concern, and Stephen realized he must've noticed the change, too, but there was little either of them could say. They had both expressed their concern earlier.

Corliss began introducing the others to Dr. Cook. The woman stepped forward and shook each of their hands. She had a warm, pleasant grasp. Her gaze met Stephen's, and she nodded politely.

Malcolm smiled at the woman, his gleaming white teeth showing off his deep, bronzed tan to perfection. "Shall we be seated?" he asked and gestured toward the table. Everyone took a chair, with Malcolm at the head and Thompson at the other end.

Foss shifted uneasily. "Excuse me if I get right to the point, but there were four more killings last night, and I'm not anxious for more." His impatience was obvious, and Stephen knew he had not given up the idea that some kind of undercover experiment was being conducted on his town.

The sheriff waved his hand toward Thompson. "On Saturday, Professor, you found evidence of this TCBA at the dump, but I'm still not sure what it proves. I didn't see the slightest hint of any poisonous vapor. It's not that I don't believe you and don't realize this TCBA is bad stuff, but how do we know we're on the right track?"

The old man nodded. "I apologize if I haven't explained myself clearly. I came here with several theories that I couldn't be sure of, but after hearing about Mr. Myers's sighting of this cloud and with the data we gathered, I now feel certain we're working in the right direction."

"I appreciate that," Foss said. "But I'm still not convinced."

"I'm afraid the aspects of this situation are quite complex."

"I understand that," Foss drawled. "Tell me about this trigger you think is responsible for all of this."

"I'll try to explain," Thompson began. "The origins of life go back to a primitive earth, surrounded by an atmosphere of ammonia, methane, hydrogen, and water. Energy, in the form of radiation from the sun and lightning discharges, broke these simple molecules into reactive fragments. These in turn combined with each other as well as with the elements found on the earth's surface to form larger molecules, eventually yielding enormously complicated compounds, some of which make up living organisms.

"Not all of these compounds are beneficial to life, however. Some, like dioxins, are powerful carcinogens. Mercifully, many of the combinations that might have proved the most deadly could not take place due to the molecular structures of the components involved. This is true of TCBA. Its formation should not have been possible.

"But there were other forces at work on the earth as well. I'm not referring to forces like the gravitational one which is a fundamental aspect around which life on this planet has evolved, but those more like the magnetic field deep within the earth's core. Ones that don't immediately appear to have much impact. Nonetheless, these basic forces exist and should not be underestimated. Given the right circumstances, they can have a formidable impact upon nature. Such is the case with the primitive evil I spoke of yesterday, It is this previously latent malign force which provided for the formation of TCBA by drastically altering the electromagnetic structures of its components."

Ezra Hunt leaned back in his chair. "I can't say I put much stock in them revolution'ry theories. How do ya know for sure it's this . . . this TCBA that's killin' our people?"

"We came to that conclusion for two reasons. Because we found traces of the chemical in the corpses. And because we have been able to determine the process by which the bodies are self-destructing. You see normally the enzymes of the body are unable to digest living cells. This is because they cannot pass through the membrane wall of the cell as long as the latter lives. When the cell dies, its membrane becomes permeable and the enzyme can then enter it and destroy the proteins within. TCBA has the unique property of being able to break down these walls prior to the cell's demise, allowing the enzymes of the victim's own body to freely eat through the stomach and began literally digesting the rest of the body as well."

Corliss nodded in agreement. "That fits with what I uncovered as well. TCBA obviously enters the bodies topically, either as a liquid or a gas."

Mildred Cook folded her hands. "I agree completely.

203

Professor Thompson is correct."

Malcolm seemed content to let the meeting run its own course, and Foss remained silent, so Thompson continued.

"Let's start with the contents of the vapor," he said. "Of course, we haven't been able to actually take samples of it, but we can guess at its makeup through the results of our tests. The main component has to be TCBA."

"It's more than the main component," Mildred interrupted. "There's no reason to assume this lethal cloud is composed of anything other than TCBA. Dr. Corliss filled me in on the test results. It's a simple gas. It's being heated and vaporized just under the surface soil, resulting in bursts of toxic steam as the inner ground pressure becomes too high. We're wasting valuable time. We need to begin testing for a chemical to defuse the TCBA at once. For a substance to be able to penetrate the cells in this manner, it has to extremely complex. One little change in its molecular structure, any minute addition, would render it harmless. It should be a straightforward task."

"May I remind you," the professor countered, "of the primitive force I spoke of. I believe there is more to this than meets the eye. We need to gather more data and proceed cautiously. I want to collect another sample of the digestive fluids from the corpses. We should test its effects, as well as those of the liquid TCBA we took from the dump, on rats and perhaps a larger mammal, such as a cow or a horse."

"As you like, Professor Thompson. But I have something at stake here too, and I plan to begin work on a formula to deactivate the chemical immediately. Speed is of the essence. The time you spend doing your 'test' could cost people their lives. You're asking these gentlemen to delay on the basis of a rather extraordinary theory, which isn't even widely acknowledged."

204

"All confirmed laws of nature began with a theory," the old man stated.

Malcolm cleared his throat. "Is there any reason why we can't go forward in both directions? It seems to me that would be the wisest course, rather than focusing all our efforts in one hope and having that hope prove futile."

The mayor looked decidedly uneasy, but Foss and Hunt agreed. Then Corliss nodded. "We need to try everything we can," he said.

Foss lit up another cigarette, and Mildred Cook looked annoyed as the gray smoke drifted in her direction.

"There are still several things that don't tie together for me," the sheriff said. "We found a shoe print in the ground next to Angela Stoddard's body and a clump of bloody human hair clutched in Louise Simmons's hand."

"There could be a hundred explanations," the female doctor admitted, "but to sit around and wait while we come up with one would be foolish. We must stop this thing before dozens more die. We don't know how fast this deadly vapor is being released, nor how far it can travel before dispersing."

A grim silence filled the room as each occupant mulled over the theories presented. Stephen glanced at Corliss. The pale physician sat motionless, his face gaunt and tired.

Foss stepped over to the water cooler and pulled down a cone-shaped cup. "I can buy what you're saying about the unusual properties of this gas, but how can you be so damn sure there isn't someone behind this? Someone letting it go from a canister or spraying it on the victims. Someone who wants us to think it came from the dump."

"What would the motive be?" Corliss asked.

"I don't know, Mike. I just don't want us to close

our minds to the other possibilities here. If you'll pardon me for saying so, it seems like the professor is a little too anxious to attribute this all to his own theory and thereby justify his own work."

"Now hold on, Bob. I've known the professor a long time. He isn't the kind of man that would do that. He's very careful and—"

Foss held up his hand in a gesture of reconciliation. "I'm sorry, Mike. It's my job to be suspicious. I've got to have doubts and ask questions."

"We're wasting time," Mildred Cook repeated. "I'm anxious to get to work. Is there a place where I can set up my equipment?"

iv.

The midmorning sun was already heating up the rolling countryside when they left the city building and headed for the morgue in Mirror County. The one placed served a two-county district. There wasn't enough business in either of the sparsely populated areas to support a second. Thompson planned to gather specimens from the victims' bones and strange gray skin as well as from the caustic pus.

The professor rode in the front seat of Foss's cruiser, beside the sheriff, while Stephen and Dr. Corliss sat in the back. Clouds of chalky dust enveloped the car as they sped over the gravel road. A steamy layer of blue haze floated over the sluggish, mud-colored water as they passed near the river. The trees were motionless. There was no hint of a breeze.

The rural scenery brought back to Stephen childhood memories of the time he'd spent here. As they bounced over the chuckholes and dips in the contour of the road, Stephen couldn't help marveling at the bizarre twists his life had taken. When he left sixteen years ago, he had never figured on returning.

The hills and fields outside the window had given way to the appearance of another small town, Almaretto according to the sign they had passed upon entering. The streets were paved and newer looking than those of Town, but the little village was just as remote. There appeared to be only four major intersections and more highway on the other side.

Foss pulled up to the curb on a shaded, tree-lined street in front of a single-story, whitewashed building labeled simply in rigid black letters: J.C. Mortuary. The lawn was overgrown and weedy, with two broken-off posts sticking out of the ground where there had once been a sign advertising the establishment.

"Perry Ellis and his wife run the place," Foss explained as they climbed out of the car. "They're both in their seventies and have to hire most of the work done. But old Perry likes to boast about how he's buried six decades of folks in this county. His father owned the business before him. They had a nice location twenty years ago, over on Central Avenue, but it burned down in a fire. Struck by lightning. The Ellises didn't have much money when they rebuilt onto this spot, and as you can see they're having a hard time keeping it up."

He gestured toward the seedy wooden structure. "It ain't much, but all told Perry's family has been in the funeral business since 1885, and that makes them sort of local celebrities. Ezra ran an article about it in the paper a few weeks ago, before this trouble started. People don't forget the things you do for them in a time of real grief. Everybody 'round here thinks well of him and his wife, but their kids have no interest in continuing the mortuary. Ain't but two dozen folks a year die in either county. I imagine it's only a matter of time till the old place closes its doors for good."

The sheriff led the party of four along a crumbling concrete walk that had turned mostly to broken bits of stone with large tufts of grass growing up through it, past a rutted gravel drive and an aging hearse, behind the funeral parlor to a small, boxlike house.

The front door stood wide open, but the screen had been left in place to keep the bugs out. The dim crackle of a radio slightly off station emanated from the dark interior.

Foss knocked loudly on the weathered framing of the screen and hollered through the mesh. "Perry, you home? It's Bob Foss."

The sound of the radio continued uninterrupted.

The sheriff knocked again, then wedged open the screen and poked his head inside. "Perry? Gladys?" He stepped cautiously over the threshold, and the others followed. The professor waited by the front door.

There were only four rooms—a living room, with a kitchenette and a bathroom to one side, and a bedroom. Stephen noted the heavy musky odor of stale carpets and drapes, and something else—that pungent, acrid smell that had become a hallmark of death. He instantly tensed, realizing they might be about to come across another grisly corpse.

Foss said nothing as he glanced about the room, but his face reflected the same concern.

Most of the furniture looked as if it had come from the Salvation Army. A worn-out sofa with patches sewn over the arms. An old tube-type television. A bent-up pole lamp. A metal table and chairs. Laundry was piled in a disheveled heap beside the table and a few stray pieces trailed into the bedroom. A steady stream of water flowed unheeded from the faucet into a rusted enamel sink.

Foss picked up an ashtray that lay upside down at his feet. Its sooty contents were spilled out across the grungy beige carpet. "I don't like it," he said. "I've never seen the place this bad before. Gladys can't get around as well as she used to since her knee operation, but she keeps it cleaner than this. Something's happened."

Stephen leaned over to shut off the water, wondering why it had been left running, and immediately recoiled from the overpowering stench in the basin. Then he saw a black mound of slimy ooze caught in the bottom of the drain. "Jesus, what's that?"

Corliss peered into the sink. "Don't touch it," he warned.

"What is it?"

Corliss hesitated. He seemed to grow paler. "I don't know," the young doctor stammered.

Foss stared at them both, quizzically. "Door's open, radio's on, water running, but there's no sign of them."

He called out the old couple's names once more and moved to the bedroom door, as though he couldn't understand why they didn't answer. The sheriff emerged again a few moments later holding a shattered glass jar of assorted change.

"Perry's coin collection," he explained. "I don't know how it got broken. There's nickels and dimes scattered all over the bed and floor. Something's definitely wrong. They must've been in some kind of trouble. Let's try the mortuary."

Foss led the way to the rear door of the funeral parlor. It was locked tight. He sent Stephen around to the car to get a set of lock-picking tools, and the two of them managed to slip back the dead bolt.

"You're pretty good," the sheriff said wryly. "If I was a betting man, I'd say you've had plenty of practice."

Stephen shrugged. "It was a long time ago."

"It couldn't have been too long ago. You aren't hardly thirty years old now."

The lawman pushed his way into the shadowy building and fumbled along the wall till he located a switch. Long parallel fluorescent tubes above them flickered slowly to life and shed a chilly, unnatural light over the surroundings.

It was clear that by going in through the back they had entered the morgue first, where the recently deceased were stored until their final viewing. It was a cold, antiseptic room covered entirely by green tile. The floor and walls were a medium green, and the ceiling was a lighter shade. The walls were lined with rectangular metal doors that resembled coin-operated lockers at a shopping mall. There was a single stainless-steel work table in the center, equipped with gutters and stirrups that could be lowered or raised as the need occasioned.

Foss took a brief look about the sterile room, then said, "I'll check the rest of the building. They've got to be around someplace. Though it doesn't seem too likely they would lock themselves in, does it?"

Thompson plodded along one of the walls with metal doors, reading the tags. The dull thump of his cane echoed softly each time it struck the floor. "Most of them are empty," he said, then stopped. "Here. This was one of the victims, wasn't it?"

Corliss confirmed his observation.

Thompson turned to Stephen. "Can you open it for me?"

Stephen swallowed his natural revulsion at the prospect of disturbing the dead and jerked the handle on the locker the old man had indicated. The door wasn't locked. The slab rolled out easily on silent casters.

Thompson drew back several inches. Corliss physically shrank and turned away, his face clay white, looking as if his eyes would explode from their sockets. But Stephen was unable to tear his gaze from the grisly sight. It was not at all what he would have expected. The skin was gone. There was no body. All that remained were whitish bones and a skull, still ghoulishly reminiscent of a human shape, poking hideously up through a pool of oily black slime that dripped onto the tile floor.

"That's the same shit we saw in the drain!" Stephen exclaimed with horror.

Professor Thompson peered into the metal tray. The stench was nauseating. "Michael, bring me the sample case. Open the other lockers."

Stephen pulled open each of the seven doors that was labeled as occupied. The results were astonishingly similar. The room was thick with the sickening sweet odor of rampant decay.

Corliss had propped himself against the outer wall for support, sweating and shaking profusely. His teeth chattered as though he suffered from an internal chill, and his skin was raised in goose bumps.

"What is it?" Stephen asked him. "What's wrong?"

"I'll be all right," he managed to answer. "I just need some air." He darted out the open door at the rear of the mortuary and into the yard like a man pursued. Stephen saw him stumble and fall to his knees. The young doctor threw back his head as he breathed in great shuddering gulps of the country air.

Foss returned from the back corridor that led into the main facilities. His expression was grim.

Thompson glanced up expectantly from his work over what was left of one of the cadavers.

"No sign of them," the sheriff said. "I've searched every room of this bloody place, outside too, and they've just plain vanished."

"Could they have gone out somewhere?" the professor asked.

"Maybe," Foss conceded. "But the car's in the garage. I'm going to see if I can raise Haskel on the radio. He's the deputy sheriff in this quadrant. I told him we were coming."

The professor nodded and went back to his task.

Foss looked past Stephen at Corliss, who was still on his knees in the weed-choked lawn, and then at the contents of the metal slabs. "Good God, what the hell is going on around here?"

Thompson replied dismally, "It may get a lot worse before it's over."

Foss grunted and headed out the door, down the walk. Just what he needed: more good news. What the devil had happened to the Ellises? Where were they? He didn't know what to think any more.

The long red needle on an ancient farm thermometer posted to one of the trees plainly displayed the temperature: ninety-eight degrees in the shade.

Just as he reached the driveway, a beat-up, canary yellow 69 Mustang convertible pulled in. A greasy, long-haired, acne-studded punk sat behind the wheel. Foss recognized his mug. He had arrested him once for driving under the influence. He also knew him as one of the Perry's hired helpers.

The kid pushed his lanky, sweat-soaked hair out of his eyes and tried to hide something under the edge of the seat as Foss drew closer, probably a beer, maybe a bag of pot. But Foss didn't care. Not today. He had other things on his mind. The least of his worries was one dirty, slightly buzzed teenager.

"You see Perry or his wife this morning?" the lawman inquired in his deep official tone.

The kid shrugged, unimpressed. "Naw. I ain't seen 'em since Friday night. They both been sick all week. When I showed up for work Saturday morning, nobody was home. That's why I'm here. The old man ain't paid me yet. I tried calling. Didn't get no answer."

"You won't get paid today, either."

"Aw shit, man. Is he dead or something?"

"No. Missing." He doubted the kid had anything to do with the disappearance. He wouldn't have come back if he did.

"Aw, fuck. I need that money tonight."

Foss stepped back from the side of the car. "Get out of here. I'll have Haskel give you a call when he turns something up."

"Man, that could be never."

"Go on. Move out before I decide to run you in for whatever's under the edge of that seat."

"All right. All right."

Foss watched, shading his eyes from the sun, as the kid pulled away and along the main drag. He took out a handkerchief and wiped the moisture from his face, then drew out a cigarette, his first in over an hour. "They're killers," he remembered old Dr. Bower saying, referring to his package of Pall Malls, but it didn't seem to matter now.

The situation appeared only to get worse. He had nine dead in his own county, three in Mirror County and two missing, a cloud filled with God knows what, a bunch of black slime, two professors with conflicting theories of chemical mutation, and damn little conclusive evidence. Thompson was right. It wasn't going to get any better in the foreseeable future.

v.

Stephen and Bob Foss dragged themselves out of the patrol car and trudged up the steps to Abigail's front porch. It was obvious from the downtrodden way they carried themselves that, though it was only two o'clock in the afternoon, they had already logged a long and difficult day.

Abigail and Laura rose from the swing to greet them. There were looks of alarm on both their faces. It was plainly bad news the two men were bringing.

"Have you eaten?" Abigail asked, her voice strong and authoritative. Food was her immediate remedy for anything that ailed mind or body.

Foss shook his head.

"I'll fix some sandwiches then. It'll only take a min-

213

ute." Without giving them the opportunity to protest, she disappeared into the house. If they had more tales of death and horror she didn't want to hear them on an empty stomach. Even Abigail's lust for gossip was beginning to sour in the wake of so many devastating killings.

Stephen and Foss sagged into a pair of rockers on the porch, willing to let her wait on them for awhile. It was the first chance they'd had to relax all day.

Laura perched herself atop the railing across from them. She wore cut-off denim shorts and a red tank top, her long legs tanned and glistening in the sun.

She's beautiful, Stephen thought. But he was too exhausted and too numb from the gruesome, mind-shattering sights at the morgue to do more than simply record the fact in his brain.

"What happened?" she asked.

Stephen glanced at Foss, and the sheriff nodded. Then Stephen went ahead and told her about their trip to Mirror County, the many things they had and hadn't found. He left out the more hideous details about how the bodies had looked when they pulled open those metal slabs, but related enough to give her the gist. His voice nearly cracked a couple of times. Those skeletons were the most terrifying things he'd ever seen, even worse than the woman he'd seen die in the hallway.

"Then Dr. Corliss collapsed," he said. It seemed like days, not hours ago.

"Why?"

"We don't know. We took him straight into the county hospital, but they didn't know either. The admitting physician thought it might be anemia. Mike was still unconscious when we left. They were planning to run some tests on him, but it looks bad."

"Dr. Corliss," she repeated. "I can't believe it. What do you suppose happened?"

Stephen shrugged. "I'm not totally surprised, though.

214

He's looked really bad for the past several days."

Laura paled. "You don't think he has . . ."

"No. Dr. Thompson hasn't ruled it out, but Mike doesn't have any of the symptoms. No lesions. No sores, flaking, or discoloration."

"Then he'll be all right," she said resolutely. "He has to be. But who's going to take over for him?"

"I imagine Professor Thompson and Mildred Cook will. They're intent on seeing this crisis out. Actually, I don't think today discouraged them at all. Both seemed more determined than ever."

"I wish I could talk mother into leaving. All the neighbors have left. She's so damn stubborn." Laura lowered her voice as her mother approached.

The plump woman burst through the door, her blue flowered housedress stretched tightly around her middle. "This'll make you feel better," she said, offering a tray with ham-and-cheese sandwiches and four tall glasses of iced lemonade. Her loose, gelatinous bulk quivered as she moved awkwardly from one to the other.

Stephen wasn't hungry, not in the least. His stomach turned at the sight of food, but he forced himself to take a sandwich, knowing he wouldn't be able to get through the day without eating something. He tried the lemonade first. It went down easy, cooling the parched, bitter taste in his throat.

Abigail settled into the swing with a glass for herself and three extra sandwiches.

"After we left the hospital," Stephen said, continuing to relate the events of the day, "we dropped Professor Thompson back at the clinic with the samples of that black stuff we'd collected. He promised to call as soon as he has any definite results."

"What does he think it is?" Abigail asked.

Rather than go into the incredible details of their conference meeting, Stephen simply replied: "He's not sure." And Stephen felt it was the truth.

"We've notified the state police about the Ellises' disapperance," Foss added. "We asked for more manpower too, and they'll be arriving tonight, but this crisis has spread over two counties. The available men will have to be divided in half."

"What about the National Guard?" Abigail prompted.

"The governor's being kept up-to-date on the situation. It may come to that before morning."

"There've been broadcasts and speculation about it all day," Laura said. "They're asking drivers to avoid the area. It's really frightening. I'll bet half of Town has moved out." She glared at her mother.

Abigail continued with her lunch. "They'll be sorry, too, if vandals break in and destroy their property. I won't feel safe till the National Guard comes in to protect our homes and the governor promises us a full reimbursement for anything that's damaged."

"That isn't going to happen, Mother."

"Then I'm not leaving."

"For heaven's sake, there are things more important than this old house and your antiques."

"Not hardly," the old woman harrumphed.

"You ought to reconsider, Abigail," Foss said gently. "Laura's right. We can't control this poisonous vapor. No one's safe. I intend to get on the radio later and recommend a complete evacuation. I'll even go to the governor with it."

"What does his majesty, the mayor, have to say about that?" Abigail asked.

"It's out of his hands really."

"Well, I can't say that depresses me. Anybody whose son would—"

"Mother!"

"I've heard about Tommy and the Stoddard girl," Foss sighed, "and it isn't true."

"I don't believe it, either," Laura said.

Abigail snorted. "Neither of you fully understands human nature. It doesn't surprise me a bit. People, especially young people, are little better than animals."

Several minutes of silence passed as they let the subject drop, then Laura spoke again. "Poor Mrs. Gorkenoff called here this morning. She's been utterly destroyed by Henry's death."

"Well, it hasn't even been twenty-four hours," Foss said. "It'll take a lot more time than that. I doubt if she'll ever get over it entirely. I don't think anyone ever does. I'll stop by and see her as soon as I get the chance."

Laura nodded. "I went by after she called. Took her one of mother's fruit salads. When I got there, she told me Mr. Gorkenoff had suffered a heart attack after he found out about Henry."

Foss let out a sharp gasp of surprise. He hadn't heard. Neither had Stephen.

"She hadn't wanted to tell me over the phone," she went on. "He's at the hospital, of course, but Mary says they think he'll be fine. They ran tests immediately, and they say there's no blockage. Apparently, it was caused by stress and age. I helped her wire her son, Andrew, in Texas. He's catching the next flight in."

Foss laid aside his plate. "We're losing," he said hotly. "No matter how hard we try to fight this thing, we can't gain any ground. I wonder if Thompson will be able to prove it was started by that toxic waste they disposed of in our ground. We ought to get a hold of that company that did the dumping and sue the pants off 'em."

The others watched as the big man rose from his chair and walked steadily across the porch. He stood with his back to them and wiped his eyes with the palm of his hand. "Problem is," he said, "by the time it got through the courts all of Town would be dead."

The phone rang in the house. It rang several more

times before anybody moved. Finally Abigail heaved herself from the swing and waddled inside. She returned a few seconds later.

"It's for you, Bob. Evelyn, down at the city building. She sounds upset."

Foss nodded and lumbered inside.

Abigail settled into the swing again.

"I wish there was something more I could do," Laura whispered. "So much of the burden for this is falling on his shoulders."

Stephen sucked in his breath. "Yeah. I've been with him the whole day, and it's just one disaster after another. It doesn't let up."

"What did he mean about toxic waste?" Abigail asked.

"It's a long story. The bottom line is that the expert Dr. Corliss brought in thinks these toxic clouds are being given off from the dump like swamp gas."

"So that's what it comes down to," Abigail retorted. "Swamp gas, indeed. They make it sound like an act of nature. It's somebody's fault, but they'll never have to own up to it. You wait and see. That's the way the world works." She picked up her third sandwich.

They waited in silence until the sheriff came out again. He stood for a moment, watching them intently, as though putting his thoughts in order. "Mrs. Gorkenoff called the office," he said. "She heard noises from the fourth floor and thinks it may be an intruder. She's alone, and she's scared. I've got to go by."

"She might be right," Stephen said. "About a week ago, Henry discovered that someone had gone up and destroyed the paintings I had stored up there. We found a couple of empty cigarette packages and an old denim jacket. It looked to me as if someone might have been living up there."

"Henry told me about it. He gave me the receipt you guys found on the floor, but I haven't been able to

218

trace it yet." Foss paused. "How the hell do you suppose he got up and down without being noticed?"

"I don't know."

"Well, I'm on my way over. I'll check it out. But that's not the worst. You remember what I said about the Stoddard case. Evelyn said she saw Cal walking around Town this morning when he should've been at work. He caused a disturbance in front of the city building and was making threats against the Malcolm boy. He can be a real hothead. Normally, I wouldn't take it too seriously—that's the way Cal is—but these aren't normal times. He's just lost both his kids."

"What do you want me to do?" Because of the emergency and how shorthanded they were, Stephen had volunteered to help in whatever ways he could.

"I had Evelyn radio Leland and send him out to the Stoddard place to see if he can intercept Cal. I've got to go to the Gorkenoff's, but I'm worried about the boy. He works at the hardware store on Petit. Could you stop in? Find out if Cal's been there and if he's made any more threats. Then warn the boy. If you find Cal, hold him. I'll have a talk with him when I get through at the Gorkenoff's. And here." He handed Stephen his Smith and Wesson .38 Chief's Special. "I've got another at the office. You might need it."

"I hope not."

"Me, too. We've got enough trouble without this."

Chapter Sixteen

Flora Malcolm carefully lifted a corner of blue-green fabric and peered out through the drawn curtains of her darkened kitchen.

They were out there, but she couldn't see them. Neighbors, friends. Did they believe her? Did anyone believe Tommy was the one sleeping with that girl?

After all the years of protecting Hube and keeping his dirty little political secrets, the lie had slipped out without thought. She had been willing to sacrifice her own son for him and his precious reputation.

She stared through the dappled shade of the huge elm dominating her front yard, certain they must know the truth. Everyone knew, and they were laughing, snickering at her behind veiled expressions of pity, waiting to see what she'd do now that IT was out in the open.

How long had IT been going on? Was Angela Stoddard the only one? Were there others?

A hateful image of young Angela Stoddard — her doe brown eyes and schoolgirl smile — flashed through Flora's tortured mind. For the rest of her days, no matter what she did, that single face, that deceitful tramp, would always be there, lurking at the edges of whatever happiness she might be able to attain.

Flora shrank back against the comforting coolness of the papered wall, wanting to disappear, swallowed up in black despair. If only she were invisible, could come and go and live out her life in absolute concealment.

Her fists tightened and silent tears spilled down her face. God, what did I do to deserve this? she asked bitterly. Haven't I been a good wife? It isn't fair! Life isn't fair.

No, it isn't, an inner voice answered.

There was a dull ache in her chest.

Flora opened her eyes and stared blearily at a half-empty bottle of Scotch on the counter. After she'd questioned Laura and poured out her wretched tale— lies, lies, lies!—to the Mortons and virtually all of Town, she'd come back and gotten drunk. What was there left for her to do?

They were out there, behind the mullioned windows and tall wooden shutters of their proper, picture-perfect homes, laughing at her. Sweet Jesus, how long had everyone known? What a fool she'd been! She had always heard the wife was the last to find out.

Cheated! Betrayed! All those years. All the pretending. The suffering in silence.

She'd been drunk when Hube had come home last night. The kids had seen the state she was in and discreetly disappeared. But Hube had been furious. She had no right to make a spectacle of herself, to indulge herself this way. No right to be human.

He had called her an ugly, soused-up hag and a disgusting excuse for a wife, while she'd lain sniveling on the sofa feeling sorry for herself. Terribly sorry.

He'd thrown things—not at her, though she'd known he wanted to—and he hadn't thrown expensive items, just things that belonged to her, ones that meant something only to her. Like the tiny, hand-blown bud vase that had belonged to her mother so many years ago. He had kept throwing stuff until she begged him to stop. Then he'd grabbed her arm and taken her up to the bedroom for her "real" punishment.

Though it made him angry when she drank, that hadn't stopped him from taking what he'd wanted. Her skin burned at the thought of his touch. Nothing stopped Hube. Men were like that. They were utterly driven by that pulsating piece of flesh that hung between their legs. It was everything to them: pride, ego, power, justification, excitement, comfort, purpose, and master.

She wiped her eyes and sniffed loudly. The alcohol hadn't helped. It had only made her head ache and her nose run and the situation temporarily more bearable. But now that she was cold sober again and the effects had worn off, in the hard light of another day, it was even more difficult to confront the wasted, meaningless existence her life had become.

She should've had an affair, too. And maybe she would. That would be a fitting revenge. What would Hube think when he found out *she* had slept with another man? Would he suffer the way she had?

Yes, that was it. She'd have an affair. It wasn't too late to get even. She'd put on some makeup and . . .

Flora rushed to the living room mirror, plans awhirl in her feverish brain. He'd be so sorry.

She stopped abruptly and cringed with disappointment at the sight that confronted her: the dull strands of lifeless brown hair streaked with gray, the sagging cheeks, her dry, lusterless skin, the infinite number of deep lines, her bulging eyes, the horrible veins and broken blood vessels around her bulbous nose.

Oh God! She knotted her hands in her hair and pulled. Oh God! The pain was incredible. How ugly she was! How she hated herself! Hube was right; no man would waste himself with her. But she hadn't always been ugly. Why hadn't Hube aged like she had?

It wasn't fair.

No.

Life had been especially hard on her. She had tried

to build a good home and do all the right things. She had joined the PTA when the kids were little, collected recipes, grown roses, run the family errands, given bedroom performances that should have won an Oscar. What woman could have done more?

And yet it wasn't enough. Life just wasn't fair. Face it, Flora Jean, she scolded herself.

But the biting agony—that painful knot in her chest, the pounding behind her eyes, the knifelike cramps in her abdomen—could not so easily be cured.

Her life was ruined.

She had been cheated.

The women at the garden center were sure to know. Her friends at the local literary club would know, too. They were scheduled to meet next Thursday at the library. But instead of debating what Tom Wolfe had meant in *Bonfire Of The Vanities,* they would be far more interested in discussing the philandering exploits of their vivacious mayor and his pathetic, rapidly aging wife.

How long had they known? Had they known last month and the month before that? How long had people been laughing?

She glanced at the clock. It was ten till five. Supper time. Hube would be home soon. Tommy was working at the hardware store; he wouldn't be home till eight or later. Kelly had gone to the lake with friends. She wouldn't be back for two days. Flora had become so conditioned over the last twenty years that five o'clock, weekend or weekday, crisis or not, meant only one thing: she needed to put food on the table.

The freezer was empty except for a package of franks and three bags of green beans. Hube hated both. She blew her nose and dabbed at her eyes with a Kleenex. Whether she wanted to or not, it was time to face the world. She couldn't hide forever.

Flora grabbed her purse and stepped into the garage.

She didn't bother with makeup or hairspray. One look in the mirror had convinced her that it was hopeless. Varicose veins and hemorrhoids were her lot. She wasn't Cinderella, but one of the ugly stepsisters.

Thanks to the convenience of automatic garage door openers, she could slip in and out of her house without having to confront any of her neighbors except at the store. Since Gorkenoff's was closed, she would have to drive to the new grocery, Big Ben's, on the edge of Town.

Though she had been dreading going out all day, she actually felt better once she got behind the wheel of their four-door Chrysler LeBaron. She had the power of a V-8 engine and all that steel behind her. She dispensed with the air conditioning and rolled down the windows instead, so she could feel the full effect of the air rushing at her face. Yes, Flora Malcolm might be ugly as hell, she might be aging at the rate of an unembalmed corpse in mid-July, but she was a lady of substance.

The Chrysler roared as she pressed her foot on the gas and screeched out of the drive. She now knew why it was that her son and all teenage boys drove like maniacs. It made them feel important, transformed them from pimple-sprouting youths with out-of-control glands into something of much greater status: Kings Of The Road.

As she stopped impatiently at the first and only traffic signal between her and the grocery, she realized that she held the power of life and death beneath her two wrinkled, arthritic hands. She was master of the universe. It was up to her to decide the fate of any fellow human being she happened to meet. Flora smiled. Never had so much rested upon her thin, stooped shoulders.

She pulled into the Big Ben's lot with a new sense of energy and purpose. She parked boldly in the first space she saw—a handicapped-only spot—and dared them to do anything about it. But once inside the store, she lost her confidence and became nothing more than Hubert Malcolm's drab wife again, here to pick out *his* supper. That same wrenching sense of self-loathing and mournful despondency set in.

Hube would always win. No matter what else she achieved, Hube would always be able to reduce her to pleading and tears whenever he chose. He had her so well trained that she lied for him, spread her legs for him, and rushed to fix his dinner amid her own personal woes. And what did he do? Her needs and desires didn't matter—least of all to him. They never had.

Nonetheless—indeed, what else could she do?—she leaned over a mound of lettuces and began examining the outer leaves and the bottoms of the cores to determine which was freshest. Hube liked a salad with his meals; it kept him regular. Yes, even Hube's bowels were of the utmost concern to her.

She carefully laid a plump, fresh head of lettuce into her cart along with a bottle of his favorite dressing, then strolled as inconspicuously as possible into the next aisle. There were very few other shoppers, for which she was extremely grateful—all the less chance of having to confront anyone in the wake of her recent humiliation. How they must be laughing! She clenched her hands around the handle and pushed her cart on, trying to remain calm. She wouldn't give Them the satisfaction of seeing her squirm.

Two stock boys in the next aisle were discussing the rash of bizarre killings plaguing the area. She had heard a report about it on the radio, but paid little attention. That must be the reason the store was so empty, though. But what did she care? It might be a blessing if a toxic cloud appeared around one of the corners and swallowed her up. As long as it wasn't too painful. She didn't want to suffer. But then again, she wouldn't mind if Hube did. Maybe the cloud would get Hube. Maybe . . .

She continued to push her way down the aisle, her eyes barely focusing, until her gaze fell across a bottle of drain cleaner. POISON, it said, in bold red letters almost as big as the brand name. Warning: contains hydrochloric acid. Handle with care.

Handle with care. A warm rush of excitement shot up her spine.

Yes. Oh God, yes.

She looked down at her cart; she had nearly everything she needed to make Hube his casserole. Beef, onions, mushrooms, noodles, garlic, red wine, everything but . . .

Not hydrochloric acid. They had used it before to clean out the bathroom pipes. It ate through damn near everything. No one would be able to swallow enough to kill himself. It would burn out his throat first.

Flora continued to study the cleaners, her ears ringing and her pulse racing. At last, she would take control of her own destiny. But what if it didn't work? A stab of fear crossed her thoughts. The poison she chose had to be strong, very potent. There couldn't be any mistakes.

It was incredible that she was even considering it, and yet . . . Hube would be surprised, really surprised. It wasn't the same as having an affair, but it was something. For so many years she had done nothing. Hube would never think she had the guts.

Mothballs, bleach, rubbing alcohol, detergent, ant and roach spray, bug powder. She paid extra care to the active ingredient in each bottle and box to see whether or not it would prove fatal if swallowed, but most didn't say. They said things like: Caution—keep out of the reach of children. Avoid breathing fumes. Do not use near food. Call Poison Control Center immediately. How was a person to know which ones would actually kill?

The long scientific chemical names on the labels meant nothing to her, and she had to be certain. None seemed really suited to her purpose. There must be a better way.

She walked back to the two stock boys. "I need something lethal," she said.

They stared in bewilderment at her.

"I need some poison," she repeated.

One stood, wiping his hands on his apron, and offered to help, while the other returned to his work. "What kind of poison do you need?"

"Well, I'm not really sure," she said with a short nervous laugh. "It's funny, I've never done this sort of thing before."

"What is it you're trying to kill?"

"Something big. The size of a deer. Maybe bigger. It's been coming around and messing in our garbage. I haven't actually seen it, but there are tracks on the ground and trash strewn all over the place. It must be something big."

"Huh." The boy scratched at a blemish on the side of his cheek, thinking.

Flora smiled. It was amazing how easily she lied.

The boy looked over the rat and roach poisonings on the shelf. "I don't think we got anything 'round here that'll kill an animal that big," he said finally. "You'd better talk to Marv. He might know; he's the manager. I'll take you up to the office."

Flora followed along meekly. Had he guessed? Were they going to call the cops?

The store manager smiled and nodded at her as the boy explained the problem. "You're Mrs. Malcolm, aren't you?" he said.

"Yes." Oh God, did he know, too?

"I thought I recognized you. I worked on your husband's first campaign when I was in high school."

"That's nice. Hube appreciates all the help he can get." She almost said, "free help."

"Well, he's a great guy. About the poison, I'm afraid Ned's right. We don't sell anything that will kill a deer. But I'll tell you what, you being the mayor's wife and all, I got some stuff in the back I can give you that'll do it."

"Really?"

"Sure. Come along."

Ned returned to the detergent aisle, and she and Marv headed toward the stockroom.

"This junk kills anything," Marv said. "We've been having trouble, too. Rats around the trash bin outside. Must be the weather. I tried what we've got on the shelf, but it didn't do any good. Finally I went over to the feed and grain, and they gave me some poison that'll kill a mule."

"How long does it take?"

"Huh?"

"How long does it take to work?"

"Oh, that depends on how much it eats. Sounds like a deer from what Ned said. Be sure you put out a lot. You shouldn't have any problem."

He swung open the back door and led the way through the aisles of boxes to the side wall. He pointed to a ten-pound bag on the floor. "Farmers use this a lot to kill mice and raccoons that get into their barns."

"How does it taste?"

Marv laughed. "I don't know, and I'll tell you I'm not about to find out. But the rats seem to like it. I only put it out one night, and we haven't had any trouble since. Take the whole bag."

"I'll pay you," she insisted.

He held up his hand in protest. "For you, Mrs. Malcolm, it's free. My pleasure."

"Oh really, you've been too kind."

"Nah. That husband of yours is one great guy."

"I know." She bent to pick up the bag.

"Here. Let me get that." He stooped over and gathered the bag at the top. "You wanta be careful with this. It's extremely poisonous."

"I will," she promised.

They headed back toward the office. "Is there anything else you need?" he asked.

"Yes. I've got a cart over there."

"I'll put this up by the registers then, and someone will help you carry it out to your car."

"Thank you ever so much."

"No problem, Mrs. Malcolm." He smiled and walked away.

On her way up to the front register, she passed a display of garden tools and pesticides. One of the labels caught her attention. WARNING: fatal, if swallowed. Keep away from food and pets. She grabbed the can and tossed it into her cart. A woman couldn't be too careful when plotting to kill her husband, especially when she was so inexperienced.

Flora watched as the pesticide rolled along the conveyer belt. Her legs felt weak and unsteady. Suppose it didn't work? Suppose it just made him sick and they took Hube to the hospital and discovered the cause? She'd have to make sure that didn't happen. Once she committed herself to it, she'd have to finish the job by whatever means.

Her heart pounded violently against her lungs. Blood rushed through her eardrums like the swell of the tide. It was over, all but over now. She remembered their wedding: "till death do us part." She had to get out of this store before she allowed her emotions to rule her body.

When the boy wheeled her groceries to her car, she was not the least bit proud of the fact she had parked in a handicapped spot, but slightly embarrassed. She saw Stella Daniels going into the store, and Stella gave her a peculiar look. Flora pretended not to notice. What did it matter? What did it matter what any of them thought? She was taking control now, and they were no longer important. This was between her and Hube.

The drive home was difficult. Tears clouded her eyes. How had their relationship deteriorated to the point where it was now? The 1958 homecoming queen of Town High and the handsome, young new owner of the Farmer's Savings and Loan Bank. How had it happened? Two beautiful children. A lovely two-story house on the edge of Town. They had nearly everything, all the components of the American dream. They should've been happy. Why hadn't it worked?

She wiped her nose with the side of her hand and pulled into the drive. No good looking back. It was over. Utterly and finally over.

What about Tommy and Kelly? Her eyes misted again. No matter what else she had been, she had been a good mother. But they were both in high school. Neither one had really needed or wanted her guidance for some time now. She had been reduced to a figurehead that signed permission slips, cooked their dinner, and washed their clothes. They would be fine without her. She'd leave a note for her sister, asking her to look after the kids until they graduated. Of course, Dorothy would anyway, even without being asked. And her parents. They would be hurt, but no more so than she herself was.

Flora grabbed the bags from the trunk and carried them into the kitchen.

Five thirty. There wasn't much time. She had only half an hour to get ready. The menu was laid out in her mind. Beef and noodle casserole with mushrooms, brown gravy, and rat poison. Key lime pie with a heavy dose of insecticide. Hube would eat anything with lots of sugar in it.

Dear God, what if it wasn't enough?

It had to be.

Don't think about that now.

She turned on the oven and opened the cupboards, pulling out pans and dumping the muffin mix into a bowl. What if it wasn't enough? She tried desperately to think of something else. What more could she add? What could she kill him with if the poison didn't work? What if Tommy came home before he was dead?

Chapter Seventeen

Like most of the houses and other buildings in Town, the outside of the Schrantz Hardware Shop was heavily laden with window cornices, old-fashioned shutters, multipaned glass, and even a narrow wrought iron balcony across the upper level.

Inside, rows of metal racks formed aisles across the plank oak floor. Hammers, nails, screwdrivers, drills, saws, lawn and garden equipment. A cash register stood by the door near a central display of paint and varnish. The interior was such a sharp contrast to the ornate Victorian decor on the outside, that Stephen couldn't help feeling as though he had stepped through a time warp.

There was a teenage boy in a red apron stocking one of the aisles. Stephen studied him briefly, but he wouldn't have known Tommy Malcolm from any other kid in Town. He went straight to the man behind the cash register.

The name Donald Schrantz was embroidered in red and white letters on the man's shirt pocket. "Can I help you, sir?" he asked, leaning against the counter.

"I'm looking for Tommy Malcolm," Stephen replied.

"He's out making a delivery. Perhaps—"

"Where?"

"I beg your pardon?"

"Where is he making the delivery?"

The man drew himself up indignantly. "You're not from around here."

"I'm helping Sheriff Foss. Has Cal Stoddard been in today?"

"Well . . ." The man hesitated, appraising Stephen's disheveled, unshaven appearance. Finally he said, "He was. About fifteen minutes ago. Is there trouble? I thought about closing. I know most of the other stores have. Maybe I should have too."

"No trouble yet, but there might be. What did Cal say? Did he make any threats against the boy?"

"Of course not. He just asked about Tommy, the same as you."

"What did you tell him?"

"Listen here. I don't like your tone." The color was rising from the man's thick neck to his ruddy cheeks.

"I'm sorry," Stephen said, trying to keep himself under control. "I'm in a hurry. I don't want anybody to get hurt."

"Does this have something to do with those deaths, what killed those kids?"

"No, it's a different matter entirely."

"Well, Cal came in and asked about Tommy. I told him the boy took a box up to Mrs. Milligan's, then Cal took off."

"Christ. Have you got a phone?"

"In the back, by the restrooms. There's a door that says . . ."

Stephen didn't wait. He ran toward the rear of the store and found a pay phone nestled in a dark corner outside the john. He flipped in a quarter and dialed the Gorkenoff's. He wondered how much danger the kid was really in. Surely, the father wouldn't kill him. But he might work him over, pound his face, break a few ribs.

"Come on, come on," he muttered impatiently. He hadn't counted, but he knew it must've rung over a

233

dozen times. He hung up. Either Foss wasn't there, or for some reason he wasn't answering.

What to do now? he asked himself. Try to find Foss, or catch up with Stoddard?

Foss must've thought there was the possibility of considerable violence or he wouldn't have given him the pistol.

Stephen darted back up to the cash register. "Which way to the Milligans'?"

The man pointed out the window. "Up that hill. First right. Down three blocks, then right again. A brown and yellow house all the way at the end of the street. It's a dead end. You can't miss it."

Stephen rushed out the door and flung his bronze Mazda RX7 into reverse and tore out of the lot. He circled around, following the storekeeper's instructions.

When he got to the house, there were no cars parked in front of it or anywhere near it. The only other vehicles in sight were sitting far down at the opposite end of the street. He'd passed them on his way; both were empty.

Stephen pulled over to the curb, keeping an eye on the house. It looked quiet. No sign of anybody on the porch.

He got out and dashed up the steps. An elderly woman with a hunched back answered the doorbell. She fiddled with the latch for what seemed like an interminable length, then finally wedged open the screen. Her parched face wrinkled into a withered, toothless smile as she asked him what he wanted.

"I'm looking for a delivery boy that was sent to your house."

"Oh yes. He was here just a few minutes ago."

"He's gone now?"

"Yes. Can I help you?"

"Do you know which way he went?"

She shook her head. "I'm sorry. He didn't stay very

long."

"Was anyone else here in the last few minutes?" He tried to keep the urgency out of his voice.

"No."

"You're sure?"

She nodded.

He thanked her and headed back to his car. He looked down the street. Still no sign of Cal Stoddard. He slid into the Mazda and slammed his fist against the wheel. Damn. What the hell was he supposed to do now?

Stephen turned over the engine and began cruising back toward the hardware store. The kid had to be around someplace. But he drove all the way back to Schrantz's shop without seeing him. He checked inside with Donald Schrantz again.

Had Tommy returned? No.

Stephen stepped back outside. His shoulders sagged. What more could he do? Stoddard must've caught up to the boy and taken him somewhere. The kid might not have any idea what was going on and might have gone with him willingly.

Stephen rubbed his hand across the sweat pooling on his forehead and stared into the somber blue sky to the west. A hazy layer of muggy stillness hovered over the sunbaked village. The long black shadows of late afternoon stretched across the cobblestone sidewalks and into the glaring heat. Traffic had dwindled over the past few days to only an occasional car here and there.

Laura was right—people were leaving, fearing for their lives amidst the latest deaths. He didn't blame them, but he knew Foss wouldn't give up. The lawman would battle it out till the bitter end, like Abigail Morton. He admired Foss's tenacity. It took the kind of guts and loyalty rarely seen these days in a primarily self-absorbed society.

Wearily, he sank onto the tan vinyl seat. He would

stick it out, too, but not out of noble sentiment. Laura was here, and he had damn few other places to go. Kat was dead. He had no family. There was nothing else that really mattered, not even his work. Not now. He jammed his key into the ignition. It was time to go tell Foss they had struck out again.

Chapter Eighteen

Six thirty-two. Flora peeked anxiously through the window at the drive. No sign of Hube. Why wasn't he home yet?

She remembered the other nights he'd been late, when he had to work or had gone out with the boys—nights when he must've been with that girl. Where did they go? Who saw them together? Better not think of that.

An icy chill raced through her veins.

What a fool I've been! My whole life. I let him push me around like a lump of clay. I never stood up to him, not for a moment. Not even for the children's sake. But now . . . why isn't he home? Where could he be?

She wrung her hands nervously, feeling the painful bite of her wedding ring against the other fingers.

There's still plenty of time, she reminded herself. Stay calm. Don't rush. Don't give him a reason to suspect anything's wrong.

Flora forced herself to take a deep breath and let it out slowly, then went on with her preparations as though it were any other meal, any other day. A matter of routine. He'd be home soon. Give it time.

The dinnerware was already laid out: a cheap set of

china they used for everyday meals, stainless steel forks and spoons, glass tumblers, a cold beer beside Hube's. Everything as it should be. Any minute, she told herself, and began putting platters of food on the table.

Then she heard a car roll into the drive. Her heart skipped a beat. Her lower lip trembled. She glanced over the covered dishes, steam escaping from around the rims — beef noodle casserole, whole wheat muffins, tossed salad, and mashed potatoes.

Flora watched from behind the drapes as Hube grabbed his briefcase and slid out of the car. An ugly scowl marred his handsome face, and she felt herself quiver. How many times had she seen that glower? What was it this time? A councilman who didn't agree with his policies? A constituent who had complained to the governor?

Maybe it was because of the girl's death. Flora's throat tightened. Did he love her? Moisture welled at the corners of her eyes, but she willed it back. Now was not the time for tears.

Hube walked with slumped shoulders, his arms hanging heavily at his sides as he plodded toward the front door. Then he heard his name called and brightened abruptly, waving to Mrs. Pearson across the street and flashing her one of his cherubic smiles.

Hube never missed an opportunity to sell himself, not even to neighborhood biddies like Clara Pearson. Flora wondered if Clara knew about Angela, if she had seen the young girl coming and going from the house at odd hours.

When he thought no one was looking, Hube resumed his gloomy posture, and Flora prepared herself. The door swung open. Hube slammed his briefcase down on the tile in the foyer and flung off his tie. "What a bitch," he grumbled to himself.

Flora wondered if he meant her, Mrs. Pearson, or the recent crisis in Town.

"Why can't they keep the goddamned kids off the street," he muttered and stalked toward the kitchen. He pulled out his chair and flipped up the tab on the beer. Flora was just taking the pie from the refrigerator.

"Bad day?" she asked, trying to control her voice and pretend that all was as it should be. She struggled to keep the bitterness out of her tone. He had never asked nor cared how her day went. All he had ever cared about was himself.

Hube grunted in reply and sipped the foam off the top of his beer, then surveyed the meal without enthusiasm. Always the same, she thought. He never appreciated her daily efforts to serve him. But soon he would wish he had.

"I went to see Howard this afternoon," he said, beginning to load up his plate, not bothering to wait until she was seated. They never said grace as they had in her parents' home when she was a girl. A person should be humble and thank the Lord for their blessings, she thought, then watched intently as he took the first bite.

"The traffic between here and Indianapolis was thicker than shit," he continued. "Took me three hours to drive up and back, but you'll be glad I went. Howard is going to save our butts." Hube stuffed a spoonful of gravy into his mouth. Flora waited, not touching her own, just stirring it slightly with a loosely held fork.

"He's found a buyer for our land north of Town. Sold it for a whopping $300,000, right before news of this trouble hit the national wire service." Hube laughed, taking a bite out of one of the muffins. She wished he would talk less and eat more.

"The buyer's already given Howard a check, so he can't get out of it. The guy wants to build apartments and a shopping center on it. He must be boiling now.

The stupid jackass ought to build a cemetery instead, then he might make a profit."

"Is it that bad?" Flora asked, hoping he wouldn't notice how quiet she was or how interested she was in each morsel that passed his lips. But then, Hube never noticed anything she did.

He nodded. "It doesn't look good. The death rate's accelerating. People are dying in Mirror County, too. But don't worry. I've made arrangements for us to get out of Town. I called the airline. You and the kids can go to your mother's. I'm making a trip—get this—to Washington, D.C. to see if I can persuade the federal government to intervene and lend us a hand—as if anybody there gives a damn about what happens here."

He shrugged and laid down the butter knife. "But you never know. If it works, I'll be a hero and maybe the government will find out what's causing this so we won't have to leave. If it doesn't work, at least we'll be safe. I figure at the end of another week, we'll know whether or not there's going to be anything worth coming back to."

"What about our friends?" She found herself thinking of that nice boy who sold her the poison, how much he like Hube. A boy like that didn't deserve to die.

"What can I do?" he argued, then shoved another spoonful of gravy into his mouth. "We've got to look out for ourselves first. You know that."

They ate in silence for several minutes, Hube's irritation passing. Finally he asked, "Where are the kids?"—only just realizing they weren't present.

"Kelly's with friends," she said. "Tommy is working."

"That's my boy. Going to be like his old man."

Hube took another bite, then grimaced. "What the hell did you put in this?"

Flora felt her face burn. "Why nothing . . . I . . ."

"It tastes like shit," he said, pushing his plate aside.

"I came home expecting a decent meal. Is that too much to ask, huh?"

She rose from her chair, beginning to panic. "I'll get you some pie," she said. "It's your favorite, key lime."

"Just get me a beer. I'm going in and read the paper. A man works hard all day, making sure your dainty little life isn't disturbed, and what do I get? The least you could do is put edible food on the table."

"I'm sorry. I tried . . ."

"Like hell. You haven't worked a day in your life. You do nothing but sit around on your fat ass, bitching with your friends and feeling sorry for yourself. Look at you. You didn't even put on any makeup. 'I'm sorry. I tried,'" he mimicked in a high-pitched voice. "Get me a beer. You disgust me."

Flora held back her own retort and stared at his plate. He'd eaten less than half of the amount he'd taken. What if it wasn't enough? Dear God, what should she do now?

Hube grabbed the newspaper from the sofa and dropped into his recliner. He opened it and began reading over the financial page.

Dazed, Flora picked up the dishes from the table to clear them away. It took every ounce of her willpower to keep herself under control. Surely he'd eaten enough to make himself sick. He'll realize what I did, she thought. A wave of panic shot through her.

She glanced over and saw that he had put down his paper. There was grave concern on his face. He leaned forward holding his gut. Beads of sweat had popped out across his forehead. She dropped her dish towel and stood watching, awash with fear and sudden excitement.

Hube didn't notice; he was too busy with his own troubles. He pushed himself up out of the chair and lurched toward the stairs.

Flora rushed around the counter into the living room. "What's wrong?"

"I'm not sure," he said, wincing in anguish. "I don't feel good. I'm going to go up and lie down."

Flora brought her hand to her mouth to hide her expression. "Is there anything I can get for you?" she asked with muffled glee.

"No, I don't think so."

She watched in fascination as he reached for the banister and began pulling himself up the steps, leaning heavily on the rail. The pain must be awful, she thought, to cause him to walk like that. Hube was so stubborn.

He's not going to win, she thought, as he reeled to the top. Not this time. So many campaigns. So many victories. But it was she and his devoted party workers who had done the real work, the grunt work.

"Flora!" he cried.

She ran up the steps, reaching the second floor landing just as he collapsed on the carpet outside their bedroom door. "Call the doctor," he gasped, rocking and clutching his middle, and she knew for once in his life Hube wasn't acting. His agony was real. "Call the doctor quick."

But she didn't move. She stood transfixed, with her hands at her sides and her back pressed to the wall, repulsed by the sight of him.

"For God's sake, hurry," he screamed.

He pulled his knees up to his chest, struggling against the tide of mounting pain. His face flushed with fever.

"What are you doing?" he howled. "Get me some help." He twisted and gritted his teeth.

Tears filled her eyes and spilled down her sagging cheeks. To think she had given her life to this loathsome man, who now writhed like a worm—had borne children and labored beside him. It was all . . . all such a waste.

"I gave you the best years of my life," Flora sobbed aloud. "You were all I thought of. Why did you do it? To torment me? Could you hate me that much?"

"What are you talking about?" The words came out in agonized bursts of pain. He groaned and rolled onto his back, knees raised, twisting his head from side to side. "I can't take it. Christ, I can't take it. Get me help."

"You can't take it!" she shouted. "What do you think it's been like for me?"

She clenched her hands and shook them over his thrashing form, shrieking with rage. "Why, Hube? To make me pay? Tell me, you bastard. Did you love that poor girl? Did she think she loved you?"

His eyes widened, and the hideous truth dawned on him. Suddenly he knew; they both knew.

"What was she like?" Flora hissed. "What did she do that I didn't do? Tell me, Hube! You owe me that much."

"Oh . . . God . . ." The words wrenched from his throat. He grunted and tried to say more, but his stomach was heaving. All he could do was retch. His eyes were bulging in fear. Mucus ran from his eyes and nose. His whole body convulsed as the contents of the poisoned supper spewed out over the carpet.

Flora shuddered and covered her mouth. It was awful. There was blood mixed with the vomit and glowing bits of white phosphorous from the rat poison. He must be bleeding internally. It was only a matter of time.

But Hube wasn't ready to die. He knotted his fists in the thick fibers of the hallway carpeting and began pulling himself toward the bedroom, using his elbows and knees to propel himself. His taut, muscular body trembled in spasmodic jerks of uncontrollable torture as he crawled steadily through the doorway.

Flora was shocked that he could keep going, and once more the fear that he would somehow survive shot through her. She scanned the room frantically and saw where he was headed. Twice he stopped and gagged, coughing up more food and blood. Her mind was a panicked blur as scenarios of Hube's recovery flashed through her mind.

He entangled his fingers in the phone cord and yanked the handset down onto the floor. Flora leapt around him and stomped on his hand. "I'm sorry, Hube. I can't let you do that."

He cried out in anguish, then grasped weakly at her ankle. His strength was gone. He was helpless before her. There was no way to save himself. He shook his head feebly and begged, "No . . . please." The terror of death was written on his face.

But Flora felt no mercy. She was glad he was going, glad her own pain would end soon. "There was a time," she admitted, "when I would've done anything for you." Then she reached over and disconnected the unit from the wall.

Hube was beyond speech. He cried like a baby, continuing to retch and vomit. Nothing was coming up but blood. It had to be almost over. She felt confident now. She could see by the look in his eyes that his spirit was broken.

She took the phone with her as she left the bedroom and went into the bathroom. Though she could still hear the sound of his labored breathing, the house felt different. She had taken control of her own destiny.

She felt very calm now, and drew one of her nighties out of the cabinet drawer. It was her prettiest: an elegant black crepe with gold embossed flowers stamped across the bodice. She held it below her chin in front of the mirror and smiled. Hube had bought it for her on their last anniversary, but she had worn it only once.

She put on the gown and combed her hair thoroughly, making it shine, then opened her cosmetic case. Hube had complained earlier because she wasn't wearing any makeup. The powder and shadow helped to alleviate some of the signs of aging, but not even they could work miracles. Still, she was satisfied when she surveyed her handiwork and applied a final coat of lipstick.

Hube would be proud. If she used her imagination, if she squinted her eyes and thought back twenty years, she looked almost as good as the day they had met. It was such a happy time then, such a grand moment, so much future ahead of them. A pity what can happen, how everything can change.

When she stepped back into the bedroom, Hube lay still. She knelt over him and put her hand against his face. Not the slightest sign of life. Stone dead. She tried to remember, to recapture the love and depth of feeling that had brought the two of them to the altar so many years ago, but it was impossible. Too much hurt had washed over the bridge.

She pulled back the coverlet on the bed. The sheets were clean and fresh. Everything was perfect. There was only one more thing to do. She took a pen and paper from Hube's desk and wrote a note to her sister asking her to look after the kids. They were almost grown now. They didn't need her, and there would be plenty of money left from the estate. Financially, they were well set. Hube had said so himself. She smiled as she thought of Kelly and Tommy. They would be all right, more so than before.

Then she rose from the chair and got a glass of water from the bathroom and her bottle of sleeping pills. The bottle was nearly full, only three missing; she'd filled it last week.

It took her five minutes to get all the pills down. She stretched out between the crisp, cool sheets, the bed entirely to herself. It felt better than she'd hoped—being free. For the first time in eighteen years, Flora slept soundly. . . .

Chapter Nineteen

i.

It was almost dark when Stephen reached the Gorkenoff's. Foss's patrol car was parked by the curb, which meant he ought to still be here. So, why hadn't someone answered the phone when he called?

He was concerned for the Malcolm boy. The kid's life could be in danger. Of course, there was a chance that Foss had heard from Leland, and Tommy was safe. But that much, he figured, was wishful thinking.

No lights were on inside the store, but that wasn't surprising. The deli had been closed since Henry's death. Several other businesses had shut down as well in the wake of the recent deaths, and yet . . . he felt uneasy. Too many things had gone wrong lately. Something about the situation made him wary of going inside. He tried to see if there were lights on in the back part of the building, but it was impossible to tell from outside.

Hesitantly, Stephen pushed against the door and found it unlocked. This gave him even more reason to believe not everyone had gone away.

The clump of brass bells overhead clanged against the glass, but unlike his previous visits, their sound elicited no response. The darkened deli fell quickly silent, and Stephen swallowed the unbidden fear that rose in his throat.

Rows of empty pastry shelves and vacant seats loomed ominously around him in the shadowy depths of the store. It was too quiet, he thought. There should have been some noise if anyone was home. The place had an almost tomblike quality in the steely gloom of impending night.

Apparently no one had heard him enter. He called out and broke the funereal secrecy. "Bob? Mrs. Gorkenoff?" It was loud enough to project into the living section of the house.

He waited. No answer.

He wondered if perhaps Foss had come and gone while he'd been out tracking the Malcolm boy. Maybe Mrs. Gorkenoff had left to visit her husband in the hospital. But then he remembered the patrol car parked outside. No, Foss was still here someplace. He just wasn't answering. Maybe they were up in the attic.

"Mrs. Gorkenoff?" he called again, and again got no response.

This time he didn't wait, but carefully edged around the corner toward the back of the store. There was a hall between the rear workroom and the deli that led to the main part of the house and Stephen saw a narrow shaft of light at the opposite end. He moved toward it through the darkness.

The glow was emanating from around a partially open door. He pushed it open and was immediately swathed in electric light. A crystal chandelier with candle-shaped bulbs twinkled above the living room from the center of a molded, plaster ceiling. He quickly glanced over the plaid sofa and overstuffed chairs, woolen blankets folded over the backs, a newspaper spread on one table.

The room was empty. Nothing out of place or beyond the ordinary, and yet it gave him an eerie feeling to walk across the polished floor and hear only the sounds of his own hollow footsteps.

He stepped back into the hall and turned the other way down the L-shaped passage. The bathroom door was wide open and clearly lit, and he became aware of a soft, watery noise—glanced inside.

It was only then that Stephen registered the smell.

Mrs. Gorkenoff was floating face down in the tub. Her dark, matted hair splayed out from her head in all directions, like seaweed. Her wet flowered housedress clung to her misshapen form, defining the terrible damage that had been done. Her skin was rent and pieces of withered gray epidermis floated atop the water along with the oily brown substance that flowed from her decimated corpse. The frothy scum seemed to crawl of its own volition as it slopped slowly onto the floor from the overflowing tub, beside a scrub brush and a can of scouring powder.

He took a blundering lunge backward, gasping for air, as though the wind had been knocked out of him. He turned and ran, mindlessly, bolting down the hall into the store—where he could breathe easier.

Christ . . . oh Christ . . . He leaned against the counter, steadying his legs. They felt like deflated balloons. Then he remembered Foss. Where was Foss? He would have to go back down that hall. He thought about calling for help, but who was there to call?

Was the deadly mist gone? He tried to comfort himself with the idea that by now it would be, and forced his legs to return past the scene of the woman's devastation.

He didn't look this time; Foss wasn't in the bathroom. He opened each of the other doors and flicked on the wall switches. It was easier with the lights on.

All of the rooms were empty.

He cut through the workroom toward the rear staircase, the only one that went all the way up to the fourth floor. He remembered following Henry up there, how they had found that jacket . . . and a layer of chalky gray dust. As far as he knew Foss still hadn't determined who the intruder had been—there was too much else occupying the sheriff's mind—but now Stephen wondered whether it had something to do with the deaths. Foss had come to the Gorkenoff's to check on noises in the attic. . . .

His mouth was as dry as cotton, and his throat wouldn't work. Somehow he managed to conquer the tremors in his limbs, and entered the dark stairwell. He flicked on the light, and his search immediately ended.

Foss lay sprawled upside down, midway on the steps, his neck and limbs twisted at grotesque angles to each other. The beefy lawman had been reduced to a crumbling, emaciated figure of bone and peeling gray flesh. The telltale yellow residue continued to drip on the dusty steps, pooling and snaking its way slowly downward in sticky rivulets. His eyes were fixed straight ahead, glassy and hard, like marbles. His cracked lips were pulled back in a cartoon grimace. His gnarled hands held tight to the gleaming service revolver he was never without, yanked from its holster. There were three bullet holes in the wall.

An awful pain lodged like a sliver of bone in Stephen's stomach. He wanted to scream until all the madness was gone out of his brain, but he couldn't. His fears turned inward, falling on the deep blackness that his emotions had left in his soul.

He felt an unnatural glacial calm. He knelt down and picked up the sheriff's hat that had fallen to the base of the stairs. It appeared damp on one side, and he was careful not to touch it.

Somberly, he closed the door and walked to the phone. His hands trembled. He reached for the receiver and dialed the operator. "Get me the city building, please."

"Which extension?"

His mind reeled with an airy nothingness. "It doesn't matter," he said. "I'll talk to whoever's there."

He waited as it continued to ring, then finally someone answered: a man. "Foss is dead," he said and hung up. Then he sat down and cried, the lawman's hat on the floor at his feet.

ii.

Stephen drank slowly from a styrofoam cup of black coffee that Mildred Cook had given him. He sat on a flat bench inside one of the many chambers on the second floor of the city building. It was utterly dark outside, but the room was well lit and Stephen found comfort in it.

Uniformed state police officers passed back and forth between the doors. It looked as if the governor had ordered in a whole command post. There were none of Town's old entourage present; Malcolm, Foss, and Corliss had been replaced by a fresh team of crisply dressed, efficient-looking, big-city experts. Though they were probably just what the situation demanded, he missed the more familiar faces he'd become accustomed to. But at least in a crowded building like this, with people continually wandering in and out, the crisis didn't seem as overwhelming, so totally void of hope, and he was finally pulling himself together again.

Cook and Thompson hovered intently over a table full of lab equipment positioned near the streetside windows. Multicolored fluids and vials were clustered about them, as well as a pair of microscopes and some distillation equipment. Samples of dirt from the dump were sealed inside glass beakers to protect against the danger of contamination and the possibility of lethal vapors seeping out.

The professor was attempting to analyze the black

251

slime they'd found at the morgue, while Mildred struggled to uncover a component to diffuse the TCBA. They'd been at it for nearly twelve hours with no luck. Sgt. Christopher Williamson stood with the two, taking notes and helping in any capacity he could.

The sergeant was the man Stephen had spoken to on the phone from the Gorkenoff's deli. The call, needless to say, had shaken everyone and put the entire department in a heightened state of never-ending alert. Williamson had taken a team of his men to the store and found Stephen alone with the two corpses. The sergeant had brought him directly back to the makeshift station.

It had taken no less than six cups of coffee to revitalize his nerves and calm the tremors in his hands. His mind was abuzz with caffeine and fear-induced adrenaline, but at least he was functioning.

Williamson strode over and offered him a cold meat sandwich.

Stephen shook his head. "No, thanks." He had no appetite.

Williamson smiled. He had a friendly, lopsided grin and small, straight teeth set in a pointed, narrow face, soft blue eyes, thick eyebrows, and rakish brown hair. Not tall, but compactly built. He wasn't the kind you envisioned becoming a cop.

"Kinda rough going, huh?" the officer said, taking a seat beside Stephen. "You people have had quite a time. Makes me wonder why anyone is still hanging around."

"Yeah."

Williamson peeled back the plastic and began eating the sandwich himself. He lifted the top piece of bread and peered underneath. "Pickleloaf. I used to eat this stuff all the time when I was a kid." He took another bite. "How long have you lived here?"

"About two weeks."

"Mmm. You're not from around Town then?"

"No, I'm from Chicago."

The sergeant grinned. "Me, too. Wheaton."

"Calumet City."

"Well, that's okay. We still allow hoodlums like you into Indiana. So why are you here in Town?"

"Just visiting." Stephen paused. "Am I under suspicion?"

The sergeant laughed. "No. I'm just trying to get a feel for what's going on. It's a pretty bizarre situation. They rounded us up at three o'clock this morning. We were briefed and have been going over the facts ever since. I read through the professor's theories. Weird shit. And there's parts of it that don't add up at all."

"I don't mean to change the subject," Stephen said, "but before I got here, I was looking for a boy, Tommy Malcolm."

Williamson nodded. "Don't worry. The kid's okay. The deputy, Bill Leland, filled us in on it. The Malcolm kid's being detained until his parents can be reached, and the guy, Cal Stoddard, is in custody."

"Was the boy hurt?"

"Not much. Stoddard had picked him up on his way back to the hardware store and taken him out to the locked-up feed-and-grain. He mostly just scared the bejesus out of him. Hit him a few times, but not bad. The kid's okay. Nothing broken. The deputy got there before any real damage was done."

"Thank God for that," Stephen muttered gratefully. One less burden on his conscience.

"Yeah. Enough's going wrong around here. But people can get like that in a crisis. They get scared and do crazy things. Like trying to stop a robbery in progress. Had some asshole do that last week. The hero got himself killed, and the punk—a fifteen year old, his first offense—is up on murder charges."

Williamson swallowed the last bite of his sandwich. "Got another piece of information you might be interested in. Before Sheriff Foss died he was working on the identity of the person who broke into the Gorkenoff's attic."

Stephen straightened and set down his coffee. "Yeah?"

"He'd taken the receipt that was found near the jacket into the hardware store and checked with the shopkeeper. The man went through his records and called back this afternoon with a name—one Evan Fielding, a forty-four-year-old farmer.

"We sent a patrol car out to the house. Nobody there. According to the local census, Evan lives with his wife and three sons. We found four of their bodies, but not the fifth. Puddles of that black shit were everywhere. The professor says it contains traces of this TCBA. I don't know." Williamson scratched the dark stubble on his chin. "This whole thing makes my skin crawl. If I didn't have to stay, I'd get the hell out of this place as fast as I could. . . ."

They were both distracted at once by a sudden stir at the lab table, and Williamson left off whatever else he was going to say. Mildred Cook had called the professor over to observe her latest results through the microscope. The two evidently disagreed, then Cook sent for the police chief. Extreme determination shone in the woman's eyes, but Thompson looked dismayed and was shaking his head, obviously trying to discourage her.

"Excuse me a minute," Williamson said. "I think something's up."

Stephen watched and listened attentively as Sergeant Williamson ambled over to see what the commotion was about. The old man leaned heavily on his cane, seeming more haggard each time Stephen looked at him. Clearly his strength was ebbing, and he would soon have to quit for the night.

The police chief burst through the door and rushed to the table with two of his officers. He was a big man, robust and silver haired, in his early fifties. "What is it?" he asked.

Mildred responded immediately. "Captain Romero, we've discovered a chemical that will inactivate the TCBA."

"But we can't be sure it will work outside the controlled environment of our equipment," the professor added.

"I must disagree," Mildred insisted. "Certainly no result is a hundred percent accurate, especially under these circumstances, but time is an important factor here. I ran the tests twice, once in isolation—with only the TCBA and the reagent—and again mixed with dirt we gathered from the site. In both instances, the acetylene solution succeeded in bonding with the TCBA and rendering it harmless."

"Yes," the professor admitted, "it worked on a desk top, on the liquid form, but it's not that simple."

"I'm not trying to simplify the problem, Doctor," Mildred objected.

"What is the point you're trying to make, Professor?" the chief asked.

"I fear other elements are involved—this evil force I spoke of earlier. It's like a form of energy, like a spark of electrical current. It can't be captured nor duplicated in a jar, but out in the open, it could be devastating. We don't know what might happen. There are too many unanswered questions for us to act on this yet."

"I don't mean to argue, Professor," Mildred said, "but no one, not even you, has ever been able to prove that this spark actually exists. I've read your thesis about the origins of life, and frankly, I'm not convinced. I'm certainly not willing to gamble these people's lives on it."

"Whether or not you agree with me is irrelevant. We haven't even seen the TCBA take a gaseous form yet," he said. "We don't know that it will. We don't have a sample of the vapor itself, and we can't possibly make a definite statement about its composition until then. It's too soon to come to conclusions."

"Any delay will cost more lives." Mildred Cook's chin lifted defiantly. "Captain, how many have died of this poisonous gas?"

"Eighteen," the chief confirmed.

She turned to the elderly doctor. "How can you suggest we wait?"

"Out of concern, my dear."

"Please, don't patronize me, Dr. Thompson. My experience may not match yours in years, but I'm sufficiently qualified to make a sound judgment in this situation."

"I'm sure you are, Dr. Cook. I meant no offense. I'm only asking that we exhibit ordinary precaution. The cow we exposed to TCBA this afternoon is not only alive, it appears to be recovering and has suffered only superficial burns."

"And the rats died immediately upon contact. I don't see what that proves. Dr. Thompson, you know as well as I that experiments done with laboratory animals are seldom directly applicable to humans. These are not ordinary circumstances, nor is this an ordinary case. The primary risk in this situation comes not from hasty actions as much as from the failure to act. Hundreds of lives are at stake."

"All right," the chief said, raising his hands to bring a halt to the argument. "I think I understand what both of you are saying. Professor, can you be more specific about the risks if we proceed with this?"

"No, not with absolute certainty. Dr. Cook might be correct. The acetylene solution may be the answer we need. On the other hand, if it isn't effective, it could result in the deaths of those who try to utilize it. Or worse, it could result in an even greater catastrophe than the one we are currently battling."

"Really, Dr. Thompson," Mildred protested. "This is no Frankenstein's creation. You know as well as I that these are basic chemicals we're dealing with. Combined in a horrifying lethal form, yes, but there is no mysterious spark involved."

"Please, Dr. Cook," the police chief interrupted. "I'm sorry, Professor. I respect what you're saying, but I have to agree with the necessity for speed. Whatever the risks of acting hastily, we'll have to take them. I hope you'll continue to help us."

The old man nodded. "Of course. I understand. It's your decision to make."

Mildred Cook looked apologetic.

"Well then, what's the next step?" the chief asked.

"We'll need to produce enough of the acetylene solution to arm all your men and coat the entire dump," Mildred said. "We'll have to hope that will do it."

"Are there any other sources of the TCBA?" the chief asked.

The old man led them toward the table where he'd been working. "I've analyzed the black residue from the morgue, and it matches those samples that Dr. Corliss sent previously. The corpses are evidently continuing to decay at an amazingly accelerated rate and are filled with a heavy concentration of TCBA. There were also minute traces of it in the black substance found on the farmer, Evan Fielding's, property. And although the quantity was small, I must say it has me extremely concerned."

The discussion continued, with Williamson and Romero's staff beginning to ask questions, but Stephen was unable to concentrate on what they were saying. The effects of the caffeine and adrenaline were wearing off. . . .

257

When Stephen finally left the city building it was 11:15 p.m. He had hung around hoping there'd be more developments, but people were getting tired and progress on the case seemed to be coming to a standstill for the night.

Mildred remained in the second-floor office attempting to produce enough of her acetylene solution to neutralize the TCBA, while the professor, his physical reserves depleted, had been forced to quit and return to Corliss's apartment, where he was staying in the doctor's absence. Chief Romero and his men, except for those remaining on duty to handle whatever emergencies might arise, had also gone.

It had been a long day. One of many. The darkness was hot and muggy as Stephen slid behind the wheel of his Mazda. The initial shock surrounding Foss's death had passed and left him feeling empty and drained. The horror and the exacting pace of the last few days were taking their toll. Gruesome images danced round in his head.

He had not eaten all day nor slept well in over a week and was suddenly hungry. He swung the Mazda around and headed toward the same restaurant Foss had taken him to yesterday. It remained open to serve the state troopers who had come to assist during the crisis.

The sidewalks were inked with the long black shadows of towering, hundred-year-old trees and gloomy, monstrous-shaped houses. As he drove through the silent streets he saw not another soul or moving car, only the dark hulks of parked vehicles. It was as if the whole population were dead or had vanished.

He became increasingly aware of how vulnerable he

was — how vulnerable they all were. His grip tightened on the wheel. He couldn't see faces through the curtain-shrouded windows, but he realized that this gaseous enemy was so stealthy and intangible that it could penetrate any window or door, and that none of them were any safer in their homes than he was in his car. At any moment, they could all fall prey to its toxic corruption.

The flickering red sign of the Roadside Cafe was like a beacon in a storm. There were four other cars in the lot and people moving around inside. He heaved an unconscious sigh of relief. It didn't matter who they were, at least he would have company for awhile.

He was looking forward to seeing Laura again when he got back to the boardinghouse, and perhaps sharing a moment of pleasure amid the suffering around them.

A young waitress greeted him at the door with a menu in hand. "Just one?" she asked.

He nodded.

"Come this way please."

She led him through the maze of tables, only three of them occupied, toward a booth in the back.

He wasn't paying close attention to who the other patrons were, simply glad of the light and the other people about — then his gaze fastened upon Marie. She was sitting alone, but there were two sets of dirty dishes in front of her, so she'd obviously had company earlier.

"Steve!" Her expression brightened, and she motioned him over.

He wondered if she'd had any more trouble from Leland. He hoped not.

"I'll sit over there," he said to the waitress. "How about a beer? Do you serve alcohol here?"

"Just Michelob and wine."

"Michelob'll be fine. And a hamburger with fries."

The waitress scrawled down his order and walked

away.

He turned to Marie. "How have you been?" he asked, sliding into the booth across from her.

The ashtray was overflowing with cigarette butts. She let out a puff and added another, then took a fresh package of cigarettes from her purse. "I'm managing," she said, tugging at the cellophane.

She was dressed as though she'd been on a date, her makeup to the hilt, her red hair curled and sprayed in place. Her sky blue dress was an off-the-shoulder number that clung seductively to her breasts and waist. "Got a light?" she asked throatily.

There was a package of matches on the table. He picked them up and lit one for her. She leaned forward and gave him a glimpse of her cleavage. She wasn't wearing anything under the dress.

She leaned back, inhaling deeply and appraising his reaction. No doubt it was just what she was looking for, he thought. He was as susceptible as the next to a beautiful woman making a pass at him, but he had no plans to take her up on it, so he broke eye contact and waited for her to speak.

She made one soft, brief laughing sound to acknowledge that she was perfectly conscious of the game they were playing, then said, "Bill and I got back together." There was a note of finality in her tone.

Stephen met her eyes again, surprised.

This time it was she who looked away. Her painted hazel eyes lowered and her mouth trembled as she took another pull on her cigarette. "I had to, damn it. I can't keep working at that tavern forever, and he wants to marry me. Ain't nobody else knocking down my door—except Joel." She laughed sarcastically again.

"Who's Joel?"

"Trouble, that's who. Forget it."

"Can I help?"

She shook her head, then finished her cigarette and

lit up another. "Bill said he wouldn't do it again. He promised. He even left his gun out in the car to prove it."

"And you believe him?"

"I don't know. I got scared when I saw his car outside my window—shaky like I was last night and ready to scream. I thought, 'This time he's gonna kill me.' He pounded on my door, but I wouldn't answer. Then he started pleading, his voice all soft and mushy, saying he was sorry, telling me how much he loved me, crying and talking about how mean his wife was when she left him. He's always afraid he's not good enough. He asks me over and over, 'Was it good enough?'"

She paused, looking directly into Stephen's eyes. "But I wasn't going to let him in, no matter how much he begged. I was tired of everybody ending up hurt, and we never seem to get anywhere. Then he asked me to marry him. He's asked before, and I guess that's why I kept seeing him. Because what it comes down to is I can't go on alone. I need somebody. I've stopped believing in fairy tales. I know I'm on a one-way street down the tubes. This is about the only shot I've got left."

Her eyes glistened with tears, and she struggled to gain control. "What happened wasn't his fault," she said. "I know that. It's me. I drive him crazy. I get drunk or high, and then . . . God knows what happens. I just can't stand it, that's all. Life is tough. Everybody has their own way of coping, you know what I mean? With me, I take a drink or a line of coke, and the pain goes away. It all gets better. It gets too much better, then I don't want to stop. But if I don't cut back, I'm gonna lose Bill, or he's gonna kill me."

They were both silent as the waitress brought his dinner. When the girl left, Marie took out a compact and corrected her lipstick.

"There are other ways out," he said quietly. "Besides

marrying Bill, I mean."

She shook her head. "Not for me, sugar. You don't understand. I've been there. I've heard the talk and promises, and they ain't worth the spit it takes to produce 'em. I'm at the end of the line."

She attempted to light up another cigarette—there must've been three or four used-up packs in the ashtray already—and burnt her finger on the match.

"Oh goddamnit! I ain't had a drink all day—and it's killing me. I can't quit shakin' inside, and all I've done is eat. I'm going to get fat as a pig."

"It takes time, Marie."

"Shit, don't I know. Listen, hon, I've got to get out of here. You've been a doll."

"I haven't done any—"

She leaned forward and cut off his words with a kiss. The lady was impulsive to say the least. Her lips pressed against his with flagrant desire. Her breasts rubbed his arm, and her sensuous perfume filled his head. Then he pulled back, and she smiled knowingly.

"See ya later, sweetheart," she whispered, and whisked toward the front door.

Stephen could still feel the blood pounding in his ears.

iv.

Joel Anderson surveyed the dark length of the dingy street as he pulled in front of the small house at 131 Mulberry Street. What a dive this place was. But then, what else would one expect from a trashy, used-up whore like Marie Sheldon O'Neal living in a piss-ant hole-in-the-wall like Town?

He had business in Cincinnati tomorrow, big business he hoped, the beginning of a whole new facet to his rapidly growing enterprise. He figured a few intimate moments with his favorite coke-mistress would put him in the right mood. He could always count on Marie.

His fist thumped heavily on her door. When it elicited no response, he pounded again, harder this time in case she was sleeping.

He saw the curtains flutter briefly, then the door opened. Marie stood facing him. He could tell how badly she needed him. Her pale expression was tight and drawn, and her hands were visibly shaking. Oh, yeah. She needed the cocaine man. And this was her lucky day because he was feeling in a generous mood.

"You're lookin' good," he drawled as he brushed past her. "You musta known I was comin', huh?"

Marie was speechless.

A calloused grin spread across Joel's impish face. The names of other whores came and went in his mind, but he always remembered Marie. How could he forget? She had double-D tits and a butt that wiggled and jiggled as she worked her mouth between his legs with the suction of a vacuum cleaner. She didn't have the best cunt in the world. After all the years of overuse, it was loose enough to drive a freight train through. But she had an exceptionally tight ass, good for a real snug fit when she was willing, and she looked like she'd be extra willing tonight.

Joel stripped off his black leather jacket and folded it neatly over the back of one of her chairs. He was a small, wiry guy with a face only a mother could love, but in this business it didn't matter. Cocaine was a social stimulant unequaled by even Robert Redford's charm. And this—this was one of the perks of the job.

His smile broadened when he saw the sofa bed was already open and waiting.

"You want anything Joel?" she stammered. "I got whiskey and—"

"I don't need any of that shit," he cajoled. "I got this." He popped out a bag of white powder and dangled it in front of him. "Now, how about yoooou? Yoooou want some?"

"Oh God, Joel." A look of inner turmoil showed in her eyes. She was obviously trying to resist, but she didn't have much strength and the battle was short lived. "How much?" she whispered.

His smile widened again.

"I just got paid," she rattled on nervously. "I got four hundred dollars in the kitchen. I can get more—"

He held up his hand for silence. "We'll get to that in a minute."

Joel opened his zipper and pulled out his dick. "You want it, you're gonna have to show me how much." He'd been waiting all day for this. Sometimes he had trouble getting his willie to stiffen, but Marie could always affect the desired result. And if she was good—if she was veerry good—he had a little psychedelic treat in his pocket that would leave her buzzing for days.

She dropped to her knees as Joel crossed over. He thought he had rarely seen such an exquisite sight. He unzipped her blue dress, and she crawled out of it wearing only a pair of black panties. Before he could even lie down, her lips wrapped around his cock and she began sucking for all she was worth. It was a delightful display of feminine talents, he thought. If there were more women like Marie, the world would have a whole lot less problems.

Joel staggered backward and fell onto the sofa bed. There was only a brief interruption and a slight gagging sound as the tip of his cock brushed the back of her throat.

Joel propped himself up to enjoy the show. Hers was a fine performance. She was truly in form tonight. Her tongue darted up and down his rod, but it was the attention she paid to his reddened german helmet that particularly got him going.

Only it was much too fast. She was too anxious. Oh

yeah. He tried to hold back, but couldn't. He jerked spasmodically as he came in her mouth. Like an obedient little whore, her lips never left him until he was finished. Anything less would've been a waste of perfectly good semen.

As he lay panting, Marie scampered away on her hands and knees toward the bag of coke he'd deposited on the chair. He grabbed her arm and yanked her back.

"Not yet," he said hoarsely. He had seldom felt so right. She really had him going tonight.

"Joel, please," she begged, desperate to have her own relief.

"Not yet I said." He pushed her down on the bed and rolled her onto her face. "I want you like this."

He straddled her backside and spread her buttocks, admiring the view. She *was* one good-looking woman. Marie knotted her hands in the sheet and groaned. Just the way he liked it. . . .

Joel was so exhausted he could scarcely move. He lay motionless for a long while, enthralled with self-absorption over his relieved member. He was only distantly aware that Marie had gotten up and cut her own lines. She had probably taken a rather large snootful, but he didn't care. She'd earned it. In fact, she'd earned the other, too.

When he was able, Joel lurched to his feet and zipped up his pants. Marie lay like a mound of jelly under the table, with a glazed smile.

Disgusted, he took the coke from beside her and re-tied the bag. "I'm going to leave this here while I run some errands," he said threateningly and dropped it into the drawer next to the sofa bed. "I don't want you messin' with it. You hear me? I'll be back in a couple of days."

Her head nodded, but he wondered whether she actually had heard. It didn't matter. Before he left he carefully administered the psychedelic he'd promised. He smiled as she shivered, and tossed her a pillow to hug. He sincerely doubted she'd be on her feet before he returned, and if she was reaaal good next time, he'd give her some more.

Tuesday, June 20

. . . a living death . . .

Chapter Twenty

i.

Stephen was sleeping, utterly spent, his arms and legs entwined with Laura's, when he heard the phone ringing downstairs. The annoying sound barely registered in his mind, and he sank down deeper in the haven of sheets and pillows, Laura's body pressed warmly to his. They had both been exhausted by the time they had gone to sleep, having taken each other repeatedly until there was nothing left to give. Her head rested against his shoulder, her soft, honey blond hair tousled and sweet smelling next to his face, and he thought how lucky he was. They had shut out the world and found their own peace.

The phone finally stopped ringing downstairs, but the silence was even more disturbing. He realized that Abigail must've answered it, which meant the old woman had gotten up.

Stephen bolted upright. Laura lay still beside him, unaware of his movement.

He knew she didn't want her mother to know about their affair, so he cautiously swung his legs down and slid out of the bed, trying not to wake her. The silvery moonlight danced off her smooth, delicate curves. She was perfect. Not tempestuous and outwardly sexual like Kat had been, but nonetheless perfect, and he loved her. He wanted to embrace her and make love all over again, but instead he reached for the door.

His stout landlady was mounting the stairs, the old wooden steps groaning under her weight.

He approached the rail, keeping out of sight. "Mrs. Morton?"

She stopped and glanced up. "It's for you," she said groggily.

"I'll be right down."

The old woman nodded and turned around. He wondered whether or not she had heard his footsteps leaving Laura's room. If she had, she gave no sign of it.

He pulled on his jeans and T-shirt and hurried down to the kitchen. Abigail had left the light on. He picked up the phone. "Hello?"

"Steve, it's Professor Thompson." The old man's breathing was labored, coming in harsh little bursts. "I'm sorry to disturb you."

"No, no. It's all right. What's up?"

"Dr. Cook just called here. She's finished her work on the acetylene solution."

"Great."

"It might be, but she doesn't want to wait until morning to test it."

"What do you mean?" The fog was beginning to clear from his brain, and Stephen sensed the alarm in the old man's tone.

"She's worried that more lethal fumes from the TCBA will accumulate and be released before dawn, causing additional loss of life. She wants to use the solution immediately. She appealed to Chief Romero to get a team of his men to go out to the dump tonight, but the chief refused. He's concerned about his men. The visibility out there would be poor even with spotlights. It's treacherous ground, you saw that yourself. And the suits might get punctured in the dark. Dr. Cook phoned to tell me she's going out by herself."

"What did Romero say to that?"

"They can't stop her, but he won't risk any of his men."

Stephen ran his fingers through his disheveled black hair, pushing it out of his eyes. "I see. What do you want me to do?"

"Go to the city building and try to intercept her. It will take her a while to gather the equipment she needs. Reason with her. I admire the doctor's work and her dedication is tremendously heroic, but frankly she's acting far too hastily. She's too personally affected. I couldn't convince her of it in the office, but I'm sure there are other elements involved — volatile forces of nature. Dr. Cook is placing herself in grave danger. If she's already gone, you might consider taking one of the suits and meeting her at the dump. But please be careful. Don't leave yourself open to any danger."

"Okay. I'll get there as fast as I can."

Stephen hung up the phone and glanced at the darkened stairway. Laura was still sleeping and he didn't want to wake her to say good-bye. But each time he left, he feared he'd never see her again. It was too good to last. Something, *something*, always goes wrong.

After a moment's hesitation, he grabbed his keys and stepped out into the darkness.

ii.

The dump had to be sprayed. It was the only way, and the sooner the better.

It took all of Mildred's determination to proceed forward and begin loading her car. She had to fight herself for each step, pushing away the cruel memory of her daughter's savage, premature death. It had to be done. That was the one thought she kept ever present in the forefront of her mind and used to chase the others away.

She had absolute faith in the solution she had devised. She had tested it over and over since Thompson's departure. Through the lens of a microscope, she had watched as the acetylene particles sought out and attached themselves to the complex TCBA molecules, rendering the enigmatic poison impotent. It worked without fail every time. So she had no doubts about that.

As to the professor's theory of primitive evil forces within the earth, of course she couldn't be certain he was wrong, but facts were facts, and in this case they proved the acetylene worked. The rest was purely speculation, scientific mumbo-jumbo — voodoo of a sophisticated form — designed to explain the presence of evil and the origins of life. The old man was dying and anxious to leave his scholarly mark upon the world.

Well, he could damn well do it at someone else's expense, she thought. The people of this community had paid enough.

With grim conviction, she reached for a cardboard box and loaded into it one of the extra white lab suits that Thompson had ordered. The helmet and filter mask went into another. She carried them out to her car, using the side door to avoid disturbing the officers downstairs.

It had to be done. The suffering had to end. She swallowed her fear and stacked the boxes into her trunk. Then she headed back to the lab for the rest of her gear.

She had brought six sprayer units from her own research center in Mirror County. They were aerosol tank sprayers similar in size and likeness to the kind used for spreading insecticide and weed killer on lawns. These were not operated by a hand pump though, but by canisters of compressed air. Thus, they would work easily with only the barest amount of pressure on the handle.

Each unit had a harness attached so that it could be carried on the back. A pliable rubber hose, ending in a four-foot metal wand with a wide-angle nozzle, made it possible to stand up to twenty feet from the intended target.

She checked over the pressurized tanks. They had already been filled with the acetylene solution, and there were spare cylinders of solution stacked on the table behind her, a sufficient quantity to spray the whole town twice over. She would take two of the units with her and leave the rest. Two were all she'd be able to handle by herself, and it would be enough to diffuse over the entire dump, which was the only source of the TCBA they had found, other than the corpses themselves.

The tanks were heavy. She groaned as she lifted the first and took it out to her car. It would be difficult to maneuver with one of these on her back. There would be little chance of escaping anything that came after her. But a man would have the same problem. It made no difference that she was a woman.

Fear still gnawed at her belly, and it was a challenge to keep herself committed. It would've been all too easy to put this off on someone else, to wait for dawn like the police were inclined to do and ignore the reality that more lives might be lost. But for Mildred Cook, there was no choice. This vicious gas had claimed her only child, and it had to be destroyed before any others suffered the same shattering loss.

Life was such a precious gift. The idea that even one additional life might be lost was unacceptable to her. She was a dedicated researcher and had spent the last fifteen years striving to advance biotechnology so that one day man would not be so restricted by the boundaries that his family's heredity had placed on him.

The last of her gear was packed into her car. She shut off the light and stood alone in the darkness, surveying the shadowed room for anything she might've forgotten.

With a sigh of self-conviction, she closed the door behind her and locked it securely.

iii.

Stephen squealed to a stop outside the city building, parking haphazardly in a space. He jumped from the car, sprinted to the building, pulled open the old glass door, and raced along the darkened corridor, straight up the stairs to the room they'd been using as a lab.

The door was shut.

He tried the knob and found it locked.

"Damn!"

The sound of fragmented voices drifted up from downstairs. He hurried back to the first floor. The noise came from the room to the left, behind the stairs. Coke machines hummed along both walls, and he could smell coffee and food from inside. A faded print of Jesus at the Last Supper hung on the wall next to the door.

The four officers on duty looked up with surprise as he strode through the lighted entry. "Where's Mildred Cook?" he inquired.

Sgt. Christopher Williamson came forward, a styrofoam cup of milk and half a doughnut in his hands. "Upstairs," he said.

"I was just there. It's locked."

Williamson shrugged. "She was still working the last I knew. Come on. We'll take a look." He sat his food on one of the tables, digging the keys from his pocket as he went.

Stephen followed him up to the second floor again.

Williamson unlocked the door. It was dark in the room. Williamson called out: "Dr. Cook?" But it was clear she wasn't there. "She must've decided to call it a night," he said.

"I doubt it. The professor phoned me. She had finished her work and wanted to spray the dump tonight before any more toxic clouds could be formed. Romero turned down the idea, and Thompson told me she was planning to go alone if necessary."

"Shit. Do you think that's where she is?"

"There's a good chance of it."

Stephen yanked open the closet where the lab suits were stored and grabbed one, then a helmet and mask.

"Where are you going?"

"To see if I can talk her into returning," Stephen said. "If not, I'm going to try to help her."

"Hang on. I'll come, too. How do we put these things on?"

"I'll show you when we get there. Do you have any high-powered spotlights?"

Williamson checked the cabinet. "Dr. Cook must've taken them."

Stephen nodded. "That's good. At least she's well prepared."

"If I'd known what she was planning to do, I'd have stopped her."

"The lady was just doing what she felt she had to. Let's see if we can give her a hand."

"We can go out the side," Williamson offered. "I've got a cruiser in the lot. It'll be faster."

iv.

Mildred Cook swung her ten-year-old Plymouth through the rusted gate and up the steep gravel lane toward the dump site. Tiny pebbles spit from beneath her tires, bouncing off the underside of her car in a chorus of jarring pings.

Her fear was coiled and tight in the back of her

275

throat as she pulled away from the illumination of Town. There were no streetlights beyond the fence, only thick blackness pierced by the glare of her headlights, as though someone had taken scissors and cut holes in the night.

It was hard not to turn around and go back in spite of herself. She felt ashamed of her weakness in the wake of the brutal torment her daughter had endured. Horrifying scenes from the past few days punished her for her selfishness, blazed on her in instant color with vivid, gruesome detail, the detail that leaps out in a sudden flash of lightning.

She groped for something out of her past that she could use now to give herself courage. But there was little in the world that could compare with the deadly menace that might await her in the dark.

It had to be done. Now. Tonight. Before any more died.

She drove slowly over the crushed stones to the top of the hill, peering carefully into the gloom for the edge of the garbage pit, her hands painfully gripping the wheel. She stopped just in time, on the brink of the crater.

Wouldn't that have been something? she thought, if I'd have driven right in and gotten stuck. She laughed, nearly hysterical, then got herself under control. It would be too easy to let her fears carry her away. She had to get in and out of here as fast as possible.

She loosened her grip on the wheel and let her hands drop, going over the steps of her impending task, coolly and logically, in the precise order they needed to be done. Then she unlocked the door and went immediately to work.

The night air was warm and soothing like a soft blanket. Not a trace of wind. But the fetid, sickish-sweet odor of decay was everywhere.

She heard crickets chirping and glanced at the stars

as she unlocked the trunk. It was quiet, peaceful . . . a beautiful evening. No reason to be afraid. The calm air would be unlikely to blow a gust of the noxious gas in her direction. It would be all right, she assured herself. She was a survivor. Strong of mind and body.

She hooked a small emergency spotlight on the latch of the raised lid of the trunk, then removed the first of the tank sprayers from the dimly lit compartment, checking over the mechanical components. She pressed lightly on the handle of the sprayer to test it and smiled with relief as a thin coat of clear fluid spread over one of her tires.

Next, she took out the protective suit and began putting it on. The odd, shiny fabric felt cool to her touch. She struggled with the closures of the bulky garment. Another person was needed to assist with the fastening of the layered suit, but there was no one to help her. She tugged in frustration at the clasps toward the back that eluded her efforts to seal them.

In the difficult process of getting herself covered up, she hadn't noticed the distant buzzing, but she heard it now, loud and hauntingly clear. Her breath caught as she searched the heavy darkness, realizing from Myers's description that another burst of the corruptive vapor must be near.

To her left. A luminous mass of the most hideous color she'd ever seen swirled over the center of the pit like a low-lying fog. The color was impossible to name and no association came to her from anything out of the normal range of the spectrum, just the single word—evil. It seemed immensely evil even at a glance.

She was startled to see how close it was and how fast it was ascending toward her. There was no wind. How could it drift so quickly? What was propelling it?

She grabbed for the helmet, quickly slipping it over her head. There was no time to even begin to fasten it on. She could taste the bitter, cutting acidity of her own fear in her mouth.

Her gloved hand gripped the metal wand of the sprayer as the kaleidoscopic mass surrounded her, wavering, and pulsating like a beating heart. The vapor instantly invaded the gaps of her suit where she had not been able to fasten the closures. She was temporarily blinded by the sheen of the intense hue and taken aback by the overpowering pain, but she fought to maintain her hold on the wand of the sprayer, desperately willing her arm to turn the nozzle toward herself.

The deadly color crawled over her, seeping into her pores as she fell to her knees. She was rapidly losing the battle. She could feel her organs succumbing to the malign intruder, beginning to dissolve under the onslaught. Her body cried out in piercing torment. The buzzing mist was a roar in her ears becoming increasingly louder until she realized it was not a buzz at all but the agonized voices of a hundred souls screaming through her veins.

In a burst of momentary strength, she squeezed the trigger on the wand. A shower of acetylene washed over her as she collapsed to the ground, the spray canister careening out of her reach. All hope escaped her with the loss of the canister.

Then the glaring mist over the face plate of her helmet began to lessen. She thought she saw movement and struggled to turn her head, hoping against all odds that someone had come to rescue her.

Her gaze fell on the emptiness of the night and the great hulking black pit that lay before her. There was nothing to save her.

But the mist was disappearing, rising and moving away from her.

Why? Had the single shot of acetylene solution been enough to destroy it or had a breeze come up and changed its direction, causing it to float up into the dark sky?

It no longer mattered to Mildred. Her half-digested form bucked and jerked, her raw, violated nerves struggling against inevitable death. Her body was powerless to repair the fatal damage that had been done. A final guttural plea escaped her lips, but it fell upon an empty night.

Sergeant Williamson and Stephen sped toward the dump in the state policeman's patrol car. A mere sliver of the moon hovered over the sleeping town, and the welcome coolness of the early morning hour provided a temporary relief from the heat of the long summer days.

Speed was of the essence. Stephen tried not to let the need for sleep dull his mind. He rolled down the window, allowing the fresh air to blow roughly into his face.

He was filled with apprehension. A myriad of unstated fears and incomplete thoughts flooded his brain. There were so many questions they had no answers to. The situation was of such horrendous magnitude that it became incomprehensible at times. He could only imagine the mental turmoil that the woman scientist must've experienced before deciding to embark on her mission alone.

The scenery outside the window passed in a blur. The streets were deserted and blackened with the night. The familiar sights and smells gave him a rare sense of normalcy amidst the ruin, but also one of dread. The town seemed to be rapidly dying, drawing in upon itself and wasting away to nothingness.

They reached the road to the dump and Williamson turned through the gate, accelerating as he forced the vehicle up the steep hill. The beams from their headlights pierced the stream of dust they raised, briefly illuminating the dried broken weeds at the sides of the gravel lane and the spread of parched undergrowth around them.

They saw Mildred's Plymouth ahead and stopped abruptly. As Williamson cut the engine, both heard her cries and knew they were too late. The tortured sound came from only a few yards in front of them. Desperate, bone-grating shrieks of misery. They caught a brief glimpse of the iridescent cloud, the insidious swirling gas, rapidly disappearing into the murky darkness of the nighttime sky.

Stephen popped open his door and rushed toward Mildred. Williamson was right on his heels. Dr. Cook lay motionless on the ground next to the massive perimeter of the garbage heap. The pale light from an emergency lantern attached to the Plymouth cast an eerie glow on her white suit.

He dropped to his knees beside her. Her pale eyes gazed lifelessly past him. Stephen was shocked to see what appeared to be an unadulterated face behind the tempered glass mask. All of the other victims had been utterly ravaged. Then he saw the bottom half of her face, mostly hidden by her position, but not quite. It looked like it had been melted by an intense heat and was stuck to the side of her helmet by the gooey seepage. Several slow streams of pus mixed with blood had begun to trickle from the gaps of her suit that she had been unable to close. Even though the damage to her body was severe, there was one outstanding difference. She had not been entirely digested. The gruesome havoc wrought by the TCBA had mysteriously stopped mid-progress.

Stephen rose slowly, grieved by yet another death. So many had perished.

Already the air had begun to fill with the characteristically nauseating stench from the TCBA, but there was another pervasive odor lingering in the air also, that of acetylene.

Williamson stepped over and retrieved the spray canister. "Do you think she had time to spray anything?" he mumbled.

Stephen shrugged. "Not much time. But it does smell like she shot a good blast or two around, doesn't it? What do you make of this? Why do you think Dr. Cook's body reacted so differently to the TCBA than everybody else's?"

"I don't know," Williamson replied, "but I doubt we're any safer out here than she was. We can relay what happened to the professor and see what he thinks of it. We'll come back when it's light and we've got our suits on. It looks like these garments are worthless if they're not airtight."

Stephen nodded in agreement, acutely aware of their present danger. Mildred Cook was obviously beyond their help. Tomorrow they'd return and maybe it would all seem less threatening then.

Chapter Twenty-one

Dr. Michael Corliss's eyelids suddenly flew open. He mustn't let IT win. His eyes bulged wide with terror. It had taken all of his remaining willpower to break from the tenacious grip of the intense sleep he had lain in for nearly three days.

His gaze darted rapidly around the darkness in panic as he tried to determine his whereabouts. A narrow strip of light glowed under the door. And more light, faint and ghostly, sifted in through the blinds at the window.

It wasn't too late. He still had time to act. If only he could . . .

He shuddered as the icy fingers within his mind tried to claim him. The coppery taste of his own blood was in his mouth.

IT mustn't—

IT mustn't—

He was not in his own room. This was not his apartment. His heart pounded madly against the walls of his chest as he tried to determined his location.

He heard footsteps outside the door and thought they were coming for him, but then the footsteps faded away, down a long hall. He inhaled the pungent smell of antiseptics and from the yet-functioning parts of his memory identified his surroundings.

He was in a hospital. But why?

He tried to remember and couldn't. His head hurt. There was a terrible aching inside his brain that threatened to overtake his mind and wipe out his consciousness. He had to fight back, to will IT away.

IT wanted his soul.

Beside the bed he saw a tall metal stand holding a pair of I.V. bottles—the substance by which he was being kept alive. Narrow plastic tubing led to a needle in the back of his hand. Another tube was clamped on his penis, where he was attached to a catheter.

A thin hospital gown was draped decorously, but not very modestly, over his long, emaciated frame. He had lost even more weight than he had imagined. There was almost nothing left of his muscles. His sallow, loose skin revealed every crevice and joint in his feet and lower legs. His splindly arms looked like knotted tree branches.

IT was winning. Hour by hour IT was draining what was left of his resources, taking over his mind and corrupting his body. A few more hours and all would be lost.

If IT won—

He shook his head, denying the possibility. He had to act fast now that he finally understood exactly what was at stake. If only there was enough time.

He tried to lift his head and failed. He was too weak. The effort nearly overwhelmed him. The room spun. He felt light-headed, almost as though he were floating.

IT mustn't—

His strength was ebbing. There was so little left. . . .

Faint and trembling, he rolled to his side, then pushed up against the mattress, gritting his teeth and ignoring the sharp stabs that pierced his head. He managed to maneuver himself to a sitting position, though his brain swam in and out of blackness. Bright spots danced before his eyes like sudden explosions. His stomach dropped and bulged out as though he had swallowed a hard round mass, while all the liquid in his body rushed straight to his bladder. A vile burning fluid rose in the back of his throat.

He pulled his legs over the edge. His feet touched the floor and he fell to his knees. The I.V. stand toppled over on top of him. It struck his back, then clattered onto the cold tile beside him.

But he hardly noticed. His entire being was consumed by what was going on inside him. His whole body heaved, and a thick stream of hot, bubbly acid poured from his mouth. He curled onto his side as jet after jet of the putrid slime spewed out.

He didn't know how long he lay there, and for awhile he didn't care. The icy coldness raged through his body seeking revenge, making his arms and legs shudder as though struck by an electrical charge.

He was surprised that no one heard, but then he realized it must be several hours before dawn. The other patients down the hall would be asleep, and the night-shift attendants were probably gathered at the nurse's station drinking coffee and talking.

There was a button dangling from a cord next to his bed, and he could have pushed it to summon one of them, but he knew they would interfere with what he needed to do. They would want him to stay and keep on fighting. Only he knew what IT wanted, craved, had to have, and how devastating the results would be if IT won.

When the vomiting stopped, he pushed himself up, taking control, and yanked the I.V. out of his hand, then disconnected the bags attached to him. He lurched toward the bathroom. There was a light switch inside the doorway. He flipped it on—

Shards of pain shot through his brain and sent him reeling. He covered his eyes with both hands and whirled back against the toilet, falling onto the seat. He rocked and cringed until his eyes adjusted to the light.

He stood and wobbled toward the sink. He scarcely recognized his own image in the mirror. He had become a gaunt old man. Three days' worth of rusty beard clung to his hollow cheeks. His sandy hair hung lifelessly across his bony forehead. Each feature was sharp and ringed with folds of sagging skin. Only his eyes were bright, his pupils narrowed to fiery points.

He found his clothes in a locker beside the bathroom. The trousers were much too big now, even with the belt. He let his white shirttail hang out over the top. He was too weak to pull on his socks and merely slipped on his shoes without them. His keys and wallet lay on the shelf, but he couldn't remember if he had brought his car since he had no recollection of coming here. He wasn't even sure where he'd go or what he was going to do, only that he couldn't let IT win. He had to stop IT somehow and save the others.

IT mustn't—

He opened the door to the hall. The long corridor was empty, but he heard voices, soft and feminine, at the far end. He crept silently out of his room, down the hall toward an exit. The door opened onto a set of stairs. There weren't too many steps, only two flights. He would be able to manage. Slowly, tightly gripping the handrail, he descended to the first floor.

There would be a guard on duty at the emergency entrance, so he slipped around to the side and out into the visitors' parking lot. The night was cold. Bitterly cold it seemed in his deteriorated condition, with his thin arms and legs.

He shivered and hugged himself, wondering what to do now. He was free from the hospital confines, but he couldn't keep IT at bay much longer.

A dozen or so automobiles and one ambulance were parked in the lot. Beyond that there was nothing, except fields of corn. The hospital was located off the highway, out in the middle of nowhere. It might be several miles to the nearest farmhouse.

He hobbled across the asphalt, stepping between each car to see if the doors were locked. Country people seldom bothered with such big-city necessities unless they'd been shopping and had something of value inside. The second car he checked, a 69 Mustang with dented doors and plastic taped over one of the windows, was unlocked.

There were no keys in the ignition.

IT had eaten away part of his brain, so that there were gaps in his memory. He couldn't remember driving or what kind of vehicle he had driven. But from somewhere out of his past, he recalled that you could start the engine by reaching under the steering column and twisting the ignition wires together.

His fingers were weak, yet still nimble. The starter ground twice, then finally the Mustang roared to life. It was noisy and must've had several holes in the exhaust system, bound to attract attention. He had to get out of the lot fast.

He stepped on the accelerator and watched the red needle on the gas gauge move upward but not very high. There was less than a quarter tank of fuel if it was registering properly.

His head was whirling with pain. He backed the car out in jerky, zigzagging motions, trying to compensate for what his memory couldn't provide. He pulled onto the highway and headed south.

An oncoming car buzzed past in a glare of lights and a jarring whir of wind that nearly sent him off the road. He pressed on the accelerator, forcing the Mustang to go as fast as it could, and weaved across both lanes, struggling to keep control. Another driver honked angrily and drove onto the berm trying to dodge his efforts.

Then IT began ITs attack upon him in earnest, sensing that he was almost beyond endurance. The icy tentacles seized his major organs all at once, paralyzing him with ITs strength. An ear-splitting scream tore from his raw throat, and his mind went nearly blank. His eyes rolled in their sockets. He feverishly fought for control, unable to steer the vehicle.

He heard brakes slamming around him, and somehow went recklessly past. He caught only streaks of scenery through his fading vision.

The evil enveloped his brain. He spun the wheel again. The tires hit the gravel at the edge of the road and plunged the car back toward the center line. Then another spasm of searing agony wrenched through his middle, and this time his heart stopped.

The blood settled in his ears. He felt the deadly silence, watched in slow motion, without emotion, as the Mustang careened out of control toward a semi-trailer, prayed for a quick, merciful end. Death had to be quick . . . before the other. He was floating . . . floating . . . as the car burst into fiery flames that reached for the sky . . . and he knew no more. . . .

Chapter Twenty-two

i.

Stephen returned to the city building and slept on one of the couches inside the lounge. He was roused shortly before dawn by a light tap on the shoulder from Professor Thompson. The old man held out a cup of black coffee. Sergeant Williamson stood next to him carrying a decontamination suit.

Stephen immediately pulled himself up, forcing himself awake, and accepted the coffee. His mouth tasted like hell, and he desperately wanted a shower, but he could tell by their somber expressions that something more had gone wrong. "What is it?" he asked, bracing himself.

"Michael Corliss is dead," Thompson answered.

Stephen sat down the coffee. "What was wrong with him?"

"We're not sure," Thompson said. "Apparently he woke in the night. The nurse found the I.V. and the catheter on the floor, but Michael was gone. He must've been delirious. He took an orderly's car from the lot. It crashed head-on into a truck and burned. There was almost nothing left of the car. Witnesses said he was driving quite erratically before the accident."

"I don't understand it," Stephen muttered in disbelief.

"We don't know why he went into the coma, nor how he came out of it, but we think he was infected by the TCBA. A vast quantity of the same oily black substance found at the Evan Fielding house was discovered on the floor of his room. We don't know how or when the exposure occurred, but his body was in a state of utter collapse. The hospital tests had revealed that he was extremely anemic and that most of his organs were functioning at less than thirty percent. He couldn't have lived much longer."

The old man was clearly upset. His deep-set eyes were watery and red. "I want to thank you for your help last night," he added. "I know you both did all you could."

The words barely penetrated Stephen's mind.

"You okay?" Williamson asked.

"Yeah, sure. Are we going back out to the dump this morning?" Stephen asked.

The professor nodded. "We're going to continue with Dr. Cook's plan to spray it."

Stephen slid off the table and forced down the coffee, though he no longer desired it. He was given a suit by one of the men. Six of the state police officers, Williamson, himself, and Professor Thompson were prepared to go to the contamination site. They had only two spare suits left, but Thompson had requested more from the governor, and they were expected to arrive that evening.

The first rose-colored streaks of dawn were beginning to cross the sky as the group left the building carrying canisters of the acetylene solution. Several additional cars were parked against the curb next to the two beige state police vans they planned to take to the dump. For a moment Stephen was puzzled as to where the cars had come from; then a clump of reporters rushed up the steps to greet them. The story of the deadly happenings in the tiny community had finally become national news.

Their questions were primarily aimed at the professor because Chief Romero had not arrived yet this morning. Two patrolmen scurried out of the building and held the reporters at bay as the team climbed into one of the vans. The other was for retrieving Mildred Cook's body.

"I'm sorry," Thompson repeated to the throng of microphones thrust at him as he boarded the van. "We have no information for you. You can contact the authorities at the county hospital about Dr. Corliss's death."

"Was it connected to the others?" a female voice shouted.

"What is TCBA?"

Thompson shook his head. "Chief Romero will issue an official statement this afternoon. I'm sorry." The old man closed the doors behind him.

Williamson grinned at Thompson. They were seated on canvas benches across from each other. "You handled 'em like a pro," he said.

Thompson nodded and took out a handkerchief to blot his forehead.

Though the trip was short, Stephen found himself struggling to keep his eyes open. The couple hours of sleep he'd gotten last night weren't going to sustain him through the day.

They parked at the top of the hill beside Mildred's blue Plymouth. Her body lay nearby. It had continued to deteriorate, rupturing and filling with the venomous fluid that was a hallmark of this affliction.

"Such a waste," the professor said, leaning on his cane as he peered down through the face plate at what was left of her.

Stephen had to look away, swallowing his revulsion. "She wasn't like this last night. Her face was only partially gone."

"Yes, I know. I read Sergeant Williamson's report. Some blood and tissue was still intact. The acetylene might be responsible—if she had time to use it. Apparently the poisonous gas overcame her before she was ready."

"She was a sitting duck. She couldn't fasten her suit completely."

Thompson nodded. "But she might have been all right if she could've gotten a good shot at it before it reached her."

Two of the officers carefully folded a leather covering around her remains. They cautiously sealed the whole bundle inside a body bag and placed it in the back of the second van.

"Will spraying the dump solve the problem?" Stephen asked Thompson.

"I don't know. I'm still convinced there's another element at work here. Nonetheless, I'm praying the acetylene diffuses the TCBA and that its destruction eliminates the toxic vapor."

"Why isn't there any deadly gas now? Why isn't the air filled with it?"

"If it is indeed coming from the TCBA, as we have theorized," the old man explained, "then the gas would be formed in the ground. It would take time for the pressure to build up to the point where more of the lethal vapor would be released."

"You said *if* it's coming from the TCBA. You think there's a different source?"

"Possibly. You actually saw the cloud leave Dr. Cook's body, didn't you?" the professor asked.

Stephen nodded.

"Did it break up and disperse, or just drift away?"

Stephen shook his head glumly. "It happened so fast I couldn't tell."

The canisters sat ready in the center of the gravel

road. Williamson and the other officers were putting on their protective garments. Stephen and the professor began pulling on theirs as well. Stephen felt less ridiculous each time he wore it. Professor Thompson wouldn't be going in the dump himself, but intended to supervise the job from the sidelines.

Williamson came over as Stephen was almost done and double-checked the closures that were hard to reach. They were all painfully aware of how crucial it was that the suits be properly sealed. "It's looks okay," he finally announced. "We're all set."

Stephen was already beginning to sweat. It was going to be another long, grueling day. He walked over and slipped one of the harnesses that held the canisters over his shoulders. It weighed at least thirty pounds, but he was able to maneuver the wand easily.

The professor set up his makeshift lab again. When they were through spraying, they would immediately begin retesting the ground. No waiting would be necessary. If the acetylene was going to work, it would do the job instantly, as it had in the lab at the city building.

Even with seven men it took them over two hours to coat the entire pit. Then, they exchanged their empty canisters for trays of glass beakers and orange markers. The retesting went quickly and with good results.

"I believe, gentlemen," Thompson announced, "that we are as sure as we can be this area no longer has any active TCBA. In all the plugs I have tested the benzanthracene has reacted with the acetylene as well. But we cannot be certain that no other site of contamination exists. Chemicals can seep into the groundwater and leach into the surrounding earth. I was told that the original industrial contamination spread throughout Town and the neighboring farmlands.

"For safety's sake, Town and the adjacent area must be checked, especially where the creeks and runoffs may have carried the benzanthracene. It will be an enormous task. More suits should be arriving this evening, and you'll be able to put more men in the field. The governor is authorizing additional manpower, and a team of federal scientists should be here within a day or two. Until then, however, we'll have to do what we can."

ii.

Sgt. Christopher Williamson led his six men along the east side of Town Creek. They continually had to fight their way through the dense brush of dry vines and brambles. Though the bulky space-age suits were hot and uncomfortable, they provided a welcome layer of armor against the thorns.

The ground was cracked and hard from lack of rain, and Williamson couldn't help wondering whether or not a little precipitation might have helped their situation and kept this monstrous gas from rising and spreading so fast. It was midday, though, and there had been no sight of the deadly gas. A good sign.

Overnight, five more deaths had been reported in Mirror County and three in Town. The death toll was substantial, but he felt they were near the end. The acetylene solution was deactivating the TCBA, and without the TCBA there would be no more poisonous clouds. Soon, he thought; as soon as we get the last of this area sprayed.

Williamson stayed in contact with Captain Romero on a hand unit, periodically reporting their progress. He had been told that the National Guard had arrived and would be joining them shortly. Everything was progressing smoothly so far, but that did not ease the tension among his men. They had seen what this thing could do, and they were not convinced it was over yet,

293

not when it still might mean their lives.

John DeSulto came up behind Williamson as he sprayed the bank and affectionately punched his padded shoulder. "I'd give my right arm for a cigarette now. How about you?"

"I'm okay." Rivulets of sweat washed down his elfish face.

"Right, Superman. You look like somebody turned on a shower in there." DeSulto laughed, pointing at the sergeant's sweat-soaked face and the coarse strands of brown hair that hung limply over his forehead.

Williamson grinned in spite of himself, longing to wipe the moisture from his eyes. "Come on. Let's keep moving. There's a lot of ground to cover."

"For Christ's sake, it's gonna take a week to spray this whole place. I'm not complaining, but—"

"Yeah?"

"Yeah!" DeSulto paused and his voice got suddenly serious. "Say, Chris, you think these suits will really protect us if we run into a patch of this shit? I mean, you know, this would be a piss-hole of a place to die. Am I right?"

Williamson studied DeSulto a moment, trying not to reveal his own fears. He had no idea if the suits were actually safe. He had only the captain's word for it, who was simply going on what the professor had said. But nobody really *knew*. Williamson had worked with DeSulto before, and the latter was always nervous under fire. Williamson worried that DeSulto's anxieties would spread to the others.

"Come on, DeSulto," he barked. "Get your ass in gear. A few more minutes and I'll start to think you're chickening out."

"Me? When have you ever known me to go chicken? Huh?"

Williamson huffed. "There's always a first time."

"No. Not me, man. I don't need this cheap shit."

DeSulto walked away grumbling and began spraying the ground under the brush.

Williamson smiled. He'd buy DeSulto a drink and apologize when all this was over. Right now, they had to get the job done.

He went back to work, leaving the creek bank and hacking his way farther into the woods. The professor had run his test on this ground and a couple of plugs had revealed extremely minute traces of benzanthracene. They hadn't found any TCBA at all, but three kids had died along here so they weren't taking any chances. The entire woods and creek bank were scheduled to be sprayed.

The task became almost routine as Williamson and his men chopped paths through the thick wood and coated the ground with acetylene. It was hot and sweaty and mostly boring. He was fairly successful at blocking the dangerous aspects of the job from his thoughts and letting his mind wander to more pleasant subjects—to his wife and kids.

He and Edwina had been separated for nine months, since he was shot during a robbery in progress. It was only a tiny graze in his right forearm that healed quickly. It wasn't much, but it wasn't the first time, and Edwina had taken the kids and left. She said she'd had enough and gave him an ultimatum: her or the job. He'd chosen the job, and things had pretty well iced over between them. Then last week she'd come over, wanting to talk, and had ended up staying the night.

Now it looked as if they might be getting back together again, and Williamson was pleased. He missed the kids, and he missed Edwina. Thinking of them made the heat and tension more bearable.

He peered up briefly at the men in front of him. All well . . .

A sudden cry: "God, look out!"

Williamson froze, his brain instantly alert, eyes taking in the whole area at once.

"Over here! Quick. It's coming at me! Oh God!"

Tim Garber was screaming at the top of his lungs in panic, hidden by the trees to Williamson's right.

Chris and the men around him headed toward the sound at a dead run, shoving their way through the low-hanging branches and vines. They could hear the loud buzzing and Tim's cries, imagining the worst.

When they got there, Garber was rolling on the ground in a narrow space between the trees, and the glowing vapor—a huge spiraling mass of gruesome color—was all over him.

Chris stood back and grabbed hold of the wand on his tank unit. He began spraying a shower of acetylene over the downed patrolmen. The others did the same. A rain of acetylene fell through the branches and leaves, covering them all.

Tim continued rolling, trying to get away, but the swirling cloud stayed right on top of him.

"Take it easy," Chris shouted above the noise. "We'll get him out of there."

Then Chris noticed the iridescent gas was changing color, becoming less bright, and there was something—something in the middle of it.

Jesus Christ. His stomach lurched. There was a second man inside the evil mist. Only the outline of his head and one leg were visible. Slowly more of him began to take shape. Chris could seen an arm, a shoulder. Then . . . then the limbs began to waver like a hologram, particles of his flesh weaving in and out of focus until it became obvious the man *was* the mist, or a part of it.

Shit! What the hell was it? "Keep spraying," Williamson yelled.

The man continued to take form. He was dressed like a farmer, wearing jeans and a flannel shirt, but he could have been the devil himself as far as Chris was concerned. The man's flesh was almost translucent, the awful hue of the luminous gas showing through the thin surface of his skin. His cheeks were hollow and sunken. His eyes were two black holes set into his face, promising of death by torture, of hot burning damnation for the soul. His mouth contorted into a savage snarl.

The image was vanishing, and the insidious color was regaining its intensity.

They continued to spray it, the onslaught of acetylene never letting up. Chris shouted instructions to his men, acting more out of instinct than anything else. He had been trained to keep his cool no matter what, but the whole scene was beyond belief.

The malign cloud was drifting upward, away from Garber. Williamson and his men turned the nozzles of the units up, but it was soon above the trees and beyond their reach.

Williamson dropped the wand and plunged forward, falling to his knees beside Tim. He tugged urgently at the fastenings on Garber's helmet and pulled off the trooper's headgear.

Tim's face was covered with tears and red from yelling, but he looked okay. He was still screaming and clutched at Williamson's suit. "I couldn't see! I couldn't see! I could hear them screaming."

"It's all right," Chris crooned, holding the patrolman against his chest. He looked up at DeSulto, who stood paralyzed with fear. "Call Romero," he said. "Tell him what happened."

DeSulto yanked the handset from his belt and shouted the emergency call numbers into it.

Williamson rocked Tim in his arms. Thank God he was unharmed, because if he hadn't been, Williamson didn't think he could live with it. Not after letting them believe the suits were safe.

iii.

Williamson turned to the captain. They were gathered in Foss's old office at the city building. "I wouldn't have believed it if I hadn't seen it for myself," he said flatly.

Tim Garber sat in the center, opposite the desk. "I heard screams," he repeated frantically, his hands still shaking uncontrollably. "Like people were caught in there. Jesus forgive me, it was the most horrible sound I've ever heard. I thought I'd been swallowed alive. Like being in the belly of a whale. I could feel its heart beating."

Williamson handed him another cigarette and lit it for him.

"Thanks."

The other four troopers stood stiffly at the back of the room, DeSulto the closest to the door, awaiting the verdict. They had all recounted their story.

Captain Romero looked askance at his men, as though he thought they were suffering from mass insanity and shared the same incredible delusion. The six state troopers shifted uncomfortably under his gaze. But Stephen had watched the professor's expression as they had related their experience. It was as if a fire had been lit inside the hunched old man.

Thompson thumped across the room with his cane and leaned against the large walnut desk in front of Garber. "What happened when you sprayed the gas, after you saw the shape of this man in the vapor?" he asked the group.

Williamson answered. "It seemed like . . ." He paused, trying to find words to describe what he'd seen.

Dr. Thompson waited patiently for him to continue.

"It seemed like the color got weaker, less bright. The man never formed all the way. Just pieces of him. Like a distorted reflection. Then the color got brighter again, and the man disappeared."

"You kept up the spray the whole time?" the professor persisted.

"Yes. It was all we could do. At that point we didn't know whether or not it had gotten to Tim."

Thompson nodded. "I understand. And the cloud drifted away—intact?"

"Yes."

Romero folded his arms across his chest, obviously perplexed. His shoulders sagged, and he shook his head. "I'm at a loss for words. I don't know what to say. It sounds incredible."

The professor agreed. "But I believe your men have given us an accurate account of what they saw. In fact, I think this finally gives us some of the answers we've been looking for. After I left the creek bank this morning, I came back to the lab. The floor of the cow's pen was covered with the same black residue we've found at several of the sites, including Michael Corliss's hospital room."

Romero raised his eyebrows. "He was definitely infected then?"

Thompson nodded.

"How was he able to leave the hospital? I thought death was instantaneous."

"Like the animals we tested in the lab, Michael contacted the liquid TCBA, not the vapor. I went to his office this afternoon and accessed his personal files."

The professor picked up a sheaf of computer paper from the desk. "Michael was a good researcher. He kept his own account of the incident and how it affected him in minute detail. The rats were too small to give us adequate results, but the cow is closer in size to a man and apparently able to withstand the initial

299

poisoning from the compound, which the rats were not."

Stephen could tell that in spite of everything, Thompson had a great deal of regard for Corliss.

Romero flipped through the stack and cleared his throat. "How did it happen?"

"From contact with bodily fluids on the girl's corpse, Sallie Ann Henderson, before he had any idea of how corrosive it was. It burned through his glove."

"Why didn't he tell anyone?"

"He didn't know exactly what it was he was dealing with at first. And he was afraid, I suspect."

Williamson interrupted. "I still don't understand. What does this have to do with the man we saw in the cloud?"

The other five state patrolmen waited silently.

"I believe the man you saw is also a victim of TCBA, probably having contacted it from the dump, which is the only active source we've found, other than the corrupted corpses.

"The liquid TCBA has an entirely different effect upon the body than the gaseous form. The liquid is actually a combination of TCBA and the primitive evil force I spoke of before. It acts as a parasite. It has no body of its own, and therefore needs a host. Though this force has always been present within the earth, it was previously latent. It was the improper disposal of the benzanthracene that enabled all of this to take place. The force caused molecular changes in the chemicals present at the dump. After that, all it needed was a host, any unfortunate who happened to touch the TCBA with his flesh—the man you saw in the mist. At that point, the balance of good versus evil was tipped, and this mutation of nature was able to begin feeding upon humanity. If it isn't stopped . . ." The professor paused. "Let it suffice to say it must be stopped."

"But how could a man become a mist?" Williamson asked.

"The man is no longer human. He doesn't live as we live. This mutation sustains its existence by feeding off of that which has life, drawing its strength from the energy of its victims, perhaps even consuming their very souls. The voices you spoke of —." He nodded toward Tim Garber, and the young patrolman shuddered.

"If you read Michael's notes, you see that his initial burn from the contact healed, but the 'disease' as he referred to it did not go away. It spread inside him like bacteria, multiplying until it eventually overtook him. Not just his body, but his mind as well."

The others remained silent, so Thompson continued. "The parasite imprisons its host, forcing him to become an ally in its grisly quest. Condemning the host, if you will, to a living death. Together they share one body. It and its host are virtually inseparable. The old vampire legends about the undead and men who turned into bats would be analogous here. During the feeding process, the mist apparently weakens and the host man materializes. This is the man Angela Stoddard struggled with and Sheriff Foss shot at. It is his hair that Louise Simmons clutched in her hand. I suspect that the host also materializes at other times, and that it was this original man, Evan Fielding, who broke into the Gorkenoff's attic. Evidently, he consumed his family, then went in search of more prey. Dr. Corliss killed himself to avoid such a fate.

"As it digests its prey, this creature leaves behind some of its own enzymes in the 'used' portion of its victims, like we would leave droplets of our saliva on a chicken bone. The enzymes are similar to our own only much more powerful. It also leaves traces of TCBA, which is the component that gives it the ability to digest living cells. It is these enzymes and the TCBA which corrupt the victim's body."

The room was quiet when Thompson finished. Stephen was as awed as the rest, but he had seen the hideous mass and heard the horrifying, pulselike buzzing that swelled within it, that could easily have been a chorus of voices or the mad beating of a heart. However unlikely the explanation might have seemed a week ago, it now made perfect sense, terrifyingly perfect sense. Slowly Stephen came to realize that all the professor had said about the nature of the crisis was true.

Apparently, Williamson did, too. His question was blunt and straightforward, but not without an edge of desperation. "How can you kill a man that is able to change to a vapor at will?"

"I think the key to that lies in the fact that the acetylene was able to weaken the cloud and cause it to return to a human shape for a while. I'd like to work on strengthening Dr. Cook's formula and see if we can't come up with something that would have a more permanent effect."

"You mean something that would cause it to permanently become a man?" Williamson asked.

"Yes."

"But it wouldn't really be a man."

"True, but it might be more vulnerable. It's a place to start." Thompson looked drained. "We're dealing with more than one cloud mass. The Ellises at the mortuary were probably infected. I imagine there are others, too. The entire population of the area will have to be accounted for. We should continue to use the acetylene to spray the surrounding land and cut down on any further chance of additional contact with the TCBA. The corpses that have already been buried will need to be exhumed and decontaminated."

"I want the rest of the population evacuated," the captain said. "Everyone who is not essential to the project."

"Some of them won't go," DeSulto said.

302

"That will be their choice for the moment. We can't force them until we get permission from the governor to declare martial law."

Chapter Twenty-three

The new stuff Joel had given her was great, but the low that had followed was worse than anything she'd previously experienced.

With legs of rubber, in a room that wouldn't stop spinning, Marie crawled across the rug to the huge bag of coke he'd left and helped herself to more. She didn't know how long she'd been wired and didn't care. She was still naked, Joel's come dried between her legs, her hair uncombed, the bed unmade, but none of that mattered as she buried her nose in another clump of the lily white powder.

She had only to get higher and higher to make the whole world go away. She inhaled deeply. This was the best moment of her life, and she hadn't really thought about what would happen when it was over. There was no reason to, yet. She'd only used a fraction of the bag, and one way or the other she'd pay Joel back; she always did.

She heard someone pounding at the door and lifted her face from the table, feeling the mystical euphoria explode in her mind.

"I'm coming," she rasped, her voice dry and raw from dehydration.

The pounding continued. It was probably Joel again, and she was ready. He could have or do anything he

304

wanted. She didn't care.

She pushed herself up and staggered toward the entrance, grabbing her robe from the bed and draping it carelessly over her shoulders. She stepped over the pile of rumpled blue fabric where her dress and panties lay and thought about what kind of pose she could strike for him as she answered the door in the buff. He'd love that.

She pulled open the door, one hand on her hip, exposing her naked torso beneath the robe. But the smile died on her lips.

Her mind carouseled with surprise. It was Bill.

His eyes darkened and flashed with murderous rage.

She knew she must look as high as she felt and stumbled backward in panic, her mouth agape, struggling to think of a lie. Any lie. She reeled back further as he lumbered toward her. He was going to kill her. She'd tried to quit. She really had. But Bill wouldn't listen. He didn't understand.

"I only had a little," she stammered, bumping into the wall behind her. "Just enough to help me sleep."

"In the middle of the day!" he shouted.

Tears sprang to her eyes. She couldn't think. There was no place to hide. No way to get away from him. She pulled the robe closed in an attempt to cover her nakedness.

"Look at you!" he shrieked. "You're nothing but an animal, a goddamned pig." He lashed out and caught her shoulder with his right hand, slamming her into the wall.

A cry of shock tore out of her mouth, and before she could stop herself, she was yelling and shaking her finger at him.

"Get out! Get out of my house, you bastard. I hate you."

"I'll get out when I'm goddamned ready." He grabbed the front of her robe in his giant fists and

305

threw her against the wall again.

Her skull collided with the flat surface, and a sharp pain cut through the haze of cocaine. She dropped to the floor, screaming, unable to defend herself against the torrent of blows that followed. She huddled in a ball and shielded her face with her arms. She was too high to maneuver; she could only crouch there and weep.

"You promised!" he bellowed. "You fucking promised. Doesn't a promise mean anything to a bitch like you?"

"I tried," she sobbed. "I did. Stop. Please. Oh God, Bill. I tried."

The blows suddenly ceased, and she looked up and saw him removing his belt and wrapping the buckle around his fist like a whip.

She swallowed the fear that threatened to close up her throat and begged. "Bill . . . you know how I am. I get the shakes. I can't—"

He swung back his arm.

She raised her hands too late.

The belt struck her face and her mouth filled with blood. She coughed and gagged, reeling inside, unable to believe this was real. It must all be a dream. A bad hallucination.

Then he yanked her up off the floor again and held her face only inches from his own. "I've had it," he spat. "I've had all the goddamn shit one man can take."

"No, Bill—"

He heaved her onto the bed, and she quickly rolled over. But before she could rise, he lashed out again with the belt, hitting her whichever way she turned. The leather snapped and whistled through the air, landing with biting strength on the soft flesh of her legs, back, shoulders, and stomach. She rolled and rolled, but there was nothing she could do to escape the brutal slaps.

She twisted and thrashed, crying out in pain. "Oh God. Stop. Please, stop. I'm sorry."

But the beating continued until she thought she'd pass out. Then he suddenly quit. She lay on the bed gasping, the welts that covered her body aching and beginning to swell.

Slowly she raised her head, terrified of what he was going to do next. She brushed the cascade of red hair from her face. He had found Joel's cocaine. He held it in his hand as though somebody had vomited on it.

"Bill, I—"

"Is this what you want?" he yelled. "It this it?"

"No, I—"

She screamed as he grabbed her hair and jerked back her head.

His huge frame towered over her. "I said, is this what you want?"

"Yes, damn it!"

His fist slammed into her jaw, and she thought she would die. She lay stunned as he pried open her mouth and shoved the entire bag in. The plastic touched the back of her throat and she started to gag. She couldn't breathe. Her air was cut off. She flailed her arms and kicked her legs, but he held her pinned to the mattress, a smile on his face.

"It's good, huh?" he said, leering down at her as her eyes bulged and her face turned purple. "Oh, you like it. You really like it. Tell me how good it is." Then he laughed and let go.

She ripped the bag from her mouth, the plastic tearing on her teeth and spilling cocaine over the bed.

He pulled out his .357. "This is it," he promised. "No more. Not for you. Not for me. I'm gonna fix you the only way I know how." Then he aimed the barrel at her forehead.

Crazed, with nothing but sheer panic in her mind,

307

she lunged for the gun, yelling. The top of her head hit his hand and sent the shot into the ceiling.

They both fell onto the floor, her on top. He fired again and hit the wall. He was as least ten times stronger than she, and she knew he was going to kill her. She was fighting for her life. She grabbed a bottle of whiskey from near the edge of the bed and struck him across the face.

He howled as the glass shattered and a bright garden of red sprung from his nose and cheeks.

She scrambled to her feet, running madly toward the rear of the house. She had to escape. She had to get away, anywhere. But there was no place to go. She flung open the bathroom door and locked herself inside, sobbing and shaking, out of her head with fear.

Then she heard him coming and crouched in a corner of the shower, not knowing if the door would stop him.

"You fucking whore!" he screamed and threw himself at the door.

The wall shook, but the frame held.

He tried twice more, then she heard gunfire, and bullets tore through the door, wood splintering and firing into the air. She screamed and buried her face in her knees. The mirror exploded. Bits of glass flew from the counter and hit the wall. It seemed an eternity before the noise ended, but the silence was just as frightening.

She could hear him breathing on the other side.

"Marie?" His voice sounded as though it were in the same room with her, soft and scared. "Marie! Can you hear me?"

She held her breath, hoping he'd think she was dead.

Finally, he let out a gut-wrenching cry, and she heard his footsteps retreat down the hall, then out the front door. She heard the engine start and tires squeal.

He was gone.

By the mercy of God, he was gone. She sagged on the bottom of the shower stall and wept.

Chapter Twenty-four

i.

Stephen swung open the screen door on the front porch of the boardinghouse. So much had happened in the past eleven days. He was filled with the urgency and danger of the situation. The wild ramblings of Tim Garber and Professor Thompson talking of captive souls rung in his mind. "It feeds off others . . . imprisons its hosts . . . condeming him to a living death . . . If it isn't stopped . . ."

The quiet, peaceful community of Town had become a hell of living torment. Like when you split the apple and saw that the interior had all gone bad, there was no good here. Not any more. No one was safe. Death stalked the streets.

It was imperative that Laura get away. That they all get away. Today. Now.

He rushed through the hall, stopping to glance in each of the rooms, but they were all empty. Then he saw her in the kitchen on the phone, leaning against the counter with her back to him. Slender and curved. She was wearing a tight pair of jeans and a sleeveless blouse. Her clean blond hair hung loose on her shoulders. So beautiful and innocent, yet she aroused such great desire in him.

He had no words to describe his feelings. He had the

310

same sense of longing every time he saw her. It was different than what he had felt for Kat. Kat was bold and enticing. She had lived and died in a world of moment to moment. Laura was someone he could feel secure in, someone he could cherish. This feeling had been badly missing from his life for so long. He couldn't take the chance of losing her now.

She smiled when she saw him, still talking into the phone, and held out her hand. He took it and slid his arm around her waist, burying his face in the silkiness of her neck. Her skin was like satin. When he touched her, she trembled and pressed herself closer. He wanted to hug her to his chest and never let loose.

"I have to go, Mrs. Murphy," she said, shutting her eyes as his fingers rubbed over her blouse. "I'll tell Mother you called when she gets back. Good-bye."

She hung up the receiver and melded into his embrace. "Oh you," she moaned. "I'm so glad to see you."

Her lips parted and her tongue thrust into his mouth. Their bodies strained to get closer, clinging to one another with instant need. He couldn't stop himself. All day there had been nothing but fear and uncertainty, and now she was in his arms. Now was all that mattered. Now. Now. Now. There was only now.

The whole lovely length of her pressed against him, and he could no longer stand it. His fingers tore at her clothes, slipping out the buttons on her blouse. It didn't matter that it was daylight and they stood in the middle of her mother's kitchen.

She was pulling him down on the floor and he went gladly. He wanted her to do more. Then the professor's words began to ring in his head again—"if it isn't stopped"—and he got control of himself at last.

"We can't do this," he whispered, lying on top of her. "There isn't time."

She kissed his lips. Her hands were on the zipper of

311

his jeans, and she wasn't listening. It was maddening, wanting her and knowing the danger they were in. "Laura, you have to pack. You have to get out of here."

"Tomorrow," she promised.

"No, now." He grasped her hands and gently pulled them away. "Laura, please. The situation in Town is extremely volatile."

"I need you, Steve. I'm frightened, and I need you." She flung her arms around his neck and kissed his face. "I don't care about anything else."

"I can't stand the thought that something might happen to you. They've ordered an immediate evacuation, and I want you to go."

She buried her face against his shoulder. "Are you leaving too?"

"No, I can't. I'm going to stay and—"

"I won't leave without you. Don't ask me to."

"For my sake."

"No."

"Please."

"No, no, no."

"Laura . . ." He sought out her mouth and kissed her deeply, their tongues meeting. "Laura, Laura . . . I love you."

He could feel her breasts through her bra, pressing against his chest. She took him in her hands and wrapped her legs around him, and he was overwhelmed once more by the power of her love. Blood rushed through his temples. He cast all reason aside as she dug her fingertips into his shoulders and pushed against him. The need was too strong.

Then the telephone rang.

Stephen jumped up as though someone had walked into the room.

"Let it ring," she whispered, holding him tight.

"No, I can't. I told them I would be here in case—"

She cut off his words with her mouth as the phone rang a third time.

He knew it was mad. They were both insane. He struggled free, pulling up his jeans, and staggered to the phone. "Myers, here," he said heavily, catching his breath, aching inside.

His head cleared immediately when he heard a woman's sobs on the other end. "Who is it?"

She was coughing and crying, trying to stop.

"Marie?"

"Bill was here," she stammered.

"What happened?"

"Oh God . . . oh God . . ." Her voice choked, and the sobs started again. "I don't know what I'm going to do."

He looked over at Laura. She had straightened her clothes and was opening the cupboard to make supper. She knew about his involvement with Marie's problems and didn't approve. The two women came from totally different worlds.

It was several moments before Marie could speak, and he knew it must be bad. He remembered the last time. Finally her cries lessened. "It was my fault," she managed to say. "I was high. Really stoned."

"Are you hurt?"

"I don't think so, but he shot the place up. I don't know what he's going to do when he finds out I'm not dead."

"Listen, I'm coming over."

"It was my fault."

"We'll talk when I get there, okay? Five minutes."

"Yeah."

Stephen hung up the phone. Laura stood at the stove. "Don't go," she said flatly. "Let her get herself out of her own mess. You don't owe her anything."

313

"She's a friend."

"She's trouble. I told you before. And I wasn't wrong, was I? She could call the police. She doesn't need you." She slammed down a pan on the burner, then filled it with water. "Marie lives the way she wants to. She's only sorry because she has to pay the fiddler's bill. Well, let her."

"It isn't that easy sometimes."

"I know. I don't want to sound heartless. It's just that I don't want to see you get involved. You can't help her. She has to do that for herself."

"Maybe she's trying. I'm not her judge."

"You're not her keeper, either, damn it. I don't trust her. She's a user. She's after something."

Stephen walked over to the stove. "I'm sorry. It's not my intention to hurt you."

Laura turned around to face him. "But you're going to see her anyway."

"Yes."

"Fine, and what about me? Shall I keep the soup hot in case you return for a bowl?"

He reached for her hand.

"Don't touch me," she hissed and spun away from him.

She leaned against the sink and stared out the window in silence for several seconds. When she spoke, her voice seemed distant. "We never made each other any promises, did we?"

"Laura, I—"

"Please don't. Let's drop it for now. It's all right. My feelings haven't changed. I'm just not sure what I want." She smiled stiffly. "I'll see you whenever you get back."

Stephen nodded; then, after a moment's hesitation, he opened the door and left.

Laura still stood at the window.

Stephen parked in front of Marie's narrow two-story. He didn't see any other traffic, and there was no sign of Bill Leland.

He looked over the house and had to admit it was one of the more run-down homes on the block—or in all of Town for that matter. The bushes and trees were scraggly and overgrown; there were no flowers in the garden; the fence was falling down; shingles were missing from the roof. If she didn't put in a few repairs on it soon, the whole thing would come tumbling down on top of her.

Stephen still had the .38 Foss had given him to go after Cal Stoddard. He pulled it from the glove compartment of the Mazda, along with an extra clip of ammo, and tucked it safely in his belt. If Leland wanted another fight, this time he'd be prepared.

From the front stoop he could hear her crying. The doorbell was out of order, so he pounded on the wood surface. When no one answered, he shouted, "Marie! It's Steve. Let me in."

He heard her struggling with the locks and sobbing. "I can't get it! I can't get it!"

Finally she flung open the door and staggered back, blinking away the daylight. She covered her eyes and nearly lost her balance.

In spite of his past experience with drug addiction—some of it personal—Stephen was taken aback by her appearance. She reeked of alcohol. Her red hair was disheveled and snarled and fell across her face in a tangled web. There was white powder clinging to her chin and spilled down her front. She was wearing a leopard-spotted robe that gaped in the middle and black lace panties, no bra. Red welts swelled across her face and abdomen.

He took her elbow and moved inside, closing the door and locking it behind him. The sofa bed in the living room was open, its rumpled sheets tossed on the floor. He saw traces of blood on the mattress, and a spot of it had soaked into the carpet, beside a broken bottle and a pile of shattered glass.

He led Marie around the bed and let her fall into a chair. "I'm going to make some coffee," he said tersely.

She nodded, her head in her hands, and began to cry again.

He headed out to the kitchen and found a pot half-filled with cold, stale coffee on the cupboard. He dumped it out. The sink was heaped with molded dishes, the same ones that had been here on his previous visit. He scrubbed the percolator and started a new pot.

There were several empty liquor bottles stacked on the table. He wondered how long it had been since she'd consumed anything other than alcohol, coffee, coke, and an endless string of cigarettes.

He moved down the hall to get something to clean up the blood on her face. The bathroom door was pierced with at least six bullet holes. Inside, the mirror above the vanity was shattered and there were five or six pockmarks in the wall. Leland must've gone completely berserk, he thought. The shower stall was still intact. That must've been where she stood during the shooting.

He reached over and turned on the hot water to let it warm up, then strode back out to the living room.

Marie still sat in the same chair, weeping. She'd gotten herself a bottle of bourbon. She tipped it up, missed her mouth, and cried as most of it ran in dribbles between her breasts.

"Come on," he said, taking her hand firmly but not roughly and pulling her to her feet. "You're going to take a shower."

She swayed unsteadily, and he caught her around the waist to keep her from falling. "I wanna drink," she sobbed. "Get me a drink. I'm so thirsty."

"Not now."

She latched onto his neck and pushed her tear-stained face against his shoulder. "Don't hurt me," she whispered. "Please don't hurt me."

"I'm just taking you to the shower," he repeated.

He sat her down on the toilet stool, while he adjusted the water temperature. She huddled abjectly against the wall and moaned.

There were no towels in the linen closet, only a box full of old medicines. He checked in the kitchen and found a couple of towels that weren't too dirty piled on top of the washing machine.

When he got back, Marie's head hung limp in the corner between the toilet and the wall, and he thought maybe she'd passed out. Her eyelids fluttered.

"Come on," he coaxed, putting her arms on his shoulders. "Just a little shower."

She mumbled incoherently to Bill as she pushed the leopard-spotted robe off her shoulders.

He cringed at the sight of all the bruises on her body. The bastard had worked her over good, but it didn't appear that she was seriously injured. She didn't need a doctor, only compassion.

"Come on," he coaxed, putting her arms on his shoulders. "Just a shower."

She clung to his neck as she stood, shivering, barely aware of where she was.

He laid the .38 from his belt on the counter, then walked her toward the shower, with little choice except to step in with her.

She gasped as the spray first hit her back and clutched him tighter about the neck, screaming.

"It's all right," he crooned, holding her against his chest and easing her further under the nozzle. "It's only water."

The moisture coursed down over both of their faces and soaked his clothes, but it seemed to help her. He saw some of the life coming back into her hazel eyes. She kept her stranglehold on his neck and tipped her head back under the spray.

"That's it," he said, smiling. "You ever take a shower with your clothes on before?" he asked to see if she understood him.

She shook her head.

"Me either," he laughed. "You know you're pretty when you're wet?"

She smiled, acknowledging the compliment, and pressed her cheek against his. He held her close as the water ran down between their noses, knowing she needed the reassurance of someone who cared for her. He didn't feel guilty about Laura, for this had nothing to do with their relationship. It was a special kind of friendship, like the one he had had with Kat long before they had even thought of becoming lovers.

He found the shampoo in a wire rack at the side of the stall and carefully, without letting go, shampooed her long red hair until it felt squeaky clean.

"How's that feel?" he murmured, holding her to his chest.

"Wonderful."

She hugged him tightly as he helped her from the shower and sat her back on the stool. He grabbed one of the towel's from the floor and wrapped it around her. She sagged like a rag doll with her head on his shoulder, nuzzling his neck.

"You know you're not making this any easier?" he

teased.

She merely nodded her head and stroked his face with her hand.

"Come on. That's enough." He bundled her up in the towel and carried her to her bedroom.

The room was clean, though worn and shabby looking. On her dresser, solid wood but cheap like they made in the fifties, were a number of porcelain ballerinas obviously saved from childhood. Many of her personal belongings were childlike: stuffed animals, cardboard music boxes, dolls with pigtails and eyes missing. The bed was neatly made with a snagged eyelet coverlet and pillows. He doubted she ever entertained her gentlemen callers in here—the sofa must've been reserved for that.

"You're gonna give me a hernia," he joked as he gently laid her on the coverlet.

She held onto his arm, trying to pull him down with her.

"Just a minute," he whispered.

Stephen quickly peeled out of his wet clothes and left them in a pile on the carpet, then climbed in beside her.

As soon as his head touched the pillow he realized how exhausted he actually was. She snuggled against him and their bodies wedged together, sharing the comfort. He closed his eyes, no longer able to keep them open. He drifted off to sleep, where he dreamed not of Laura or Kat or Marie but of nothing at all. His mind sank into a void of utter stillness, as heavy and tomblike as death.

iii.

Bill Leland sat alone at a table in Danny's Saloon,

chugging his sixth beer. He'd come here not knowing where to go or what to do. Tears of regret rolled down his broad cheeks and into his mouth. If only he hadn't gone over there . . . she'd still be alive.

He rubbed his coarse hand over his watery eyes and let out a choked sob of self-pity. He wanted to tear the place apart with his bare hands, anything to get rid of the pent-up rage in his chest. It hurt so goddamn bad. Why did she have to do it? Why tonight, when she knew he was coming over? Oh Christ, if only she hadn't been high. He sobbed again and took another swallow of beer.

He knew she was dead. She had to be. There was no way anyone could've survived the number of bullets he pumped through that door. His career, his whole life, everything was ruined now. He kept a watch on the entrance of the saloon, expecting at any moment for a barrage of state policemen to come bursting through and arrest him for murder.

He'd warned her over and over, but that hadn't worked. He'd gotten tough and knocked her around, but that hadn't helped either. She just wouldn't listen. She was bound and determined to destroy everything they had that was good. His big shoulders shook with grief. Jesus Christ, what the hell was he going to do now?

Without Foss, there was nobody for him to turn to. Nobody at all. Soon the whole Town would learn what he'd done, and no one would have any sympathy for him. They'd never understand the months of torment he'd gone through with that woman. He'd done everything he could to save her.

He finished the beer and brushed away the snot under his nose. He stared past the other empty tables. Maybe she wasn't dead. Maybe she'd only been wounded and was in the hospital someplace dying. He could find out with a few calls. Then he could talk to her, and maybe she'd forgive him. Maybe he hadn't even hit her. . . .

Bill shoved back his chair and tossed down a ten-dollar bill. It was a longshot, but he had to find out. If she was alive . . . he staggered toward the door. If only she were alive. . . .

iv.

Stephen opened his eyes, his head pounding from the sudden awakening out of a deep sleep. He didn't know how long he had slept, nor what had brought him out of it.

The room was completely dark. He glanced around and tried to come to grip with his surroundings, focusing on shadowy shapes of furniture in the murky interior, but it was difficult to see anything in the thick blackness. Then he remembered with immediate trepidation that he had left his gun in the bathroom.

Stephen quickly untangled himself from Marie's slumbering embrace and groped his way through the darkness into the bathroom. The .38 still lay on the counter where he'd left it. He thanked God that Leland had not returned while they were asleep; then he listened for any threatening noises from the other parts of the house. There was nothing but the sound of Marie rolling over in bed.

He made his way out to the kitchen to check the time. It had to be late, or early, as the case might be. He saw a red glow from the percolator on the stove and flipped on the range light above it. The coffee was burnt. He dumped it out and looked at the clock over the sink: 3:05.

Laura would be asleep, and no doubt pissed as hell.

321

If Marie hadn't been in such bad shape earlier, he could have taken her back to the boardinghouse to spend the night and that might have appeased Laura, but it was too late now.

His clothes were still sopping wet when he retrieved them from the bedroom. He was struggling into his damp jeans when the phone rang.

"Goddamn it," he muttered under his breath and tried to hurry.

Marie bolted up and cried out in panic.

"It's just the phone," he said. "I'll get it."

"Is it Bill?" she asked, trembling.

"If it's Bill, I'll take care of it. Don't worry." And he thought to himself — if it is Bill, I'll kill the son of a bitch. A cold hatred like the one he'd felt for Kat's murderer flooded over him.

He hopped out to the living room, pulling on one of his socks, and picked up the receiver. He waited to let the caller speak first. He could hear someone breathing, rattling heavily, then finally a catch of air.

"Marie? Marie, is that you, honey?" The voice was Bill Leland's, raw and panicked, maybe a little drunk.

It took all the restraint Stephen could manage to keep his anger under control as he spoke. "This is Steve Myers. What do you want?"

There was a second's silence as the deputy reassessed the situation. Then he asked wretchedly, his voice cracking: "Is she dead?"

"No. And damned lucky she's not."

"Is she hurt?"

"You oughta know. You slugged her enough times." Stephen's anger was mounting, but he relented a bit when he heard a sob on the other end.

"I didn't mean to hurt her," the man cried loudly. "She just won't listen. She keeps taking that fucking crap." There were several choked sobs before Leland

322

was able to continue. "Can I talk to her?" he begged.

Stephen swallowed his hatred and softened his tone. "No, I don't think so. Let her rest. She's had a rough day."

"But she'll be all right?"

"Yeah, I think so. In a week or two."

"Oh Christ," the man cried, obviously relieved. "You don't know what I've been through. What did she say about me? Was she mad?"

Stephen shut his eyes to refrain from shouting. "You come in here and beat the shit out of her, then ask if she's mad? What do you really want to know, whether or not she's going to file charges?"

"It ain't that," the man said quickly, taken aback.

"Then what is it?"

"I-I . . . I love her."

"Believe me, it shows." It was then that Stephen lost all control because he could see how the whole lousy scenario was going to play out. "I don't know what she's going to do," he shouted. "She was a mess when I got here. It'll take her a couple of days just to recover. After that, it's up to her. Maybe she'll take you back, and maybe next time you'll kill her."

"Who the hell do you think you are?" Leland screamed. "God Almighty? You don't know all the things I done for that bitch. But I know what you are! I know what you want! You fucker, you hear me? You've got her in bed, don't you? You're fucking her brains out, ain'tcha? You found yourself an easy mark and you're over there screwing her inside out! I'm gonna come cut your stinking prick off —"

Stephen slammed down the receiver. He'd let the slimy asshole get the better of him. If he'd handled it right he might've talked the guy into staying away from Marie for a few days.

He heard a sound from the hall and looked up.

Marie stood at the corner, wrapped in a sheet. She was shaking; she knew who it was he'd been yelling at.

"Come on," he said gently, taking her arm. "Go back to bed. It's all right now."

"What did he say?" she asked.

"He wanted to know how you are."

"Is he going to kill me?" She'd come out from under most of the effect of the drugs, and the look in her eyes was sincere.

There wasn't much he could tell her. Leland might damn well be on his way over. But he smiled, anyway, and kissed the tip of her nose. "Not while I'm here," he promised. "Okay?"

In the back of his mind, he was wondering: what happens when I leave? When she's had time to be alone and get desperate again, will she take him back?

Perhaps Laura was right, perhaps there was no way to save Marie. Because first you had to save her from herself.

Chapter Twenty-five

i.

Bill Leland slammed the door on the phone booth and battered his huge fists against the plexiglass, sobbing hard and viciously.

"Cut his stinking prick off! Cut his stinking prick . . ."

The words gave way to even greater sobs of pain as a wave of utter despair seized him. The large man threw himself at the side of the booth and slid slowly to the ground, cries of anguish racking his big frame.

What the Jesus H. Christ does that fucker know about my life? What the hell does he know? Had his wife walked out on him? Had she laughed in his face when he couldn't get it up? Had she waved her naked ass in front of him knowing there was nothing he could do about it?

It was different with Marie, he thought, as the tears rolled down his craggy face. Marie understood. She was gentle and kind and patient, ready to do whatever was necessary.

If only it weren't for the drugs. The damned drugs. When she got high it was no good. She'd get so stoned she only lay there, laughing or humming to herself, completely incapable of rendering the warmth and compassion he needed. If it weren't for the drugs.

He didn't know how to get her to quit. He'd almost killed her twice in the process, and now she'd taken up with someone new. That was the thanks he got for trying to help her, for all the flowers and money and sweet talk.

That fucking artist from Chicago. Hotshot prick.

Bill clenched his hands. He'd cut the bastard's balls off. He'd kill them both, the rutting, fucking pair of them. That's what he'd do. He pulled himself up from the ground and started toward his patrol car.

See how brave Mr. Big Shot is when he's looking down the barrel of a .357. Bill laughed through his tears. Yeah, fucker. Gonna watch ya eat a little lead. See your eye pop out and watch you crap in your pants. See what she thinks of you then, with your drawers full of stinkin' shit.

God, it was lovely. He felt better immediately. The taste of sweet revenge.

He scooted behind the wheel and turned the engine over, then spun out of the parking lot. You motherfucker.

He remembered the look on Marie's face when he'd pulled out his revolver. Even in a drug-induced haze, she'd known what death was. Her bright hazel eyes had lit with terror.

Bill laughed and wiped his nose with the back of his hand.

Her hero was probably holding her now. Tellin' her, "there, there, baby, daddy's gonna save ya," and all the while grabbing her ass and filling it up. Using her like most of the scum she slept with.

He himself was the only one who had ever really cared for her and loved her. Someplace in the pit of her stupid brain she had to know that. She was only doing this to pay him back 'cause he wouldn't let her snort her rotten drugs.

Well, the hell with her, the goddamned cunt.

Bill swung into the lot of the J.P. Liquor Store, nearly taking out the signpost with the front of his bumper and narrowly missing a large brown dumpster. He skidded and ground to a halt squarely in front of the solitary business.

The two-story building on the edge of Town was as dark and empty as a graveyard breeze. Old J.P. and his wife, Roberta, had left Town with the other cowards at the first word of trouble. What with the fucking evacuation they had announced that afternoon, everyone would soon be hitting the road, leaving Town prey to any low-life crud that happened by.

Nobody in the whole goddamned area had the slightest idea what they were doing. They were all a bunch of mealymouthed pinheads like Malcolm. But Malcolm got his. Poisoned by his own wife. Christ, wasn't that something? Thank God I lived long enough to see the day.

Bill heaved himself out of the car. The liquor shop door was heavily padlocked with a chain and a wrought iron gate, but the windows were unbarred and there was a carefully arranged display of whiskey and vodka bottles.

The deputy glanced around. The street was deserted, no traffic in either direction. He picked up a baseball-sized stone from the curb and hurled it through the glass.

An alarm went off as the fragments of glass shot out over the sidewalk, but there was no one to hear it. It might as well have been ringing in the heart of the Amazon Jungle. The deputy simply reached in and pulled out three bottles of each. He twisted the cap off one of the Jack Daniels and tucked the rest away in the trunk of his car.

The raw liquor eased the ache in his throat. He sat

327

for several minutes belting it down, swallow after swallow, till his brain began to swim in a mire of alcohol.

Goddamned whore. Fucking pig. She deserved everything he gave her and worse.

He took the .357 and a fresh box of ammo from under the seat. His hands shook as he loaded it. This time . . . this time . . .

Tears welled in his eyes. Oh God, Marie. I love you. His shoulders sagged, and his face fell against the wheel, huge sobs of despair tearing from deep in his chest. If only . . .

He'd shoot her, that's what he'd do. Visions of the bullet ripping into her flesh passed through his mind. At first he pictured the scenario with a hole pumped neatly into her forehead and glassy blank eyes staring up at him in surprise. Then he imagined torturing her, so bit by bit she could feel death coming and suffer the same pain he was experiencing.

ii.

Leland woke suddenly. His patrol car was still parked in front of the liquor store. A sharp burning had pierced his skin and invaded his brain. The heat of molten lava rushed through his veins. A loud buzzing rang in his ears, and all around him raged a blinding light of hideous, demonic color.

He thrashed against the seat in a vain attempt to ward off the weightless enemy. The iridescent mist was inside him, devouring him, reducing his entrails to tarlike residue.

His arms and hands flailed wildly. His fingers touched on the butt of his pistol, and for a second, the irony of his own death instead of Marie's registered. Then the thought was lost, dwarfed by the intense surges of mounting pain, by the blackness threatening to swallow his soul.

His grip tightened on the .357. With great effort, he brought the weapon up and placed the barrel in his mouth, then squeezed the trigger. . . .

Wednesday, June 21

. . . screams of the souls forever bound . . .

Chapter Twenty-six

Laura's door was open when Stephen got back, and a suitcase was spread out on her bed. She was busily shoving the articles from her dresser into it.

He'd already talked to Mrs. Morton, who sat tearfully in the kitchen. The old woman refused to evacuate her beloved home and had begged her daughter to reconsider. He understood how Mrs. Morton felt. It hurt to see Laura leaving, in spite of the fact he'd urged her to go and knew it was for the best. He wanted to leave with her, but he felt his responsibility to this town wasn't over yet.

Stephen rapped lightly on the door frame.

Laura stopped and looked up.

He smiled. "Hi."

She nodded, forcing herself to return his smile, then went on with her packing. "I have to get out of this town," she said dryly. "It has nothing to do with last night. I should've done it a long time ago."

"Pursuing your dreams?"

"Something like that. And you?"

"I'm going to call over to the city building in a few minutes and see if they need help."

"Still playing hero?" She paused. "Sorry. I didn't mean that. I'm just worried. Be careful, huh?"

"Sure." He watched as she finished loading a duffel bag. He had the feeling he was losing her, and he wanted desperately to hang on, but he didn't know how. "Still mad?"

"No. It's all right. I'm not going to ask about Marie. It doesn't matter."

He walked over and sat on the edge of the bed as she zipped up the suitcase. "What's wrong then?"

She turned and stared out the window at the street below. "I'm scared."

"About what's happening in Town?"

She shook her head. "About us."

"I don't understand."

"This is new for me—all these feelings between you and me. I guess I got jealous last night."

He smiled. "It's okay. Happens to the best of us."

"Not to me. It made me realize how involved I'm getting, how much you mean to me. All my life I've lived in this same little town, wondering what it'd be like to get out, to fall in love, to be somebody independent, and now I'm so goddamned scared I can feel my knees knocking. I don't know what I want. I love you. I love you very much, but I'm frightened to death of giving up my future."

"It doesn't have to be like that. Love isn't a ball and chain."

"I know." She sat beside him, and he drew her into his arms, holding her snugly against his chest. "I'm scared of failing. I'm scared I'll go out there and fall flat on my face."

"Not you."

"I don't want to end up like mother. So full of regrets, so bitter. Stuck in a place like this with nothing to do but prey on other people's trouble, with nothing but a dozen photo albums of what life could've been." She laughed, but he could hear the tears at the edge of her voice. "I don't know what I want. I'm just not ready," she cried, and clutched him tighter.

"It's all right," he said, rubbing her shoulder. "You don't have to decide today. Give it time. Where are you going?"

"To my aunt's in Iowa. I'll stay there for awhile and sort things out. I've applied to the university."

"I remember."

"When this is over, will you write me?"

He nodded and kissed her. "Every day. Till you're sick of reading my letters."

"This is so hard," she whispered. "Hold me. Hold me tighter."

They sat in silence for several minutes, kissing and embracing. Finally she pulled away. "I've got to go. If I don't leave now, I'll never be able to. Will you help me with this stuff?"

"Sure." He picked up her suitcase and the small bag she'd packed. "Anything else?"

"No. This is it for now. I'll come back for the rest someday when I'm ready."

They walked down the stairs. Abigail was waiting for them on the porch. "I made you a lunch," she said, her voice quivering, "peanut butter sandwiches and celery. I put them on the front seat. You should stay a few weeks and buy a new car before you go. You'll never make it to Aunt Sue's in that."

"It'll be all right, Mother."

"If you say so." The old woman's eyes were watery and red from crying. Abigail hugged her daughter, then hurried back into the house, the screen door slamming shut behind her.

Stephen carried Laura's suitcases to the rusted yellow Volkswagen and loaded them into the trunk. "You know your mother's right about this car."

"Now don't you start in, too," she said, laughing and wiping a tear from her cheek. She glanced back toward the house a final time. "I'll miss her. I'll even miss this

335

town. I just can't live here any more. Love me?"

He nodded, his throat growing too tight for words.

"You won't forget to write?"

"No," he said thickly.

"I hope it all works out for everybody here."

"Me, too."

She slid behind the wheel, and he stepped back as the engine started up. He tried telling himself that her departure was for the best, but still it was one of the hardest things he'd ever experienced, almost as hard as the day they found Kat's body. He waved as she honked and drove away, wondering if and when he'd ever see her again.

Chapter Twenty-seven

i.

"We are hoping to achieve a more permanent effect," the professor explained. He stood at the head of the table in the third-floor chamber of the city building. State police chief Romero had called in all the volunteers, National Guardsmen, and troopers he had on hand when the professor announced that he had finally produced the more powerful formula they needed to combat the man-filled mist preying on the area.

A sharp blade of fear penetrated the room as everyone concentrated with grim awareness on the seriousness of the situation and listened intently to what was being said. Stephen sat at the far end, thankful that Laura had left and was no longer in danger. He watched Sergeant Williamson's reaction as the professor continued.

"The acetylene was able to attach itself to the TCBA molecules for a long enough period to cause part of the host's shape to appear, but the evil force at work in the mass quickly compensated for the reaction, and the mist escaped.

"What I have done," the professor said, lifting a cylinder of the new solution onto the table, "is to combine oxonium ions to the previous formula. They should have a longer-lasting result.

"Unfortunately, this solution cannot be tested in the laboratory. We were forced to destroy the infected lab animals because they posed a threat. But, as demonstrated yesterday, the airtight suits should provide adequate protection."

"Excuse me, Professor," Williamson interrupted, "but what happens when this cloud becomes a man? I mean, how do we destroy it then? Will this formula kill it?"

The old man shook his head. "No. I don't even know for how long it will bind the vapor, or for certain that it will. But if it does, then we may be able to find a means of eliminating it. It is my theory that the host body itself can be destroyed. And because of the parasitic nature of the creature, I assume it cannot survive without the host."

"I see," the sergeant mumbled, though it was clear he didn't completely.

"Could the host be killed by gunfire?" Romero asked.

"That is my hope," the professor admitted. "The host may still be limited to some of its human structure. Though," he cautioned, "not for a minute should it be thought of as human. The physiological changes that have occurred in its body may make it impossible to defeat by ordinary means. But even if we succeed in confining it to that manlike form, we will have won a minor victory. Battles like these are not won quickly."

"I understand," Romero said.

"Have the additional suits arrived?" Thompson asked.

Romero nodded. "There's enough for everyone in the room. And tank units, too. God help us. Most of the residents in the two counties have been evacuated, but several deaths were reported last night, and we have no idea how many unreported fatalities are out there."

Thompson nodded. "If we aren't fast, the numbers will increase and spread to other counties."

Romero whispered something to the man next to him,

who got up and left; then he turned back to the group. "We're set to go outside. A thorough search needs to be made of both counties and any other areas where these deaths have been reported. We need to keep careful track of the number of mortalities. There can be no letup until all of this is over."

Romero rose and the entourage began to file out. Stephen stood slowly. A sudden premonition of fear shot through him like an electric needle, but it was gone almost as quickly as it had come.

ii.

Stephen and Sergeant Williamson went out together, starting on West First Street and heading toward Mulberry in a house-by-house search. Every garage and outbuilding had to be checked, too. They were looking for bodies, traces of the black residue, and any signs of the supernatural vapor.

They were not alone. There were teams of two or three men posted on every street in Town and more covering the woods and miles of farmlands. It would be a long, tedious process in the bulky space-age suits, carrying the heavy tank units on their backs with .45s in holsters on their hips. The buildings they didn't have keys for they were forced to break into, then make a note of it, so they could be boarded up until the owners returned.

No one was home at the first three residences they checked, and there was no sign of anything out of the ordinary. Only three beautiful, antique homes filled with modest furnishings, tidied up as though the families had left on vacation. The counters were wiped clean, the rugs vacuumed, the wastebaskets emptied. It was as if at any moment the owners would come running in, the children quarreling, the parents worrying, and life would resume as normal.

But the fourth house . . .

They didn't expect to find anyone, but still they knocked. When no one answered, Williamson waited at the front while Stephen ran around to the back. He managed to jimmy the lock, and entered through the kitchen.

Dishes were laid out on the table for a meal, just as though the family were about to sit down and eat. But the food in the bowls was hard and dry like it had been there for some time.

Stephen cautiously stepped through the arch into the dining room. It was dark. Nothing but dusty furniture and a few withered houseplants at the window. Wary, he entered the living room.

He flinched when he saw the figure on the couch—a man's skeletal form dressed in work clothes, black with dried pus and decay. The figure was outstretched in obvious agony, although the moment of its torture had long passed. Its hands clutched at the cushions in a futile struggle to resist death. The corpse was, he assumed, from those he'd seen at the mortuary, three or four days old. The black bile had almost entirely eroded through the flaky gray covering of its skin. The eyes had shriveled and fallen within the sockets.

Stephen checked down the list of those reported missing and found the address: 616 West First Street, John and Rita Glover, two children.

Oh God.

Williamson was pounding at the front door. "Steve?" he yelled.

"Coming."

The thirty-three-year-old artist unbolted the lock. "In here," he said, directing Williamson's attention to the sofa. "That's the only one I've found so far. The whole family is registered on the list as possibly missing."

"How many?"

"Three more. Two of them kids."

"Christ."

"You look around down here," Stephen said. "I'll get the upstairs."

"Be careful."

"Yeah." But he suspected the danger had long since passed. The suit would protect him from any contact with secretions from the bodies. It was only the dead who had anything to fear, their souls now imprisoned within the creature.

The stairs were dark and creaked with each step. Near the top, he called out but got no reply. He braced himself for the worst.

The bedroom to the right was the master suite, a conical-shaped room with a sitting area. It was neatly decorated in maroon and lace to go with the home's Victorian vintage. There was no sign of the woman, only a few clothes laid out in the bathroom and a cracked mirror. No evidence of the disaster that must've taken place within these walls.

There was a den and a sewing room, both empty, then—his hand froze on the knob. This had to be it—the children's bedroom—there were no others. They didn't necessarily die here, he told himself. The woman might've taken the kids and fled. She might've escaped. . . .

With what remained of his nerve, he thrust the door open. It was messy as most kids' rooms are. Stuffed toys scattered across the floor. Barbie dolls and their miniature clothes. The list didn't say so, but it was clear both children were girls, between five and ten years old, he guessed. Posters of Mickey Mouse and Snow White hung on the walls.

Stephen walked around the small table and chairs and

examined the bunk beds. He threw off all the blankets in a flurry of movement, determined to get it over with. To his relief, both beds were empty. Then he looked underneath — empty there, too.

He turned and saw Williamson in the doorway. "Any sign of the woman or kids?" he asked.

The sergeant shook his head.

"None here, either."

Then Stephen pulled open the closet. . . .

Dead, both little girls were huddled together on the floor where they had tried to hide, forever entwined in a hideous pose of petrified terror, smiling Barbies clutched in their rigid arms. A sticky black slime of decaying matter coated their shrunken frames and congealed in a darkened pool around them.

Stephen drew a deep breath and staggered back, reeling with shock.

He heard Williamson gasp. The sergeant rushed up and flung the closet door shut, as though that would somehow make it untrue.

The two of them stared at each other as they grappled with the grim reality of witnessing so much carnage and suffering. Stephen's mind whirled in pain. This couldn't be happening. Nothing this monstrous could be real. It didn't seem possible. But somewhere deep inside, he knew it was.

The situation got worse when they searched additional houses and found more dead. Stephen and Williamson listened on their hand units as the other volunteers reported similar findings. Entire families reduced to moldering remnants of humanity. One group reported finding Bill Leland's body. He, too, was a victim. The death toll was greater than any had thought possible.

The gruesome spectacle of the ever-increasing corpses was not something either man could displace from his brain. No amount of self-denial could compensate. It filled their minds and souls till both were sickened and literally numb with horror. It didn't seem possible to go farther, and it was only sheer willpower and the intimate knowledge of how awful this thing was that drove them onward.

iii.

Thus far none of the patrols had sighted the gaseous enemy, but plenty of bodies had been found, twenty-three at last count. Stephen and Sergeant Williamson had turned onto Mulberry and were headed toward the railroad tracks on the edge of Town, only a few blocks from Marie's. They were walking along the left side of the street when Stephen spotted a rusty yellow Volkswagen stopped in front of the crossing.

Recognition hit him immediately. "That's Laura's car," he screamed. With an overpowering sense of dread, he lunged forward, bent under the weight of the canister on his back.

Williamson stood puzzled, then quickly followed on Stephen's heels.

Stephen raced toward the automobile, his heart pounding and his chest aching with the exertion. He couldn't think; he just ran, hoping she wouldn't be there.

He let the harness slide from his shoulders and allowed the sprayer to drop to the ground as he neared the car. The vehicle looked empty, but the passenger door was ajar.

His muscles tightened with a terrible fear as he scrambled around to the other side. Then he saw her. Half-in, half-out, dangling from the seat, her head on the pavement. She had tried to flee her grisly fate, but had not succeeded.

A cry of anguish wrenched itself from his throat. Stephen fell to his knees beside her, tears streaming down his cheeks. The exhausting efforts of the last few days now hit him with overwhelming power. His hands shook as he grasped Laura under the arms and tried to pull her free from the vehicle that had become her tomb.

Her face and arms had burst with a multitude of lesions as her skin had withered and torn. Her eyes were cloudy and coated with the thick, darkening fluid that dripped from her body. Her silky blond hair that he had run his fingers through only hours before was matted and caked with sediment.

Williamson abruptly halted as he swung around the rear fender. "Oh shit," he muttered.

But Stephen was oblivious to the officer's presence, engulfed by a world of his own pain. He took the grossly mutilated figure of the young woman into his arms and cradled the limp form, the white metallic suit protecting him from the putrid pus that poured through the tears in her shriveled flesh.

"She must've stopped for a train," Williamson said lamely. "It must've got her then."

Stephen didn't answer. He gave no sign that he had even heard.

Williamson knelt beside him and laid his hand on the artist's shoulder. "There's nothing more you can do for her," he said. "Let her go."

Stephen shook the hand away and clenched Laura's body tighter, not wanting to relinquish it. This was all that he had left of her now, all that he would ever have.

"Leave me alone," he croaked. He didn't care if they found the God-cursed man or not. It could go on killing and killing forever. Let it destroy the whole planet.

Laura was dead, and that was all that mattered. Dead.

A strangled sound of grief worked its way to the surface. His heart hammered and the blood pumped ferociously through his brain so that he thought his head might explode.

Laura was dead.

He didn't know how long he sat in the road, holding her for the last time. Finally, as though in a trance, he allowed Williamson to pry her loose from his arms.

The sergeant led him away, and he staggered along the edge of the street, unsure of where he would go or what he would do. He took off his helmet, unable to breathe, and threw it on the ground. His stomach heaved.

Williamson stood beside him as he vomited onto the grass. . . .

iv.

With desperation, on the precarious edge of sanity, they resumed the hunt, if for no other reason than it had to be done. Stephen blanked his mind of all other thoughts with a forcefulness of determination he hadn't known he possessed, and a rage unequalled filled his brain.

He followed Williamson down Mulberry to the first house past the tracks. His mind was so absorbed with anger that he didn't hear the woman's screams. But the sergeant stopped, instantly alert. Stephen realized something was wrong, and when the sound came again, only moments later, he heard it. It wasn't a cry of alarm or even a shriek of pain; it was the base sound of terror.

The screams continued, panicked and wild. They both ran toward the noise. As they drew closer, Stephen realized it was coming from Marie's house.

345

Williamson got there first. The door was bolted, but he didn't bother to knock. He jumped back and fired at the lock with his .45, then kicked in the splintered frame. Stephen followed him inside.

A skinny, long-haired man kicked and flapped on the sofa bed. The demonic cloud hovered over him, rapidly digesting his tortured organs. His body convulsed in a hideous puppet's dance, his pants caught down around his ankles, his sex act brought to a premature end he could never have anticipated. The syrupy liquid bile gushed through a number of open lesions on his form as well as out his mouth and down his chin. He struggled for breath, gasping, his hands waving frantically amidst the oppressive ruin claiming his body with deadly thirst.

Stephen and Williamson had begun to shower the sofa with the acetylene solution. Stephen was distantly aware that Marie crouched against the far wall, shaking hysterically.

"Stay where you are," he shouted in warning, his heart pounding like a jackhammer.

The acetylene spray washed over the luminous mist. The monstrous vapor wavered and pulsed slower. The iridescent haze became murky, its unnatural glow beginning to fade.

Stephen saw the vague outline of a person suspended in the hue, the ghostly image of a man riddled with the bacteria of the undead. Spiraling veins of the hideous color seemed to shoot into him. His mottled flesh resembled moldy cheese. Entire chunks of it had fallen away in places, revealing the gruesome parasitic force that seethed underneath. His eyes blazed with a molten darkness that reflected no light whatsoever.

Slowly the man took shape. His face contorted with evil.

Williamson stopped spraying and tore out his re-

346

volver, but before he could shoot, the horrible apparition of the man leapt upon him and knocked him backward onto the floor.

Stephen ripped his .45 from the holster on his hip. The grisly man had wrapped his hands around Chris's neck.

He aimed for the creature's torso and squeezed the trigger. It was difficult to get a clear shot; he was terrified of hitting Williamson.

He blew four wide holes in its back, all to no effect. Small streams of the monstrously colored mist hissed from the wounds, snaking upward in eerie tendrils and clinging to the ceiling like fog.

Stephen continued to fire. He drew another round from his belt, but the bullets seemed useless. There was no blood or bones in this thing; it was entirely filled with the malevolent color.

Chris was gagging. His jaw was broken and the creature was crushing his windpipe. Frantic, Stephen aimed again. This time he shot at its head, narrowly missing the bloodied sergeant.

Black mucus began to leach slowly from the punctured flesh of the assailant's face, and Stephen kept firing. Then he heard screams. The deafening sirens of anguish splintered the air. They were a sound that no human could make. It was the screams of the souls forever bound in the black, tarlike substance spewing from the creature's brain. The oily blackness gushed out, coursing over the repulsive man's eyes, nose, and mouth.

The diabolical figure began to collapse. It grabbed and thrashed at the air in a frenzy to escape its own horrible demise. Gaping ulcers erupted and spread like fire across the ruinous form. Steam and dark froth boiled from the open fissures. Its moldering hands clenched and unclenched in spasms as the man crumbled and twisted, coiling inward upon himself. He was slowly melting, his face distorting as his features ran and blended together.

Suddenly, the inhuman executioner burst into a geyser of hot blackness. The air was alive with heat. The blaze began to burn downward, torching through the carpet and flooring beneath. The earth opened up, exposing a huge abyss bubbling with the demonic color. The fiendish mass plunged into it, vanishing, taking his tormented captive souls with him.

Epilogue

i.

Stephen put the last of the cardboard boxes he'd packed into his trunk and shut the lid, then stood beside his car to take a final look at Town. The street was empty. There was not a voice to be heard or a person to be seen other than old Abigail Morton, who rocked silently in a wicker chair on her front porch, watching him go.

She had survived the crisis and remained in her home, but there wouldn't be much for her now. Laura was gone, and so was almost everyone else. Fifty-six dead between the two counties. Many others had fled in terror. Some would be back, but more than a few had moved permanently and put their property up for sale. It would be a long time before anything sold. Though given enough time, this area would come to life again.

But he would never be back. Neither would he ever forget.

They had gone on the other night to destroy six more parasitic host mutations. In the last five days there had been no more deaths. All those on the missing list had been accounted for. Chief Romero had declared the crisis officially ended this morning, and with those final words Stephen was leaving.

He was headed back to Chicago. Back to the dream. To the same apartment he had shared with Kat. But he would not be bitter or remorseful this time. Instead, he looked forward to living up to the new expectations he had set for himself. Kat would not be there, and neither would Laura, but he would begin over, and after this he would not so easily be defeated. Not by a negligent legal system, financial troubles, or a changing world.

His experience had taught him how precious life can be. Though he had loved and lost twice, he was not going to stop living. He could admit to himself now that when he'd come to Town, he'd come to retreat, and he'd been wrong. You can't retreat until the end, until the devil himself comes to get you.

He opened the door and slid in the car. Marie sat in the passenger seat, waiting.

"That's everything," he said.

She nodded as she lit another cigarette. Most of the bruises on her face had healed. There was only a small scar above her left eye where Bill had hit her the last time.

Stephen turned over the engine and slowly shifted into gear. "We'll stop for breakfast when we get to Indianapolis, okay?"

"Sure," she whispered. Her voice was still hoarse, but she was recovering. They both were.

ii.

Dr. Corliss awoke and stretched. His muscles were cramped and tight, and his skin felt as though it would burst. In several places it had cracked and flaked, and a strange fluid trickled out. Oh God, how long had he been asleep? An hour, a few days?

He checked his watch.

June 26. Six days!

God Almighty. How had he slept so long?

He glanced around his surroundings—and began to remember. He was in the Gothard's barn, under an old tarp at the top of the loft. He shook off the canvas covering and crawled across the hay. The sun shining through slats in the window hurt his eyes. How had he gotten here?

A vision of the crash flashed through his mind. Searing orange flames that shot high in the sky. Burning metal and upholstery. Oh yes . . . in the last few seconds, as the car careened out of control, he had felt himself changing, becoming thinner, insubstantial, no more than a curl of smoke on the breeze. He had drifted out through the window into the summer air and watched the fiery wreck of his stolen automobile.

He remembered being like that for hours, in and out of consciousness, until he'd found this barn. He had come here to rest, but now six days had gone by. He had to get back to the clinic, to his patients. He crept toward the ladder, then stopped. How had he floated out of the window?

A streak of terror cut through his mind. He had changed. He was no longer . . . as he had been. Michael stared down at his hands. They were his hands, but they were ashen and dry, somehow not right.

He touched his flesh.

It was cold.

He felt for a pulse.

There was none.

And the hunger. The hunger was absolutely incredible. He shuddered and felt himself shake, squeezing up inside and reverting back into the luminous mist. He knew he must feed soon. . . .

THRILLERS BY WILLIAM W. JOHNSTONE

THE DEVIL'S CAT (2091, $3.95)

The town was alive with all kinds of cats. Black, white, fat, scrawny. They lived in the streets, in backyards, in the swamps of Becancour. Sam, Nydia, and Little Sam had never seen so many cats. The cats' eyes were glowing slits as they watched the newcomers. The town was ripe with evil. It seemed to waft in from the swamps with the hot, fetid breeze and breed in the minds of Becancour's citizens. Soon Sam, Nydia, and Little Sam would battle the forces of darkness. Standing alone against the ultimate predator—The Devil's Cat.

THE DEVIL'S HEART (2110, $3.95)

Now it was summer again in Whitfield. The town was peaceful, quiet, and unprepared for the atrocities to come. Eternal life, everlasting youth, an orgy that would span time—that was what the Lord of Darkness was promising the coven members in return for their pledge of love. The few who had fought against his hideous powers before, believed it could never happen again. Then the hot wind began to blow—as black as evil as The Devil's Heart.

THE DEVIL'S TOUCH (2111, $3.95)

Once the carnage begins, there's no time for anything but terror. Hollow-eyed, hungry corpses rise from unearthly tombs to gorge themselves on living flesh and spawn a new generation of restless Undead. The demons of Hell cavort with Satan's unholy disciples in blood-soaked rituals and fevered orgies. The Balons have faced the red, glowing eyes of the Master before, and they know what must be done. But there can be no salvation for those marked by The Devil's Touch.